■ □ ■ □ ■

PERVERZION

Writings from an Unbound Europe

■ □ ■ □ ■

YURI ANDRUKHOVYCH

PERVERZION

Translated from the Ukrainian and with
an introduction by Michael M. Naydan

NORTHWESTERN UNIVERSITY PRESS

EVANSTON, ILLINOIS

Northwestern University Press
Evanston, Illinois 60208-4170

Printed in the United States of America

10 9 8 7 6 5 4 3 2 1

ISBN 0-8101-1963-3 (CLOTH)
ISBN 0-8101-1964-1 (PAPER)

Library of Congress Cataloging-in-Publication data are available
from the Library of Congress.

The paper used in this publication meets the minimum requirements of the American
National Standard for Information Sciences—Permanence of Paper for Printed Library
Materials, ANSI Z39.48-1992.

CONTENTS

■ □ ■ □ ■

TRANSLATOR'S ACKNOWLEDGMENTS

Several of the pieces here have been published previously in journals and are reprinted here with permission from the publishers. Chapter 10 appeared in *AGNI* 48 under the title "The Testament of Antonio Delcampo." Part 10 of the novel was published in *Exquisite Corpse* 8 with the title "Guardians a di Joiman Gate." A fragment of "Publisher's Foreword" along with parts 1 and 2 of the novel have been published in the summer 2001 issue of *Pequod* 44. And part 31 appeared in *Absinthe: New European Writing* 2 under the title "Stakh's Demise."

I owe my greatest debt of thanks to Yuri Andrukhovych for being such a cooperative and congenial author and for being so generous with his time in providing detailed answers to my innumerable questions by e-mail as well as in person. In addition, he spent countless hours combing through the final version of the translation with me to both emend my erring ways and to help me convey intricate nuances of his original. I, of course, take full responsibility for errors or omissions that may have slipped through. Special thanks also to the Fulbright Visiting Scholar Program, which made Yuri Andrukhovych's visit to Penn State in the 2000 to 2001 academic year possible.

As always in my work, I am indebted to many people who have helped make this a better translation. Many thanks to Sasha Hrytsenko for assisting me with cultural and translation questions in my initial work on chapters 1 through 10. My gratitude to Adrian Wanner for reading through an earlier version of the manuscript to check German and Italian spellings for me. Bianca Maria Colosimo was kind enough to fix several of the myriad Italian spellings for me.

Askold Melnyczuk, editor of the journal *AGNI*, was immensely helpful in editing chapter 10, which appeared in volume 48 (fall 1998) of *AGNI*. I am especially grateful to Lida Stefanowska for her moral support on the project and for her taking the time to answer many of my translation conundra. I also have a great debt of gratitude to linguist Antonina Berezovenko for illuminating me on numerous questions regarding the nuances of contemporary Ukrainian. Rhetorician Christine Skolnik has been very helpful on questions of style in English. Thanks to Maria Hablevych for some very appropriate suggestions that I was able to incorporate in this final version. And I am extremely thankful to Lee Carpenter for her editorial emendations on an earlier version. Thanks also to the editors at Northwestern University Press for their meticulousness in checking the many intricacies of the novel for this final published version.

This translation is dedicated to Roxy and Lila.

YURI ANDRUKHOVYCH: WRITING
AT THE EDGE OF THE NEW EUROPE

A postmodernist author of great depth and dimension, Yuri Andrukhovych is one of today's leading Ukrainian prose writers. Born in
1960 in the picturesque provincial city of Ivano-Frankivsk (former-
ly called Stanislaviv) in western Ukraine, he grew up and was educated in a land bordering the still-untamed Carpathian Mountains.
He received his undergraduate degree in philology from the
Polygraphics Institute in Lviv, which to many is the cultural capital
of Ukraine, a city that has always had close ties to Europe and the
West. The markedly medieval city, whose name means "city of
lions," served as a great inspiration and locus for much of Andrukhovych's literary activities and for his growth as an artist. Following
his undergraduate studies, Andrukhovych completed his doctorate
in Ukrainian philology at the Subcarpathian University in Ivano-
Frankivsk, writing his dissertation on the great Ukrainian poet from
the Lemko region of Poland—Bohdan Ihor Antonych—whose life
and work have served as a profound inspiration for Andrukhovych.

The Ukrainian literary critic Bohdan Rubchak places Antonych
in the "Orphic strain" of Ukrainian poets, who gravitate to the natural music of language.[1] Thus the allure of Antonych for Andrukhovych, an Orpheus in prose who has even included an opera,
Orpheus in Venice, as an elemental component of his novel *Perverzion,* is quite understandable. This western borderland of what has
become independent Ukraine has given inspiration to a bevy of writers from its multicultural soil, including such luminaries as Joseph
Roth, Paul Celan, and Bruno Schulz. Andrukhovych is one of the

most talented in a long line of innovative literary voices from the region.

Andrukhovych began his literary career as a poet. To date he has authored four books in this genre—*The Sky and City Squares* (1985), *The Center of the City* (1989), *Exotic Birds and Plants* (1991), and *Exotic Birds and Plants with an Addendum "India"* (1997). The best of his poetry is in the Orphic strain, with a focus on subtle sound and the musicality of words. But many of his poems additionally are bombastic and iconoclastic. They break clichés and taboos, gibing at cultural sacred cows of every ilk.

Andrukhovych was conscripted into the Soviet army in 1983, and his two obligatory years of service provided the raw material for his initial foray into prose. He penned seven often harshly realistic short stories based on army life, which were published in 1989, as well as a screenplay drawn from his army experiences. A. Donchyk's film *Oxygen Starvation* (1991) was based on the latter. From 1989 to 1991 Andrukhovych received a stipend for postgraduate study at the Maxim Gorky Literary Institute in Moscow. His experiences in the Soviet capital became material for his second novel—*The Moscoviad: A Horror Novel*—about a crumbling, dysfunctional empire that is empty at its core. His latest novel, *The Twelve Rings*, was published in 2003.

Andrukhovych is best known for his trilogy of novels: *Recreations* (1992), *The Moscoviad* (1993), and *Perverzion* (1996). The first two deal with the final death throes of the Soviet empire and the third with the aftermath of the empire's collapse and the newfound freedom that independence wrought. *Perverzion* received the novel of the year award for 1996 from the preeminent Kyiv-based journal *Suchasnist.*

An engaging essayist, Andrukhovych partly honed his essay-writing skills as a cultural columnist for the Kyiv newspaper *The Day* and published a number of his contemplative culturological essays, *Disorientation in Locality,* in 1999. His profoundly thoughtful essay "Within Time, Down a River" appeared in English translation in 2001 in the American literary journal *AGNI.* A translator of considerable talent, Andrukhovych has translated, among many other works and authors, Shakespeare's *Hamlet,* the New York School poets, and the Beats.

Andrukhovych is the anointed "patriarch" and cofounder of the influential Bu-Ba-Bu literary performance group. The group's name is formed from the first two letters of the Ukrainian words meaning buffoonery (*bufonada*), farce (*balahan*), and burlesque (*burlesk*). Together with his coconspirators—the poet Viktor Neborak and the satirist Oleksandr Irvanets—Andrukhovych performed his carnivalized works for crowds numbering in the thousands in the late 1980s and early 1990s. A particularly impressive performance was a two-day poetry and operatic "happening" in 1992 called Chrysler Imperial, which delighted audiences at the sold-out Lviv Opera House.

Andrukhovych has a burgeoning reputation in his homeland and abroad as a superb stylist and innovative writer of great imagination. His works have already been translated into English, German, French, Polish, Russian, Bulgarian, and Finnish. The Canadian Institute of Ukrainian Studies published Andrukhovych's novel *Recreations* in Marko Pavlyshyn's translation in 1998, and his poetry and prose have appeared in English translation in *AGNI, Pequod, Glas, Salt Hill, Exquisite Corpse,* and *Absinthe: New European Writing.* In Vienna, Austria, in 2001 Andrukhovych received the prestigious Herder Prize in Literature and that same year was awarded the Antonovych Prize in Literature in Kyiv, Ukraine, for his expansive contributions to Ukrainian culture. He continues to reside in Ivano-Frankivsk, on the physical periphery (of Ukrainian political life and culture) that gives him the aesthetic distance he needs as an artist.

The novel *Perverzion* is many things. It is a mystery that attempts to solve the riddle of the disappearance of Ukrainian poet Stanislav "Stakh" Perfetsky. Yuri Andrukhovych has collected everything he could find regarding the mysterious disappearance of his friend in the dark waters of the Grand Canal in Venice. Andrukhovych re-creates the life of Perfetsky modeled after a saint's life, culling information from various sources. He follows Perfetsky's path by train from Lviv, Ukraine, near the Polish border through the new Eastern Europe; then from Germany to Italy through the Alps by car, and through the waterways of Venice by gondola, accompanied for most of the journey by the profoundest love of his life, Ada Zitrone, who over the course of the novel periodically sends encoded reports on Perfetsky's activities to a mysterious patron named Monsignore.

The novel comprises a collection, a miscellany of various narratives, of versions and *per*versions: first-person, third-person, surreptitiously heard and seen narration, recorded narration (video- and audiotapes), diaries, computer files, and published artifacts. In many respects the novel is voyeuristic because the reader has access to the most intimate details. This postmodernist saint's life, with technological innovations providing the means for gathering information, gives the reader both filtered and unfiltered access to moments in Perfetsky's life, allowing the reader to determine which versions ring truest.

The novel also can be read as a philosophical novel, in many ways like Bulgakov's *The Master and Margarita,* to which it has been compared: *Perverzion* deals with the powerful questions of life and death, of killing or not killing, of the immortality of the soul, of good versus evil, of Hamletian being or not being. It is also an intimate and profound love story with Ada (aka Cerina in her hypostasis as the secret agent monitoring Perfetsky's activities) central to the plot. Rather than giving answers to the unanswerable questions, the novel, in postmodernist fashion, gives choices, possibilities, and impossibilities.

The novel largely parodies the notions, the -isms, the absurdities, and the excesses of politically correct Western civilization. What else *could* happen at a conference in Venice called "The Post-Carnival Absurdity of the World: What Is on the Horizon?" Demonic forces are at work at the conclave to transfer earthly power to a new chief terrestrial demon, Tsutsu Mavropule, and to make new converts, especially among the conference participants who, of course, are ripe for being transformed into their immortal but evil true selves.

The notion of performance, or what I call performance text, comprises one of the most striking features of the novel. There are lectures, both staid and riotous; television, radio, and newspaper interviews; a pastiche opera, *Orpheus in Venice;* reggae and rap performances; a Third World cult ceremony; Black Mass rites; a dramatic demonic possession; a threesome sex scene suggestive of performance; multiple dramatic and comic masks; and a staged, tape-recorded exit from this life by the hero Perfetsky.

While the novel is replete with humor and satire, scatological language, and the breaking of many taboos, it also conveys the serious theme of the quest for identity of both the individual and a nation against the larger backdrop of European civilization. The author knows the Western and Third Worlds intimately, but he and his homeland remain inconspicuous to those civilizations. This, of course, is a blessing and a curse, for it gives him the opportunity to control his own self-definition—to shape his own narrative and to make himself and his homeland conspicuous.

Translating this novel has been both a delight and a vexation for me. It has been delightful because, in the process of translation, I have made many discoveries about the nuances and intricacies of Andrukhovych's fascinating prose. It has been vexing to try and figure out how to convey those qualities of the original in English. The problem, in a nutshell, is that Andrukhovych is Rabelaisian, Gogolian, Joycean, Nabokovian (take your pick) in his mischievous wordplay. He sets many delightful traps for his reader in a polyglotic polyphony of voices and tongues. He is a poet writing prose, who constantly explores the intrinsic semantics and ontology of sound. The result is a fascinating universe constructed by his artful use of words.

Like all translations, this one comprises only a shade, a semblance, of the original, which can only remotely represent the unique aesthetic effects created by the author. All translations do remind us of the fact that nothing surpasses the magic and power of the original. My colleague John Fizer has described my approach to translating *Perverzion* as a translation of correspondences, one that seeks to find functional equivalents of the original in the target language. My goal, however, has not been to "domesticate" the original in English, as some theoreticians of translation would put it, but rather to find a golden mean to convey what the Ukrainian reader finds in the text. Readers in English, whenever possible, should laugh where the Ukrainian reader laughs and should find poetry where there is poetry in the original. Thus, one will not find dutiful literalism in various parts of my translation, but rather creative solutions to make the novel accessible in its polyphony of unique voices and sounds in English.

I have chosen the English title *Perverzion* with a *z* instead of the standard *s* for particular reasons. First, the novel is not just about sexual perversion, but it is a philosophical novel about different versions of narrative with both satirical and serious implications. The eminent Ukrainian linguist George Shevelov has suggested that the title *Perverziia* in the original historically should have been spelled with an *s*; in his mind it comprises a mild perversion of the Ukrainian word. Thus I feel that my slight perversion of the title in English constitutes a realized metaphor and is in the spirit of the author's design.

Michael M. Naydan

Notes

1. In his introduction to Bohdan Antonych, *Square of Angels: Selected Poems*, trans. Mark Rudman and Paul Nemser with Bohdan Boychuk (Ann Arbor: Ardis, 1977), ix.

■ □ ■ □ ■

PERVERZION

*For
John
Siddhartha,
the wandering
Nottingham
prisoner*

Italy,
blessed
Italy,
lay
before me.
—*IZDRYK*

■ □ ■ □ ■

PUBLISHER'S FOREWORD

THE MYSTERIOUS AND OBVIOUSLY PREMATURE DISAPPEARANCE OF
Stanislav Perfetsky from sight that occurred at the beginning of
March last year in Venice unfortunately failed to stir the depths of
our contemporary society. It failed even to stir the surfaces of it—
with the exception of several appropriate statements on the TV news
and in one or two short notes in street tabloids according to the
model "Don't Do Venice, Ukrainian Poets!" (the *Daily Blurb*
April 8 and *Kyiv Stuff* April 10 the same year), only the Lviv *New
Millennium News* responded to this event (antievent?) with extensive commentary that gravitated more toward a necrology through
its completely unmasked pathetics.[1]

Not the diplomatic service or the law enforcement agencies or
the special services[2] of our country pertinent to this apparently
intervened. The Italian organs of internal affairs were satisfied with
the calm from the Ukrainian side and with the inconclusive material evidence gathered in Perfetsky's hotel room after his disappearance. There were hatched (with all possible carelessness) two
parallel versions—of murder and suicide, from which a third—
joint—line failed to develop: coerced suicide. Having analyzed the
entire slew of evidence left by Perfetsky himself (dictated audiotapes, notebooks, computer diskettes, etc.) and completely having
failed to notice the absence of the main corpus delicti, the very body
of the poet, for which experienced Venetian divers over the course
of a week searched in vain in the darkness of the Grand Canal, the
investigation was capriciously stopped.

Surprisingly promptly on March 21 a penetratingly emotion-
laden article under the title "Ciao, Perfetsky?!" appeared in the

columns of *New Millennium News*. Signed with the name Bilynkevych[3] that till that time had been unknown to readers (it, I surmise, unequivocally, must be a pseudonym), this thing was an almost morbid generic mishmash. However, I cannot restrain from the temptation to publish it here in its entirety—with all the positives and negatives, retaining even the not always correct orthography and word usage. I feel that this will help us in curbing the further avalanche of texts that this semisensational book contains within itself.

CIAO, PERFETSKY?!

Early, early in the morning of the eleventh of March from the window of his room in the Venice hotel the White Lion, there was hurled out into the eternity of the waters of the Grand Canal the well-known (in Lviv) Ukrainian poet and the culturologist of the younger generation, born in the town of Chortopil[4]—Stas Perfetsky. He took almost nothing with him to the beyond, even leaving his eyeglasses on his desk, and his shoes on the eaten by wormwood and mold windowsill of a flung open—into the unknown—gate of the window, tips turned "to the exit." Will we ever find out what his last words were? . . .

Stakh always wore a smile, like a Japanese. We knew him as gracious and often despondent, open in everything most superficial and at the same time completely closed in the most essential. I was lucky at one point to have been his school chum, and he always remembered this.

Stakh arrived in Lviv to conquer it as a green youth. With all assuredness I can now say that he managed to do this. He knew countless languages marvelously well—both English and German. He had countless faces and countless names. In the circles of the new bohemian society, they called him not just Perfetsky. Jonah of the Fish, Carp Loverboysky, Sheatfish Saintlymansky, Pepperman, Hunkman, Antipode, Bimber Bibamus, Pierre Fukinsky, Kamal Manchmal, Johann Cohan as well as Gluck, Bloom, Vrubl, and Strudel . . .[5] And this is far from a complete list.

Have you noticed how much our city landscape has lost from his absence? He, oh, he knew how to fly above the streets and rock up the coffeehouses like no one else, like a young demon eternally changing his appearance and filling us up each time with new genial poems! On the appended photograph here you see his appearance from the period, as he himself described it, of "Kozak[6] dandyism"—with a smoothly shaved, all the way to his scalp lock on the peak, head, with a monocle in his left eye and a tuxedo, where, it's true, instead of a bow tie, it wasn't difficult to recognize a desiccated chicken foot as a symbol of protest against the nuclear threat.

He constantly risked his wealth, his talent, his life. Almost all his actions, these escapades of audacity, acted out publicly, surrounded by television crews and video pirates, assured complete failure, yet were consummated with absolute triumph. It's worth just looking at the horrifically sweet and widely sponsored by patrons "Resurrection of Barbara Langisz,"[7] performed a certain midnight before one of the half-ruined gravestones in the Lychakivsky Cemetery, when from twelve cardboard towers there were released into the rainy Lviv skies countless pigeons, balloons, condoms, crows, and poetic metaphors?! (*Our newspaper at that time contained reports about this multivalenced action.—The Editor.*) Or the unforgettable flight above the rooftops and squares, fearlessly begun from the heights of the highest point in Lviv Vysoky Zamok[8]—"A Young Poet in the Claws of a Delta Glider?!"

Now he didn't just recite poetry this Stakh Perfetsky. He played and sang with rock groups, symphonic quartets, street jazz musicians, with choirs and orchestras (the oratorio "Nights of Incarceration"), with itinerant Peruvian musicians and Gypsy-Armenian bandit bands from the neighborhood of Lviv, with Chortopil jaws harp players, whom he brought one time to Lviv right from the highlands with three military helicopters, and also with Elton John, who that year happened to spend time in our city incognito. Stas could play almost every musical instrument, but with the utmost accomplishment he played our souls—on the strings, completely invisible to the naked eye, of those who revered him as well as his enemies. . . .

But about his enemies—not a word.

At times he'd disappear for a long while. And everyone knew: new poetry was being written, new ideas being tossed about, this is the bitter oxygen of being beaten on the chest—all the way to eternal paroxysm. Where did he disappear? To the Carpathian forests, to the Arabian deserts? Perhaps he was preparing strange dank nests from old manuscripts and ladies' stockings for himself in the unexplored garrets of Lviv? And right now, where had he disappeared?

He was a planet, and forty satellites circled around him, he was a star. Sometimes—a lonely star. Especially when he was left without money. By his lonesome in our big, indifferent city.

He abandoned this city—as it was revealed today, forever—in the early spring of '92, organizing a farewell performance at the train station—"The Twelve Most Beautiful Lovers." And to each one of them he left something of himself, a certain little part, *a kind of magic.*[9] One received the latest notebook of poetry, another a prewar harmonica with which an unknown soldier of the Wehrmacht had gone into battle, a third—a plaster facsimile cast of his penis. He, Perfetsky, loved to give gifts. His possessions, thoughts, images, body, and soul. We, favored by gifts from him, didn't even notice as we walked about. Until he no longer was with us.

On that curly headed morning, as our other great poet once wrote, "the twelve most beautiful lovers lamented." As always smiling and squinting from being nearsighted, Stakh Perfetsky waved his hand from the running board of the car, slowly disappearing in the distance. But that train 75, as it turned out, did not go according to the route designated in advance—Lviv to Przemysl. It took our Stakh not to the neighboring Polish town, but to . . . NOWHERE.

What did you do, Friend, between that early fall and the next early spring, when you made the decision, without asking us, settling all accounts with life in Venice, suffused with centuries-old culture and salty vapor? And what was the name of your last artistic performance—free fall from a hotel window? Answer. He's not answering!

What is left? Several summations, several recollections.

Books of poetry that flew out like stones from his spiritual fling (*here, undoubtedly, a typesetter's mistake: instead of "fling" it should be "sling"—Yu. A.*). Here they are, in order of publication: *Astrology for Used People* (Lviv-Chortopil, 1989), *Robbery in the Hotel George* (Lviv, 1990), *Scoring* (Lviv-Paris-Munich, 1990), *Be Attentive* (Lviv, 1991), *Life as Death* (New York-Ternopil, 1992).

His literary essays—mostly distributed in samizdat form: *Concrete Reading Material* (1991), *The Building of a Boudoir* (1992).

The most renowned activities (from which all are not documented—our eternal disorganization!—and they have a clear attachment to dates): "Stryisky Park of the Jurassic Period,"[10] "Love for Three Harlequins," "The Resurrection of Barbara Langisz," "The Arrival of His Majesty the Kaiser Franz Josef I to Lviv in the Summer of 1855," "A Young Poet in the Claws of a Delta Glider," "Jubilee Banquet in the Anatomical Theater," "Devouring of the Great Fish."

Concerts, soirees, discussions, drunken carousing, scandals.

What else? . . .

Let's take another look at the photograph. Barely smiling, a bit ironic, yet gentle, in a dress coat unnaturally sticking out in every direction, Stas bores sharply through us via a monocle over his left eye. The right eye looks warm and affable, streaming with love. Might this not be because he could see almost nothing without his eyeglasses? And perhaps, to the contrary—precisely because he could see everything. And now he sees everything. From there.

I. BILYNKEVYCH

P.S. As it became known to experts of the editorial board from quite well informed sources, the disappearance (suicide?) of Stas Perfetsky was noticed on the morning after his birthday that, by irony of fate, always fell on the tenth of March. On that day he was . . . But anyway, that doesn't matter."

This was a publication in *New Millennium News*. One would guess that after its printing the chief editor immediately encountered significant problems, since already in the next issue dated January 28, an editorial disclaimer in tiny type squirreled away in a lower corner of a page was published: "The editors in advance spurn and refute all rumors and insinuations linked to the name of a certain St. Perfetsky. We ask our respected readers to refrain from contacting us regarding this."

Such an announcement in and of itself is quite telling as regards the true order of things with freedom of the press in our democratic country, and it provoked me to conduct particular searches and an intentionally unannounced private inquiry. Besides this, I considered myself duty bound to do this as one of those who personally knew Perfetsky well and one to whom even the idea of one of Stas's names belonged (Antinoah and not Antipode as the dubious Mr. "Bilynkevych" allows himself to make up). And, if the subject has turned toward fantasy, speculation, and falsifications of the latter, then it's worthwhile now to rectify the most glaring of them: the Hotel Leon Bianco (and not the White Lion, the way it is in Bilynkevych), from the window out of which Perfetsky purportedly threw himself, had been closed permanently some two hundred years ago, although all kinds of monarch types and their mistresses used to love to spend time there over the course of the seventeenth and eighteenth centuries.

But let's return to Perfetsky.

Over the course of several years with intensity I followed the development of this extraordinary subject, at times I took part in his performances and provocations and, sincerely speaking, could not help but love him.

Taking advantage of several of my acquaintances in neighboring European countries, I managed to gather up certain news about Stakh's activity from that mysterious period, which, not without cheap ornamentations, the author in *New Millennium News* laid out "between that early fall and the next early spring." The facts to which I wish to concentrate on consist mostly of press reports, depositions of eyewitnesses, postcards, programs, posters, and other things. One should believe all this with the most zealous carefulness, but nonetheless believe.

The graphomaniacally lauded by Bilynkevych (ha-ha) train 75 did arrive that day in Przemysl, and Perfetsky got off it. I confirm this because already three days after on Sunday the twentieth of September there was a performance by Stas Perfetsky for the Ukrainian community of the city. Numerous listeners (the general number 37), following the end of a Divine Liturgy in the local Greek Catholic cathedral (a former Polish garrison church), ended up at a meeting with (as the periodical of Ukrainians in Poland, *The Belch*,[11] reports) "a famous guest from Leo's city and his poetic muse." Besides several of the latest poems that were completely incomprehensible to those present, Perfetsky performed a few acrobatic études, and also answered questions about the situation in Ukraine; out of the entire program the acrobatic etudes had the greatest success, especially when he walked on his hands. As regards the muse, Eva may have been she, a student of astrophysics, a crazy Cracowian and longtime friend of Stakh's.

The entire further path of Perfetsky, followed by me nearly to the minutest details, is a dogged, unceasing, and unerring push to the West with its delicate congested twilight. The city lights, squares, bridges seemingly wink in a kaleidoscope, cathedral towers and university gates, shady pubs, clap infested poor houses, and five-star hotels. How did he manage to cross the border? I know little about that. But—it hits you in the face—not a single step to the East! This is like the completion of some grand mission, whose profound meaning is only known in the unreachable and cold strategic height.

Just unfold any of the maps of Europe available today. There a trip, delightful in its amplitude, awaiting us, which the author of a novel for teenagers might call "Along the Tracks of a Poet Who Vanished."

Next after Przemysl was Cracow—a city sufficiently inured by history to originality and curiosities. Perfetsky, a.k.a. Jonah of the Fish, felt like a fish in water in it. At first for five hundred students of Jagellonian University he read an extremely heremeticized but brilliant lecture about the quantitative-qualitative systems of versification. From other sources, in truth, it has surfaced that there weren't five hundred students, but thirteen who listened to this enchanting lecture (the text of it has not been found so far). In any case, his performance had so much undeniable success that Perfetsky wanted to live in Cracow for a while longer. Secured by the support of two or three local hooligans and criminal elements, over the course of the next several days and nights he bacchanalized the neighborhoods of the Market Square and adjacent Jewish Quarter, calling this risky contrivance "A Tartar in the City: Scenes from the History of Cracow." The result of the performance was the breaking of four store display windows on Florian Street, two spontaneous fights on St. Jan's Street and Franciscan Street, a reading at night of the most controversial excerpts of Shevchenko's long poem "Haidamaky"[12] before the monument to Mickiewicz, and also an entire truckload of empty bottles of juniper gin, walnut liquor, pepper vodka, lemon vodka, saffron vodka, Okocim[13] beer, and other Slavic beverages, in which Perfetsky, a.k.a. Bimber Bibamus, drowned himself and his nameless acquaintances, not failing to miss a single Cracow passerby. The completion of the performance had already occurred at the jailhouse, where, explaining his exotic actions, Perfetsky could assure them of just one thing: by his own admissions, the spirit of the legendary Tartar horseman had settled in him, the one who in the times of the late Middle Ages with a shot from his bow on a half note cut off the life of the ardent trumpeter from the Mariacka Tower.[14] This version didn't exceedingly convince the police of the city of Cracow, so the affair moved forward, it seems, to trial, until one day in an unknown manner and completely without a trace Perfetsky (a.k.a. Carp Loverboysky) managed to slip through from behind the gratings and, desperately working his fins, dissolved in the impassable unknown.

Licking his wounds and coming to himself from the precipice of completely nervous exhaustion, Stakh stayed one or two weeks in a small mountain monastery of the Redemptorist Fathers near the Polish-Slovak border. The superior of the cloister was a certain Father Remigiusz, in the recent past expelled from Lviv Polytechnic for the simultaneous creation of three secret groups with separate aims. Perfetsky in the past had known him from Lviv (joint participation in the protests of 1990),[15] but it was right here, in the peaceful homestead amid the primordial October forest of the Tatra Mountains, they came together in spirit and struck a deep friendship, idling their days in virtue, in spiritual peace, in Latin and Krishna song, in meditations, in the picking of late strawberries, and also in quiet conversations about beekeeping and cheese making.

In the second half of October Stakh Perfetsky, renewed and illuminated, emerged (he was already Sheatfish Saintlymansky) from the waters of the Danube onto the shores of Bratislava, where, without success, he endeavored to have a public lecture "The Slovaks as an Ethnic Branch of the Ukrainian Nation." The poster was even preserved, true, ferociously trashed, evidently by some Slovak nationalist. Nothing more happened in Bratislava, if you don't count the unlikely plausible fact that it was there that Perfetsky succeeded in obtaining an Austrian visa (and not at the embassy as is the habit of all sojourners to do, but at the Samarkandian gypsy Yashkin's, with whom our Orpheusky had come to an understanding like two dogs sniffing each other's butt in some dump outside the city).

And so Vienna, this entirely other world, rises on the path of the hero of our narration. In Vienna he appears at formal receptions, often springs up at the opera, each time in a different loge seat and with a different entourage, he shows up in TV fluff footage (Perfetsky's perfect knowledge of German and of all the tense forms of the verb in English fashions the opinion of him as a cheerful and interesting conversationalist). But in a completely unforeseen way he disappeared one day from the surface of the earth and dove into turbid and dense, murky depths. Further, we have two versions about his continued Vienna vacation.

Concordant with the first, he spent several evenings in a row in a certain conspirational apartment, and it's unknown with whom he met and why. By the way, habitations of this sort were scattered all over Vienna in hordes, which is one of the fatal residues of the empire.

Concordant with the second version, which appears more probable, Stas Perfetsky got a job as a male dancer in a quasi-legal strip club on Margaretengürtel Street, where every evening, a.k.a. as Pierre Fukinsky, he performed complicated erotic moves for the satisfaction of regular customer older ladies.

However it was, during the winter of that year that Perfetsky is found in Prague, which he reached with a forged passport by dressing as a woman. In fact, all these numerous secret agent attributes do not seem completely appropriate, for at that time Prague had long been waiting for him anxiously and with a weighty invitation: in the Central European University he was supposed to read a series of lectures under the general title, "Revelations on the Expectorated Margins." The first of the lectures simply turned out to be a shock for the initially skeptically inclined listeners. Perfetsky celebrated his minor victory with delectation, over the course of the next two weeks, without crawling out of the noisy and vile-smelling beer hall "Dachovy posranec"[16] somewhere in Zhizhkov. All kinds of well-known Czechs like Vaclav Havel and Egon Bondi went there to take a look at him. Stakh Perfetsky, a.k.a. as Johann Cohan, startled them with his wittiness and directness, and, additionally, taught all the drunks of Zhizhkov several Ukrainian songs and the toast "Down the hatch!"

But, when after two weeks the second lecture from the cycle "Revelations on the Expectorated Margins" resounded in the university walls, the reaction of the auditorium, overstuffed with all kinds of rabble, turned out to be markedly more restrained. This, however, for Perfetsky didn't serve as an alert, and after a day he self-ignoredly (in order not to say "self-assuredly") ventured to do a third lecture, although he himself certainly had no idea what he had to say. Punishment arrived with absolute irreversibility: right after the fourth sentence uttered by Stakh, with whistling and catcalls rotten tomatoes flew at him as well as curse words in the various languages of Europe. Nothing more kept him in Prague.

For Christmas he, Kamal Manchmal, ended up this way in Berlin where, undoubtedly, he had to get to through Dresden. But we don't know to this day whether he made a stop in Dresden. Berlin struck him with its endless number of lights, hanging in the bare trees, and not less—the stout streetwalkers in riding boots and with whips in their hands that with the approach of dusk completely took control over all the entrances and exits in the vicinity of Savigny Platz and Charlottenburg. Stas, however, didn't give in to their excessively transparent insinuations to fondle them, at that time having warmed up a seat for himself in a small inexpensive leftist restaurant Terzo Mondo, run by a Zeus-like Greek by the name of Costas and served by a countless number of young Greek girls, each of whom was related to the owner somehow. To one of them, Zoe—one should note, the most beautiful, with such buxom breasts, his spirit was slain right at first sight—Stakh Perfetsky, a.k.a. Pepperman, became benumbed from something much akin to love. Sitting for hours at his little table in the gloom of the Third World Restaurant reeking of wine and marijuana, he, like a starving cat, met and followed with an uneasy, myopic gaze every appearance of the beauteous Dionysian female, who, moreover, remained nearly indifferent to him, bringing him, however, from time to time, a goblet of complimentary red *imiglikos*. Each time Stakh dove deeper into a melancholic numbness, all the more convincing himself of his complete worthlessness for anyone in this world. At times Costas, the owner of the establishment, sat down next to him and, understanding everything perfectly, as though reading from the palm of his hand, advised him anyhow to forget about Zoe, who soon had to go home to Greece, where, for the right to become her husband, two fiancés were competing. The old Greek sympathized with Perfetsky, but warned him if he has *that* in mind, by the ancient custom of all southern peoples, he would be castrated. Perfetsky thanked him and suggested they sing something together.

It happened that a certain Nachtigal von Ramensdorf came to his table, but this tragic actor from the rabble, a descendant of knights and usurers, who was able to imitate the voice of Edith Piaf or Ella Fitzgerald, could not, however, soothe the melancholy Stakh with anything. Thus in solitude and mortiferousness he greeted the New Year, having, by the way, prepared for the Berlin Academy a sensitive paper on the topic "Ancient Greek Culture and the Greek Girl of Today: Convexities and Concavities." Eight professors heedfully listened to him, skeptically blinking their eyeglass lenses, but in the end thanked him with applause—as sparse as possible for eight professors.

And at this intolerable hour of life, when tormented by insomnia and Zoe's eyes, Perfetsky began to think about the propositions of the ladies of the street in riding boots, an invitation from Munich found him. Someone Invisible was concerned about him, straightening out his wings and each time arranging a new rescuing turn. From the invitation it surfaced that a certain institution of a sort of a Maecenas very much wanted to see him as their stipend holder, it also offered him complete expenses for the term of three months with housing not far from Munich, right next to the Alps, *schöne Umgebung*,[17] a five-hundred-year-old tradition of beer, a frozen lake, hot baths, enchanted swans, post cards to all the corners of the earth, a stone hall, candles, marmalade, an encrusted harpsichord for practicing well-tempered music, vigilant care, *bayrische Spezialitäten*,[18] rare species of trees, park sculptures, the lady of the house in head wrap and gaiters, immense stacks of hay, bird's milk, fresh eggs, white rumps of hills, *Kirche, Kinder, Küche*, all the gold of the world, porcelain, majolica, toccatas and fugues, sonnets and octaves, museums, museums, museums, museums, *ja-ja, eine gute Idee, jo-jo, eine Starnberger See, und eine feine Blechmusik, und meine kleine Nachtbumsik, und Hofbräuhaus, und Nazisraus, und besser ist, dass es München gibt—mit Franzl und Platzl und Kindl und Rudl—willkommen am Stachus, Herr Stach, lieber Strudel!* . . .[19]

On the twenty-third of January Stakh Perfetsky, a.k.a. Strudel, stepped onto the platform of the main yard in the free Bavarian capital. He disappears from our field of vision from that time. All my attempts at finding out anything about his Munich tour have been in vain for a long time.

The next news of Stas was, unfortunately, what we began with: March, Venice, an inexplicable disappearance, a step through an early-morning window . . .

We live according to the law of coupled systems.[20] Any movement, even the quietest one, compulsively finds its echo.

Several weeks ago my acquaintance, a fairly well known artist Bohdan Br. returned from a nearly half-year internship in Venice, where they taught him a love for old objects and recent vintage wine. One day a stranger visited him at his house, who barely spoke broken Ukrainian and who had a large package filled with all kinds of things for him. This package, in his words (but more in gestures), one ought to pass along "Ukraine."

The uninvited guy couldn't explain anything more because of his severely insufficient store of vocabulary. However, he distinctly uttered my name several times.

After the return of Bohdan Br. from Venice, the package from the stammerer ended up with me in this way.

What you will find subsequently in this book comes from the above-mentioned package and concerns the Venetian Adventure of Stas Perfetsky. I collected everything here—and in the sequence in which, in my opinion, the action unfolded.

But just what are these materials? What's their origin? I would divide them into several rubrics.

First, these are copies (if not originals) of those documents that ended up at the disposal of the police after the disappearance of Perfetsky and after a complete inspection of everything that he had left behind in his hotel room. As already stated, these were notebooks, audiocassettes, with texts spoken by Perfetsky himself, a printout of several computer texts, that, obviously, were on Stakh's diskettes. All this—is from the person of Stakh himself, and, I must say, the most wrangling textological analysis would support my conviction that it wasn't a fake, that these words, these phrases, this vision belonged to him, Stakh Perfetsky. But such materials are far from being the majority, perhaps not even a third of them.

Second, these are texts that were and remain generally accessible and completely officially published, but each of them has a direct relationship to the story that interests us. These are invitations, programs, reportages, newspaper interviews, given by Perfetsky in Venice and published still before his disappearance on the tenth of March.

Third, this is a series of quite strange documents that in spots recalls work dispatches; at the top they have a mysterious cipher, put together partly in Italian, partly in German, partly in English, and written, it appears, by various persons, but most often by a particular woman.

Fourth, these are depictions of several other people about episodes that they experienced while accompanying Stakh Perfetsky. They had to be translated, too.

And finally, fifth. Bits and pieces (also in various languages), but it is unknown who made them. It's as though they have been noted by that conventional "teller," or rather "observer," or perhaps "narrator," who knows everything about everyone, who simultaneously is everywhere and who is nowhere other than in literature. Who is the author of these bits and pieces?

A completely separate case—a videocassette taped by a hidden camera.

I set out two versions immediately. And then, each of You, esteemed readers, has the right to his or her own. Or for several of his or her own versions. Let's not rush with them.

The numeration of each of the published documents, marked by me in the upper right corner, belongs, clearly, to me, in as much as the sequence of publication of the documents is proposed by me. It would be interesting, how much different could this sequence be?

Besides numeration, there are no textual (or extratextual) changes. And before finishing this, believe me, introduction that is quite difficult for me, I want to thank the most respected Ms. Mariana Prokopovych (for translations from Italian), and Mr. Yurko Pr. (for translations from German), and Oleh Mokhnaty[21] (for translations from English)—their assistance was unpaid, but not fruitless. With not the least thankfulness I bow before everyone who in one or another way has served to help the appearance into the world of this disquieting book, especially Mr. Oleh Zayachkivsky, and through his intercession, Mr. Francesco Apolloni and Mr. Rossano Rossi, each of whom, without knowing it, brilliantly fulfilled the mission of my secret agent in Venice.

December 1994
Yu. A.

■ □ ■ □ ■

1

HER NAME IS ADA ZITRONE[1] AND HIS JANUS MARIA RIESENBOCK. I'M sitting in their Alfa Romeo, and we're speeding along the autobahn from Munich to Venice. From Munich. To Venice.

This happened to me the day before yesterday, Ash Wednesday, the first day following the end of carnival. It was a stroll through Munich in the hopes of seeing the remains of a yet untidied up holiday: piles of garbage, broken bottles, trampled tails and wings, torn, painted masks. I didn't find anything of the like, because I started off to town only after noon. The streets and city squares had been cleaned up, probably, before dawn. . . .

I found short-lived refuge in the coffeehouse Luitpold, which I found by a map on Briennerstrasse (or as they say here, "shtraahzze") II, where I permitted myself one after the other double Remi Martins (the first in honor of Rilke, the second—of Stefan George). When I got nice and warm, I crawled out of the coffeehouse and started off slowly in the direction of Schwabing,[2] passing by Odeonplatz and Ludwigstrasse, flooded with the first twilight. The shop windows promised everything in the world, even immortality. No one had their foreheads anointed with ashes.[3] Thousands of passersby moved side by side with me in this toylike megalopolis. But decent people have to take communion with fish on this day: Ash Wednesday (as Eliot called it), *Aschermittwoch,* ashes, sorrow, melancholy, and fish. This is the way the fast begins. . . .

Now, one lyrical moment. Without having yet reached the university and the Triumphal Gates, I sensed that spring was beginning. It was all together in one: a warm wind, a bit of snow just beginning to melt in spots, my unbuttoned raincoat, the dangling of my scarf, a new shirt, the scent of a new shirt, roasted chestnuts, sharp spices, the scent of something else, of some kind of women, men, that flowed next to me, music from around the corner, a tightening in my chest—I stopped for less than a moment, and no way, I didn't stop, I simply understood—but what I "understood," when this is entirely not the right word, and "sensed" is not the right word, and no one will tell me the word I need—I felt something, some kind of great changes, at least one, something like. . . .

Her name is Ada, his Dr. Riesenbock, private urology in Possenhoffen. And they're taking me to Venice in their car. I came to my senses a bit just before the Austrian border. It was just then that almost by touch I recognized the need to say something into this Dictaphone.

So, the day before yesterday, during the evening of the Wednesday of the beginning of the Great Fast, I finally stepped out into Schwabing, onto Leopoldstrasse flooded with irritating lights. I was ready for adventures, so that I was even jumping inside my own body. Adventure did find me here right away: a squat and red-lipped mulatto woman, short legged and in a short skirt, with wild curves, covered in bangles, in a tight, trimmed-with-spangles, décolleté dress, a streetwalker from some other cheerful quarter, because Schwabing now isn't the same one from the times of Symbolism and Kaiser Wilhelm. She stood in the gate beneath a street lamp and looked to be a face indispensable to the crowd. In fact, it turned out this way for me, I saw her light up, she smiled, I understood everything, it became hellishly cold in my chest, just ten more steps were left, not even a whole hundred marks in my wallet that I had with me, so there was no guarantee for our contract, five steps away from her I heard: *"Hallo, kommst du mit?"* Two more steps I kept silent and blurted out right at her: *"Ja, ich komme mit, Liebling, wieviel?"* She didn't answer *"Wieviel,"* she whirled on her sadomasochistic heels, took me by the hand and led me to the gate. But she turned out to be a local, she opened the gate with a key, procured from her stunning décolleté dress for the sake of *special effect,*[4] and so we stopped in a building where she led me up the stairs, from time to time looking back and smiling with her thick lips, I also felt how there surged and rebelled in me all the abstinence of the last months, even years, these bangles on her were just unbearable, I was ready to drive into her right here on the steps, squeezing her against the handrails and tearing her purely symbolic, short-tailed[5] red silk skirt. But she maintained a safe distance and kept leading me somewhere upstairs, onto some ninth or so floor, during which time she sang in some tropical language, maybe Amharic.[6] So finally we ended up in living quarters filled with people, with smoke and incense and all kinds of equatorial aromas, illuminated by green and red lamps, where everyone without exception was singing . . .

. . . Oho, I didn't even notice us cross the Austrian border. I just managed to read KIEFERSFELDEN[7] or something like that, some kind of fields of beetles. Stone walls along both sides of the boulevard, finally mountains, we drove into the mountains, everywhere there was a shitload of snow falling, even Dr. Riesenbock—this is me about you, about you—had to put on his protective glasses. He's sitting behind the wheel and doesn't know a word of Ukrainian. His wife is another thing. She understands everything, a Ukrainian herself by birth, she's next to him on the front seat, as she should be, Frau Riesenbock, dressed completely in black and dark cherry colors, but she doesn't hear me. . . .

I apparently didn't get what kind of apartment this was right away. My chest filled up with sweet smoke, I felt myself to be almost made of wax, voices singing floated from everywhere, from all the rooms, all these people were still walking around today in carnival rags, it was as though they had collected them from the garbage after yesterday, my bronze-colored temptress dissolved among the other mulatto, Arab, Turkish, Chinese, and Indian women, they decorated the apartment with living green branches, with strips of hot-colored fabric and countless holy pictures, at which I was completely unable to look; moving from room to room, I kept trying to grab her by the bottom, why have you brought me here, I respect the customs of all people, rites and so forth, but you've gone too far, nocturnal bird, I would say to her, but in every room there were sitting on rugs, benches, and right on the floor lots of carnival dressers, anachronistic carnival revelers, and they all were singing, endlessly from the time I wound up there, nonstop songs in broken German, something like psalms or hymns, the grammatical clumsiness struck even my ear, but the melody was nice enough, an insanely nice melody, exquisite, a mixture of Celtic and Coptic with additions of Brazilian, Armenian, Maghrebi, and Romanian. I went wacko from that music, I tried to howl along with it myself, but from time to time one of the singers glanced at me reproachfully, as if saying, Don't stick your nose in this, it's not your thing, so I shut up. . . .

The first thing that I always do when I stop at a place I don't know is to look for a musical instrument. I love the piano, guitar, violoncello, accordion, the maracas, the flute, I love countless other musical instruments. So I began to look for them. But nowhere was there anything of the like—just voices, female and male, children's and elders', some kind of half-crazed prayer to another god, something there about forests, honey, groves, fields, orchards, mountains, meadows, grasses, gates. In the meanwhile, with a little more intense concentration, I looked over the apartment; it was one of the typical rental rooms from the past century. In Lviv there are thousands of these kind, they had already erected them even before the secession, in the days of stormy eclectics in ideas, it was as if the architect had competed with the material, contriving for himself as many problems as possible and cramming the apartment with all kinds of nooks, niches, pavilions, mezzanines, and, besides the singing human crowd, nothing else was there and no one, well, okay, there were several sofa beds, odds and ends, couches, some kind of rugs—everything as though it had just been brought, all foreign and random, and generally—just bare walls and floors; one does not live or even pray in these kinds of conditions, but here, as is evident, they both lived and prayed. And also—these lamps, red and green, something in between a discotheque and a Byzantine cathedral, and also aromas, aromas everywhere—from candles and incensors, the latter in the hands of Peruvian, Korean, Malagasian, Moroccan, and Filipino women who danced by from time to time; somewhere my ample-lipped havoc ambled her way among them, but I would already not recognize her in this overgrown flower garden; after some time it came to my mind that this wasn't just a single apartment, but rather several former living quarters, between which the walls were knocked down, the entire floor, the seventh heaven of the chimerical presecession building on Leopoldstrasse, or, perhaps, on one of the side alleys—I didn't notice. . . .

Wow, now pay attention! Gray sky. Bald-spotted snow. Towers. Crows above the city hall's ridge tile. Yellow walls. Silence, ten, no, eleven in the morning, Friday, cold, highmountain, Highalps, what else? Heavy down comforters, bedrooms in locks frozen overnight, coffee with milk, hot wine, school children at recess, a distant bell, chimneys, smoke above the chimneys, invisible wings—Whose? This is Innsbruck, my friends. To my right in the valley. I'd like to be here for a while. Hey, *Achtung, Achtung, mein lieber Riesenbock, bitte, auf ein Moment stoppen! . . . Ich habe manche Problemen. . . .*[8]

Well there. I was able at least to intimate something, at least with something, or what? Maintain this status, this Innsbruck? At times I feel friggin' bad: how much of everything I've let go, a hole-filled collector, how much I've lost, forgotten, especially there, at home. There remains with me (in me?) some kind of just dark courtyards, corridors, damp garrets, trampled dandelions, unfilled ditches, lime-covered tree trunks. . . . This is already here, in other countries, I began to work by my entire self, by all that I am. I disappeared in the wild abysses of moods, I wasn't keeping up with them and took such a fright that, just as at home, I'd almost lose everything. In the end, you can live more peacefully with this. Consider everything lost extraneous. Everything not lost (a tiny little thing) indispensable. That is, inevitable. But I had an inkling. Even earlier in Lviv, and even in Chortopil, I was afraid that chance was using us constantly every day. I'd want to be able to do something to oppose it.

So the idea of this Dictaphone came up. Always to have it with me. To speak, to be silent, to speak again. To cram into it equally as much of everything as is crammed in our language. It's clear that even it won't save us. But it can intimate, give something, without knowing it itself. Oh, fuck, such wise thoughts, I hate myself! Well good.

I return to the day before yesterday's story. While I remember it. Too bad that Ada isn't listening to this. Because I wanted her to like me. But she packed a bag for herself filled with Italian operas and all the way from Munich has been sitting with her headphones on, sometimes amplifying the prima donnas with her raspy voice. "O don Fatale."[9] In Italian. She knows Italian. She's lived in Rome and Ravenna, in Pisa and Assisi. Enough of that.

For a good hour I had been groping through these quarters, at every step startling all kinds of Malaysians, Persians, Ethiopians, they continued to sing, I deciphered just individual, mutilated phrases, something like, "An wi go to di radiance a di Joiman gate wid a young son wid a greaaat floaaating fish til di king scatta wi grain pan blood mek di lightning strike dem an it gi we a gyadín a di Joiman gate whe dem have bread and beer an apple a di golden cockerel glory to di Fada so wi wooda get loaded in di celestiality a di silva wine a wi ignarance butta gi wi some butta an beer an di spirit a di great fish glory to di Fada tase wi an oshun doshun boshunu[10] mek di lightning strike dem mek di lightning strike dem cause wi gwine inna di radiance a di Joiman gate wid a young son wid a greaaat floaatting fish til di king scatta wi grain pan blood mek di lightning strike dem an it gi wi a gyadín a di Joiman gate whe dem have bread an beer an apple a di golden cockerel glory to di Fada"[11]—this is the way they clacked their voices with their far-from-perfect language of the realm,[12] these people dressed as Moors and Monks, Knights and Seminarians, Rhinoceroses and Astrologers, Minnesingers[13] and Nibelungen, Indonesians, Kurds, Pakistanis (or maybe Palestinians), and Albanians, too, Bosnians, Moors, and Khmer, among which there were, categorically, Haitians, Tahitians, Cretans, Cypriots, Congolese, Bangladeshis, Côte d'Ivoirians, and Burkina Fasoans, and all of them entirely not too badly bore this most complex of melodies, uttering something like, "Di herbal gaadín a di Joiman gate stan before wi and be wid wi, mek we knife fall an fill all a wi—wid a young son a big fish, wid di spirit af enchantment, wid di enchantment af spirit, iyan an cannan crawl inna it aze, lick mi wounds, an fi him, fi har, an she to, grow fi wi like temptation inna di guts ar guts inna di temptation glory to di Fada so we gwine get loaded inna di hole a di sun di celestiality a wi clear ignarance meat gi wi meat an schnapps an ja-ja a greaaat fish glory to di Fada an oshun doshun boshunu mek di lightning strike dem mek di lightning strike dem di herbal gyadín a di Joiman gate stan before wi an be wid wi, mek wi knife fall an fill all a wi—as a young sahn great fish, wid di spirit af enchantment, wid di enchantment af spirit, iyan an cannan crawl inna it aze, lick mi wounds, an fi him, fi har, an she to, grow fi wi like temptation inna di guts ar guts inna di temptation be glorified di new Isaac"—I would have hated myself for the rest of my days, if I would have attempted to escape from here, even though the sense of danger continued to grow in me, all the more so since no one planned even to talk or somehow to come to an understanding with me—a guest—the men sang on, sitting about on the floor, rugs and sofas, and clapped as well to the beat with their palms, and the women also sang on, carrying out of the side corridors newer and newer branches of ferns, cocoa nuts, swatches of fabric, bangles, small holy pictures, broken records. . . . But you've really gone crazy, I got unstrung, though without hate or scorn, for all around something grand was really happening, a harmonious ritual of all the wronged from the entire world, they had to invent another god for themselves, they were battered with hunger and bombs, epidemics, AIDS, chemicals, the most polluted wells, and the cheapest bordellos were filled with them, they had weapons and patience tested on them, they had their forests burned and their deserts trampled, they were driven out from every direction from the moment they were born; how did they answer—with jazz, with marijuana, with a hundred methods of making love? . . . I walked among the refugees, half poisoned with the aromas, with the green and red flashes, the songs, it's easy to poison me—with everything thought up by these passportless searchers of the rich German god, the Sovereign of the German Gate, to which they managed to force their way through at the last minute—some through a ship's pier glasses, some through louse-infested benches, through truths and untruths, through bribes, payoffs, killings, pleading, begging, through thrusting out their vaginas, rear ends, through playing on a leather flute, through Lviv, through Poland, through the throat, through the lungs, through eighteen borders and thirty customs checkpoints— as emigrants, musicians, journeyman laborers, sorcerers, sex machines, victims of burned-down houses, dissidents, bandits, rebels, garbagemen, shit carriers, sellers of roses in restaurants, croupiers, communists, Maoists, students of law and philosophy—

thus they managed, succeeded, defrauded, tore off this land for themselves, this Germany, this good life, these sleeping bags in underground passageways, they made these cities more colorful, this good, hardworking, self-sacrificing Germany warmed them and fed them and gave them to drink and so forth, but they want something else from it, they're pleading for something else from their shared, though invented, god—what do they want: the forests, the Alpine mountaintops, the castles, the museums, a visa extension, blood, warmth, sensitivity, money, cars, maybe they want citizenship? . . .

I walked among them stunned, as though I were guilty of everything, as though I were the cause of the causes for this screwed up world. . . . I'll rest a bit.

The checking of passports at the Brennero Pass didn't last longer than three minutes. Even my Sovok[14] booklet didn't arouse in the Italian guy any kind of conspicuous emotion.

Then we madly rolled downhill—Janus Maria gassed his Porsche, or whatever it was he had, nearly to two hundred kilometers an hour, we tore into a region where there was no more snow, where there was green grass, this is the kind of earth: *"Wo die Zitronen bluhn"*[15] (and you, Zitrone, have you bloomed in this land?—what an idiotic last name, I've fallen in love with your very name Mrs. Riesenbock),[16] the sun poured into our eyes, cliffs flew on both sides of the road, but everywhere there were roadside signs of human presence: a bridge over a stream, a chapel, cows in the grass, a Madonna, a ruined tower, a battered wall, several sheep, a school around the corner, a Madonna, a scarecrow in the garden, a robber's castle, a hunter's restaurant, a gas station, a Madonna, a chapel, a beehive, a fisherman's inn, a water mill, a cemetery, a Madonna, a girl with a basket, a robber's castle, a hotel with geraniums (gardenias? hortensias?) in the windows, a cheese-making shop, a smashed-up Opel Kadett without any passengers, a woman in black, a Madonna. . . .

Riesenbock got nervous: much too often Italian road workers, who weren't in much of a hurry, popped up, and he had to slow down to forty or fifty, to look for detours around them, breaking every second. The Italians in work clothes were unnaturally calm.

And Riesenbock—yes, I'm talking about you, about you—looks nervous—he has big and bony hands, he has a beard, bald spots on his head and a little bit of roving in his eyes. From his appearance he looks like he's in the middle of his life's journey: wearied by life, but still ravenous for it. I like these kinds of guys.

We stopped for a few minutes between Bressanone and Bolzano. Ada drove the car from there. Don't look back. Now, when you've got to take off the headphones, I'll continue my story just for you. It was that way from there on.

Finally everyone readily turned their attention to me. Four girls appeared next to me—a Thai, a Samoan, a Trinidadian, and a Lesbian—moving to the rhythm of the collective song without interrupting their singing, they quite tenderly, but commandingly, began to take off my coat. I decided not to resist and experience everything to the very end. Maybe to atone for something. Or just to learn. All the more, the end of the action was approaching, from behind "a di Joiman gate" sung by the horde, several symptoms flashed from time to time, my head was swirling from the fragrant smoke, the song was becoming louder and higher, the refrains more frequent—me, without my coat, take note, without chest armor—they led me to the largest of rooms where everyone was crawling one by one, there were countless numbers of them, it seemed there was no way whatsoever to make room for them all, and somehow they did not fit in dressed in their carnival costumes. They left the middle of the room open.

Yes, I also suspect that this is some kind of new sect, absolutely.

Then the following occurs. Several strange characters with buck and bull horns on their heads, dancing closer to me, they carry out to the middle of the room a small sacred felt rug (the kind we use to wipe our feet on), and before it, together with the final ecstasies of song ("a di Joiman gate gi wi to swim past like a greaat fish") for the sake of the common rapture they put out a bust: gold-plated bronze with somewhat increased proportions (in regard to natural proportions, obviously), and I understand that this is their deity, their idol, their divinity, better to say some kind of pithecanthropus, or a Buddha, or a German philosopher-materialist, he was the Guardian of the German Gate, either Egir, Grungnir, or Fafnir,[17] a guard of the enchanted garden. . . .

All those present besides me solemnly kneeled before his divine presence. When I had the impulse to kneel, then the girls, all four of my overseers, simply kept me from doing it, grabbing every piece of me from every direction. With the last rhythms of the great psalm, inasmuch as I understood, the High Holy One or something similar appeared before our eyes—a really robust lad of unknown race, for certain some kind of mixture of a Papuan guy with a Laplander, with a bag on his head, with only cutouts for his eyes, ears and mouth. Shaking his entire body, he finally fell face down to the deity and crawled before it along the small rug. At this point the several-hour-long hymn finally cooled down. But here, however, a common *murmurando* was born, similar to the buzzing of millions of flies. Once again, clearly, everyone other than me was humming, because I was banned from doing even that, although I really had the urge to hum with them. . . .

After Trento the doctor of urology again took the wheel. Ada, just as earlier, dove into her Italian operas. Rossini, Verdi, Leoncavallo, Donizetti, Pinzetti. And also Mozart, Mozart, Mozart, who really must have been an Italian, at least half. German women, especially from the south, really love Italians. They come just from hearing the Italian names, especially the double or triple ones. This is the way immaculate conceptions begin. This is the way Mozart was born, the great possessor of my heart.

But I probably won't last till Venice. Too much of everything—these mountains, the green grass, which hasn't been seen since September, these arias, this bony Janus, who from time to time mild-naturedly curses someone in German, this view with fallen towers, this speed, this Ada, half turned away, here's her ear, her sweet ear, illuminated all the way through, is filling up with the nectar of music, with the warm sperm of music, with Italian voices, here the line of her neck passes to her shoulder, here's her hair, it seems, colored, bright chestnut colored, and now—her arms, her palms, two birds that lie on the front panel, they sometimes spring up in time with the music heard by no one else in the world.

I was bullshitting you. It's better this way, with the music heard by the entire world.

Now: attention one more time! Verses from which I must free myself. This is improvisation. I can make a mistake here and there. Well then. O Italy, what reason do I love you so? Six foot iambic, cool! O Italy, what reason do I love you so? O Italy, what reason do I love you so? Because you blow into the butt of a boat. Utter nonsense, and it's not six foot. Well good, let's go on. O Italy, what reason do I love you so? Because you blow into the butt of a boat. Because you are like a harbor for a boat! And I'll always, believe me, love you: when I love, I love even when I'm barfing! When I compose this song of mine, Like a nightingale happy in the grove, Then I feel like I'm in paradise, Where beautiful sluts whisper to me "Stanislav, I love you!" Around me—the mountains and the Tyrol! Here what's not a word is *parole*! I'd *porol*—bang you, *geeoorgeous*![18] Your king has begun to sulk like a troll. Why, Tyrol, are you so wondrous? Why, king, are you so lecherous? Why these cliffs, these monasteries, these oak trees? I'd lick your neck with the tip of . . . Pardon me, maybe I'm getting too loud.

They're husband and wife. She's maybe thirty. This isn't my business.

Well look. Our Ferrari runs mile after mile, we've jumped out of Alto Adige, not a single mountain robber attacked us, not a single of my barons enjoyed our blood, and the landscapes are becoming more unbelievable, this is the South, the South, the South, this is cedars and pines, and laurels, and the peonies along the Autostrade, this is the scent of coffee from everywhere, this is aloe, myrtle, and sweet rush, this is a simple enumeration which one can arrange in writing in two columns, each one of them will mean something completely unforgettable, but at the same time—define orientations along both sides of the road; I'm thrilled just from naming, that's why I just want to name, just to enumerate, this is a simple enumeration, from which your innermost bowels spasm, and I can't venture to violate its wonderful internal sequence:

a flower garden
a balcony
a church

a city square
a fountain
a kiosk
steps in the bushes
a lantern
a gate
a pillar
a stained-glass window
mcdonald's
a display window
a cornice
vegetables
a sidewalk
a sidewalk
a donkey

a pigeon
Saint Thomas
swallow's nests

Saint Peter
Saint Luke
a girl in a window
Saint Francis

Saint Roch[19]
Saint Spirit,[20]

    I tear off everything from myself besides my shirt, as though I'm a saint, and finally give me a swig of alcohol, even better—two swigs, so that I won't die prematurely from excessive heat.

    And what's that ahead? Verona?!

I should somehow finish the day before yesterday's story, shouldn't I?

    So, at the height of the loudest humming, I'll say it like this, the horned men appeared who were mentioned above, I understood that they're priests or of this persuasion. The main one raised his head from the rug and began to shake upon seeing what they were carrying: it was an aquarium, an enormous one, like a large vat, without plants, without seashells, without little stones on the sand, just with water and with a big living fish, a fish, it was, perhaps, maybe even a carp or a sheatfish, or a bream, or a white *amur,* say, a pike, and here, together with the compression of ahs of the entire crowd, they strike this aquarium to the floor (here the director dictated slow motion of the film), the aquarium falls for a long, long time, but breaks up anyway, splashing out green streams in every direction (everything dries up in me), this is awful, for the priests with their dark tongues capture the splashes, in me it's as though something is breaking down, I see how the fish is jumping in pain on the little rug among the broken pieces of the aquarium, I see how the High Priest has procured a sharpened hatchet from his belt, and I know what will happen next, my legs give way, I'm no longer made of wax, I'm already cotton, I'm already not even made of cotton, I'm made of air, the first blow with the hatchet—and the fish is split through, but it's still shaking (I'm knocked off my feet), a second blow—everyone shouts "A-ah!" the fish has a broken pond, but it's still shaking (I'm no longer breathing, the air is escaping from me as though from a punctured ball), the third blow—everyone is screaming "U-ukh!" right at the fish's heart, it will flap a bit more and grow silent, and I: that's it darkness bottom zero button hook not a peep.

Just today I came to my senses right before the Austrian border. The police found not me, but my body—at night Wednesday, apparently at about three o'clock, beneath the Kennedy Bridge near the English Park, I lay with my head pointed to the west, the way all decent corpses lie. They brought me back to semiconsciousness, but I was almost unable to explain anything to anyone. All of me hurt, I felt faint inside, I felt like vomiting, there was a ringing in my head, but I didn't succeed in falling asleep, someone had warned me, someone had warned me. The police kept me to 10 A.M., until that miracle-working pair appeared—he and she, Ada and Riesenbock, I had never known or seen them, but they explained to the police that I'm the famous Pepperman, and that, it turns out, everyone is waiting for me in Venice, everyone is just pissing in their pants without me in that Venice, everybody just got freaked out and is raging without me, and all of Venice is chanting: "Per-fe-tsky! Per-fe-tsky!"—they so want to touch me in that Venice; Ada and Riesenbock shoved at them some kind of scented, rustling papers on sky blue and pink forms with a winged lion, entangled like Laocoön, in serpents; they vouched for me, drove me to their place in Possenhoffen, packed for their villa, and the doctor gave me all kinds of sleeping pills—in connection with which I crashed on their nuptial bed the rest of the day and another night until morning, and they, Ada and Riesenbock, in the meantime took care of my affairs, drove to the Italian consulate for a visa for me, picked out some new glasses for me, bought all kind of trifles for the road and phoned someone deep into the night, explaining something, convincing someone of something, all while I slept (didn't sleep) on their wide bed, scattered all over with crumbs, red-hot nails, and nutshells.

I don't know what all this was about. I had to end up in Venice— and today I'm stopping over there in some two to three hours, or maybe even sooner. It's difficult for me to think up any explanations. It's easier for me simply to contemplate and list them in a whisper: the steering wheel, the road, the grass, her neck, shoulder, a half turn, a half bend, a half dream, a half call, a half love.

The vineyards first appeared between Verona and Padua.

■ □ ■ □ ■

2

Venice,
March 1, 1993

Most Respected Mr. Perfekcy![1]

Our mutual and good acquaintance, doctor of a psychiatry Frank
Popel (Lawsanne, Swatzerland) recommended You as a potential
unit from Ukrania for participation in an internashional seminar of
cultural-spiritual activists, which our foundation *La morte di
Venezia* is organizing together with individual intellectual, commer-
cially active and sacral circles. The theme of the seminar is "The
Post-Carnival Absurditi of the World: What Is on the Horizon?"
    If you are prepared to attest your interest in the upper-noted sem-
inar, then we ask that you bowingly come to Venice no later than
the fifth of March year of our Lord and make an appearance with a
word on one of the themes underscored below (the length of your
talk must not exceed seven or eight pages of computerial typescript).
It could be on the theme of death in Ukraninian culture. Or: also,
the theme of love of the erotic and of the thanatic, but touching the
problematics of Oriental Europe, or, in general, the absurditty of
life. It can be your look into the feminist or masculinist. Or into the
postcommunist. It could also be a model of a new analysus of the
processes that just recently have begun existifying in your country,
for example casinos and night klubs. Or also the uncovering of the
essence of the Ukraninian mentaliti, on the background of certain
others known to the world. It can also be a certain magical or demi-
urgic or even surgical act that attests to some current absurditti of

the world. It can also be anything that You suggest, dear Mr. Perfekcy. If, for example, you feel like relating something about Ukraninian nuclear arms, that would be wonderful. Or You might want to inform us about Dostoevsky, Gorkee, Bulgakov, Sakharov[2] and other of Your writers—that would be okay. Like, for example, Your desire to think about the schools and movements in Ukraninian nice art or in politics, like, for example, nashunalism. Finally, we would even be interested to hear from you a report about this year's epidemic of cholera in Ukrania.

Your constant guide-companion and helper will be the sweet Mrs. Ada Zitrone, a collaboratress with our foundation, through the body of which from here we are passing along this invitation. The organizers will take on themselves all Your expenses, will gwarantee your hotel and bedding, daily diets, degustations, hygienes and medical sanitaria. And even more we will guarantee You for Your informative address recompense in the amount of one million lire Italian.

Mr. Perfekcy, with great imtolerance we await You. As they say in your homeland—COMEWELL PLEASE![3]

Yourses to eternity
Dr. Leonardo di Merryhouse, President
La morte di Venezia Foundation
Amerigo Dappertutto,[4] Technical Secretary of the Foundation

THE POSTCARNIVAL ABSURDITY OF THE WORLD: WHAT IS ON THE HORIZON?[5]
An Enclosure for Participants

Today we live under the sign of the sad word "post-." Faithful to our nature and technology, we do not want to perceive that this is the possible end, so it emerges, from all the surrounding attributes, signs and indications. Step by step we become more commonplace in the grand absurdity of repetition and self-repetition. And even nonvirological changes that from recent times have limited the face of reality have not brought the expected breach. The most original of ideas, generated by the spiritless spirit of our time (permit us the unhappy play on words)—this is the idea of the total and of course totalitarian imitativeness of everything, deadly and grand. Quotation, collage, and deconstruction have displaced something more distant in time, more primordial, and more authentic. Have they displaced it forever?

Is the fact of the matter going to a spiritual death? Do we have hope for development? Is something quite ordinary demanded of us—like a return to God, for example? Or either to some other? Our ship must be oriented on the certainty of the horizon. Where can we obtain it? Is it worthwhile to live to yet another millennium?

We in Venice are inclined to think that the loss of Carnival has occurred. We can see this. Almost no one can see this—for Carnival exists, it occurs year after year, several times, for various reasons, with fires and masks, with wine and dance. Carnival exists, anyone will tell you from among those who still (or already) do not see and of which they are of countless number. Carnival is becoming bigger and bigger, it's everywhere and uninterrupted, others who are of evil persuasion will tell you.

But is it really this way? Or is it only measured by what is gulped down and devoured? Or with unbelievable swarms of tourists, Japanese, hotel services, amusements, or with the return of money and losses on pyrotechnics? And is this already only bare mechanics, machinery, cold industry, massive consumption, permanent parasitic behavior? What if it is just a trap?

It appears that together with Carnival we lose our very selves. Are we still capable of loving, laughing, or crying? Are we sufficiently alive in order to live? Or to do something else? Here's a question that it's worth it to . . .

We invite you to Venice, a city on water, a city-ship, a city of apparition, the first week after the end of the traditional Great Holy Day. Just then, when the last, drunken convulsions make their last sound, orchestras and choirs will stop reverberating, colored bundles of hemp will fly from the balconies and gates of churches, legions of the world's tramps and newly arrived traveling clerks (both of whom now strangely can't be distinguished one from another—that's a sign of the times!) will vanish, and then, in peace and profundity, in the short-lived interlude of the Great Fast of circumspection, let us contemplate together, deep in the Benedictine silence of the glorious San Giorgio Maggiore, about us, about the

Carnival that has flitted past, about chances and possibilities, about the resistance of absurdity, about the absurdity of resistance.

Our gathering will hardly save the world, hardly save carnival, it won't even save Venice, or even us. But we will gather together—right now and right here in this place, overfilled with reverberations and quotations, in the middle of the Great Quotation, the embodiment of our final "post-."

With greetings from San Marco and its winged lion—
Leonardo di Casallegra

ORIENTATIONAL PROGRAM OF THE SEMINAR
With a Listing of the Participants

The seminar "The Post-Carnival Absurdity of the World: What Is on the Horizon?" will take place from the sixth to the tenth of March this year in Venice, on the island of San Giorgio Maggiore, in the halls of the monastery of San Giorgio. The program of the seminar foresees only official activities (papers and discussions), leaving the participants endless possibilities for getting acquainted with the city, its female and male inhabitants, with the local color, with its smells and tastes. The beginning of official activities every day at 10 A.M. We ask the participants not to be late and to plan their time according to the plan given below.

SATURDAY, MARCH 6
Solemn opening of the seminar. Appearance of the participants. Arrival of gondolas. The surrealism of human relations. General toast. Hostesses will invite you to dance.

Introductory paper: "The World after Everything and the World Before Everything from the Point of View at the World of the Old as the World Venetian"—Leonardo di Casallegra, Doctor of Thanatology, Scholarly Carnivalist, Honorary Head of the Department of Blood Transfusion and Incest of the Cagliostro Secret University of Venice.

Discussion with the speaker.

Coffee and cookies. Continued discussion. Completion of discussion.

Dishes of the day: tortellini, braised tunny fish, orange-tomato sauce "Piazzetta."

Drink of the day: Mozart Chocolate Liqueur.

SUNDAY, MARCH 7
Opportunity to swim with the hostesses. Exchange of ideas. Light snacks with video film show.

Paper: "The Chimera of Choreography as a Dancing Phantom in the Shadow of the World Tree"—Gaston Dejavu, France, ballet theoretician, independent researcher of allergic (corrected) allegorical phenomena.

Paper: "Postmodernism in Politics. Sarajevo as a Quotation."—Alborak Djabraili, Sweden, emigrant and dissident, stipend holder, publicist, winner of the award "For Honesty with Yourself."[6]

Discussion with panelists.

Cola and crackers. Dizzying discussion.

Dishes of the day: fillet of anchovy, bean[7] consommé, omar-crab (khayyam).

Drink of the day: Absolut vodka.

MONDAY, MARCH 8 (International Day)
Opportunity to fix teeth; costs covered by the foundation. Consultation with hostesses. Massage of injured organs. Prophylaxis. Eclectics.

Paper: "Listen to Reggae, Die beneath the Sky, Smell the Scent of the Grass"—John Paul Oshchyrko, Jamaica, teacher of the underground, three times enlightened, a free botanist and musicmon.

Paper: "Sex without Cudgels, or Little Red Riding Hood on the Right Road"—Liza Sheila Shalizer, U.S.A., professor of Yoknapathaupha University, head of the Awakened Housewives initiative, nonfiction star, nonstop-televishun-oridginal-soap-opera-producer (*The Hard Road of Deborah Icekream*, 665 episodes up to now!).

Discussion with panelists or without them.

Ice cream, oysters. The kindling of discussion. Shrimp.

Dishes of the day: Big Mac, hot dog, popcorn, salted nuts, red-hot chili peppers.

Drink of the day: Johnny Walker (maybe even Bizon vodka!).[8]

TUESDAY, MARCH 9
Badminton with the hostesses. Collective smoking of incense. Exchange of ideas. Transition to the critique of pure reason.

Paper: Tsutsu Mavropule,[9] Bessarabia—Transylvania, heresiarch and ventriloquist, fire-eater, honorary academician of Bu-Ba-Bu,[10] a knight of the Order of the Flying Head, a champion of Galicia (corrected) the Galaxy in black magic in the class of Black Mass competitions, a personal healer of Michael Jackson and federal Chancellor Cabbage,[11] prince.

The topic of the paper does not yield to formulation.

Paper: Stanislao Perfemsky, Russia (crossed out at the last moment) Ukrainia, author. The topic of the paper TBA.

NO DISCUSSION.

Eggs Chinese style. Zitrone (corrected with red pencil to "Lemon"). There will be no discussion. Cocoa-flavored flakes.

A magnificent dinner on the occasion of the completion of the papers at Casa Farfarello (see the attached map).

Dishes of the day: borscht, sour *ciorba* soup, olives, haddock, hemlock.

Drink of the day: *tsuica* plum brandy "Gorbachev."

WEDNESDAY, MARCH 10

Final day. Opportunity to say farewell to the hostesses.

Tips.

Summational discussion. The deliberation for the making and acceptance of a general memorandum "Carnival Must Continue On, Otherwise It's Going to End!"

Farewell dinner-*maestoso* in the monastery of San Giorgio.

Dishes of the day: large pepperoni pizza, a smaller lazzaroni pizza, omeletto Veneziano, spaghetti Napolitano, cutlets Bolognese, swordfish in dough, broccoli, calamari "octopus," goose Roman style, Corsican sardines Sicilian style, torte "Tintoretto."

Drinks of the day: grappa "Candolino," Tuscany, Roman, Campagno, Apulean, Ligurian, red, white, black, semisweet, dessert wines.

The coming of night. Darkness.

THURSDAY, MARCH 11

Departure of participants from Venice.

Among the honored guests of the carnival (crossed out) seminar: François Mitterrand, Jacoponi do Todi, Albert Gore, Kobo Abe,

Luciano Benetton, Oksana Baiul, Giorgio Armani, Jodie Foster, Michael Schumacher, *Freddie Mercury Jr.*, Yves St. Laurent, Sophia Loren, Sophie Marceau, Marcel Marceau, Ewa Cumlin, Michel Anderson, King Olelko II, Benazir Bhutto, *Woldemar Zhirinovsky*, Joe Cocker, Wim Wenders, Franco Baresi, Frank Costello, Elvis Presley, Elvis Costello, Juan Antonio Samaranch, Salman Rushdie, Anatoly Kashpirovsky, Cicciolina, *Wolf Messing*, the Mavrodi brothers, the Richynsky sisters and dozens of other famous figures of contemporaneity and the past.[12]

WE EXPECT THE ARRIVAL OF . . . FRANK SINATRA!

The organizers once more humbly ask You to firmly observe all the items of the orientation program. Eventual changes will be announced separately.

With wishes for fruitful work and the strongest impressions in the charm-filled city of palaces, gondolas, Titian, and Vivaldi—

Sincerely Yours Amerigo Dappertutto,

Technical Secretary

■ □ ■ □ ■

3

srbms-pq
For Monsignore's[1] information I report:

1. The prevailing stay of the Respondent in Munich to this time has not been distinguished by anything extraordinary.

2. The Doctor and I succeeded in finding the Respondent just on Thursday, March 4, anno 1993, close to ten in the morning, in Police Ward 305, where the Respondent ended up on the night of the third to the fourth of March, dead drunk and unconscious.

3. The entire next day on the fourth of March, as well as the night from the fourth to the fifth, the Respondent slept through an unwakeable sleep at the Melusine villa in the area of Possenhofen, where the Doctor put him to bed, stimulating sleep with a risky dose of herbal and other hallucinogenic means (morphini hydrochloridum, scopolamini hydrobromidum, aconitum, solanum, etc., ibid.).

4. Fifth of March, near nine in the morning, together with the Respondent we set off for Venice in a fourth-generation all-purpose car of the Manticore series.[2]

5. It is a fact that all the way to the Austrian border the Respondent did not exhibit any interest in the surrounding situation.

6. Regaining consciousness already in Austrian territory, the Respondent came to life, calling himself "historically a subject of the local country"[3] and in conjunction with this began to demand "a few swigs of alcohol." He got them from me (white Bacardi rum—a shot, then another).

7. In the area of Innsbruck, the Respondent noticeably began to stir, asked to stop the car and, driving off the Autobahn, even to return to the city where he had, he said, a druggist acquaintance whom he had to see. I have been unable till now to explain the person of the above-mentioned druggist as well as whether such a subject existed at all.

8. At the Austro-Italian border (the Brennero Pass) the Respondent properly exhibited a short-lived anxiety, which is typical for all his compatriots at the border stoppage: whether everything was all right with his documents and whether they would allow him to enter Italy. However the ironic attitude of the border people dissipated all his fears.

9. In the territory of Alto Adige the Respondent grew more animated and with unresisting annoyance repeated his demand regarding "two to three swigs," which he finally got (Chantreau brandy, pocket flask).

10. Almost the entire road to Bressanone the joyful Respondent talked about a baron acquaintance who had his own castle somewhere not far away in the southern Tyrol.

11. Particularly noticeable facts regarding the baron (for elucidation to the Fourth Bureau of the Informational Subdepartment): relatively young age; a war fighter—till recently he had led persistent military actions against a neighboring bishop; he shoots well from a crossbow; married, his wife is a young, attractive Portuguese whom he keeps locked up faithfully in a well-guarded tower of his castle; recently the baron has been in a lethargic stupor as the result of a bite last summer from an unknown fly.

12. During a short stop between Bressanone and Bolzano the Respondent became interested in whether the Doctor and I know where the village named Tenno was. The doctor really did find the location of the designated village, spreading out a detailed road map with that aim. The Respondent announced that "for this we need to drink" and following unconvincing exhortations he received his (a glass of Martell).

[No number]. In light of the fact that the Doctor had grown weary of fulfilling his immediate obligations, I took the wheel from him. With this, I had to listen to a not completely decorous narrative without end or beginning from the Respondent about his drinking bout with some refugees in Munich in Schwabing (one should understand that it's the very drinking bout which resulted in his ending up later at the police station).

14. After Trento the Doctor again was at the wheel (the feeling of obligation once more won out). The Respondent became all the more active. From a particular moment the Respondent began to sing. He sang about eight or nine Ukrainian songs of a mostly folk content. I remembered a song with an often-repeated refrain "du-du," "du-du." Clarify for the Subsection of National Creative Arts and Ethnography.

15. Before reaching Verona, the Respondent took to quoting Shakespeare in not entirely precise English, and also in Ukrainian, Polish and Russian. He asked for a comparison of the quality of the translation. The Doctor (as a result of this?) nearly struck an oncoming Opel Kadett.

16. Between Verona and Padua the Respondent first noticed the vineyards, although they had appeared earlier. The Respondent became furiously active, every minute asking us to stop the car, to catch a breath of air, to sing together with him, to give him "something cool" (Jim Beam whiskey, a quarter right from the bottle).

17. Not far from the interchange right before Mestre-Marghera (Highway E70), the Respondent beckoned us to pick up some crazy young Italian girl who was trying to flag down a car. The Respondent with this announced that he hadn't seen in a long while such powerful, stretched in black, female legs.

18. Right after Mestre I succeeded in finally convincing the Respondent that it wasn't worth turning back for the above-mentioned woman (girl?). This was achieved at the cost of pouring into the Respondent a successive dose, which the Respondent demanded with tripled compliance (the well-known-to-Monsignore Falling Star liqueur, watered down by three parts [!] of Lucifer mineral water).

19. After consuming the indicated drink, the Respondent was in fact taciturn all the way to Venice. Even the well-known Ponte della Liberta on entry onto the Islands failed to strike him.

20. Near 1700 hours we reached the Islands and parked in the area of Tronchetto. The Respondent reasonably recuperated along the road from the parking lot to the stop for water tram 1 (further—the vaporetto).

21. At the stop (the last one, Tronchetto) there was quite a large throng of inhabitants and guests of Venice. The Respondent again livened up upon sitting in the vaporetto, when he heard nearby in the jostling someone calling someone else a *putana*. The Respondent announced here that Italians are quite like Ukrainians.

22. During the boat ride from Tronchetto to Piazzale Roma the Respondent noted that Venice is a completely uninteresting city.

23. On Piazzale Roma the Respondent gave up his seat to some woman in a poncho and stockings, and informed me and the Doctor that the Venetian women look right into your eyes, after which all the way to the Ferrovia he tried to catch the glances of the women present on the deck and kept turning his head the entire time.

24. At the Ferrovia the Respondent expressed wild surprise at the fact that Venice had a train station. The Respondent said that "this alters certain moments."

25. Floating beneath the Scalzi Bridge, the Respondent announced that a boy named Skalsky had gone to school with him.

26. Turning the Respondent's attention to the first notable structure—the Church of San Geremia to the left, I heard from him an impromptu poem, in which Jeremiah rhymed with pariah, and Aquarian with vegetarian.

27. Still more passengers got on at Riva di Biasio, so that it became quite cramped, the result of which the Respondent began to wink at a freckled redhead with a chickenlike appearance, in a backpack and hiking shoes, apparently a Hollander, wide necked and so short that with her beak she was leaning up against the Respondent's stomach. With regard to this the Respondent was not up to the splendors of the Corner-Contarini Palazzo, to which I wanted to turn his attention with all my efforts.

28. At San Marcuola I considered it necessary to tug the Respondent by the sleeve and point to the Natural History Museum, hearing in answer from the Respondent that this is exactly what was needed and for the sake of which, he said, he had come here. Undoubtedly, the Respondent was telling an untruth.

29. After the stop at San Marcuola there were more seats in the vaporetto; however the above-mentioned redheaded Dutch clucker did not withdraw from the Respondent's body, as though she had

become glued to him. Jumping ahead, I will state that she rubbed up against him all the way to the Ca' d'Oro.[4]

30. When to the left of us the Palazzo of Vendramin-Calergi floated past us with all its delicateness, in the windows of which the first evening lights had lit up, I related to the Respondent the fact that to the end of March a casino was ensconced here, one of the chanciest in the world. In answer the Respondent became interested in whether the ghost of the composer Wagner sometimes appears above its green tables, by which he expressed a certain familiarity with the situation.

31. To Santa Stae[5] we passed yet several more less-important palaces that appeared on both sides of the Grand Canal. Every time more electric lights lit up around us, particularly outlining the features of the Respondent's face, his narrow lips, his left eyebrow.

32. To the right of us were the palaces Battagia, Tron, Priuli. To the left: Erizzo and Barbarigo, and then the Gusson.

33. Showing the Respondent the illuminated Ca' Pesaro, I didn't forget to say that there were two galleries in it now, although, as it seemed to me, the Respondent was completely inattentive to this. True, already after a minute, when the baroque style Corner della Regina had appeared before us, the Respondent tossed out in passing that it wouldn't be too bad to leave your soul in its walls. From the words of the Respondent I conclude: the Respondent has already been informed by someone about the fact that nowadays there is a pawn shop in the walls of the Corner della Regina.

34. The redheaded shitbag finally got off at the Ca' d'Oro. An erection, if I may be so bold to surmise, didn't occur, and then the Respondent, suspiciously enlivened, thrust out a series of questions, to every one of which I was unable to give an answer immediately. It interested the Respondent to know: what's the average depth of the Grand Canal? How deep is the deepest spot? How many islands comprise Venice? Are there any standard lengths that gondolas should not exceed? If it's true that Venice is gradually sinking into the abyss of the sea, then how quickly will this happen? In a year? In an hour? In a second? Are there any certain measures being taken to keep Venice from sinking? If they are being taken, then what kind of measures? Are there fish in the canals? How does the Venetian sewage system work? Is the presence of impurities in the city waters checked

with the help of special apparati? Or isn't it checked? And why was it just now that he began to realize that my eyes are green?

35. I answered that Venice was founded by fugitives, saving themselves from the Huns and the Longobards; that the Byzantine influences from the early Middle Ages have been felt till now; that all the gold of the world floated here over the course of centuries; that everyone without exception feared Venice in the Old World, including the Vikings and Seljuk Turks; that only Napoleon managed to deprive it of its virginity; that the illuminated palace behind us— was that, namely, Ca'd'Oro, where in the interior courtyard, paved in bricks with reddish walls, on the background of which the marble steps are painted white, in the summer of '86 I saw a live unicorn, and that unicorn was doleful voiced, that is unicornis absurdus—not recorded practically anywhere and an undescribed semispectral subspecies, and it touched my bosom; that I just noticed how long the Respondent's exquisite fingers were.

36. And while the questions-answers were going on, we passed by the Ca'da Mosto, about which I had wanted to say that it was once the famous Hotel Leon Bianco, in whose rooms even to this day you can happen upon things forgotten by careless guests from the previous several centuries, such as, for example, fans, toothpicks, needles for jabbing rivals, ribbons and garters, bows and ostrich feathers, and indestructible spots on the linen witness certain intimate aspects in the life of many persons of the crown, additionally, for example, the Russian tsarevich Paul, who stayed over here with an unknown female traveling companion; in these very walls a nice little erotic comedy was filmed about this story. The Respondent replied to this that it was his, the tsarevich's, wife, the princess, apparently of Pomerania and Schleswig-Holstein or something similar.

37. I already haven't mentioned anything here about the Palazzos of the Fontana, Sagredo, Michele delle Colonne, and, additionally, about Morosini-Brandolin.

38. I cannot, true, help but mention the Palazzo dei Camerlenghi.

39. I can't help from mentioning the Doctor either: during the entire boat trip he was silent and overtired, for which I was terribly grateful to him.

40. At the Rialto Bridge the promenade had already begun in the light of the first street lamps. The Respondent informed me that a

similar gathering of people had been seen here only 550 years ago. I request the Third Chancery of the Research-Investigation Subsection to explain why he said this.

41. After Rialto the number of passengers again approached a catastrophic amount, we also didn't have the tiniest opportunity to exchange even a few sentences not only all the way to San Silvestro, but even to San Angelo.

42. From San Angelo it emptied a bit, because a good ten passengers, it seems, disembarked for the theater. I felt like telling the Respondent the touching story of Palazzo Grimani, that overwhelmed and loomed with its immensity. In my opinion, the Respondent didn't quite understand something, for keeping silent all the way to San Tomà, finally asking a question, whose answer I was forced to think about until the Ca' Rezzonico, namely: is my love for Venice not linked to some erotic core and—continuing—have I not tried to cure myself of this love with the help of certain exercises of the body?

43. With this I wasn't able to say a word about Moscenigo, or the Ca'Foscari, and the Moro-Lin or Giustiniani. And only next to the Ca'Rezzonico was I able to inform him that we just had one more stop, right after which some kind of extremely nervous music for chamber orchestra splashed out from the half-illuminated windows of the palace.

44. Also when we were exiting near the Ponte Accademia, the music still reached us.

45. The cupolas of Santa Maria della Salute crowned with sculptures were partly illuminated from below. Stepping onto the bridge of the Accademia, the Respondent uttered a mysterious word combination, "povny pincet."[6] Please decipher.

46. On the bridge of the Accademia the Respondent suddenly asked whether it's true that Italian women don't stop lovemaking even during their geranium blossom time. That depends on the Italian men, I answered, you'll have to ask somebody else.

47. With such conversations and thoughts we finally approached the establishment well known to Monsignore. The Doctor walked in front of us a bit, like a great bony servant with a torch above his head and a stiletto at his side.

48. By the gate beneath the green lantern the approaching *giovinetto*[7] of the hotel, diabolically furrowed with an alcoholic's

wrinkles in a tricornered cap with a feather, which he saucily took off at our appearance, as though he were greeting us, but in truth demanding handouts. The Doctor quite decisively avoided him, the Respondent, instead, cheerfully poured an entire fistful of all kinds of coins in the form of Austrian groschen, Slovak gellers, or Romanian bani into the bottomless abyss of the cap's triangle.

49. Upon hearing from me that this modest but glorious inn has been operating since the times of the *gotico fiorito*,[8] the Respondent asked if the local spittoons, toilet bowls, bidets, electrical outlets, the on-off switches, and telephones also correspond to the noted style.

50. At the reception desk we were served by an almost two-meter-tall, well-toothed black man dressed like one of the Magi,[9] but looking more like an NBA superstar. After receiving the appropriate keys, the Doctor moved to look over our quarters with him.

51. In the meantime I accompanied the Respondent to his room, one floor up. I informed him that at various times Immanuel Kant, Edgar Allan Poe, and Pierre Menard had stayed in this room.[10]

52. The Respondent carelessly answered that in the name of the future this list must be expanded. He had in mind himself.

53. Without taking off his raincoat, the Respondent walked around the room, looking at and touching everything, lighting up chandeliers, brackets, lamps, lanterns, nightlights—everything that could be lit. The room was turned into a hall flooded with lights.

54. In the next instant I understood the aim the Respondent had pursued with this. In one of the partitions he came across a not very big, though sufficiently nice-sounding, spinet.

55. Remaining there further by the cloak, the Respondent slightly lifted the darkened top of the spinet and without the least attention to the surrounding situation, as well as to me personally, he performed the D Major[11] Sonata no. 15 (according to Kirkpatrick's classification) by Scarlatti. Following it the Respondent played something from the English virginalists, but it didn't go as well for him.

56. At the end of the music there was silence. And I coughed.

57. The Respondent whirled on his tabouret (African elephant bone, late Renaissance) with his face pointed toward me.

58. I slowly moved up to the Respondent, turning off appropriate lamps along the way. A satyr and a dryad from a tapestry behind

the Respondent's back plunged into the gloom. The satyr winked at me. I began to quiver.

59. I walked right up close to the Respondent. I plunged my hand in his hair. The Respondent's hair is silk to the touch.

60. I took the Respondent's glasses off and placed them on the spinet. Without his glasses the Respondent has completely different eyes. They looked at me from below and nearly didn't see me.

61. My coat crawled off my shoulders onto the floor. I took off my scarf and, tossing it around the Respondent's neck, I pulled his handsome head to me.

62. We grew still. This lasted for quite a long time.

63. Until I sensed that the Respondent had grabbed me just a touch below my buttocks with his long, beautiful fingers.

64. Then the Respondent took a breath with his entire body and finally rose up from the tabouret, without releasing me from his arms, and to the contrary—lifting me above himself and strongly squeezing me to himself.

65. I shut my eyes. The Respondent blindly carried me in front of himself. He could have stumbled at any step.

66. But I sensed that he was putting me down on my back on a hard and smooth surface (a writing desk, ebony wood, fourteenth century).

67. I helped the Respondent free me of my skirt, stockings, and underwear. This took nearly a lifetime. The Respondent rustled his coat above me, like a dragon its wings.

68. From certain of the Respondent's inexperience in undressing and other things, I came to the conclusion that the Respondent long ago (never?) had been with a woman.

69. We were reflected in a large wall mirror (the island of Murano, the beginning of the seventeenth century), where I, closing my eyes, saw myself with my head thrown back and spread legs to meet the Respondent.

70. I also saw in the mirror the raised collar of the Respondent's coat, his forehead covered with tiny droplets, his thin lips, his left eyebrow, slightly raised above his eye, his eye itself.

71. I also saw the door to the room behind the Respondent's back. The Doctor could appear in that door at any moment, clearly he'd cough to alert me or knock.

72. But I was indifferent.

73. For I also had seen the unicorn, and he touched my bosom, and entered into me, although this entry had taken nine and a half centuries—not less.

74. And for the entire time we didn't say a word. . . . .
. . . .
. . . .
. . . .
. . . .
. . . .
. . . .
. . . .
. . . .
. . . .
. . . .
. . . .
. . . .

99. After a warm shower I went to have dinner at a trattoria on Campiello Loredan. The Doctor and the Respondent were already seated there.

100. I will continue observation of the Respondent. By established means I will inform Monsignore regarding his further activities.

To Monsignore I pay my respects—

Cerina

■ □ ■ □ ■

4

I AWOKE FROM THE SURROUNDING MORNING NOISES WITH SUCH regret and sorrow inside that, even having opened my eyes, for a long time I remained motionless, without the strength to shake myself and to remove this torpor, uninvited just before dawn. What did I dream? I didn't know what I had dreamt.

After all, these sad awakenings are familiar to me. It happens like this when I dream of Her. Certain fragments of these two or three years, deprived of their own time and space, sometimes it's only sounds, but most often—some kind of foolish pursuit and constant failure, some kind of bounding from buses to trolley buses, running into gateway entrances, searching for a safe courtyard, shelter beneath a tree or simply—in the darkness. Certain judging glances of passers-by, as it were, about what they are doing here together. Dogs that tear away at their chains on catching sight of us, foreign breeds and two-legged ones, in their zone of protection, the summoning of the police by some invisible observer glued to the window who remembers every step of the suspicious pair below. Concealment from patrols— behind the stump of a tree, around the corner of a building addition, behind hanging laundry, behind garbage cans. Thus the similar motifs that I can't help but dream, for these were moments of my highest and most tender love for Her—right at the time it began with Her, we were running to doctors and healers, we stood in endless lines by the offices of clinics, to add to it they also turned us away, and we were forced to leave home at seven in the morning, and return not earlier than midnight, we also hung around town and didn't manage to go anywhere, and sometimes for five or six hours we had nowhere to go, because it was impossible to return home. She constantly felt nauseous, She fainted in jam-packed (as well as in empty) buses, sometimes someone gave up their seat by the window for Her, but this didn't save Her, I held Her by the hand, although the lingering grayness had gathered on Her face, we jumped off at the stop and flew into the first-best gate, where She finally erupted with her long suppressed vomit, poor girl, homeless and ill, and I circled around Her like a sentinel, like a raven, like a protector, like a slave, like a master.

It happens that I dream of something different. I'm invited to some kind of place. I know that She will come there right away. This is to be our first meeting after a long separation. I sit down in an armchair and wait—She will appear straight away. Some very influential companions have arranged this impossible possibility for us. In my memory a prepared phrase pulses, with which I will return to Her. I hear footsteps on the stairs or the screeching of the entrance doors. But it's not Her. No one comes to the room where I'm waiting. And it's this way to the very time I awake—over the course of four, five hours, I wait, the chances melt away. I listen to every sob of the surrounding silence, but She doesn't come.

There are also dreams filled with people's faces: entire crowds of friends, good old friends, buddies, and girlfriends (besides in many of them the external appearance is definitely not the same as it is in reality), some kind of drunken carousing, dancing, cigarette smoke, a row of masks, laughter, crampedness, I struggled to find Her among this brood, they grab me by the arms, they pour me booze, I penetrate through this sweaty thicket, they tempt me with conversations, with song, and I pretend (alas dreams are this way) that She interests me the least, that I'm not seeking Her, but at that very same time in a panic I determine how much more time is at my disposal (until awakening), in order to overcome all these innumerable overpopulated living quarters and find Her. Once I dreamt that I had found Her, but the entire time she turned her back to me, and right before awakening, I thought that I wouldn't call Her—this is risky, for really the being that I see just from the back can turn out to be not Her, and what then?

But today I didn't dream of Her. And this sorrow, this sadness, this sense of being torn apart inside can't be explained by anything.

I ended up in Venice. I awoke in an antique bed, on multicolored sheets that smelled of quince and dry apricot blossoms. A high and clean ceiling is above me with an ornamental decoration, which doesn't remind me of anything. Around me is an entire collection of fine objects made of silver, walnut, ebony, sandalwood, ivory, bronze, terra-cotta, lace, velvet. Before me—five entire days and nights in this reality more like a hallucination.

Yesterday I strayed with a woman I hardly knew. She's married to someone else. Then the three of us had dinner in a trattoria, this lasted till far into the night, we drank a really great amount of Chianti, but the wine behaved with restraint, like water. We parted in front of the doors to their bedroom. Afterward I was alone.

Is this sufficient reason for sorrow in the morning? If it's so, then I'm done. I'm a goner.

But all the same there is salvation: you just have to get up out of bed and live on. A *completo*[1] of morning procedures, a bathtub made of pink stone (Abyssinian? Mauritanian?), towels that retain the scent of lilies and oranges all the time, in everything the presence of the clear music of Benedetto Marcello, a half hour of choosing a shirt and tie, the coming to life of the Grand Canal beneath the windows, transitions from a minor to a major key and vice versa, a close look at myself in the mirror, rejection of a tie, the scent of something edible that comes from who knows where, a reminder about breakfast at nine.

Thus I will indulge in this city. I will try to experience the hottest, the sharpest in it. I will find the most mysterious spot in it where they can't reach me. Not the carabinieri, not the police, not the devil himself.

But today it's still early. Today at nine is the beginning, the getting acquainted and the endeavor to be liked by everyone, per favore, Perfezki, I absolutely have to take a gondola, otherwise it's not worth even a rat's ass[2] to come here.

A strand of sun on the furniture, on the mirrors, on the silverware, *mio caro signore, tutto e per Lei,*[3] we begin the traditional Venetian exhibition named "Joy of Life, or Dolce Vita." At your disposal: the splashing of water, the scent of perfumes, almond baked goods, chapels on piles, a Rilke poem dedicated to Richard Beer-Hofmann, sharp-quilled grass in inner courtyards, a thimbleful of tarry hellish coffee, scholarly erudites and book lovers, fleeting women who gaze into your eyes, ten thousand churches, palaces, wine cellars, museums, bordellos, four hundred bridges, and from each one they suggest you spit, schools of unknown trades, songs of street romancers and, clearly, the most triumphal of the Venetian sights—the omnipresent quivering of a never-drying wash!

It is left for me to be serious. That is, to look at myself in the mirror one more time. Not to forget to pick up Ada's shawl. To remember the beginning of canto 21 of Dante's *Inferno*. To close the door behind me, to lock it. And, whistling, to move on to meet enticements.

■ □ ■ □ ■

5

MY RECOUNTING OF THE FIRST DAY OF THE VENETIAN SEMINAR "The Postfestal Anarchy of the World: What's Next?"—I'll begin from the window of the beautiful monastery library on the settlement of San Giorgio Maggiore. Namely here, in these walls, forever smelling of the dampness of manuscripts and incunabula, over the course of the immediate next four days, things will be expounded that are most necessary for culture and civilization and for all of humankind. Even nicer is the fact that, indeed, a delegate from our, as well as your, fervently beloved Ukraine is also represented today.

At ten o'clock, looking out from my window onto the rarely clear perspective of the Canal di San Marco and Piazzetta with two of its Syrian columns, I notice a quick, light motorboat, which is driven out from behind the Fondamenta della Salute and the Customs. After a few minutes the motorboat is rushing along the spacious reaches of Bacino di San Marco. The entire time it's getting closer and, obviously, getting larger, until it allowed us to distinguish in it, other than the reliable steersman experienced in the ways of the world, the figures of the passengers, of which there were three. Up front a silent and petrified gentleman sat in a bright coffee-colored hunter's jacket, and the closer it gets from him to Your observer, a beard becomes all the more distinct on him and . . . certain signs of thinning hair on his head, that we quite delicately call "highbrowed," and about such men, bearers of the just-noted high brow, we say "baldish" in sympathy. Right away I assumed that this is Mr. Perfetsky, a representative of Ukraine, whose arrival everyone here is expecting with impatience.

In back of him, standing on the flat part, like a monument of the times of classicism, a quite attractive couple in different colored coats, so loose that they sway after the movement of the motorboat like flags. I pleasantly note the red and black colors on the unfamiliar woman. Regarding the figure of a fairly tall youth in dark glasses, then I carry the impression that he must truly be close to the already-mentioned woman, for otherwise the way in which he was holding her by the elbow, you could decidedly classify as ill manners.

The entire trio looks the best and could even serve as an example for a tourist advertisement about trips on the waves of the Adriatic.

Landing at the island's terra firma right before the main gate of the Church of San Giorgio, so as to step onto the small mosaic square right in the middle between the statues of Saint George and Saint Stephen, situated in niches of the facade, the visitors dispatched the helmsman of the motorboat with a God bless you and moved along the right to the monastery's buildings. After a brief minute they were greeted in the great hall of the refectory, called Cenacolo,[1] where elegant hostesses in Venetian costumes of the sixteenth century with certain frivolous details, which, betray their, I'll put it this way, courtesanship, they approached each person in turn and accompanied them further. Among the hostesses several shapely blondes stuck out, thus we were involuntarily reminded of the Slavic (proto-Ukrainian) origin of the Venetian people.

From that moment I approach the newly arrived small group and stand next to them till the very end of the deliberations.

And here the first surprise for me. The quite attractive and efficacious mistress, described by me above in red and black colors, acquaints those present with Mr. Stanislav Perfetsky, who turns out to be . . . a not particularly ripe-aged tall bespectacled guy! Instead, the bearded intellectual in the coffee-colored jacket turns out to be the husband of the noted lady, translator and participant of the seminar, Ada Zitrone. Additionally, her husband, if I heard correctly, is a germy man. This is how Your correspondent messed up at the very beginning of the undertaking!

The first to appear before Mr. Perfetsky was the host himself, a tiny riled up Italian of uncertain age, beneath his moustache, perhaps, glued on, and with an eternal cigarette in the corner of his mouth, Mr. Dappertutto, the secretary of the foundation, active and a fidgety freewheel, or, I'll put it this way, mercurial.

"How was your trip, Mr. Persitsky, how did you sleep, how was your breakfast, what do you think of Venice, what do you think of my girls, I guess you're in a good mood, Ada, you look phantasmagoric, let's begin right away!" Mr. Dappertutto said in his usual way and flitted off further, encircled by a dozen prattling hostesses as beautiful as flowers.

Perhaps Mr. Perfetsky would have wanted to relate something to him, in response to that quick-shooting line without transition, but for the poor soul there already wasn't anyone to relate it to! . . .

But our blossoming Mrs. Zitrone accompanied him to a new circle of guests, among which at that time there was a lank and hook-shaped female member in some kind of semimasculine and quite elegant suit with tie, a colorful young man in a woven cap and hair in thousands of braids, with slacks torn in several spots and with a multistrapped large bag across his shoulder, and besides these first two—one more guest with a large red mouth outlined in lipstick, Politeness herself, eternally gazing into Affable Clarity and the Virtues of Petty Sufficiency. When after a minute we find out with the assistance of the aromatic Mrs. Zitrone, the speakers of the seminar in turn will be Mrs. Shalizer from the Incorporated Countries of America, John Paul Oshchyrko (someone in the family must have definitely been Ukrainian!) from Jamaica and the world-renowned Frenchman Dejavu.

They spoke mostly in English in further conversation, during which Mr. Perfetsky, a representative of Ukraine, exhibited quite good knowledge of that complicated language.

"*Hi, man!*" the stringy-haired racially mixed guy greeted him. "My name is John Paul. And yours?"

"Stakh," Mr. Perfetsky answered quite correctly.

"*Great!*" The dark-skinned man delighted in showing his entire mouthful of teeth.

"*Very nice!*" And Mr. Perfetsky didn't err here.

"*Oh shit!*" Mrs. Shalizer half shut her eyes at this. "He speaks so well! Tell me, Stakh, how are things today *in your country?*"

"*It's all right, ma'am,*" Mr. Perfetsky allayed her. "*We are the cham-*

pions. First we take Manhattan, then we take Berlin. Dead can dance, ma'am. . . ."

After these words, the company began to laugh rambunctiously at his jest except for Mrs. Shalizer, who, if I'm not mistaken, didn't particularly care for Perfetsky's use of "ma'am" in his address.

Mr. Dejavu, precipitously taking up the topic with his red lips, suggested a Free Society, the transition to which is the embodiment of Difficulty itself, especially in those countries where till now Unfreedom and Oppression still dominate, that shameful pair of sardonic Lovers on the body of Mature Humanity. The reforms introduced in the captive nations, in the opinion of Mr. Dejavu, can in no way emerge onto the real Road to the Market, for that reason the Bear of Totalitarianism, releasing its victims as though to a New Order, in reality as the Panther watches and waits for each small Grain of their Erroneousness, to turn back the Wheel of History at the slightest opportunity. Finally, if our famous colleague Mavropule would arrive right now, he would have something to add to such a bold theme, Dejavu completed his short, but meaningful lecture.

And all the conversationalists sorrowfully shook their heads: too bad that Mavropule hasn't arrived yet.

"And do you know, friend, how one should call our John Paul in Venetian?" Dejavu interrupted a brief inopportune pause.

"*How?*" again Perfetsky did not come off a loser.

"Zanípolo!"[2] Dejavu shouted with all his strength and slapped Perfetsky on his back.

The entire circle again laughed a bit, now this time including Mrs. Shalizer, who, finally, taking our Stanislav a bit off to the side and looking right into his eyeglasses, whispered the following:

"*Dear friend,* would you like us to do a two-hour tête-à-tête? A long and passionate one. I don't know if you know about me. I write nonfiction. I do bestsellers, blockbusters, brainbreakers. I want to write about your reforms. I want to invite you over to my hotel. I want a tête-à-tête. I want to. I want to do you."

Following this speech, giving our nonresistant countryman her Venice address on a piece of paper, she smiled with sterile teeth and added:

"I have really good tapes. I have drinks with ice. I have my own publishing house. I have a suitcase of condoms. Please translate." She flashed an eye toward Ada.

Then, without even giving a sign of confusion, our scalawag Perfetsky squeezed her large masculine hand and with all his strength slapped her on the back, from which the American woman even lost her breath, and the Jamaican black man quickly had to make her a roll-your-own cigarette, procuring his smoker's apparatus from his multistrapped backpack to everyone's alarm.

"The old whore," the resolute Ada remarked to that, taking Perfetsky by the elbow and smiling to everyone in departing, especially to Mrs. Shalizer.

Now we will turn our attention to Herr Dr. Riesenbock, who long had not been seen by us. As all mutes he perfectly knows how to manage in life and does not allow anybody to pull the wool over his eyes. Thus as Ada was taking Perfetsky around the hall, acquainting him with the company, our bearded guy moves immediately along the extraordinarily interesting table with drinks and cold hors d'oeuvres, plying onto the delectables directly beneath a grand painting of *The Marriage of the Virgin,* beautifully prepared by the brushes of Jacopo Tintoretto, an artist-painter famous in the sixteenth century.

A look at him and at the painting—and all right, we move further, behind the real heroes of the narrative.

Here and there people famous in the world circle around them, among whom I couldn't help but recognize several (right on the spot!) ministers, a stripper, a hypnotist, a matador, a terrorist, a prima donna, and a cardinal. All abide as though in expectation of something central, that is, if I'm not mistaken, a general toast fixed in the program. However, Secretary Dappertutto, who meteorically leaps from time to time here and there, does not begin the ceremony for some reason. What kind of fish is this that forces you to wait for him for so long?

"The old whore," Ada repeats her irritating definition. "John Paul isn't enough? Not enough hostesses? Do you really want to go to her, kiddo?"

"To make love with her? Maybe under general anesthesia!" Perfetsky calmed down his female colleague. "I guess this is a satisfaction for those stronger than me in spirit."

"But she could pay you well. For a two-hour conversation."

"Really? Then that changes things. I'll visit her tomorrow at midnight while she's lying on her bed moist from anticipation. Taking off her fake lashes. Putting her false teeth into a glass. Taking off her wig. I'll bring an entire collection of all kinds of artificial stimulators. You know, those elastics, dildos, vibrators, tweezers. . . ."

"Stop, Casanova," Ada says coldly.

"But I won't arrive alone," our fantasizer Perfetsky leads on. "You'll be there with me. And together we'll crawl into her crocodile beddy. . . ."

"Hold on, stud," Ada says to him, although, it's possible it wasn't to him, since an Arabian racing stallion had just appeared in the hall on long thin legs, led by the bridle by a swarthy incognito who was greeting everyone.

"Alborak Djabraili" was the name of the latter, as he held the horse right in front of Ada and Perfetsky.

The horse stood up nearly stock still, and just as we were recognizing something else in it: it turns out to be a bicycle, and also a very good brand, at that.

"I rode on it all the way from Sweden," Mr. Alborak explained. In the Baltic Sea I had to pack him up on a ship. He got seasick and totally refused to eat oats.

"But how did you manage to get him here, all the way to the island?" Mrs. Ada expressed a polite interest.

"Oh, it went much easier here!" Mr. Alborak was moved by such a sign of attention. "The fact of the matter is that we both swim marvelously."

However, after all this, it was evident that our Ada and Stakh didn't particularly believe all this—as their interlocutor, as well as their two-wheeled acquaintance, didn't look as if they had just bathed in the Venetian waters. Stakh, in fact, fondled the wise horse's snout with his hand and with all possible politeness formulated the following question: "What's the name of your beauty, sir?"

"Rocinante, of course." Djabraili smiled even wider. "To the point, respected friends, do you know anything about Mr. Mavropule? Has he arrived yet, or not?"

"I seem to think not," Ada gave to understand.

"There, when Mr. Mavropule arrives, everything will begin,"

Alborak Djabraili mysteriously pronounced and, amiably tinkling to say farewell with the bicycle's bell, departed with his own cares.

For a while Ada and Perfetsky listened to the clear clopping of horseshoes behind them.

Like a tiny demon his secretariness Mr. Dappertutto jumped out again in front of them with an imperishable cigarette and, without slowing down the motion of his legs, managed to pose a question to Stas (winking to Ada): "Mr. Parfyansky, are you ready now to give us the topic of your lecture?"

Then, however, he was whisked away by a cloud of slender hostesses, without hearing the answer. And there was no answer anyway.

In the meantime, having perfectly understood the situation, Mr. Riesenbock devoured coffee with cookies, sprinkling crumbs all over the floor.

And what notable guests are weaving all around, what celebrities walk right past us! Among them I recognize: George Sand, and Barbra Streisand, and two or three Amands, and someone else in baggy Turkish pants, and I equally turn my attention to other such distinguished persons that our current Ukrainian monarch is not as unassuming among them. I manage occasionally to ask something of His Regal Grace. Here is the flash interview:

"What feelings do You have upon arriving in Venice, Your Grace?"

"The invitation here, to this magical assemblage of scholars and activists, I value as an acknowledgment, each time more extensive, of my country and my people."

"And how did You, Your Grace, manage to get to Venice?"

"I was taken by a special airplane of the Spanish military to Marco Polo Airport. From there I took a taxi."

"And the last question, Your Grace. In which hotel are you staying?"

"I'm not staying at a hotel, but at my colleague's, the King of Sardinia's place, who has a pretty nice apartment on Lido Island."

"I sincerely thank you, Your Regal Grace."

"My pleasure. Pass this along to my subjects in Ukraine."

Moving along subtly like a reporter, catching up to Ada and Perfetsky, who swayed through the Cenacolo Hall, each time getting to know more and more new acquaintances. Who was that old gray man, stooped over and hunchbacked, sitting on a bench by the wall, and the two nimble eighteen-year-old hostesses with their dexterous hands massaging his knees? He looks at least a hundred years old and smiles so tenderly to everyone that saliva is even dripping from his lips. And this, my loved ones, so that you should know, is Messeur himself, the very professor di Casallegra, the president of the foundation denoted above.

"My feet are really freezing," the old man says to Ada and Perfetsky instead of greeting them.

"That's nothing." Ada calms him down and kisses his dried-up hand, maybe even his ring.

"You, Mr. Perfekcy, from which direction have you come to Venice?" The patriarch became interested without any introduction.

"From the direction of Mestre, patron," Ada hastily answered.

"In some kind of unknown model car, granddad," our quite direct Mr. Perfetsky adds, but in translation for some reason Mrs. Zitrone leaves out the last word.

"Oh, then you haven't seen Venice yet!" The old man is pleased as a child, his eyes were even rolling, although, perhaps, it was from the fact that the indiscreet saucy hostesses were massaging him in the wrong spot. "You have to arrive in Venice by sea, young lad."

And after these words he grew silent for a long time.

"Can we go?" Stakh asks Ada.

"No. He wants to talk to you."

"Then let him talk!"

"He talks this way. Awfully slowly. Sentence after sentence. He thinks while he speaks."

"He reminds me of the departed Yeshkil Zontakh, the Hebrew teacher from the Chortopil High School." Stakh shrugs his shoulders.

"Be attentive," Ada remarks to him, having noticed how the old man's lips were beginning to quiver slightly at the sign of attention that something would come out of him. That's what happened.

"Venice, Venice," said the professor.

Ada had just translated this phrase of his when the following darted out of him.

"You are still quite young, Mr. Perfekcy."

"And you are already really old," our countryman wanted to react to this, I venture to think, although Ada would have never translated it anyway.

"Venice is dying, Mr. Perfekcy. I sense this with all the old bones in my body. She's dying. Lucia, massage me higher! Concita, don't be so enthusiastic!

And making his subsequent maestro's pauses, Mr. Casallegra said the following (for the sign of a pause I use the symbol "[. . .]" and present it in the translation of Mrs. Zitrone).

"Venice was first infected five hundred years ago when the idiot Columbus discovered his illusory America [. . .]."

"A great sea power in an instant stopped being great [. . .]."

"Changes occurred on the map of the world's travels and campaigns [. . .]."

"All the gold of the Old World, collected by Venice, weighed nothing compared to the gold of the New World [. . .].

"To stretch to the shores of America, to those golden empires of the West, to cross the Atlantic—we weren't able [. . .]."

"Before then it was getting more difficult with our conquests in the Mediterranean waters [. . .].

"The Turks, Spaniards, Genoans. The increase of piracy [. . .]."

"A noticeable worsening of the surrounding climate: storms, fog, siroccos, smashed ships [. . .]."

"The inundation of entire islands, churches, buildings, underground galleries and wine cellars [. . .]."

"The inundation of storehouses, garrets, cellars with treasures and contraband [. . .]."

"A sickness that can wear down a stone. Mold like aggression. The pollution of the sky, slicks on the water, August's foul odor of alleys and museums. The crumbling of walls. The ruining of the landscapes [. . .].

"Ada, translate precisely. I want him to know. . . . [. . .]."

"However, we knew how not ever to worry about the present order of things [. . .]."

"Against every act of oppression—psychic, physical, moral, that is, foreign, against conditions and conquerors, against venereal diseases and madness, against the East and against the West, against everything in the world and against the entire world we had a Holiday [. . .]."

"We imagined marvelous perversions for ourselves, people were amazed at us, they came to us to study: love, painting, seafaring, the slave trade, music, chiromancy, wine making, blood transfusion, architecture, sodomy, the culinary arts, inquisition, the arranging of horoscopes, and violin concerts, all kinds of other trades, such as jewelry making, spying, and glassblowing, but most of all, again and again, love, oral, anal, any kind, but always pure, fiery, and lofty [. . .]."

"Thanks to this we've survived. I remember Byron, visiting the Fiesta del Redentore,[3] who said something like the following: "Leonardo, this makes you invincible!" [. . .].

"Byron?" Stakh queried.

"Byron." The old man stubbornly nodded his head. "Does this surprise you? Yes, I knew him. And even earlier—Pope Alexander III and Friedrick Barbarossa. And Saint Mark, the Evangelist. I have the right to call myself as old as the world, young man [. . .]."

After this the most honorable elder began to laugh dryly and then, each time exhaling more impetuously, continued his speech, the pauses a bit shorter, so that poor Ada wasn't able to keep up with her translation, nor the hostesses with their massage.

"The true death of Venice will happen not from swallowing by the sea or sand, not from floods or heavenly thunder [. . .]. All this is only external, that is, apparent, that is nonessential [. . .]. Entire institutions exist that have been summoned to save Venice [. . .]. They stirred up a multitude of ideas, each more clever than the next [. . .]. And now—for the sake of saving this stone, this gold, this marble, these stuccos and mosaics, this pigeon dung—several eggheads even propose to move this entire Venice to some safer and drier place [. . .]. The monuments that will perish in these dirty waters, as it were, are dearer than [. . .]. Otherwise, asses would have wanted to chase away everything living from here including the shitty pigeons and to preserve everything here in perpetuity [. . .]. They contend that no one should be living here in twenty-five years. Such an, you know, accident zone [. . .]. So that only ghosts of people should rush along the canals on ghosts of gondolas [. . .]. I have completely antithetical principles [. . .]. Lucia, sweetheart, a bit more restraint [. . .]. Concita, that's better now, honeychild [. . .]."

"In reality they're saving the wrong thing entirely [. . .]. For first of all they should be saving themselves [. . .]. An epidemic is drawing near, more ferocious than the one from 1630, when just swollen bodies were floating along the canals, and I looked at all this from the loggia of the Palazzo Dario, exactly where the King of the Plague had a banquet with his family accompanied by wild music [. . .]. An epidemic of dehumanization is drawing near. Venice is turning out to be just an unsuccessful attempt. A hopeless attempt at the eternal flowering of humankind [. . .]. You won't stop its fall with anything anymore, for this—is the fall of humanity among people [. . .]. It's simplest to express it this way: existence is being rid of its eternal dramatism [. . .]. People are completely satisfied with the way they live. To them it seems they are living. They like what they drink and eat, what they wear, they've gotten used to the free choice of a sexual partner or a television channel, they're gotten used to amenities, pleasures, comfort, the early morning paper, and late-night porno [. . .]. Living blood more and more slowly flows in these absolutely drowsy arteries. Each time it becomes faded and more often loses its red color. Leukemia—is that what this feebleness is called [. . .]?"

"Translate for him that my thinking is just about the same," our Perfetsky related to Ada. "But, shoot, I have the impression that a paralytic stroke soon will rout the old devil from such an active massage."

"Don't worry, kiddo." Ada didn't even wink at this.

As for Mr. Casallegra, he really got hot and spoke further with more passion and expressiveness: "I've seen ten thousand carnivals! . . . I've been at every one of them! . . . I've seen those eyes! . . . Those masks! . . . Those slits in the dresses, those swords! . . . Those legs, those bare shoulders, those snatches! . . . Those dances! I've brought together male and female lovers, I've mixed their bodies, it was dough! . . . I've brought together rivals! I've put death as the judge between them! . . . I've sniffed like a hungry dog, the senses poured out all over! . . . Exactly this way, the senses. The senses. Do you know what these are? You, present-day people? O-o-o-o [. . .]! The senses. . . ."

After expressing his favorite word the hundredth time, the honorable professor froze in motionlessness for yet another minute, rolling (what was this from?) his eyes. He was transported into some kind of other worlds. He soared there beneath the clouds like a phoenix. Just by the corners of his mouth could you recognize any kind of presence in this body of a scrap of spirit.

However he took control of himself in barely a minute and returned to our beloved Stas and Ada, quietly finishing: "I'll speak about it today."

After this he smacked both of his assistants on their conveniently upturned fannies and announced they were on their own for now. First Lucia then Concita fluttered to the middle of the hall like baby birds from their nest.

"My great-granddaughters," Casallegra said. "They've literally grown up on my knees. Now from time to time they warm up an old man."

Stas followed both of them with a mistrustful (when it wasn't lustful) gaze.

"I'm pleased, Mr. Perfekcy, that an individual of such stature as you did not refuse to be present," Casallegra changed his somewhat prophetic intonation. "I, unfortunately, do not know your wonderful language. But I translated the invitation for you myself, using forty-four dictionaries. Did I make a lot of mistakes?"

"Trifles. Not even in every word," Perfetsky remained honest.

"There weren't any mistakes," Ada translated.

"I'm pleased, pleased, Mr. Perfektsy! My beloved Ada, just warn our dear guest to be especially cautious with you, kitten. You're a femme fatale." Following these words he again smiled cordially.

"He said that your talk is planned for Tuesday," Mrs. Zitrone translated.

"It seemed to me that he said I might fall in love with you," Perfetsky contradicted her.

And he was right, as you and I know.

Ada was already preparing to say something sarcastic, but fanfares began to play from every direction, and everything all around grew quiet.

"And what about Mavropule, hasn't he shown up?" The old gray head reminded himself amid the complete silence. "Too bad we have to begin without him. . . . Well, go on along, children, don't stand like pillars over an old man. . . ."

And with a certain kind of gesture it was as though he were releasing both of our doves, or even blessing them.

Then the secretary's voice began to buzz throughout the Cenacolo Hall—Mr. Dappertutto called everyone to a toast, extending a goblet, obviously made of Venetian glass and filled with something red, in his right hand. The guests and hostesses grew silent, the ladies and gentlemen, and even Mike Bongiorno. Some with goblets, some without, those who were without scrambled to the buffet tables, but too late, so our Ada with Stakh, as the Ukrainians say, "sewed themselves buffoon's clothes." However, Riesenbock even had two glasses, and he, this artfully pliant close-mouth, filled his jowls with Gorgonzola cheese.

And this was a spectacle and not a toast! A certain illegibility and lack of clarity, and further on just simply moaning and groaning, half whispers half lispers, and generally—nothing other than cackling and clattering, which instantly turned into sobbing and snorting, and also into rustling and brustling. And the words were something like words, but then again not, but simply just mutterings and smutterings, rustling, crackling, hacking, drumming, though not strumming. And this lasted for a long time and to such a degree until the artful Mr. Dappertutto had himself crawled into the toaster's role, when one of the ladies present, apparently Jacqueline Onassis, fainted at the fifteenth minute, crashing to the floor with the full force of her body. And while all this was going on, everyone endured it in their own way. Some had trembling legs, others breasts, one suffered from a nosebleed, another from an allergy, yet another from lethargy, someone just stood there benumbed, and in others their eyes just flashed with a yellow glow. . . .

And our Stas, the pride and glory of Ukraine, sneaked up to the musicians (an entire *cappella* had been brought since morning because a dance had been promised!) and he conspiratorially grabbed a golden trumpet from the first trumpeter. And—just as Dappertutto was finishing up rasping out his stuff, droning and barking (for everything has its time and the end is coming, and the end is the proof of the pudding)—as our Perfetsky bellowed Jericho-like, as though on his native *trembita*,[4] as though he had released a black angel beneath the heavenly vault. . . .

Here from that point it had just begun, although the fervently awaited Mavropule hadn't arrived on time, without whom nothing should have begun.

For that's the way it is in life—as in a long planted field, if there's one out of seven missing, then the others won't wait for him.

And I, my beloved readership, at this instructive moment (the hostesses have not yet escorted the men present as well as me to dance), I should complete my excessively detailed report. I had to leave our respected heroes a bit on the side, since there was a parade at a long table of all kinds of tarts, tortes, roulettes, and . . . of course, *frutti di mare!*[5]

■ □ ■ □ ■

6

I'M SUNK, SUNK, SUNK—PELL-MELL, CATEGORICALLY, I'M SUNK, I WAS lost head over heels, I'm trashed, I burned up and crashed. The end awaits me, kaput, the edge, *finale apotheoso,* the X-hour, the starry hour.

I spent all afternoon and evening with Ada. After all those schizophrenic discussions on the island, they put our entire coterie-crew on a spacious *motoscafo*¹ and took us somewhere to the depths of Venice. There everyone could do what they wanted. Riesenbock, for example, had a fancy for looking for some new rare fish for his collection. Riesenbock buys aquariums, fishbowls, tiny fish, algae, and shells everywhere in the world. He sends them home by special delivery mail—from Cairo and Buenos Aires, Singapore and Istanbul, although most often from Venice. He has connections with similar ichthiophiles. It's like a mysterious network from which it's impossible to come out alive.

So the two of us were left alone, and Ada escorted me though a part of the city where a dog would break a leg walking around. To add to this, it had gotten cold, the afternoon sun had escaped somewhere in the direction of Naples, the sky turned completely gray. So I was sunk. Yes, I was sunk.

What happened that day? A spider's web of alleys, roaming, dead ends, uninhabited places by walls, the quietest green of March in secret enclosed yards, the scent of the canals, disorientation, the inability to find the simplest path, to find the most complicated path, any kind of path, returning to the point of departure (the very same beggar appeared before us for the second time, for the second time shouting out his *carita*)—this meant that we had been circling around something, which, perhaps, we don't recall, some kind of mystical epicenter was somewhere here next to us, behind these curtains, behind this gate, it was worth it just to cross the little bridge and either three times or three times three times, by a prearranged sign, to knock on the door. We really wanted to come out onto San Marco Square, and what could be simpler?

There also were several cups of coffee, which we used to warm ourselves up, not to forget the cognac, the infinitely large number of coffee shops moved in our tracks, repeating our mistakes, our straying from the road, returning to their places and together moving with us again. Ada began to seethe, the numbers marked four times on the walls just irritated us, and the street signs to San Marco, it seemed, had been just set up by carousing wise guys— insofar as all this was uncertain and contradictory, which just distanced us from our goal. Ada cursed right away in several languages because she had forgotten her map in the hotel, otherwise we wouldn't be knocking around here with these sleep deprived alcoholics and retired prostitutes, from whom you can't find out anything, either because of bad diction, or dialectisms, or something else, or everything all together was the reason for this—it's unclear. At the end of the tirade, the magical word-question "*Capito?*" came up, and we, not getting anything, gave up the ghost, nodded our heads and said "*Grazie.*"

Then another pause came over us during coffee, the host put a burning candle in front of us, because it was really getting dark in the building, and here the thought struck me: this woman, this candle, this coffee, this cigarette, this ephemerality, this passage, this terminality, this is only "here and right now." In this way I first, apparently, touched upon the greatest of the mysteries of the West (somewhere beyond Naples the sun was setting)—it is not for us to understand all the depths of this unhappiness, these depressions of sweet sojourn, however just the sojourn and nothing more—the World permits you, gathers its enticements—in streetlights, flowers, fragrances, candles, passing bodies—and then, then it begins to take all this away, gradually and with knowledge of the matter, ridding of bodies, candles, fragrances, flowers, streetlights, one day to turn off the remains of dark light in your Neapolitan eyes. We envy— fiercely and blackly, as though we were lost children, for those western people, for these inhabitants of blessed evening gardens, their food, their profits, their diversions, their cars, we are ready day and night to gather oranges for them or to wash their spittoons, just to enter, to filter through, to be admitted, to be closer, but every one of them, poor buggers, returning from the office, crouched up beneath an illuminated sign, took the cheapest burger for themselves with ketchup and, washing it down with cola, nearly began to cry: Why this world? . . .

There was Ada. There was Ada on this day. Strictly speaking, that which I saw in her, but not completely. Half turned, half profile, half stooped. From time to time a bold intention pierced me, to reach to her ear with my warm lips. She wouldn't resist. But I didn't do it a single time.

We managed to do quite a bit over the course of the afternoon: we took a boat ride, imperceptibly violating the borders of the *sestiere,* we spent time where we could, all the previous epochs were accessible, and the Byzantine fluidly transformed into the Romanesque, we could talk about Veronese, about his jesters and dogs, about lots of other things like rugs, masks, cutting knives, or Middle Age condoms, about culture, about Canaletto and Canareggio, about Caravaggio. We could simply utter these words out loud, these notions, these names—in this way it is absolutely quite possible to reach nirvana, or at least illumination, the way Hindus reach it from a permanent "Om," thusly, attention: o Canova Casanova and San Cosma San Felice la Fenice o Carpaccio catenaccio Negroponte o Pozzetto Pozzolongo Falier and Venier Castelfranco Bergamasco Scarpagnino Ghirlandaio Malamocco mantecato and staccato and barocco Pergolezi Pellegrini Pordenone and Pontormo Vivarini and Vivaldi Barbarigo Brandolin mandolino mandarini and Manolesso and Manín and Marangona; o risotto de peoci Sernagiotto and Perducci; and: Santa Maria dei Miracoli Santa Maria della Pietá Santa Maria della Salute and Santa Maria dei Carmini Santa Maria del Giglio and Santa Maria Gloriosa dei Frati Santa Maria Zobenigo and Santa Maria Formosa Santa Maria Assunta and Santa Maria e Donato and Santa Maria Mater Domini; and Maddalena Madonnetta Malapaga Malipiero and Calle Acqua Minerale and Sansovino Paul Sorvino and Santo Vino and Santa Grappa and Santi Tortellini and Santa Pasta and Piazza di Santa Pizza and that's enough, basta!

YURI ANDRUKHOVYCH

From now on this is my daily Venetian prayer. I want to pray, for I want to prosper. For I'm sunk—entirely and hopelessly, and in this city of my hallucinations I have to do something depraved with my own soul, that's why I'm summoning, I'm asking, I'm imploring Your support, O Lady, Your intercession, O my patroness, O Serenissima! . . .[2]

Ada purchased an exit from the labyrinth for a few hundred lire: it was a kiosk, and in it finally a map—not quite the kind that she had forgotten in the hotel, no, this one looked considerably older, printed sometime in the 1550s, when geographers believed in the Goatfish, the Fishchicken, in Dagon and Eight-eyed Sea Serpents, for all these beings were depicted on the just-purchased map—in the waters, immediately adjacent to the lagoon, drawn in the minutest physiographic detail and in motion; and there was even a nereid rising from the waters of the Grand Canal not far from today's post office and vegetable market. In general one could contemplate the map endlessly, there were not only all the canals, streets, squares, and shores on it. Here and there we also found depictions of inner courtyards, separate buildings, loggias, trees, bushes, and beyond these— discrete passersby or people in rowboats, among which musicians especially stood out, who just had steered to the right of Rio di San Barnaba, and therefore warned other boaters with deep, throaty shouts. The musicians were with oboes, flutes and tambourines in their hands. Among them there were all kinds—young and old, juvenile boys and wind-worn guys furrowed with scars with criminals' but not musicians' faces, some kind of pirates from Dalmatia or from somewhere else, with earrings in their ears and sex-crazed drunken eyes. I thought that once I surely end up in musicians' hell, and just these types surround me there, the kind depicted on the ancient Venetian map, we'll guzzle down certain black unearthly libations with them, and then we'll put on such a jam that the saints will go marching in.

We indeed exited from the labyrinth with the assistance of that map. This turned out to be quite simple: several dozen meters away, and to that point unnoticed by us, the Merceria, teeming with people and filled with temptations, glowed with the first evening lights. It was quite easy to exit onto San Marco through it—you just had to keep from deviating from it anywhere. However Ada, believing neither herself nor the map, nor, even more so, my premonitions, every minute tore out ahead, inquired of people she came across and again hurried on, again inquired, I tried to hold onto her by her hands, by her neck or waist—this nearly didn't succeed, she rushed on like a manticore, forward, she slipped out as though she were covered with scales, and I was left only to repeat: I'm sunk, I'm sunk, I'm sunk, I was lost with all my heart and penis, I crashed and burned.

Is it possible to confirm that at 6 P.M. on March 6 Stanislav Perfetsky definitively became convinced of his feelings for Ada Zitrone?
Yes, it is. Approximately at 6 P.M. the realization came to Perfetsky that his life would be intolerable without this woman. The day before, when the paths to a retreat remained, Ada succeeded in tempting him. This act might not have meant anything if not for the rare ability of Perfetsky to fall in love with a woman's fidelity. Like all narcissists, in everything he always saw his own reflection, that's why women made their way through to his inner kingdom in the instance when they first manifested their attraction to him. Ada did this more than persuasively: she gave herself—in all the meanings and connotations of this wonderful verb. Not to speak here about the corporeal side of the above-mentioned act, we must accentuate that for Perfetsky it became a great emotional surge and led to a quite sensitive spiritual arousal.

However, the further intensifying feeling of Perfetsky promptly acquired a sad coloring. All the more distinctly he understood that soon, in several days, he'd have to part, and all too soon—the parting would be forever. In the meantime, walking out of the Merceria[1] onto San Marco Square beneath the clock tower (Torro dell' Orologio), to the left of the Old Procuratie, unexpectedly and distinctly he sensed he'd never want to part with this woman, that he'd want her by his side for the rest of his life, and that he'd want to die together with her one day.

What most did Perfetsky like in Ada?
As was noted already, fidelity in love, more precisely in lovemaking. Her temperament. And not last in turn—her voice. He liked her

entire body, sufficiently strong and tender, without any territories neglected or defective regions. He really liked her backside, in no way was it too large, and it was so perfectly built into the rest of her body that for Perfetsky it could become a source of inexhaustible fantasies and joys. In general, that entire part of Ada that began below her belt was best known to Perfetsky, and he blessed it with gratitude just on seeing it, or even if he didn't see it—he touched it. As concerning, for example, her breasts, Perfetsky knew less about them, although he could say that they obediently fit like cups into his large palms—perhaps, he thought, Ada dealt with their care completely separately.

There were also her eyes the color of a green river. Certain hints of the sensuality of her mouth and ears. And also—one should especially pay attention to this—the half turn of her head and the half slant of her neck, that turns into her shoulder. That is why Perfetsky loved to stand a half step away from Ada and talk to her from behind her back.

Did Perfetsky try somehow to get closer to Ada when they were alone together?
He tried many times. Sometimes he madly wanted to touch her. Or even to kiss her—on a bridge, near a stone wall, in a coffeehouse, in front of a gate, by the monument to Goldoni, by the laundry drying in the wind—on the ear, on the cheek, on the lips, on the neck, on the shoulder. But he didn't do this a single time: Ada was different, not that kind—as though it was not she yesterday who had placed his large weak-eyed head on the meadow of her stomach.

To what did they turn their attention when they entered beneath the vault of the Basilica of San Marco?
At the bronze gate with lions' heads; at the thrice-carved ark that closes the portal and on it carries the earth, the sea and symbolic animals, which are bulls and griffins; at the mosaic of the Judgment Day; at Christ-the-Vine-Grower surrounded by the prophets; at the triumphal quadriga, again bronze and blackened; Perfetsky especially turned his attention to two fishermen in a boat and the bustling about of stone fish in the depths beneath them, at the

appearance of an angel before Saint Mark the Evangelist in his dream, at the tanned warm stripe of Ada's neck that opened up after the lowering of her coat's collar, at all this boundlessness, the oversaturation, the inaccessibility.

What was known about the above-mentioned dream of Saint Mark?
Saint Mark, giving a sermon on the teachings of Christ, once had returned from Aquileia to Rome in order to move from there to lands considerably further south—to Ethiopia and Egypt. Here it's as though a terrible storm had deliberately begun—the streams of water poured from the heavens, and the winds arose from all directions, serpents of whirlwinds began to swirl on the water, overturning the fishing and the sentry vessels. In order somehow to pass through this time of misfortune, Saint Mark was washed toward the shores of Rialto and fell asleep there, weakened by the difficult battle with the elements. In his dream he saw an angel who addressed him in the Name of the Lord: "Here you will find peace, Mark, My evangelist!" Besides this, already dissolving in the hazy substance of Mark's half awakening, the emissary of the Lord still managed to prophesy the appearance of a glorious and splendiferous city on the surrounding islands. As we are persuaded by this example, one should believe in dreams, especially those in which angels speak.

What impressed Perfetsky most inside the basilica itself?
A typical Byzantine structure that is based on the form of a Greek cross, it didn't impress him. Also, the darkness of the gold or the marble of the walls or the alabaster of the columns. The perusal of several of the mosaics took longer: such as, for example, the Tree of the Mother of God with all its Hebraic spreading growth. Or the Descent of the Holy Spirit, at which you have to look for a long time, throwing your head back in order to discern beneath the circle of the twelve apostles all the extinct tribes of the Old World including the Asians, the Heretics and the Arimaspians. Or again, the Ascension of Christ, filled with angels, apostles, all sixteen virtues, the four evangelists, and the waters of the Biblical rivers. Since Perfetsky really loved to look at water, he wanted to live in it. He also loved old medallions with deer, dogs, eagles, and pigeons,

with bushes and stones, he loved all manner of images, he loved the red marble from Verona or the trophies of the Crusades, especially chalices and small chests, small chests and chalices. He loved Ada.

Ada moreover remained in the baptistery where for a certain time she meditated before Salome in her cherry-colored cape (we've already paused on Ada's passion for black and cherry colors, but it's just worth adding that Ada appeared without exception every day in different clothes, however the above-mentioned two colors were the most frequent of her combinations). The head of John the Baptist didn't make a particularly great impression on Ada, unlike the cherry-colored cape of the young harlot.

Let's return then to Perfetsky, who, moving from the atrium to the presbytery, from transept to transept, from one nave to the next, from Tesoro to Cappella del Sacramento and steadily approaching the Golden Altar, thought at that time about all the layers of this giant torte, which it was impossible to feel to the bottom, about a woman with a violin, a winged steed, about a lion that rends a wolf, about the gold of glory and the glory of gold, about the complete absence of feeling, as though you—in God's Temple—this scurrying around of Japanese, American, Australian, and Russian swarms with cameras, this excess of aesthetic, which isn't overly justified, all this can sooner remind you of the Train Station of All Times. Perfetsky thought about this without reproach and pretension, without overstraining, splashed by the wandering flashes of the ornaments, lights and real jewels, he moved sluggishly inside this thousand-year-old basin; he also thought about Ada without reproach, who from time to time rose up next to him, and then again left him alone—why? Then she sometimes related something to him—about Venice, about the basilica, about herself.

What did Ada tell Perfetsky about herself?
Ada told him she was born in America, that she lost her mother at an early age, and her father gave her up to be educated beyond the ocean, to a convent of the nuns of Saint Clare in the Lombardian Alps, not far from Como. That she stayed in the nunnery until the age of seventeen and completed her basic schooling there, where she was taught the Romance languages, embroidering with golden threads, and special secret prayers, from which your hair grows

quicker and your teeth stop hurting. From the age of seventeen Ada studied on her father's money—partly in France, partly in Italy, as well as in Bavaria. Her first husband was a Frenchman, more accurately a Jew from Marseilles, a child of the Sephardic tribe, the same age as she and a student, agile and really slim; they attended the same classes and colloquia and were absorbed by the same incomprehensible disciplines like comparative sociopathology, the hermeneutics of semiology, or the history of the theory of linguotherapy. At the age of twenty Ada escaped from him to Rome, where a seventy-five-year-old professor of mnemonotechnics soon wedded her, one of the pillars of a sacrilegious society "To the Highest Radiance," a brilliant lover and a capricious man, the owner of several bountiful estates in Calabria. The Ada of back then turned out to be that pliant clay, from which he sculpted the her of today— her soul, her body, her mind. He taught her to be strong, to make love in 118 different positions, and to take care of enemies with the help of certain deadly flowers (an art which Ada did not make use of even once). When one morning he died, Ada turned blue from despair, she pounded the walls and mirrors, after the funeral the servants had to put her in a straitjacket for two weeks: everyone around her feared that she definitely would raise her hand against herself— and not necessarily with something sharp or combustible, it was sufficient simply to take a good whiff of the flowers she knew about from her deceased professor. But with time all the wounds healed, and Ada once again began to roam. In Munich, where she instructed uncensored Middle Age Latin and comparative chronoscopics for especially gifted adepts, her current husband met her—Janus Maria, one of the favorites and followers of her dead husband in his time. The great commonality of the past, completely concentrated in the exceptional figure of the professor who had been spent before his time, patched the two of them together. But the era of mutual understanding and pleasant coexistence in the shadow of the professor's grandeur didn't last for very long. The destructive passion of Riesenbock for aquariums and decorative fish caused his almost complete neglect of all other aspects of family life. Beyond this, Ada furthermore came to the conclusion that for her third husband a young boy of corresponding proclivities would be better suited in love than poor her. Wishing only for happiness for dear Riesenbock,

Ada herself even strove to find him a young acquaintance some-where in Belgium or in Denmark. But first they had to divorce, and since both of them were bound by a church marriage, then right after the end of the seminar they planned on driving to Rome to take care of the business of the divorce in the chanceries of the Holy Father.

Besides this, Ada related that since childhood she had danced Ukrainian dances, that's why she had so much strength and flexibil-ity in her legs. She could listen to any kind of music, but always to her favorite: two or three Italian operas, including *Don Giovanni;* Neapolitan songs, Nat King Cole, Maria Callas, and Bruno Maderna. She knew French better than Spanish, but knew Italian best. She got terribly used to Europe, although inevitably she'll return somewhere to California or Virginia, where she'll begin her life anew, she'll open an astrology parlor or a school of Ukrainian dance and will thumb her nose at everything. And that's that.

What else did Ada tell to Perfetsky?
The story about how the dream of Saint Mark came true. More than seven centuries have passed from the time when he accepted a martyr's death in northern Africa, in Egyptian Alexandria, where before this he had founded Christ's Church. The body of the unde-composing saint lay in the gloom of a sacred place there, in a wretched and cold sarcophagus. But the taking of the city by the Saracens gave birth to unrest in Christian souls: the oppressive foreboding of a great blasphemy hung above Alexandria. Then two zealous Venetians—citizen Rustico from the island of Torcello and citizen Buono from Malamocco—set off to sea to fulfill God's will and save the remains of the saint's body. Their journey turned out to be quite difficult—it seemed that hell had thrown all its might into the battle just to impede the holy mission. Three times while they were sailing they came upon the fiercest storms, from which not a single other sailor would have come out alive. Three times bloodthirsty Algerian pirates followed them, and each time both reckless men managed to escape. Three times a Leviathan, the master of the sea's abysses, rose out of the water on their path, and three times it opened its reeking maw wide to swallow them to-gether with the ship and their two-month supply of lard, but coura-

geous bearing and sincere prayer always saved the bold ones. After they got to Alexandria, Rustico and Buono dressed in rags, tossed bags over their heads with holes for their eyes and hung tiny bells on their neck. In this way they feigned being lepers, which allowed them to enter the sacred place with Mark's body without any impediments. All the Saracens without exception believe that lepers are God's chosen, and for that reason do not dare touch them. And after carrying the relics onto their vessel, Rustico and Buono again set out their sail, a winged lion appeared above them. And thus it accompanied them over the course of the entire return journey, defending them from robbers, storms and vile sea serpents. After twenty-five days of traveling they arrived in their native Venice, where they were noisily met on the bank, the entire government with doge Partecipazio at the head, all the patricians, all the citizens. This way the body of Saint Mark the Evangelist, the disciple of the Holy Apostle Peter, finally found eternal peace for itself, as was foretold by the Lord through his night messenger seven and a half centuries earlier.

What was the further fate of citizens Rustico and Buono?

Not much more is known about them. Rustico was elected to the Consiglio dei Dieci,[2] that is, the Council of Ten; however, not a single time was he elected to the Cappa del Consiglio dei Dieci, that is, to the secret triumvirate. Living to a ripe old age, he had fourteen children and fifty-six nephews, of which he remembered the names of only the first five.

Buono went on military expeditions to the East, to the lands of Gog and Magog, during one of which he ended up a prisoner of the Koprophagi,[3] he picked up leprosy there and soon after died, having fallen apart in bits and pieces.

To this day the memory of both is revered in Venice.

You can attest to the truthfulness of everything related here in front of the facade of the basilica, where above the four entrances to the temple this story is laid out and again composed in the tiny stones of the mosaics, thus just about everything in the world is composed of its own stones, bricks, blocks, atoms—it's important just to have the knowledge to fit them with the others and with the Great Surrounding.

What didn't Ada tell Perfetsky about herself?

That her family roots also are from Chortopil. That the first mention of Tsytryns[4] in the town register there comes from the sixteenth century and concerns a half-crazed alchemist and a planetarian Georgy Tsetryna (at that time the name was spelled with an "e"), of the Greek faith, later an Arianist,[5] a pupil of Bologna and Padua, who in the fifty-first year of his life was viciously slaughtered by three robbers who demanded some of the king's moonshine from him: he was immersed in a vat with a solution of sulfuric kvass near the exit from his own cave-laboratory.

Ada's father Hermogenes Zitrone (*Tsytryna*) ran away from home in his early childhood, not long before the outbreak of World War II. This resulted from the fact that the world-renowned Vagabondo traveling circus drifted into Chortopil. The boy was so charming to everyone who saw him at the performance that he hooked up immediately with the tricksters who took care of the animals and who mended worn gymnastic tricot. True, after several years of uninterrupted blundering through the European theater of military operations, the young Zitrone began to exhibit extraordinary mesmerizing abilities, then finally the director of the circus, the telepath Ananda, entrusted him with a number, giving him the sinister artist's pseudonym Azril de Frankenstein.

After the end of the war the circus troop, saving itself from accusations of collaboration and the court of the victors, was forced to leave for America, where from the 1950s the mad ascent of the great Azril began. Following the tragic demise of the director Ananda (he was slashed to pieces by the sword-swallower drunkard), Hermogenes Zitrone embraced the directorship of the entire circus. One day at a New York subway station he picked up a homeless Ukrainian girl, who, accompanied by a hurdy-gurdy, sang the first part of "A Song about an Embroidered Cloth," which in those times was becoming popular. This was Solomia Bizarrsky.[6] In a short time she learned to fly beneath the vault of the circus (trouble-free mechanisms carried her upward on cables during the time that the orchestra inimitably struck up Herbert L. Clark's "The Carnival of Venice") and, dancing on the trapeze, performed popular things from the repertoire of the World's Greatest Jazz Band. This enjoyed enough good success—the riskiness of the number was complemented by the not-quite-correct American pronunciation of Solomia that caused a mixed, horribly comic effect. With the beginning of the '60s Solomia gave birth to Azril's daughter Ada. In a year or two she renewed her performances in the arena, but the era of her music had already passed, she needed to take command of new rhythms and new tunes, America was being shaken by The Velvet Underground and groups from the West Coast. Failure after failure forced Azril to reject Solomia's solo; without the circus she clearly withered, she resorted to alcohol and took on the habit of frightening her little daughter with all kinds of stories about giants who eat their own heads. Ada grew up impressionable from this excess; in addition, she openly feared her mother, for whom she personified the end of her airborne gymnastics career. Azril more than once sent his wife for treatment to the best Ukrainian experts (professing the golden rule "use what you know"), but none of them managed to make the situation better, restricting himself to the advice regarding "her most active participation in social life as in the League of Ukrainian Women." When Ada turned fourteen, the inevitable happened: moving secretly and stealthing her way to the circus one morning, Solomia Bizarrsky, quietly singing "The Carnival of Venice," clambered along the cables up to the very vault of the tent and, spreading her shoulders for the final flight, decisively threw herself from there down.

Saving the child from spiritual and psychic catastrophe, her father decided to send her far from America. Here the convent of Saint Clare in the north of Italy became useful, where the abbess was a former Frankensteinian love, the onetime acrobat named Le from the previous cast of the Vagabondo circus troop.

Thus Ada Zitrone for the first and for a long time ended up in Europe?

Did Ada tell everything about her relations with men?
It's clear, far from everything and not how it really was. Besides, it was untrue that she ran away from her first husband, a student. One day he simply went mad and began to call himself Vol de Flèche.[7] His sick imagination progressed so quickly that after eight days the poor guy could only whistle, being simultaneously the subject as such, and the condition of the subject, and its essence, and

even its possibility. He was hastily delivered to a semisecret clinic that researched anomalies, where, locked in a hermetic box, he's still whistling to this very day.

Ada's second husband, a professor and mnemometrician from Rome, taught her the habit of making love impetuously in the most unexpected places. Especially propitious for this were the nooks of his Calabrian palaces, as though they were intentionally planned for a similar sort of amusements, flavored with honey, petals, and *zitrone* juice. Maintaining in his seventy-five years a strong impeccable springiness, he often took trips to all manner of congresses and conferences on all the mainlands and continents of the world. From the moment of marriage Ada was his constant companion and even helper. During these undertakings the professor acquainted her with many of her friends, the same kind of old oddballs and capricious men, inexhaustible mistagogs and strategists, eternal demagogues, among whom appeared the Venetian baron Leonardo di Casallegra with his incomprehensible foundation.

Ada didn't even say anything about certain circumstances of the sudden death of her second husband, accentuating more her suffering after it. The body of the old man, charred and painfully shriveled, was found in the morning in his office, on an undamaged rug, right in front of a window thrown completely open. The cause of death was determined to have been a lightning bolt—and, in fact, the night before, a thunderstorm had passed through, and the old man quite often and riskily had been experimenting with the elements the past few years.

Concerning her third husband, Riesenbock, Ada concealed almost nothing, with the exception of one of his favorite pastimes, which could have interested Perfetsky. It happened after Friday evening soirees, the usual *party*,[8] and consisted of the fact that Janus Maria convoked an entire villa of all kinds of monsters, to which he demonstrated one and the same spectacle: a giant aquarium with water was filled with countless fish of the most valuable assortments, and then he threw several large fish-predators into it and, when they had destroyed the entire aquarium's small fry, several bigger predators appeared, who swallowed the previous predators, and so it went on until the king of the predators was carried out of the tub, the one and only mighty Fish, that ate the last pair of large predators. Immediately after this, the Fish was caught and killed in the kitchen. Then the cook prepared it for dinner for the entire company—together with the schools swallowed by it as well as tinier schools of small, smaller, and even smaller fish.

Was the current number of Ada's lovers restricted to the number of her husbands?
Of course, no. Beyond all doubts, there were more of them, something like twelve. We can't know about all of them in detail—every woman has the right to keep such things secret.

The first three sprang forth on motorcycles from out of the hills while she was still living in America, in the middle of the '70s, not far from cherry plantings, where the thirteen-year-old Ada with her friend Susan were picking juicy and sweet berries on that June cherry-colored midday. They were on motorcycles, still teenagers, two or three years older than Ada, without moustaches and sharp as knives, in black leather and army helmets with dragon-eye goggles, they boldly stopped near the girls with lips sticky from the cherries and impatiently said "hello"; then it happened that two of them took the girls on their motorcycles, and the third flew ahead alone, as though he were pointing the path to the Garden of Eden, they had a tape player with them, which here began to sing "Riders on the Storm" in the voice of Jim Morrison, and then a violent and warm June storm really hit—the kind you come across on a Sunday after lunch; Ada was just slightly afraid, but the rain lashed so stubbornly, that there only remained for her to more gustily press into the hard leather back of the wild angel in front of her, and it enraged her so much to have to be the eternal caretaker of her mother, that she agreed to everything, and when "Riders on the Storm" was over, at that instant the downpour passed, again it smelled of the sun, they swerved to the woods (Jim Morrison began "Waiting for the Sun"), the Harleys were marvelous, they tore above the pathless roads, already under the power of some kind of new dimensions; there was an entire island of dry moss, and they finally stopped there, and lay down, and each one of the three spent some time with each girl, and Jim Morrison sang "The End" for all of them, and several new ones were added to the cherry stains, and that's how it happened.

Spending time later in the convent, Ada developed the rare ability to daydream of love. This happened during endless masses or daily lectures. In this way she managed to close up her consciousness and soul, her entire self, that one step from the pulpit, before the very countenances of the saints and prophets, wafted by the sweet fragrances and strewn with stained-glass spangles, she sensed how dark-eyed boys were kissing her, whispering her something in unknown languages and touching her everywhere, reaching her, rousing her, until one day, having fixed a moistening look at the naked Saint Sebastian, she recognized the fact that a pleasure, till that time unknown to her, was happening right here, the saint had a taut muscular stomach, supple thighs and half-opened lips, completely sown with the arrows of pagans, he held himself strong and taut as a tree, he was worthy of becoming her lover and became him, and with a moan she started to crawl on the granite slabs of the floor, and several girlfriends led her, completely blissful, outside.

Who else to name in this enumeration? Perhaps Bertrand, the dark-skinned university friend from the times of Ada's first marriage, who made love to her between the library stacks, spreading out a ten-volume set of Voltaire in soft cover beneath her? Or Dino, a thick-lipped oboist from the chamber cappella of her second husband, who could wind her up and lead her to unconsciousness with just a high C note? Or the nameless naval officer, with whom she rode in the same compartment from Rome to Geneva, and who turned out to be as though he were poured out of hot marble? Or the unicorn, who appeared out of nowhere, as though out of her very own fantasies, in the inner courtyard of the Ca'd'Oro?

And finally, completely separately stands the night of loving, spent once in the bed of the abbess, who in the past was the famous circus acrobat Le.

And it is impossible even for us to know everything.

What remained for Perfetsky and Ada after viewing the basilica?
To exit onto the square. To listen to living Venice. To look at the waters of the lagoon. To identify several constellations in the sky; if they were not to appear in the sky—to identify them in the city's illumination, in the electric flashes. Leisurely, coffeehouse after coffeehouse, moving in the direction of the hotel. Telling each other

about each other. Listening that entire evening about their great need for one another.

How was it really?
Ada again was a bit in front, raising the collar of her coat. Pleading a migraine, she wanted to get to the hotel all the more quickly, to take some pills and hide under the covers. With this she said that Stakh was not obligated to accompany her, the entire city was at his service, she would find him a map and, if need be, money, too.

What did Stakh say to this?
He walked further after her. Mostly he was silent. When he found himself in a bright area—beneath a street lamp or near a shop window—it was abundantly evident how he so wanted to take her at least by the hand. But he didn't do this a single time.

Why?
Nobody knows.

8

THE ABUNDANT RINGING OF THE SIXTY-THREE CHURCHES OF OLD
Venice hung above the city since morning: Sunday. Our motor
launch pushed on slowly, as though it were groping—an impenetrable fog settled on the shores, just here and there leaving a tiny
opening for a cupola, a loggia, a tower. It seemed that till now
Someone had been sprinkling layers of flour and cotton from above,
although Giovedi Grasso,[1] intentionally planned for this ritual, had
passed already a week and a half ago. I missed it.

Venice plunged into nothingness. Reaching the shores of San
Giorgio Maggiore, we saw just remnants and rags—it was as though
the foundations of buildings, guzzled by the fog, did not exist. And
just an angel on the very top of the bell tower continued its eternal
turning, an unreachable guardian of the Islands.

And what if there's this kind of fog on Tuesday?

And what if there isn't this kind of fog on Tuesday?

What then?

We stepped onto the shore and, taking each other's hands so as
not to get lost, moved toward the monastery buildings. Someone
was complaining out loud that no bathing with the hostesses had
taken place. Someone else contradicted this and said that, in fact, it
had occurred and had not been too bad at all. A third said that he
had lost his horse. I wanted to see Ada, but it was impossible,
although she, certainly, was walking right next to me. Dappertutto
met us at the gate with embraces, the hostesses, and a cigarette. He
managed to demonstrate his attention and amiability to each.
Calling me Parfumsky, he asked if I had come across Senior Mavropule, who, as it were, apparently, had already arrived in Venice,

perhaps held up for a day or two in the bloated with scandals atmosphere of the Vendramin-Calergi winter casino. Senior Mavropule loves games of chance, and he always is wildly lucky at roulette.

Everyone looked liked each other. Casallegra majestically floated through, supported on both sides by his great-granddaughters, dangling his head, bent forward—apparently he was still sleeping. Shalizer, hanging on the shoulder of the shorter John Paul, heron-like, moved his long shanks in unpressed pants, as though till now she had not seen the road and was fearful of stumbling on a skull with snakes. John Paul, dragging a good half of Mrs. Shalizer on him, was somewhere else at the same time, and the aged wall paintings, certainly seemed to be for him some golden forests on the shores of Jamaica. Stooped over both of today's speakers hanging together—Gaston Dejavu, Preparedness and Collectedness, covered tightly in a gray ballet tricot, in a short cloak made of black silk, and Alborak Djabraili, dressed almost in military garb, in a beret riddled with bullet holes.

The shadow of Eleonora Duze rustled.

Everyone was seated here.

I didn't see Ada.

We were seated at a single, although immense, oval table, over which I'll bend to describe it in more detail sometime: it seemed something was sitting inside it.

The presiding Casallegra in his own particular manner, making ten-minute pauses between sentences, all the same announced the beginning of the second day, and regarding the summaries of the first day, designated it as a complete success, particularly his talk. The guests applauded a bit. Then with great sadness they announced the further absence of Tsutsu Mavropule, fervently expected by all. Taking the floor, Mrs. Shalizer announced that yesterday after lunch, as it seemed to her, she saw him, leaning against a wall of the Palace of Doges. He was awfully drunk and couldn't move. He reminded her of the biblical Noah. Mrs. Shalizer's remarks were heard out with courtesy.

Then, finally, the floor went to Gaston Dejavu, he announced his topic, dancing a bit on the podium, I attached the headphones for synchronous translation and submerged into my own thing.

Ada, I spoke my thoughts, beseeched, prayed, and begged, like a beaten dog. Ada, Ada, Ada, where are you, Ada.

Ada where you who you Ada?
O Ada. Oasisiada.
O you Ada.
It's me Ada where you, Ada?
Jawohl Ada: ja ja Ada.
Ada's Ada: I want some ada.
Ave Ada. Hiya Ada.
I'm nichts without you lieber Ada.
My ode to Ada. My enchilAda.
Do you want to do me Ada?[2]
Where're you who're you come here Ada.
Come here softly sweetly Ada.
Me and Ada—Meandada.
Either Ada or I'm nada.
Where are you Ada
Cause I'm sad, ah?
I was Adam's now I'm Ada's.
I was me now I'm Ada's.
I was one now I'm Ada's.
I was fine now I'm Ada's.
All the depths of Hades Ada.[3]
With no Ada there's no strAda.
Si do Ada sol do Ada re do Ada Eldorado.
She's my Ada my stumbling blockAda!
She's my life my acqua Ada!

"Two expressions immediately serve"—in the meanwhile Dejavu flowed off into his mission—"as the motto for my restorative searchings, each of them belongs to a person, incontestably, of World Measure. I don't know whether it's accidental or not, but Both have come from the very same nation, and I am not at fault for the fact that this nation has so harmed Others, indeed, and has done a great deal for Them. Both expressions concern the subject of my many years of Research—Allegory. The first of them belongs to Goethe, who in his "Maxims and Reflections" in number 742 and 743 pronounces the following: "Allegory transforms a phenomenon into a concept and a concept into an image, but in such a way that the concept always is determined and entirely is encompassed by this image, is apportioned by it and appears through it. The symbol transforms a phenomenon into an idea and an idea into an image, but in such a way that the idea, contained in the image, forever remains boundlessly active and unreachable, and, even being expressed by all languages, it all the same remains unexpressed." The next Quotation is sharper and more candid in Its—I allow myself to give an Evaluation—obstinate Antiallegoriality. It comes from the well-known and, unfortunately, Often-Quoted Sermon of Luther "*De captivitate babylonica ecclesiae praeludium*" and sounds approximately like this: "All these allegorical studies are diversions of people, plunged in idleness and in idle prattling. Can you not guess that I would not have managed to play allegory on the topic of any kind of God's creation? And will just a single snub-nosed, incompetent person be found anywhere to strew allegories in all directions, like the magpie with its cawing?"[4]

"Goethe—in definite Form, that is delicate, imputes to Allegory a certain limitation and I'll say it like this, its Scholastic Sterility. Luther—in polemic Form, that is insulting, imputes to Allegory its complete Emptiness and Insignificance. Today I resolve to defend the Honor of Allegory, although I was not judged by History to be the Most Brilliant Soldier in this Grand Battle.

No later than Yesterday, wandering along Museum Venice, several times and not just once or twice, I halted before the most eloquent Testimonies to the Honor of Allegory. I have in mind Immortality, which descended upon me from the canvasses and frescoes, sculptures and statues: *Justice that Delivers the Sword and Thorns to Doge Priuli* by Tintoretto the father and *Neptune Bringing Gifts to Venice* by Tintoretto the son. *Doge Grimani on His Knees Before the Symbol of Fidelity* by Titian and *Allegory of Faith* or *Venice on the Throne Surrounded by Justice and Peace* by Veronese, and finally *The Doge Cicogna before Christ Surrounded by Faith, Peace and Justice* by Palma the Younger. I could continue This Series. Because right here in this City-Palace, Allegory reached its Highest Privilege. And where, if not in Venice, could I venture, an ordinary dancer, a Child of the Ballet, stand to the Defense of It from the desires of our eastern neighbor? . . ."

The last rhetorical figure was met with laughter and applause. Dejavu bowed in every direction and moved to the Main Part, but here something intolerable began to crackle in my headphones and I, fortunately, stopped understanding him.

Outside the windows the fog grew thinner. From patches of it, taking on all the more visible solid concreteness, the bell tower of San Marco slowly emerged, the winged lion, the arcades of the Palace of Doges. Lots of people scattered on the Piazzetta, buying flowers, postcards, wine, looked in our direction, began to flirt, tempted others, and were tempted themselves. But I could only conjecture about this. Just as about the fact that among them she definitely had to have been jostling about, a tourist in dark glasses and in a sweater below her knees, with phrase books, with maps, with a Dictaphone, with strong legs, with newspapers beneath her arm, Eva from Poland. For once we agreed that we'll get together in Venice. For the second day she's already been looking for me in all the hotels and hostels. Yesterday I saw her several times in passing. But I didn't call out to her. For well-known reasons. I'm just that way.

Casallegra dozed, taking his large gray head in his hands. Taking advantage of this, Lucia and Concita openly flirted with some handsome guy across from them, who looked a lot like Freddy Krueger. Alborak with his beret, crushed in half and pinned beneath his epaulette, was boldly writing something of his on the empty writing pads of the foundation, from time to time angrily shaking his head and snorting. John Paul, closing his eyes and biting his lip, was listening to Bob Marley. Liza Sheila was very ardently (but in a whisper) convincing her neighbor to the left, an Italian minister of social care, of something, leaning so hard against his ear, that he had to swing his head up and down frenetically, agreeing with her on everything. Greta Garbo was drinking small gulps of orangeade, and Caruso was drawing a fat woman in his copybook. Dappertutto first disappeared, then appeared, he phoned somewhere from a neighboring room, at the doors met those who had arrived late, returned with a cup of coffee, then with a glass of water, then with a sandwich, then with a Snickers bar, then with a caramel, then with a waffle cookie, then with a cream cone, then with marzipan, but always with a cigarette. And who then listened to the poor Dejavu? Who?

"Beauty, Tenderness and Whiteness," he continued in the meantime, when again I pressed to the headphones, "being Essentials, the essence of Unity: all that is Beautiful, or Tender, or White must be mutually linked, for it has One and The Same Basis for its Existence, One and the Same Meaning for, let's say, God. These Peculiarities are what these Things are, the Very Kernel of their Being. Our Thought can see them this way—each time, when It returns to the Sagacity of the Savage, the Child, the Poet and Mystic, for Whom the Natural Properties of Things are comprised namely in These General Individualities. But such an Interrelationship just then takes on Actual Meaning and the Fullness of a mystical sense, when in a Unifying Chain, that is, in a Given Individuality, the hidden Presence of Both Terms of symbolic Comparison; in other words, when Redness and Whiteness are simply considered Signs of physical Differentiation according to a quantitative principle, but are examined as Realia, as Facts of Reality. Through the Existence of the same Characteristics: Beauty, Tenderness, Purity, the Bloody Redness of roses, those same ones, that the Martyrs or the Chaste had. How does this Assimilation occur? Posthistorical Intellect immediately sees the Symbolic sense Here: the Chaste and Martyrs Shine in beauty In the captivity of Their tormentors. Red and White Roses bloom in the Captivity of Thorns. The Symbolic Assimilation on the Basis of commonality of dissimilar Characteristics has SeNSE oNly Then, When these CharACTERistics are fOr GiveN THinGs something eXISTential, When the PRoPErTIes that cOnTrOl them like a SYMBOL, as well as what is SYMBOLIZED, are exAMINed IN the QUALITY OF THEIR ACTUAL ESSENCE. . . ."

Far too many capital letters were popping out. In addition, I understood that the synchronous translation was delivered back to front—perhaps intentionally, and perhaps through Dappertutto's oversight. Dejavu spoke measuredly, underscoring every division, smoothly gesticulating. His short black cape fluttered from every movement completed in his deliberation.

Last night V. arrived. I didn't expect that this would happen right away. V. reiterated: it begins tomorrow. They're gathering in Venice just for three days. Ministers as ministers from all of Europe.

Everything has been kept secret, but the press has sniffed out some of it. Our friends, too, of course. V. said that they're everywhere. Monday and Tuesday. For Monday they're inviting us to an evening theater performance. There I'll find out if N. has arrived. His seat is in one of the loges of the first balcony. My seat in one of the upper balconies. I'll have to supply binoculars. I mentioned my sight. V. answered that it doesn't concern him. These are my problems, V. said. On Tuesday they'll take them in several boats to Lido. I understood: telescopic sight, etc. V. was very uneasy. He glanced at the door, asked three times whether the room was bugged. I wanted it to be bugged. I treated V. to some liquor. We downed the bottle with a big, shaggy orange. V. told me that in the theater—this was by the way—I have to be careful. There will be operatives there—one or two, not more—but they'll be there without fail. I uncorked a new bottle in the hope of dragging something more out of V. V. refused the liquor. V. said that it was time for him to go. It was close to three in the morning. V. put on the mask of a Kyno-kephalos.⁵ Through the bathroom window he tossed a rope ladder into the yard. He lowered himself along it onto the ground. He disappeared in the fog.

The fog opened up large chunks of shoreline Venice a bit more. In the windy territories and fields cleansed by the sun each time more clearly there became visible the southern facade of the palace, the wall of the Marciana Library and the Zecca, three poles with flags, even a tower with a clock and the cusp of the Loggetta, even the Bridge of Sighs—a bit in the depth to the right of the palace. But in this entire view there was no place for Ada. There was no place for Ada anywhere at all. I didn't see her in the sky, on the square, I also didn't see her in the waters. She wasn't: buying mimosas, watching the pigeons, riding in a motorboat, in a gondola, eating pizza, posing for street portraits, flirting with the carabinieri, going into churches, going out of them, having her hair done in a salon. She was not even standing on the step board. And this gnawed at me the most.

"However the Flow of one Thing from Another," said Dejavu, once again establishing a certain amount of order in the capital letters that were about to rebel, "we will examine just in the light of the naive principle of the Immediate Multiplication or the Ramification of the Tree—That Very one, to the Rustling of the Leaves Of

Which we have been listening to for several tens of thousands of years. The Harmonic Bond invariably unites all the Territories of Thought. That, which occurs in the Old Testament, presages and anticipates That, which occurs in the New; World History is filled with Their reflections. Every Act and every Tiniest of Action can and must have its Higher Explanation, emerging as a symbol, as a Sign, as an Allegory. When a priest, accepting Communion, becomes similar to the Lord's Sepulchre, for the Host is Christ, therefore I, using Milk with Flakes for Breakfast, also make myself similar to Something or Someone, for example, to Zeus, if it's goat's milk. But you can always find at least One property for Assimilation. Everything presages Everything with itself and even Nothing. I often recall a certain game of Childhood Years, when friends and I guessed the most unexpected Allegorical Pairs, leading ourselves to Complete Exhaustion by their, at first glance, Idiocy. So, we loved to say that a Wolf is Candidness, a Hare—Goodness, and an Owl—Fallacy, a Fox—Endurance, a Turtle—Affectability, a Bear—Joy, and a Falcon—Mercy. And now I want to ask, my dearest friends, in These Comparisons is there less Sense than in the traditional ones: the Wolf is Fleet-footedness, the Hare Squint-eyedness, the Owl Vigilance, the Fox Giddiness, the Turtle Guardedness, the Bear Lasciviousness, and the Falcon Above-cloudiness? No way, the Distinction only in the fact that we've gotten used to the Latter, and to the Former still haven't managed to do so. This, however, does not mean that the Latter have Sense, and the Former are completely stupid. Just for that very reason they have Sense in that they are stupid, Tertullian, that Master of Paradoxes, would have joked on this occasion! . . ."

The audience livened up a bit. From a side room a quartet of musicians was led in, dressed at the same time as the Four Seasons, the Four Corners of the World, the Four Tetrarchs, and the Four Seas of Italy (Ionic, Adriatic, Ligurian, and Tyrrhenian). It seemed to be clearer: the ballet will begin immediately, that is a short dance number with Allegoric Figures, promised by Dejavu for the closing of his talk. Dappertutto impatiently puffed smoke, gazing at the clock to mark the start.

"The Symbolic Comparison remains a far from adequate Means for the revealing of Constant Interconnections!" The lector began to hurry, summing up what had been Squeezed out of his Brain. We are conscious of this, gazing at the Dance in the Shadow: 'For now we see through a glass, darkly,' the Apostle Paul wrote to the Corinthians on this account.[6] Understanding that the Riddle arises before our vision, we deal with It all the more this way and, striving to look into the Mirror of reflection, explaining Visions Alone with the help of Others, laying out the Mirrors One against the Other. The entire World arises before us in the Images of the Personified: this is the Season of Withering and Overripeness. Thinking has been made overly dependent on Embodiment in Images; a visual aspect, so important for the era of the late Middle Ages, today has become All Powerful (the movies, TV, video). Everything Visible and Invisible (that is Thought) is remade into the Plastic and the Pictured. A posthistorical perception of the World will attain a state of complete Peace—this is as though the Hall, filled to the brim with the Glow of the Moon, the Thought inside of Which could finally plunge into a Dream."

The applause had not yet managed to thunder, Dappertutto had not managed to circle among the guests with clean ashtrays, I failed to manage to think that somewhere and at some time I had already once read something very similar, as Dejavu slapped his palm, and together with the first beats of the music, Seven Hostesses appeared, dressed so that from the front each looked like one of the Cardinal Sins, and from the back—like the Opposite to It Virtue, being, besides this, one of the Seven Days of the Week and one of the Seven Provinces of Northern Italy. The lecturer himself put on a mask (which could embody Death, Time, Night, and AIDS at the same time) and with light ballet jumps set off to meet the hostesses.

In answer to such an open *pas,* the entire quartet of musicians ignited in sounds, as though they had moved uniformly from where they were standing into a march. And some kind of pavane began to reverberate—but not quite a pavane, a galliard but not quite a galliard, and not a sarabande, and not an allemande, but rather a chaconne. And Dejavu flew over the bookcases and shelves, blowing away the thick clouds of sweet dust from the tops of the folio volumes with the wings of his cape. And then each of the Seven Hostesses, choosing a dancer for themselves according to their taste, scooted over to ask him. As though intentionally, my lot fell on

Miss Tuesday, additionally the province of Piedmont. But most vexing was the fact that from the front she was the heaviest of the sins, that is Pride.

"Well why, why have you come to me?" I asked throughout the dance, straining to swirl her around her axis and turn her significantly more chaste backside to me, that is Humility. But the girl quickly untied herself from my spider embraces and again appeared to me as Pride, with her highly upturned nose and breasts.

"This is not me, this is you," she answered several times when I repeated my question.

All around other pairs soared, and Avarice turned into Generosity, and Kindness into Wrath and vice versa, also when everything whirled at the peak of the incited undulation of the musical theme, which, in fact, was further becoming wilder, each time recalling less the good, old chaconne, I finally caught up to the entire impenetrable depth of the author's conception of Monsieur Dejavu: in this circling, flickering, and shimmering, in this tugging and havoc, it was already impossible to explain, to determine, or to separate anything—envy from purity, covetousness from kindness, moderation from idleness, lust from vigilance. However, he remained at the center of everything, Gaston Dejavu himself, Death, Time, Space. . . .

With the final chords Pride stuck her lips to my neck and hung on me this way. In order to make her a bit more discreet, I was even forced to smack her on the rump of Humility. Just after this she fell off. In addition, the reasons for her falling off could have been different, say, the piercing voice of Dappertutto, who shouted out a brief intermission. The breathless guests wandered about in search of cookies and drinks. Dejavu artfully accepted congratulations and immediately gave several interviews. The musicians put away their lutes and violas in their cases and, dejectedly bent over like prisoners on their way to capital punishment, exited one by one: spring, summer, fall, winter.

I sat down near the window in hopes of at least seeing something: a seagull on the crest of waves, a fish, a cloud, a piece of an oar. Or, for example, Ada. But Shallow Shalizer appeared at this point above me and proclaimed something like I "fantastically beautifully dance."

"*When?*" She asked me.

"*What?*" I pretended naively.

"*Shit!*" She snickered, and, slapping me hard on my shoulder, stepped away.

"Whew!" I snickered in her tracks and even waved.

Go cram it, my love from beyond the ocean.

I can handle anything. I can handle anything. I repeated this one hundred and fifteen times: I can handle it. At the hundred and sixteenth time the word was conferred to Alborak Djabraili.

I didn't particularly listen to him, although his beret, shot through where the cockade was, and the speckled camouflage, and an old Soviet gas mask on his side struck a note that Alborak was saying something about "postmodernism in politics," stressing at the beginning that he had arrived directly from the "territory of battle action," but I didn't quite hear who was battling against whom and why. In addition, yesterday he said that apparently he had arrived by bicycle from Sweden.

Alborak's text was a laborious mixture of allusions, of foreign language citations, expressions in quotation marks, inside of which other quotation marks appeared, there were more quotation marks than any other signs taken all together, he took out of the brackets the most unessential, and he modestly hid the most important in brackets, as though it was just a semiextraneous addition; he also began to play with words from his very first sentence when he recalled how "in 1914 in Sarajevo the Austrian Archduke from Princip(le) had been shot." This figure of average piloting was supported by the applause of those present—this way an audience well versed in jazz reacts in the middle of the composition to any peculiarly broken septachord. Not long after this the winged Alborak cleverly rhymed "Balkan" with "vulcan," reviling the capital of Albania as "till recently a city of tyrants," compared Yugoslavia with a pizza cut into pieces (obviously remembering that in Slovenian "pizza" with one "z" means something else, wet and mysterious, then he called Austro-Hungary "a text, which no one has ever read to the end as a result of its eclecticness," at the same time moving, like pieces on a chessboard, ancient and Biblical heroes, he harshly judged some "asses from Oslo," as though he had unintentionally mixed up Venice with Vienna, he compared Latin America with a cannibal restaurant, where the main house dish was "cannon fodder," he called democratic Russia baked ice, about Europe he articulated that it has "Aesop's Complex," and he introduced the year of the world ruin of Carnival with the aid of a separate formula

$$\frac{x \cdot y^z}{n},$$

where x is the period of the incomplete building of the Tower of Babel, y—the rapidity of the spreading of the thousand-year Kingdom, z—the Number of the Beast (the constant), and n—the ordinal number of civilization.

He finished with a stormy announcement on the occasion of the abduction in Venice of his "alter ego and closest friend," with whom he has traveled to ninety-three countries of the world and crossed the equator seven times "at the hottest points." The loss of such an emblem, he continued, can be appraised "either as a political provocation, or as a criminal act, that has as its aim a brutal attack against national (Alborak Djabraili) and biological (his horse) minorities." The speaker warned of "the possibility of petitioning to "international" "law" "institutions." He added that everything "relies" on "healthy" reason and "human" feelings of unknown ("?") evil-minded people and far "from" that, "or" to accuse of action that "occurred," all the amiable "Venetian people." Liza Sheila Shalizer was the first to put her signature at the bottom of the document that had been read, Alborak remarked, and gave to understand that everyone should join in.

The city police already know about this unpleasant case, Secretary Dappertutto assured in answer. Photographs of the horse were passed out to all the precincts. There exist, true, certain complications tied to the fact that the two-wheeled acquaintance of our friend could have been snatched by Islamic terrorists (here read—the red brigades) as a hostage. And anyway—however it might be, the most professional investigators have already taken up the matter. It remains for us to take heart and in spite of everything continue our seminar, maintaining firmness and hope that tomorrow the illustrious Rocinante will greet us by these walls with his joyful neighing.

"Everyone is free until tomorrow," the chairing Casallegra creaked from his seat, without opening his eyes.

ΣΩΔΞ–ςϑ
To Monsignore I humbly dispatch:

On Sunday, March 7, the care of the Respondent was taken over by me (as a result of Cerina's supposed illness). For her own reasons (Monsignore will excuse a certain indelicateness), apparently cramps, Cerina categorically refused to leave the hotel (she did not allow herself to be examined, which cause my doubts to the reality of her illness to emerge). Thus I accompanied the Respondent and over the course of long hours never was far from him (which the Respondent couldn't even guess). Taking advantage of the climatic conditions (a thick fog had taken possession of Venice since morning), I sat on the Respondent's tail and remained with him for as long as I could (till late in the afternoon, in other words toward evening). This does not solely belong to my duties (about which Monsignore may have been incorrectly informed). But in working for Monsignore, I have already gotten used to executing not just my own duties (I ask that you not take this as a complaint).

The early-morning Respondent looked bad (general weakness, crinkled face, puffiness around the eyes and eyelids). There was the impression that he had slept badly or too little. The conduct of the Respondent during the seminar talks can be characterized as indeterminate (often glancing at the window, chronic inattention, the absence of facial expression). At the same time the Respondent was evidently longing for someone (I could guess who, but I won't). As far as dispersion of the fog (the weather further was sunny), the Respondent acquired certain characteristics typical for him (roaming grins, wiping of his eyeglasses, and others). During the dance offered for the participants (the relative nature of sins and virtues), the Respondent was asked to dance by Pride-Humility (Txss). The Respondent conducted himself lustfully like a billy goat (I ask the Monsignore's forgiveness). His poor partner was barely able to free herself from these spider embraces (once again forgive me) only through the merit of her lost maiden's virtue. At the end of the dance, the Respondent latched on to a different person with female sexual characteristics (also a participant in the seminar, her real last name Zuckerkandel). Permitting myself unbecoming expressions and gestures, the Respondent induced Zuckerkandel to coitus (see the hour and place of their meeting in the next notification).

With this, the seminar lectures were ended (some kind of misunderstanding with the Centaur, I suspect discord in the actions of the Accidents Sector and the Robbery Subdivision).

Further, the surveillance of the Respondent for me became quite linked to the complete dispersal of the fog and the impossibility of close accompaniment (I ask Monsignore to at least consider this in the distribution of tips). Sent off with everyone through the San Marco Canal, the Respondent then disembarked at the Riva degli Schiavoni (the call of blood?) and went east to the San Zaccaria stop. There for a time he studied a map that he had pulled out of his pocket (eyeing the surrounding women more). Finally the Respondent flicked his hand (at what?) and moved on foot in a northerly direction (I walked at a distance of ten meters behind him). Walking in sight of the Respondent was quite difficult, since the Respondent does not walk like other respondents (I ask you to weigh my experience in this matter). The Respondent has the habit of suddenly stopping, turning, pulling out a map, walking back, once more looking at the map, losing his orientation, concentrating his attention on all kinds of silly trifles (paper flowers, garbage cans, drying women's underwear—the Anomalies Sector should check on the matter of fetishism). The Respondent barely dragged his way to Campo San Zaccaria, then he entered the church of the same name, where he spent thirty-one minutes to unknown purpose (I remained in the square). Coming out of the church, the Respondent blasphemously crossed himself (shame!) and nodded (it'd be interesting to know to whom?).

From San Zaccaria to the Fondamenta del Osmarin, the Respondent continued his path to the north, but not to the Orthodox church of San Giorgio dei Greci (how could one suppose from his, he-he—prayerful mood) and not to the police *questura* (as one could expect in his condition). The Respondent chose Ruga Giuffo for his movement, from which I deduced the next aim of his route—the Church of Santa Maria Formosa (and I've not made a mistake). True, for a short time the Respondent walked hesitantly back and forth in front of the building of the Querini-Stampalia Museum, from time to time looking at his watch and counting something in a whisper (I can guess what). But a visit to the museum could not enter into the Respondent's plans anyway (through which he moved further). In the Church of Santa Maria Formoza the Respondent spent an even longer time than in the previous one (nearly forty minutes). On the square I managed to drink up a small bottle of Bardolino and to eat *zucca barucca*[1] (the vileness of which you'd have to go far to find!). I assume that Cerina was not ill at all, and simply wanted to heap onto me the entire range of the job (I thought about this on the Santa Maria Formoza Square while eating the thrice-damned baked melon, excuse me, Monsignore).

From the above-mentioned square the Respondent (finally leaving the church) took a bit of an easterly direction (along the Calle Lunga) and, intersecting the bridge above the Rio di San Giovanni Laterano, he directed his precious steps, clearly (Monsignore has already surmised), to the Church of San Zanipòlo (that really designates not one, but two saints concurrently). Near the church his attention was taken for a long time (three minutes) by an equestrian monument of condottiere Bartolomeo Colleone (nothing other than the fact that he liked the horse's ass, excuse me). Here two female Japanese tourists rolled up to the Respondent with the request that he photograph them on the backdrop of the monument (the Respondent faded away in a friendly smile). Both geishas burst out in laughter from one of his jokes (one can guess, fat and salty). Finally the Respondent convinced them to take the picture not in front, but behind the monument, on the backdrop of the above-mentioned horse's ass (confirmation of my version—you can check on the matter of zoophilia).

Having satisfied the playful Japanese women, the Respondent grinningly parted with them and, once again becoming serious, he went (as Monsignore had not doubted) inside the Church of San

Zanipòlo (I remained on the square). While the Respondent following in turn "prayed" (hmm-hmm), I observed the arrival to the shore of an ambulance boat, the unloading of a sick man (a sharp kidney stone attack, although the operative intervention, in my view, is still not obligatory), and the transportation of the body to the hospital building (the former Scuola di San Marco). Cerina further is getting more used to the fact that Monsignore favors her, I thought (excuse me, Monsignore).

After a good half hour the Respondent came out of the church (alongside the hospital building) again took steeply to the north (along the Fondamenta dei Mendicanti). He met several nice large Swedish women, who stopped him to ask something (with a carefreeness peculiar to Swedes, taking the Respondent for a Venetian). Over the course of five and a half minutes the Respondent fooled them, pretending that he spoke Italian (in answer to which the Swedes sonorously and appealingly laughed). Then the Respondent finally switched to English and graciously (but was it correct?) explained to the light-haired beasts where they had to move further. The Respondent waved his hand in the direction of Rialto, from which Monsignore can make the conclusion about the further aim of the procession of the unknown Swedish women (but I will restrain because this does not enter into my overly inflated obligations). Some person allows herself to lie on her hotel bed for days at a time (listening to all kinds of Italian operas), and I must exert myself for two just because Monsignore places great hopes on me (and not in vain).

Making his way along the Fondamenta dei Mendicanti, the Respondent all the more often looked at his watch (version: the Respondent has an agreement about a meeting with someone). However, getting up to the Church of San Lazzaro dei Mendicanti, the Respondent could not restrain himself from the temptation and (as Monsignore already understands) went inside. I awaited this quarter hour in a garden adjoining the church, where on the young grass I observed the ball playing of several active teenagers (I especially recall the oldest of them with long legs and a well-developed torso). I immediately wanted to step closer and meet the young guy; however, at that moment the Respondent (again—br-r-r—crossing himself) came out of the church and continued his movement to the north (obviously, to the Fondamenta Nuove). The little guy, it seems, sensed from my side (kicking back the balls, each time it was as though he were showing off his skill), and somehow even openly and quickly glanced into my eyes, even burning after this. With unpleasantness I had to walk after the Respondent. The boy looked at me leaving (as I heard, his name was Cherubino), yes, he looked at me leaving, shielding himself from the sun with his strong and simultaneously tender palm. But otherwise, it was just the scent of the spring earth that so subdued me (Monsignore, absolutely, knows how the head can swirl from such scents).

I anticipated that, getting off at the Fondamenta Nuove, the Respondent would take a northwestern direction (and not a southeastern one—to the Arsenal). That's the way it happened (intuition plus analytical abilities). In conjunction with my confirmed outlines I ask Monsignore to consider the following version (and extend it as you are able). We marvelously know the catastrophic financial situation of the Respondent (an audit by the Eighth Financial Chancery came up with a final amount, from which your hair would stand on end (even though I'm not at liberty to know). The Respondent's crusade to the churches can be seen (in this way) as an attempt to take possession of something extremely valuable from the church's wealth (a painting of Palma the Elder or Younger, Bellini, Tiepolo; objects of church decor; chalices, pyxes, monstrances, boxes, etc.). If the Respondent succeeded (and it's not excluded that he succeeded) in stealing any of the five hundred-year-old reliquary (the same as urns with the skin of the heroic Bragadin, torn off at the command of Sultan Mustafa), then he (I have in mind the Respondent) could easily rid himself of his financial problems. I don't lay a claim to the infallibility of my supposition, but I'm unable in any other way to explain this stubborn Respondent's "pilgrimage" (he-he).

At the Fondamenta Nuove I had to lag behind (please, Monsignore, don't only think that I stopped trailing to return immediately to that boy practicing with the ball). The following happened: at the Fondamenta Nuove landing a passenger boat of line 5 just arrived (from the direction of Cannaregio). I first got cracking, understanding that the Respondent intended to get on it (buying a ticket on the landing). However, almost immediately, I changed my decision (for the sake of maintaining secretiveness). There were so few passengers on the deck of the vaporetto (soldiers and a girl, a bluish-gray-nosed priest, a woman dressed in mourning clothes with an armful of dried flowers), that it would have been impossible to remain further unnoticed to the Respondent (although he is half blind, sorry). Of two evils—to be noticed, uncovered, and mess up the business or to lose the Respondent from my field of vision (temporarily)—I chose the lesser, and therefore restrained myself from further remaining near the Respondent (I also went back along that fantastic garden with the teenagers and grass).

The vaporetto with the Respondent on the deck floated away in the direction of its further route (the islands of San Michele and Murano). I surmise that from the island of Murano the Respondent could have decided on an even more distant trip (to the islands of Burano and Torcello). The reason for the Respondent's travel by boat was still unclear to me (although my supposition about robbing the church remains in effect—because the churches there are everywhere like manure)! For my failure I ask that Cerina be most harshly punished (if I'm not mistaken, Monsignore, to be sure, has entrusted the greatest part of the matter to her). Lately Cerina actively has been taking advantage of her essentially feminine influences, as a result of which you forgive her too much (pardon my directness). If Monsignore were harsher with such (I don't want to use a stronger word) feather-brained dames, then the most assiduous and devoted to Monsignore individuals (I have here in mind not particularly myself even) would not need to do double (many times triple) the amount of work. It seems that it would also be worthwhile to have Cerina's conduct examined by the Third Special Subcommittee (for the time being with a prophylactic aim).

In concluding I want to share with Monsignore my great joy: I succeeded in acquiring several extremely rare specimens (which makes me nearly happy). They are: *astronotus ocellatus*—a brown background with black speckles, a thick and soft skin, seemingly velvet, on a tailed fin—an expressive black eye framed in red; besides that, *synodontis angelicus*—a charming fat sheatfish, white peas on a velvet-black background; and finally, finally—red piranha (*serrasalmus nattereri*) with a bright red anal fin. I managed to find a pair of each type (although they say that synodontises don't re-produce in aquariums).

Ready to the death (he-he) to serve Monsignore—
The Doctor

P.S. Only Monsignore is able to evaluate my efforts equitably (I have here in mind not necessarily a raise).

■ □ ■ □ ■

1 0

I, ANTONIO DELCAMPO, SIXTY-NINE YEARS OLD, VICAR OF THE
Church of San Michele, an inhabitant of the *sestiere* Cannaregio,
have the need and consider it my duty to recount a meeting that
occurred in the evening of the first week after Great Lenten
Wednesday, namely on the seventh of March this year. First and
foremost the fact impels me to do this that not too long ago,
although with great delay, I found out about a certain inexplicable
disappearance, for which many are inclined to suggest suicide.
Perhaps my narration will help to pour more light on this story and
will uncover certain new circumstances regarding it.

As is well known, the island of San Michele, where I happen to
conduct a mass in a church by the same name, belongs to the most
dismal islands not only of our lighthearted city, but even, perhaps,
of all the Lord's World. Thus, a city cemetery is situated on it, for
the reason of which it is fittingly called the city of the dead. The living come here to pay their respects to the dead, to be next to them
for a while in silence, in sorrow, and in the eternal green of the
cypresses, to pray for their souls and at least to meditate a bit on
the unseen. Over the course of twenty-eight years, I have been on
the island nearly every week and with the Lord's help have performed all the necessary rituals inside of the church, as well as in the
Emiliani Chapel or at the burial spots, and have become accustomed to the island's peacefulness, to the cypresses and birds there.

On that day I arrived on the island after noon, because ahead of
me there was only an evening service, which we call the Angel of the
Lord, for the memory of all the dead. In the church there were only
a handful of people—the undertaking was getting close to Sunday

evening, outside it was barely dusk, and the daily visitors to the graves already had managed mostly to sail away to the city.

At the end of the service I was supposed to stay in the church an hour or two. Besides me, there was no one in it, if you don't count the old man Angelico, the church handyman and watchman. As it ought to be on that day (I remind you that everything was happening on the first Sunday after Ash Wednesday, which is the beginning of the Great Fast), I had plunged deep into thought on the theme of the fourteenth chapter of the Gospel of Matthew, verses 22 and 23. The following lines took on an especially great meaning for me: "And when he had sent the multitudes away, he went up into a mountain apart to pray: and when the evening was come, he was there alone." At that time there came into the church a stranger on the better side of thirty—one of those people on whom you naturally direct your watchful attention even in a crowd. I first noticed this newcomer two hours earlier, because we'd sailed to San Michele on that same boat. Getting off then on the shore, he moved to the depths of the cemetery, although, undoubtedly, no one he knew was buried there. I took him for some kind of tourist who, lagging behind the group—intentionally or by accident— seeks out his own impressions without assistance.

Having greeted me in a quiet and somehow constrained voice (here I was convinced that he was a foreigner), the young man began to examine the church. I must say that the temple of San Michele, in which I am grateful to serve the Lord, truly deserves the most spirited examination, built during the Renaissance according to the plans of Mauro Codussi, whom I consider the most expressive of the Venetian architects of that time. However, over the course of long years of pastoral work, I learned to be attentive and to understand not only people's words, but their movements, gestures, their manner of breathing and looking, too. My experience suggested that it wasn't the architectural charms and not the inner arrangement of the church that interested the lonely foreigner at the moment. From his face I read unrest and turmoil, as well as indecision and doubts. I confess, there was even a moment when inadvertently I suspected him of something bad, robbery maybe. Fortunately, my suspicions turned out to be groundless. Sometimes I caught his quick glances at me. I knew something should happen, but I didn't rush things and didn't meddle for the time being, giving his disturbed soul the opportunity to ripen with his own efforts.

Suddenly rising before me, he asked if he could speak to me in English. I answered him in broken English that, unfortunately, I didn't know more than fifty English words, therefore I wasn't sure if such a conversation would be fruitful. But if he knew German, too, then we could have a decent conversation—in my youth, when I wasn't a priest yet, I had lived a good number of years in Frankfurt, where I played and sang in a little restaurant called Mamma Rosa. The foreigner was pleased by this and, easily shifting to German, called himself Stanislav. "I would like to confess, Father Antonio," he shot out, right after I gave my name to him. "I'm walking from church to church and I can't find a priest anywhere who understands me. Finally I came across you, Father!" After taking my seat in the confessional and blessing him, he suddenly said: "Pardon me, Father Antonio, but would you be able to violate the mystery of my confession?" I didn't quite understand him, thinking that the long years of not using German had really twisted things in my mind. So I confirmed that the mystery of holy confession is inviolable. "But I, I myself, I'd want you to violate it!"—Stanislav expressed himself more clearly. "It's the first time I've ever heard anything like this, my son," I harshly answered to let him understand the utter bizarreness and inadmissibility of such a wish. "Believe me, Father Antonio, this is very important. I allow you, for a certain time, to tell everyone you think should know, what I'm about to say here," he stubbornly insisted. "You allow me?"—I wagged my head. "How do you dare to allow or not allow me something beyond your right? Do you know that when one of God's great mysteries is at work, then we, slaves and servants of the Lord, mustn't interfere with our obstinate self-will?" He was silent for a bit, and then again he threw me into confusion: "In that case, Father Antonio, I ask you not to consider this a confession in the canonical church sense. Let it be just our conversation." "But in that case," I came up with an answer, "this will just be a conversation of two ordinary people. And nothing more. And you will not be adorned by God's grace and will not receive forgiveness for your sins." "But it's important that you hear me out," Stanislav insisted. "For this you don't necessarily have to go to church." I shook my head. "Just spill everything out to the first-best drunk from the public house and you'll have what you need." I sensed that I'd hurt him—he grew silent, wounded by my implacability, and I, too, as a result of a brief spiritual battle, mellowed somewhat and offered to relate it for him. The strength of following the Lord lies not in the letter. Saint Thomas Aquinas taught the meaning of exceptions for spiritual practice. And even if he hadn't, let's assume, that even without Aquinas, I'd act by the prompting of my heart—isn't this a sufficient argument?

"I'm a great sinner, Father Antonio," Stanislav began his conversation. "Of all the Lord's commandments, there's only one I haven't violated. I don't remember which number it is, but I remember that it's 'Don't kill.'" "That's the fifth commandment, my son," I reminded him, for he truly could have been my son. "Thank you, Father, I also thought it was the fifth," he continued. "But soon I plan on violating even it!"

This forced me to shudder and to listen with all possible attentiveness—with my inner alertness. "I've come here from a really distant land. Maybe you don't even know about it, Father Antonio. Suffice to say I was born in a little town in the mountains, quite close to the center of Europe," said Stanislav. At this point it seemed to me that he wasn't completely rational. "What are you saying?" I was surprised. "Is it so far from here? Isn't the center of Europe somewhere in Switzerland?" "No, Father, amid different, entirely different mountains, far from here!" He insisted. "Perhaps in the Ural Mountains?" I myself remembered something from school lectures on geography. "No, not the Urals, but in the Carpathian Mountains, Father," he corrected me. "Some of you still call them the Caucasus." "Wait a minute, wait a minute." Something stirred in my memory. "I've heard about those mountains! That's where they get lots of snow not just on the peaks, but also in the valleys?" "Yes, Father," he answered, "sometimes so much snow falls that we're forced to plow through it up to the neck, digging it out in front of us with special light shovels. And we get such cold winters that all the people for months sit in their houses and don't even stick out their nose anywhere, because it would freeze and fall off straight away."

This terribly interested me, and I decided to find out something more from Stanislav about his strange land. "And what do the inhabitants of your homeland look like?" I asked. "They're like me, Father" was the answer. "Or they're not like me. There are different kinds. However, in general, all of us are more alike than not. In fact, my teeth are a bit better than most of theirs. Though my sight is considerably worse." "And do they honor our Lord Jesus Christ there?" I tread closer to the main topic. "Or, perhaps, do they pray to some kind of stone idols? How, for example, do your people celebrate Christmas Eve the day before the Birth of Christ?" "This among our people is one of our main holidays," Stanislav asserted. "All day before this we fast and pray, and just as the first star appears in the heavens, we sit down to a mystical supper. For supper only meatless dishes are served, but there have to be twelve of them, after the number of holy apostles, for each dish personifies one of the apostles and therefore at the table it's not permitted to identify each one by its own name, but by an apostle's. So you can't ask 'And please pass me the stewed cabbage,' just 'Pass me James the son of Alphaeus,' and you can't ask 'And pass me some ground poppy seed,' just 'Pass me Matthew the publican.'" "What superstition! I couldn't restrain myself, perhaps inadvertently insulting his familial feelings. "Besides this," he proceeded, "on Christmas Eve it's not permitted to shake hands with one another across a threshold, to spill salt, or to break mirrors. Besides this, it's not permitted to say 'soup,' but only 'borscht,' for over the course of the coming year in the house there will be misery. Also, a husband that evening dare not touch his wife with the index finger of his left hand, but must eat only from her plates, finishing what she leaves. That evening one must sing Christmas songs, which we call *haivky*, or grove songs,[1] for, according to our beliefs, the Virgin Mary gave birth to the Child of God not in a cave, but in a sacred grove not far from Bethlehem. As concerning the Epiphany, this, too, is an extraordinarily splendid holiday. On this day the most severe frosts occur, so cold that not only the rivers and lakes are covered with ice, but also both seas—the Black and Azov. From an icy block they chop out a giant ice cross (a "chrismo")[2] and, sprinkling it with red Greek wine, they set it up plumb beneath the light of the sun, from which the cross flashes with a ruby fire. The wine must be Greek, for we belong to the Greek rite, as you know, Father Antonio." "Now I know!" It became clear to me. "I remembered when and from whom I already heard something similar. My uncle, my father's brother, the elder brother of my father, Michele Delcampo, one of the first Italian pilots, who once set off for your lands, where he went down during World War I. He described something similar in his letters! Do you know this name, foreigner, Michele Scipio Delcampo?" "Everyone in our land deeply respects him." Stanislav bowed his head.

Then I decided to be better disposed to him and talk about what was on his mind. "You are seeking reconciliation with God and peace for your soul, my son," I reminded him. "Can you talk more about your worries and pangs of conscience? "Happily, Father Antonio." As always, Stanislav began from far away. "To talk about myself is one of my greatest pleasures. I so love this that even the hardest confession would not bring me suffering but satisfaction." "Forget about confession," I cautioned him. "We're just chatting." Then I'd ask your permission first to play the organ a bit, Father Antonio," Stanislav revealed. "You play the organ?" I didn't hide my shock. "In my land nearly everyone knows how to play the organ," Stanislav explained. "Some worse, some better. I'm average." This quite interested me and I, stepping out of the confessional, led him upstairs, where I showed him a not very big instrument, but a precision one, dependent only on good maestros. After this I went downstairs again, and Stanislav, practicing no longer than five minutes, suddenly and without any special evident efforts or noticeable transgressions re-created the well-known Canzona no. 3 in G Major by Frescobaldi, after which with even more assurance and, I would say, even with affectation—his again, Frescobaldi's, toccata "Per l'Elevazione."[3] "Each time you amaze me, foreigner," I admitted when he had come down, stretching his long, musical fingers. If that's average in your land, then what's the best?" "I studied music with an old woman organist from my hometown. She was Jewish and died at one hundred and eight. But maybe she didn't die," Stanislav answered enigmatically.

And a not so bad idea struck me. "Listen, maybe we should step out a bit in the fresh air?" I proposed. "The evening today is warm and quiet, the cypresses smell nice, Venice on the other shore is already lighting its lights. Nearby I have an observation point from which you can see half the city." "How about the dead?" My guest asked. "You really are superstitious in your strange land!" I calmed him down. "So what of the dead? We won't disturb them for nothing!"

Then I shouted to Angelico to prepare everything we needed, and in a short time we were already sitting beneath the cypresses, not far from the cemetery's wall, with several bottles of Valpolicella, a head of cheese, and other good snacks, having before us the quiet waters of the lagoon, the warm dusk and flashes of lights in the buildings of the city, and beyond the wall—the biers falling into the darkness.

"Listen." I turned to him with all the seriousness of which I was capable, after each of us in his own way had prayed. "Although Bede the Venerable (or maybe somebody else) maintains, it's bad to mention the Lord while drinking, I don't believe it's an insult to Him. So I would like to raise this first goblet for the number one, for the Unique Oneness, for the only God the Father, the Almighty, creator of heaven and earth and all things visible and invisible, and in this way—for the first of the Lord's commandments. All this beauty"—I pointed my hand around—"and this quiet belongs to Him, and we also belong to Him and let us not ever forget about this with gratitude!"

The wine was princely, and the cheese and fruits sustained this feeling in us. Without delay I refilled the goblets so that in a suitable manner we could praise the number two, that is to drink for the two natures of the Lord our Jesus Christ, for the two worlds— the visible and invisible, for the two main commandments of love, for the two Mysteries of the dead, for the Second Coming, for Deuteronomy, for Cain and Abel, for bread and wine, for the two fish (unfortunately, we didn't have more on the table).

"I see that you're not a vacuous man," I said to Stanislav, breaking off a bit of fish, which he refused. "When did you end up here, foreigner? What brought you?" "Great loneliness, Father Antonio," he answered. "I don't have a home, or friends, or relatives. I just wander through the world and speak to God from various churches and cathedrals." I liked his answer and I continued: "Don't you, such a man of the world, have a wife?" "Once I had one, Father Antonio. And I really loved her." Following these words he pulled out a medallion from under his shirt and, opening it up, showed me a miniature oval portrait of an altogether young woman, a half child, but I wasn't able to see the rest, for it was already getting quite dark. "Is she beautiful?" the stranger asked. "Like an angel." I wasn't lying.

"Now I know, Father Antonio, what we are drinking to," Stanislav said after a minute of silence. "For number three, that is for the Holy Trinity!" "Absolutely," I agreed, "but not just for that. For the number three is a sacred and a perfect number. This is the first of the numbers that has a complete structure: a beginning, a middle and an end. This is a symbolic number and with much meaning. Also let us drink not just for the three Persons of God, about which you've already quite properly spoken, but also for the three kings from the East, who came to adore the tiny Jesus. In addition, for the three days and three nights, spent by Jonah in the belly of the whale, and then for the Third Day in general, for this is the day of Resurrection. We can also mention here Shem, Ham and Japheth or, we can say, Daniel, David, and Solomon." Drinking after these words, I shouted to old Angelico for him to bring out of the sacristy a lantern and a few musical instruments. At the same time I asked the foreigner: "In your land are all the girls as pretty?" "They're departing from my land," he answered. "Soon there won't be a single one left. Any kind. You know, Father Antonio, it's the same way with miniskirts. First only the good-looking girls with nice legs wear them. A bit later—ugly girls with nice legs. And still later—good-looking girls with ugly legs. After them—ugly girls with ugly legs. And then finally—all the other girls." I praised him for his sharp syllogism, although this, perhaps, wasn't a syllogism, and then, taking into my hands the mandolin brought by the old devil Angelico, as a gift to my guest I played the most beautiful little madrigal "Si, si, ch'io v'amo!" composed to the blessed memory of Claudio Monteverdi at the beginning of the seventeenth century. When, having listened to it, my young companion began to clap loudly with his palms, I made the observation that he should conduct himself a bit more quietly because we were at a cemetery, and he immediately assumed an air of gravity.

So an appropriate pause for a new filling of the goblets arose— above us the number four was being painted. "For the four Holy Gospels," Stanislav began. "But not just," I added. "For there are also four moral virtues—wisdom, righteousness, courage, and abstinence. Besides this, there are the four last things that we all must honor: death, judgment, heaven, and hell. Beyond this there are four sins that call for heavenly retribution, among which there are intentional killing, sodomy, wronging of the defenseless, and—I don't know why—delaying payment to someone for work.[4] However, so as not to end on this threatening note, let's drink for the four six-winged beings that everywhere accompany the holy Evangelists—the Angel, the Ox, the Eagle—and certainly—the Lion!"

A distinct shadow of anguish and sorrow ran across Stanislav's face after drinking up. Accustomed to observations even of the shadows of shadows, I understood that the reason was in the reminding him of the sins calling for heavenly retribution. I decided bit by bit to draw something out of him, but deliberately—it was important that he come forth himself.

While Angelico was carrying away the emptied bottles and bringing a new one—just not Valpolicella, but Soave—my guest Stanislav took up a smallish delicate bandoleon and played a bit of his melodies—however, soon he came to the right tone to perform (without any noticeable inaccuracies) "La Venenosa" and suddenly after it "La Lusignola" by the unforgettable Tarquinio Meruli. I praised him highly for his playing—somewhat too brusque for Italian music, but unique. "Do you also have love songs?" I became interested. "Our love songs are abandoning us together with our girls. They want to live in other countries" was the answer. "Did your wife leave for another country?" "Yes, but not for America" was the answer. "May she live well there," I sighed, renewing the contents of our goblets with young Soave. "Except for the Pentateuch, I don't know what else we should be drinking for," the perplexed Stanislav confessed. "What?" I prodded him. "How about the five living Mysteries? And the five loaves of bread? And the five openings of the human face created by God? And the five church fathers I love the most: Clement of Alexandria—one, Hippolytus of Rome—two, Ambrose of Milan—three, Xenon of Verona—four, and Augustine of Hippo—five, even though this fifth one was disapproving of music? . . ."

My enumeration stirred him, and we drained the goblets. Not long past the number five, I asked: "By the way, you began today by saying you're planning to violate the fifth commandment?" "I must, Father Antonio," he said with a mouth stuffed to the brim with ewe cheese. "And are you conscious of the fact that you inevitably will be punished for this—even if you manage to fool the earthly courts a hundred times? Are you aware that to attain forgiveness and salvation for such a heavy sin is incredibly difficult? That this is one of the shortest roads to the ruin of the soul, and consequently, to hell? That, depriving someone of their life, a person consciously repeats the crime of Cain? Might it be worth not doing it? Is there really so little strength in you that you're incapable of overcoming this serpent-murderer?" "But if I don't do this, then they'll kill me" was the answer.

I needed to reflect a bit and refilled the goblets for the sixth time. Around us the vast darkness had thickened. Only the lantern brought by Angelico illuminated our little wooden table and the nice objects on it—bottles, bread, cheese, fish, some onions, and grapes. A pale half-moon lowered over Venice. Somewhere from beneath the graves, from behind us, viscous gray smoke was curling. Again it promised night fog. It was getting cold, and we huddled in our coats more tightly. Then we honored the number six, drinking for the six higher truths of faith, for the six days of God's creation of the world, for Abel, Isaac, Joseph, Moses, the Paschal Lamb and the bronze serpent. "For six times one hundred and eleven." Stanislav winked at me from the darkness. I grabbed his scalp lock, bushy and silky to the touch, with my hand and tugged it to cause him pain. "I'll box your ears for that kind of joke," I warned him, and we both laughed wildly, then calmed down in unison.

"Over the past several years I've gotten used to cemeteries, Father Antonio," Stanislav again began to speak after several minutes of silence. "There was a time when I worked as a grave digger. I understand cemeteries better than anything. And here today I wandered about in the afternoon a good two hours. It seems to me that the dead listen to us. "Endowed with such sensitivity of soul, with musicality, with an inner inclination to good, do you really suppose you're capable of killing?" I walked up to him from the other side. "I don't know, Father. Perhaps you think too well of me. Thank you for this." And taking the mandolin from me, with intimate understanding, Stanislav strummed "Trying a String" on it, by the good-for-nothing Gianambrosio Dalza—a work not too capricious, but quite rare, when speaking of all kind of repertoire collections from the rare music shops, and then he performed a song in the language of his country, the content of which he later related to me. It was about a boy, who, out of great love poisoned his girl (an analogous case occurred in Bergamo two and a half years ago), for which he got seven years of hard labor. The boy's name was Hryts⁵—in honor of the Eastern saint Gregory the Theologian, I think. In the course of each of the seven years Hryts encountered a successive mystery. Initiated in the mysteries and changed, he returned home, having served his term of punishment. And here he found his beloved alive—it turns out that she had slept for seven years in a deep sleep, much like death. So they were happily reunited. The melody was quite sweet, and one could almost like the music of the words if not for the excess of hushing sounds.

"Here we've come, friend," I said after that, without forgetting our goblets, "to a special and truly symbolic number, that heralds perfection and completeness. In honoring it, what do we remember first and foremost?" "The seven heavens." Stanislav wasn't timid. "But also the seven circles of hell and seven circles of purgatory." I pointed my index finger up. "But also the seven holy Mysteries, the seven gifts of the Holy Spirit, the seven acts of mercy of the soul, and the seven acts of mercy for the body; the seven entreaties of the Lord's prayer and the seven universal epistles; the seven churches of Asia, and further, the seven stars and the seven golden lampions; the five loaves and two fishes and the seven filled baskets," I finished. "And also the seven sleeping Ephesian youths," my guest reminded me quite appropriately. And gladdened by his proficiency, I slapped him on the back, although I could barely see in the darkness. After this we drank up.

Then, set to play the guitar brought by Angelico, I decided to call to mind some things from my youth, when I wasn't older than my foreign friend. And one after another I played "Che penae questal cor," "Adiu, adiu," and "I'vo bene."⁶ In response to this Stanislav, having grabbed a lute from somewhere in the bushes, marvelously re-created "Dove," "Ahi! Filli,"⁷ four ricercare, one villanelle, and one saltarello. "You vile slime," I said greatly moved, "having such a heart for music, you still dare to speak—no, to think—about some kind of murder? May your hand of genius dry up and shrivel!" "Then chop it off." He stretched his right hand to me. "Angelico!" I bellowed to half the cemetery, for which I repent. "Bring an ax or a saw here. Something sharp!"

After a while having emerged right next to us, the old guy was greatly surprised by my request. However, from his shed he brought not only an ax, two saws, garden shears, and a rusted saber of the doge Dandolo, but also an enormous cutlass for fish. "What have you contrived, your eminence?" Angelico suspiciously asked. "I want to deprive the blockhead of his right hand. So it won't tempt him too much!" I explained to the old man. "But first listen to how he plays!" Then Stanislav delivered "Oh, come vaghi!" and "Oh, viva fiamma!"[8] over which even the partly deaf Angelico shed several tears. So that he wouldn't have to come twice, I poured out the rest of the Soave in the goblets and in this way we approached— now the three of us—the number eight. "For the eight Gospel sanctities!" I finally recollected, and then, straining, added: "The number eight, which contains within itself the power of the Resurrection, is the original image of the future world, says Origen. The number eight is the fulfillment of our hope, Saint Ambrose subscribes to it, so I zealously esteem him." "For the eight immortals," Stanislav decided to toss in, but I declined his idea, because I didn't know anything about any eight immortals.

When Angelico disappeared in the darkness with the empty bottles to fill them up—this time just not with Soave, but finally with something stronger—dark Venetian Tokay, when we again were left together, I asked of my invisible interlocutor: "If you want, I can hide you from your enemies so that no one will know where you disappeared?" "Not that." Stanislav shuddered. "My enemies are so powerful that they can destroy even you, Father Antonio!" Upon hearing such nonsense, I frankly began to laugh boisterously. "And I can sneeze at their all-powerfulness!" I exploded, after I stopped cackling. "The Lord teaches us to be courageous and unbreakable in defense of the truth and righteousness. If the saintly martyrs had not feared being broken on the rack and torn to pieces, if the prophet Daniel, relying on God, had not feared being in the same pit with hungry lions, then what can you scare me with? What should I fear?" "Not what, but whom," my guest said firmly. "Them. They're everywhere. Even here." This was said in such a way that I sensed goose bumps along my spine. Angelico arrived just in time with the refilled bottles. "So you still haven't been hacked up?" He took an interest, glancing at Stanislav. "You don't understand anything, old salt." I contritely wagged my head, and Angelico, muttering something, moved off into the fog.

"But can't you escape from this city to the devil knows where?" In anger I started cursing and, to correct my transgression, recalled the grandeur and power of the number nine. "Here's still one more of the Lord's numbers. Do you remember, dear Stanislav, how solemnly and with dignity we honored the number three today? So here, imagine that the number nine should be honored with the same, but triple the dignity! Because this is the triad of triads, and some even say that, painting three nines on the wall, we give up our home to the vigilant care of the Lord." "For three nines!" Stanislav accepted, saluting me with his goblet. "For the nine fruits of the Holy Spirit," I indicated. "For the nine angelic orders. For the suitability of the heavenly army in the earthly battle. I have in mind three undefeatable threes, about which we read the poet: "Angels fly like resurrected pilots, in threes." Thus for King Arthur, Charlemagne, and Godfrey of Bouillon—the three greatest knights of Christianity! For Joshua the son of Nun, for King David, and for Judas Maccabee—the most successful of the Judaic warriors! For Hector, for Alexander the Macedonian, and for Julius Caesar—the noblest leaders of the pagans!" The turning to the glorious names so strengthened my spirit that after this, as we drank up, I added: "No shit can dare to claim your life, dear Stanislav, otherwise he'll have to deal with me! And with me there's no joking!" I lifted up my big strong fist to his glasses so he could see it. "What do you say about this?" I asked victoriously. "I'd guess more than one nose has been flattened with that thing," Stanislav clearly answered. "Right!" I confirmed his accuracy and we both began to laugh.

Then, reminding himself why we're sitting here, Stanislav grabbed the guitar and without the strain that sometimes appears with foreigners, he boldly sang "Ogni amante è guerrier."[9] "Somehow it seems to me, my friend Stanislav, that you're in love. Is that so or not?" I decided to disclose. "I have an ill-fated love, Father

PERVERZION

119
▼

Antonio" was the answer. "That is?" I wasn't satisfied with his answer. "My love is a married woman. I coveted the wife of a friend. I'm ready to do everything in the world for her." Following these words he hiccuped. "And what else?" I gave him no peace. "She gave me her body once. But now it seems to me that her soul has remained unrelinquished." "Thus you didn't manage to deal with her body well enough," I concluded. "Tell me in more detail how it happened." I did everything for her that I could, and it was incredibly good for her. The table she was lying on was shaking." "Don't sink to these kind of details, boy," I noted. "I don't need to know your modus coiti with her. Better to tell me how she looks at you: with devotion, with courtesy, or with reservation?" "I'd say with courteous reservation, Father Antonio," he answered this. "Then I congratulate you! She loves you!" I assured him. And I put the question point blank: "Do you want to do away with her husband?" "What are you saying, Father?" He dispelled my suspicions. "They're getting a divorce even without this. Soon they're driving to Rome for an annulment." "Then all the more don't *cave in*! And always put your hope in God," I reminded him. "And in Saint Valentine, who helps in these affairs!" After which I recalled that the time had come to honor the number ten, the goblets were also filled to the brim. "For the ten commandments," I began, but for a long time couldn't think of any other example of ten. Finally I came up with yet one more. "For the ten Egyptian punishments!" And also after a minute added: "And for the ten bridges of Palestine."

When the number ten was honored in a suitable way, and the goblets dry, I picked up the lute again and strummed "Duolsi la vita," and then—without any kind of transition—"Ecco la primavera,"[10] however the lute, the devil knows why, stopped being docile with me, perhaps because it was getting colder each time and my fingers were turning numb, and I was confusing the words as well. "And tell me, boy, I forgot your name," I addressed the foreigner after a minute, "don't you need some kind of weapon for self-defense? I can give you, for example, this saber. Or a pistol. I have a good pistol! We can shoot a bit from it at that tree over there. Take it, I'll buy myself a new one." However Stanislav very politely thanked me and flatly refused the weapons. "Then what else can I do for you?" I insisted. "Forgive my sins, Father," he said. "Well then I forgive you!" I waved my hand, and he gratefully kissed each phalange of my finger. His lips were warm and soft from the wine. I hugged him, and we drank up again, although with eleven, things got more complicated, and I endeavored to make a toast for the eleventh part of the Symbol of Faith (although it was truly the key one, for it states "I await the resurrection of the dead")." "I await the resurrection of the dead," Stanislav repeated and began to quiver from the cold. I guessed that after these words they'd truly arise one after another, but at the cemetery everything remained as it was, although an owl began to screech and the fog became more dense. Venice was no longer visible and it seemed that only the two of us were left, the last ones, for the final pronouncement. Stanislav, surely, also sensed something similar, for suddenly he struck up Tromboncino's famous "Ave Maria" with his not especially strong but wondrously sweet to the ear scratchy baritone voice. I couldn't help but follow him with my barely cracked tenor voice, for which in the seminary they called me not "Delcampo" but "Belcanto?" Thus our voices were the only thing that linked us here, in this unpopulated and voracious world. But to glorify the Most Holy Madonna with song is never a sin. And so we felt ourselves to be amid the waters of the Oceans in a tiny boat, which she protects and about the salvation of which she eternally implores her Son.

I felt Stanislav's face and kissed him right on a teardrop, unable to quell a surge in my chest and throat. "It's not a sinner I've kissed, but a good musician," I said in Italian, though he understood all the same. We splashed out the rest of the wine to the goblets. Midnight was approaching and we needed to get to the number twelve. "For the twelve holy apostles." Stanislav understood me. "And for the twelve sons of Jacob, then the twelve tribes of Israel," I continued. "For the twelve gates and twelve pearls, and twelve foundations, and twelve names that are written on the foundations. For the six holy women and the six holy men that in sum also come out to twelve. For the lambs of Saint Agnes. For the tower of Saint Irene. For the heart of Saint Theresa. For the hair of Saint Mary Magdalene. For the nakedness of Saint Mary of Egypt. For the shoulders of Saint Catherine, for her stomach, for her entire body. For the arrows of Saint Egidius. For the dances of Saint Vitus. For the lashes of Saint Peter. For the flowers of Saint Francis. For the temptations of Saint Anthony, my patron and intercessor. For the dogs of Saint George!"

We drank up the last drops and, stumbling, supporting one another, moved along the shore of the island back to the church. Beyond the fog its white-stoned facade had disappeared, divided by pilasters into three parts, with a statue of the Madonna and Child above the entrance. Stanislav carried the lantern in his hand and repeated over and over: "You can't see anything through the fog!" We wandered along blindly, and right before the church we stumbled on old Angelico, who was standing stock still on the path like a pillar of salt. "Are you my guard?" I reproached him, shaking the guitar in the air. "What are you standing there, like a pillar of the church year?" But the old guy tried to convince me to sleep in his shed. The fog had hung like such an impenetrable porridge, that no boat could be found to get us to Venice.

Everything that happened (if it happened) afterward was shrouded for me as a mystery, for I remember almost nothing—the long day's weariness and poor visibility worried me to death. I know that the old devil put me to bed for the night at his place. To where Stanislav left that night, I don't know. I hope that all the same he came across some chance boatman, and made his way with him to his hotel which, as he said, was somewhere on the Grand Canal, not far from the Ponte Accademia.

I remember only as I shouted into the fog, following his light steps: "Remember your soul!" And as his answer flew back to me: "How could a horse's ass like me forget!" I covered the spot in space where this horse's ass was, with a sign of the Holy Cross.

■ □ ■ □ ■

11

MY GUEST, OH, ALL OF AMERICA KNOWS MY GUEST! HER INCLINATION
for quasi-masculine hairstyles and clothing. She has nineteen cars, each
one of them is a champion of the highway. Her television channel, her
network of restaurants and nonstop markets. Her books, each of which
functions as a demolition explosion, and always scandals, lawsuits, sui-
cides and premature retirements. Her sextuple-meaninged accounts
and leftist convictions. Among the closest of her friends—anarchists,
senators, football stars. She acknowledges only absinthe and Lucky
Strike without filters. About her they say "irate Liza." About her they
say "intolerable Liza." About her with love they say "our irate intolerable Liza Sheila." Enough introductions. My guest—Liza Sheila
Shalizer! We are doing our broadcast *live*[1] from the International
Center of Culture and Civilization on San Giorgio Maggiore. Today it's
already the third day of the superseminar for intellectuals and notables,
dedicated to the problems of Venice. Mrs. Shalizer, my first question is:
what is your opinion on this extraordinary assemblage?

"*Oh, fucking shit!*" [*Bursting laughter.*] My opinion! My opinion
doesn't want to be expressed! It's a really harsh opinion and unpleasant. Ask me something more pleasant, *baby!*"

"How do you like Venice, Mrs. Shalizer?"

"Just call me 'Liza!' I can't stand these *shitty* bourgeois hierarchies!
[*Devastating laughter.*] Venice? It *stinks!* Everywhere it's filled with
junk, stray dogs, a lot of poor people. Venice is a great big *asshole*.
It's a crime against humanity!"

"All the same. What's your strongest impression, Liza?"

"Strongest impression? [*Laughter that turns into baying.*] Better
this way: what surprises me the most? And do you know what it is?

I ask you, I, blunt Sheila, I ask you here in this city: how can you *screw* your entire life in these eternally damp beds? Why don't the women here liberate themselves? Why do they sit in this dankness like inside a *cunt*? . . ."

"Here there's really something to think about, Liza. . . ."

"Here there's nothing to think about, *dolly!* Everything's clear and how! This city is dying. On the top floors of the palaces all the windows are already boarded up. Forever! No one will go there!"

"As I'm aware, this problem indicates the purpose of today's seminar. Soon, in an hour or two, your lecture will resound here in these walls. What are you going to talk about?"

"Oh, they'll remember it! It will be about the end. About the end of phallocentrism, my *pussy.* We've succeeded in living at a unique crossroads of epochs. Woman is becoming self-sufficient. The phallus is ceasing to rule the world."

"Does this end mean some kind of beginning? The beginning of vaginocentrism, for example?"

"This means that the *dick* is declining in shame and retreating to insignificance. After all, from time to time we can simply buy or rent one—nothing more. We have emerged from under its dependence! . . . We now have the true possibility of choice. We just go to a sex shop and bring that thing home, nicely packaged and, in fact, much more realistic than a worthless living *cock!* . . . I salute you with this, as a free woman salutes a free woman. I salute all our female listeners. . . ."

"Thank you, Liza. I don't think you're acquainting many of us with very pleasant news."

"Be sure of this! Haven't you really been disgusted at eternally being raped? And by whom? By these big-gutted *dorks,* who really don't even need to ejaculate, just a good helping of macaroni and beer!" [*Satirical laughter.*]

"But, Sheila, they're spreading rumors about you that you're in a certain, as you put it, dependence. Let's say a certain illustrated weekly published a quite candid report about the inner goings-on at one of your mansions in San Felipe, California. There they describe the frenzied *wild parties,* that you have the habit of holding in the company of your chauffeurs, stable boys, masseurs, guards, and lawnmower men."

"That's not true! That's *bullshit*. I'm free. I'm free to make use of them the way I want. I'm just interested in the size of their *foreskins*. Any minute I can suspend, fire, trade in any one of them. Even for a robot. Or for a rhinoceros!" [*Sardonic laughter.*]

"But in conjunction with this can you say that you hate men?"

"Hate? Some of my best friends are men. There are exceptions among them, worthy of respect. Some are even present here, at this *fucking* seminar. For example, that fantastic gypsy Mavropule. Too bad he hasn't arrived yet. Oh, he's a phenomenal *cuntchaser*! Or my colored brother and friend John Paul. He's also going to give a speech about liberation. Freedom and equality—these are the two things over which we get bent out of shape and for the sake of which we tolerate this *slimy* city."

"But again they're spreading gossip that John Paul is something more than a brother and friend to you. . . ."

"I know, I know, *catty*! I know what's going on here! That's because it's accepted to think that all black boys without exception have an apparatus that extends all the way to their knees! I have to admit that you're close to the truth on this!" [*Nymphlike joyful laughter.*]

"If we've already begun to speak about the most intimate things, then say something, please, apropos of yet one more category of rumors that since this morning have been circulating in seminar-associated spheres. It's about your tangled relations with that young Russian Perfetsky."

"I like the incline of his large head. His left brow. It's a bit raised above his eye and sumptuous. He's pliant enough, that is, he holds his body not too badly. Turn your attention: there he is standing against the opposite wall, like a *movie star*. This pose really grabs your attention. He looks like an archangel! He holds a goblet with some kind of *crap* in it with his thin and sensitive fingers. You can love him most for his fingers! Besides that, his country interests me. It's the country of my parents. They fled from it a really long time ago. The regime there persecuted them just because their last name was Zuckerkandel. . . ."

"That's terrible! All those regimes! . . . But let's return to Perfetsky. This morning here much has been made of the fact that last night he was seen in your hotel. . . ."

"Not true! Last night he was dead drunk! I don't want to chat anymore on this topic. In addition, today, I see that monkey, the daughter of the circus swindler is accompanying him. Turn your attention to how she is glued to his shoulder like a jellyfish. . . ."

"As much as I understand—I'm saying this for our listeners—you're talking about the coordinator of the seminar Mrs. Ada Zitrone."

"Yes, about that *whore*. . . . He's constantly prattling about her. He only thinks about her."

"Maybe it's linked to some kind of mysterious circumstances?"

"There's nothing mysterious! It's linked only to her *cunt*. Also to her *ass*. He's completely lost his head, that cretin."

"Our listeners would be very much interested also in finding out about. . . ."

"He sat in an armchair, for three hours he sat in an armchair, and his head constantly hung down. I ordered some really strong coffee for him, but he only spilled it. It seems he didn't even see me. That I was sitting right in front of him. That he came to me. There, where I'm residing. . . ."

"Thank you for the interview, Sheila, allow me. . . ."

"He barely turned his tongue, his completely deprived of senses softened from the wine *goddamned* tongue, but everything that he said without exception was about her, about that *slut*. He said her name a thousand times! I said to myself: 'Okay, Sheila, be patient.' I brought him another pillow and a robe. . . ."

"Dear Liza, I guess that our time on the air. . . ."

"He didn't hear anything, but just described her body. He said that her *ass*—is a tunnel with blinding light at the end! Who did he say this to? Me! That her *cunt*—is the American dream! That her *boobs* are like young melons. I was ready to fall on my knees before him—if only he would stop grinding with his wooden tongue, his thin sensitive tongue. . . . I even wanted to disguise myself as her, so that he would think that I'm her, but I didn't have those *shitty* cherry colors. . . ."

"Thus at the end of our conversation. . . ."

"I wanted to lift him from the armchair and put him in bed. I believed I could lift him and carry him a bit in my arms. But he became so heavy! Then I dragged him right onto the floor, I slapped him on his cheeks and took off his eyeglasses, I felt some kind of medallion under his shirt, I wanted to tear that medallion away so that he could finally come to his senses. . . ."

"And with this, dear listeners, we thank our famous guest for. . . ."

"This changed him! He himself jumped up onto his erect legs and grabbed his glasses from me and with his hands tore away that that that housecoat and ran out first into the loggia then to the bathroom then to yet another room where John Paul was sleeping and where it smelled of grass he guessed that he'd find the exit but the exit was just to jump through the window and he had already been standing on the ledge when I pulled him by the bottom of his coat by his pants by everything he had then he suddenly began laughing boisterously and fell back into the room he fell backward because I pulled and this was enough for me to end up on him I sat down on him I pressed his sides with my knees and he couldn't move anywhere John Paul said something in sleep and I became master of him him him and had already crawled into his clothing I'd take off that clothing from him I'd take that skin off him but saw then he was sleeping that he had fallen asleep just fallen asleep that he was like a dead man that I had no chance and I just spat and so I left him there on the floor and went to phone that little Giulio from the first floor. . . ."

"I remind you, this was Liza Sheila Shalizer, our guest from America. We laud her with International Women's Day and wish her the greatest possible success today at the seminar. Just now secretary Amerigo Dappertutto announced the beginning of the third day. From other news of the seminar: the quest for the horse continues, on which one of the participants, Alborak Djabraili, came to our city. According to an investigator's version, another participant, Tsutsu Mavropule, had taken possession of the horse, inasmuch as he, first of all, is a gypsy, and second, still was absent from the seminar till now. There also exists a parallel version about the complete nonimplication of Mr. Mavropule in this, already sufficiently tumultuous, "bicycle" affair. And in the evening one of the central activities of the program awaits the guests and participants: a visit to the Teatro La Fenice,[2] where the premiere of the opera *Whorfeus in Venice* is taking place. As for what concerns us, I end my report with this and return you to the studio. Keep tuned to our wavelength! Ciao!

■ □ ■ ■

1 2

JOHN PAUL OSHCHYRKO WITH HAIR IN A THOUSAND THINLY WOVEN dreads. John Paul with headphones on his ears. John Paul with a cotton duck sack over his shoulder. John Paul in oversized baggy clothes. John Paul Beyondomeasuro wagged his handsome black head to the rhythm of his inner music. And everyone heard words from him that only John Paul could express.*

To listen to reggae, to die beneath the sky, to breathe in the scent of the grass, mon. To listen to the sky, to die to reggae, to breath in the leaves of the grass, mon. To breath in reggae, to listen in the sky, to die to the scent of the grass, mon. To listen to the grass, to breathe in reggae, to die beneath the sky of scents, mon. To die with the sky, to listen and breathe in: reggae, grass, the scent, mon. To listen and breath in, to die and listen: the scent of reggae, the sky of the grass.

To fall into reggae, to die beneath the sky, to breathe in the scent of the grass, mon. To fall into hell, to sleep without you, to breathe in the scent of the grass, mon. To fall with hell, to sleep with you, to feel the scent of the grass. To fall into you, to sleep above hell, to feel the saliva of the grass, mon. To fall into saliva, to dream of you, to feel the hell of the living, mon.

To fall into the sea, to dream of you, to feel the hell of the living, mon. To fall into the sea, to dream of the green, to feel the hell of the living, mon. To fall into the sea, to dream of the green, to feel the wounds of the living, mon. To fall into the sea, to dream of the green, to feel the wounds of the fish, mon. To dream of the sea, to fall into the green, to feel the wounds of the fish, mon. To dream of the sea,

*Readers not inclined to linguo-cabalistic expressions can painlessly omit this section.

to lick the green, to feel the wounds of the fish, mon. To feel the sea, to lick the green, to believe in the wounds of the fish, mon.

To come in wounds, to lick the sea, to believe in the green of the fish, mon.

To fall in love with the wounds, to love the sea, to sow the green for the fish, mon.

To love the peak of the wound, to love the vale of the sea, to begin to sow all the fish with the green, mon.

To love the peak of a woman, the peak of the sea, the peak of the green of the fish, mon.

To make love with the vale, the vale of a woman, with the vale of the sea, with the vale of the peak of the green of the fish.

To sow yourself in the vale of the green of a woman, in the vale of the green of the sea, in the darkness of the vale of the peak of the green of the fish. To be strewn as grass in the vale of the green of a woman, in the dry vale of the green of the sea, in the glow of the darkness of the vale of the peak of the green of the fish. To be strewn as grass and tenderness in the green of the vale of a woman, in the dry black vale of the green of the sea, in the sun and the glow of the darkness of the vale of the peak of the green of the fish, mon.

To be strewn as grass and tenderness and silence in the vale of the green of a woman, in the dry and the black and the tight vale of the green of the sea, in the sun and the moon and the glow of the darkness of the peak of the green of the fish. To be strewn as grass and as tenderness and as silence and with force in the vale of a woman, in the dry and black and tight and bloody vale of the green of the sea, in the sun and the moon and the stars and the milk in the glow of the darkness of the vale of the peak of the green of the fish. To be strewn as grass and tenderness and silence and with force and with fear in the vale of the green of a woman, in the dry and black and tight and bloody vale of the green of the sea, in the sun and the moon and the stars and the milk of the glow of the darkness of the vale of the peak of the green of the fish. To be strewn as grass and tenderness and silence and with force and with fear and flesh in the vale of the green of a woman, in the dry and black and tight and bloody and joyful and painful vale of the green of the sea, in the sun and moon and stars and milk and sperm of the glow of the darkness of the vale of the peak of the green of the fish. To be strewn as grass and tenderness and silence

and with force and with fear and flesh and the eternal spirit in the vale
of the green of a woman, in the dry and black and tight and bloody
and joyful and painful and like skeletons frail vale of the green of the
sea, in the sun and moon and stars and milk and the sperm like nectar for the golden pee of the glow of the darkness of the vale of the peak
of the green of a fish. To be strewn into dust by grass and tenderness
and silence and with force and with fear and flesh and the eternal spirit and the tip of the tongue in the vale of the green of a woman, in the
dry as a chalice and black as a hole and bloody as vestments and joyful as a stone and painful as an anus like skeletons of the forest for the
frail and like the place of birth of the beast for the damp vale of the
green of the sea, in the sun and the moon and the stars and milk and
the sperm and like nectar for golden pee and like the sky of the vigil of
God for an empty river of the glow of darkness of the vale of the peak
of the green of the fish.
To break into bits:
as a coffin as a mask as a bird and thunder and honey and a prick
and a mint womb and dread fish in the green cave
of the world.
in the empty as a skull and warm as lips and cold as gates and
unquenched as a voice and as headstrong as a martyr and the dull
as a shell of a flood and the mysterious as the summer inside a
beast the green memory of the sea,
in anger and kindness and hopes and trees and saliva and the blue
as a hosanna vein and as a crown of the abiding of the Father the
sealed language of the flux to the wasteland of water fire
of the green female wound.
To break into bits:
as a coffin no lid and as the mask of the church and the bird of
a tower, with the scent of thunder and stolen honey and as a prick
used in vain and the minty womb of queens and the mortal dread
of a drunken fish
in the cave of the world green as stalks of the meadow,
in the empty as a faded skull and warm as lips between legs and
cold for a killer as gates and unquenched from the light as a voice
and headstrong with your tenderness like a martyr and dull as the
first and last shell of the flood and the mysterious as the summer of
blood inside a beast

YURI ANDRUKHOVYCH

130
▾

in the memory of the sea green as an angel, an angel of the moss,

in anger without limits and kindness without beginning and wicked hopes and timely trees and the saliva of all orgasms and the blue as a hosanna dawn the vein of twilight and as a crown of the restless abiding of the Father forever sealed lucid language of the nocturnal tide of the dreary wasteland of the boundlessness of water of the measurelessness of fire

of the green female wound.

To break into bits:

as a coffin no lid (but not a bed no body), not the flower of loins (but the mask of the church), as a bird of the tower (but not as a tower of tin)[1] and with the scent of thunder (but not the flash of caraway) and as stolen honey (but not a found garden) and not a square mirror (but as a prick used in vain) and the mint womb of queens (but not with the singing throats of slaves) and with a mortal dread of a drunken fish (but not the flowery sigh of flowing clay)

in the green as stalks (but not as thighs of hops) cave of the world, in the empty as a faded skull and warm as lips between legs (but not as a blossoming graveyard and warm as a fruit between your lips) and the cold for a killer as gates (but not for a prophet as a word) and unquenched not from despair as the plague (but from light like a voice) and headstrong with his tenderness as a death rower (but not with his presence as a speaker) and not meager as the first and last droplet of semen (but dull as the first and last shell of the flood) and mysterious as the summer of blood (but not a sieve of glory) inside of the beast (but not a tiger)

to the green as the angel of moss (but not as a shore of rain) memory of the sea, in anger without bounds (but not without regret) and kindness without beginning (but not without sense) and not in pure oils (but in wicked hopes) and timely trees (but not weak roots) and not in the crap of all peoples (but in the saliva of all orgasms) and blue as a hosanna of the dawn (but not like a chapel of night) the vein of twilight (but not the mystery of coition) and in sealed forever not as a storehouse of the boundless infidelity of the Bull (but like a crown of the restless abiding of the Father) the lucid language (but not the dark roaring laughter) of the night tide of the dreary wasteland (but not the slow burning of ships) the boundlessnesses of water and fire (but scads of sand of countless stars)

of the green female wound.
To break into bits:
and as a coffin no lid and a bed no body but also a corpse no nuts
and the flower of loins and the mask of a church but also the
message of a sign
and a bird of a tower and the tower of tin but also the fly of a
rose
and the scent of thunder and the flash of caraway but also the
dust
of the ground
and stolen honey and a garden found but a
backside sold
and a mirror square and a prick used in vain but
a clot flying
and the singing throat of slaves and the mint womb of queens
but also the sleepy motion of butts
and the mortal dread of the drunken fish and the blooming sigh
of flowing clay but also the guilty taste of a blue plum
in the green as stalks meadow and like thighs of hops but also
like
the ceilings of the stalks of the cave of the world,
in the empty as a faded skull and like a blooming cemetery
but also as a pregnant stump
and warm as lips between legs and dark as a fruit in between
lips but also silent as hands between breasts
and cold for a killer as a gate and for a prophet as
a word but also for a pilgrim like a city
and unquenched from despair like a wound and from light like
a voice but also from rage
and headstrong with your tenderness like a death rower and with
your
presence as a speaker but also with your patience like
a pagan
and the meager as the first and last droplet of semen and dull
as the first and last shell of the flood and hoarse as
the first and last blare of a vision
and mysterious as the summer of blood and like the sieve of
glory but also like

the rye of the field inside a beast and inside a tiger but also
inside a whirlwind
green as an angel of moss and like a shore of rain but also like
nests
of trees
the memory of the sea,
in anger without bound and without regret but also without anger
in kindness without beginning and without sense but also without kindness
and in pure oils and in wicked hopes but also in beaten
crucibles
and timely trees and weak roots but also in prayers
gone out
and in the crap of all peoples and in the saliva of all orgasms but
also in
the dew of all impregnations
and the blue as a hosanna of the dawn and like a chapel of the
night
but also like a chapel of a hosanna
the vein of twilight and the mystery of coition but also the froth
of gluing together
and the sealed forever as a storehouse of the boundless infidelity
of the Bull (but like a crown of the restless abiding of the Father)
but like a column of a bottomless
flowing across of Blessedness
the lucid language and the dark roaring laughter but also a sorrowful whisper
of the night tide of the dreary wasteland and slow
burning of ships but also the tall building of bridges in
the morning approaching to the littoral
the boundlessness of water of the measurelessness of fire and
scads of sand
of countless stars but also the visible-invisible scattering of
pearls
of the green female wound.
To break into bits:
and as a lid without a coffin and as a body without a bed and as
nuts without

a corpse
and with the loins of a flower and the church of a mask or also
a sign of a message
and the tower of a bird and the tin of a tower but also the rose
of a fly
and as the dust of thunder and the scent of caraway but also the
flash
of thorns
and as sold honey and a stolen garden but also
a backside found
and as a mirror fleeting and a prick square but also
as a clot used in vain
and a sleepy throat of queens and the mint movement of slaves
and
the singing womb of butts
and a guilty dread of the dark blue fish and the blooming taste
of a flowing plum but also the mortal sigh of drunken clay
in the green as thighs meadow and like walls of hops but also as
the stalks of the stalks of the cave of the world,
in the empty as a pregnant skull and like a pale cemetery
but also like a blooming stump
and the warm as lips in between lips and the dark as a fruit in
between breasts but also the quiet as hands between legs
and the cold for a killer like the city and for a prophet like
a gate but also for a pilgrim like a word
and the unquenched from despair like a body and from light like
a wound or also from rage like a voice
and headstrong with your presence like a pagan and
with your patience like a death rower but also with your
tenderness like a speaker
and the meager like the first and last shell of the flood, and in the
hoarse
as the first and last droplet of semen or also the dull as
the first and last blare of a vision
and the mysterious as the summer of the field and like the rye of
glory but also like
the sieve of blood inside a beast and inside a tiger and inside of
a whirlwind

YURI ANDRUKHOVYCH

134
▼

green as nests of moss and like an angel of rain but also like a
shore
of trees of the memory of the sea,
in anger without anger but also without bound without regret
in the kindness without kindness but without beginning without
sense
and in wicked oils and in beaten hopes but also in pure
crucibles
and in the trees put out and in the timely roots but also in weak
prayers
and in the crap of all impregnations and in the saliva of all peoples but
also in the dew of all orgasms
and the blue as a hosanna chapel and like a chapel of the dawn
but also like the chapel of a chapel
the vein of twilight and the mystery of being glued together but
also the froth of copulation
and the sealed forever like a storehouse of the restless
abiding of Blessedness and like the crown of the boundless
flowing across of the Bull but also like a column of the bottomless
infidelity of the Father
the dark language and heavy roaring laughter but also the clear
whisper
of the tall tide of bridges and the night building
of a morning wasteland but also a slow burning of littorals in
the dreary approaching to ships
of scads of fire of water of sand of stars of pearls but also
the visible-invisible scattering of countless boundless
measurelessness
of the green female wound.
To break into bits:
and with a lid and body but also with nuts
and loins and a church but also with a letter
and a tower and tin but also with a fly
and thunder and a garden and caraway and honey and thorns
and a backside and
a mirror and a prick and a clot and a throat and a womb and

a movement and a guilty sigh and a blooming dread and
mortal taste
in the green as thighs like ceilings like stalks of the cave of the
world,
in the empty and warm and dark and quiet and cold and
unquenched and headstrong and meager and hoarse and dull
and
mysterious
green memory of the sea,
without anger without kindness without end without sense
in hopes oils crap dew saliva
like a storehouse column crown
in the flowing toward an infidelity abiding of
Blessedness the Father the Bull
in language roaring laughter a whisper
in the tide building and approaching
and also in the burning of boundlessness measurelessness count-
lessness of darkness
without end
of the green female wound.

To break into bits as dread in the green cave of the world, in the
empty green memory of the sea, in the anger of fire of the green
female wound.

To listen to the dread in the green cave of the world, to die in the
empty green memory of the sea, to breathe in the scent of the green
female wound. To listen to the dread in the green cave of hell, to
die in memory of the sea beneath the sky, to breathe in the scent of
the female wound of grass. To listen to the dread in the fish cave of
reggae, to die in the sea of grass beneath the sky, to breathe in the
female scent of the sea. To listen to the dread of the cave of reggae,
to die as the grass of death beneath the sky, to breathe in the female
scent of fish. To listen to the dread of reggae, to die as the sky above
the grass, to breathe in the female scent of death. To listen to the
dread of grass, to die beneath the sky together with the sky, to
breathe in the scent of death. To listen to reggae, to die beneath the
sky, to breathe in the scent of grass.

■ □ ■ □ ■

1 3

WHEN THE PODIUM WAS PASSED TO LIZA SHEILA UNBRIDLED, THE
audience present in the library was still coming to its senses after the
psychedelic attack of John Paul, waving their fans (the ladies) and
smoking (the gentlemen, too) with cigarette lighters in quivering
hands. Many points of her lecture should have interested and even
fascinated Stanislav Perfetsky, but he, from the wee hours of the
morning, gray, as though he were a clot of the nocturnal Venetian
fog, reviving more and more with the skin on his face and with gri-
maces (not without the influence on these processes of Ada sitting
opposite him in black and cherry red) and adamantly cursing the
previous night spent by him on the floor of someone else's room of
someone else's hotel, he had been incredibly careless. The record in
two columns below allows us to assess the level of his carelessness for
comparison's sake. The record, from all the variety of activities that
in reality have a synchronic development, focuses just on a bit of
them.

Ending up on the podium,
Liza Sheila decisively looked
over the auditorium and, not
even using the appropriate for
such occasions *dear friends,* she
immediately took the principal
of the bulls by the . . . no, not
by the horns: "I have been
asked here, to Venice, to let my
thoughts be heard on subjects,

Ending up across from Ada,
Perfetsky was divided in two
and tattered. On the one hand,
he was happy with the innocent opportunity to be next to
her, to look at her first with a
furtive glance, then openly, to
breathe in her scent, it is a mixture of scents, the basis for
which could be the scent of

so widely and often discussed in new societies from Marx and Freud to Marcuse and Fellini, and still as unclear in some things even to this day and—I use a word intolerable for me—mysteries: about sex and about the male organ, as well as about the liberation of female structures from under it, as we will see, not a motivated oppression. I am aware of the fact that many of you categorically may dislike what I will be saying further. I am prepared for your protests and at the same time remind you of the sacred right of each to express their own opinion, and even more, one that borders on the truth. And if you on the periphery still accept this not quite categorically, then for us Americans, there already have been no questions here for two hundred years.

First and foremost we must answer the following question of our contemporaneity: is the presence in today's world of this—not tolerated by me and those who think like me—male organ truly unavoidable, decisive and necessary for creation, continuation and renewal? Or, perhaps, are rumors about its irreplaceability somewhat exaggerated? Or do we have the

grass. On the other hand, he wasn't sure whether he was insulting her this way: crumpled and swollen after the adventures of last night.

And in such turbulent moments he received a note from Ada, where he read:

"Stanislav! Sorry, but I couldn't devote yesterday to you. You know that sometimes I collapse into a certain overwhelming drowsiness. I fall asleep and sleep, and sleep, and sleep—and no one can wake me."

"Why didn't you say so earlier?" Perfetsky wrote back. "I would have gone to wake you."

"Today it all passed," she had written on a new scrap of paper. "Again I'm at your service, my genial prick! "Where

bases already today to state the accomplishment of a certain stage of human existence, which one can designate by the much promising word "prehistory?" If I can belletrize the topic of my short lecture, then it would sound like "The Rise and Fall of Mr. Ph," where under Mr. Ph one should understand a subject well known to the majority of you, which by its externality in its best moments recalls a cane, a rod, a pillar, a ray, a vector, a direction, a spear, an unopened morning tulip, a rocket carrier, but first, a staff, that is, a cudgel, and in its worst moments something entirely pitiable, as, for example, a thrashed bird. Its complete name is Phallus, and in the pantheons of nearly all civilizations of the past it belongs to the most revered idols. I underscore: of the past. I want to bring to your attention the fact that it has no future. Daring to speak about this even here, in this enchanted and dying city, where monuments are erected to it in the form of the bell tower of St. Mark's and countless columns, in the city where its cult is present invisibly, in genes and in passing glances, in the city, which in its time gave birth to one of the

have you been roaming last night, Orpheus?"

"I was wandering through Venice till morning and thinking about you," was his answer.

"I'll pretend that I believe you," Ada wrote back. "What was it you were thinking about me?"

"I thought about how to wake you."

"And how would you?"

Perfetsky drew an unopened morning tulip.
"Oho?!"

"Yes! And then I thought about the agile and close devotion of your body."
"Oho-ho?!"

"Because I love you. With all of me. All that I am. All that I'm made of."
"And first of all . . ."
"And with that too, of course."
"Who are you talking about here?"

staunchest priests and great martyrs of his, Mr. Ph's, cruel cult—I have here in mind, of course, the well-known sex terrorist Casallegra, eh-eh, pardon me, Casanova, with the boisterous life of whom countless trifles, legends and gossip not tolerated by me are tied.

I dare to speak on this teasing topic for the simple reason that my name today is widely defamed thanks to my many years of research of the phenomenon of Mr. Ph as well as my multifaceted familiarity with each of his emanations. It is enough just to bring up the fact that, as the majority of you must be aware, in my Miami home you can find, perhaps, the largest collection in the world of male members, those actual embodiments of Mr. Ph, each of which I had to buy for fantastic sums in the anatomical theaters of various continents. For example, acquired a month ago at Sotheby's auction, for the organ of African king Joshua (Mbobo) the Twelfth I had to part with . . . three hundred thousand dollars! However, if we're speaking about the truth, about recognition, about the keys to the future, then no price is too great or able to stop me!

"About us."

Ada, having read this, thought something over for a while. Then she wrote for a long time. Then she crossed out almost everything that had been written. And then she crossed out even what had remained uncrossed out. She crumpled the paper and made a ball from it. She put away the ball in her handbag. On another piece of paper she wrote something completely different. Namely:

"He-he."

Having read the contents of the last note, Stas also took a long time to write back. He stopped often, hastily glanced over following every completed sentence. Finally he folded the sheet of paper and made a ball out of it, which he shot in Ada's direction.

[Applause, somewhat ironic.]

You have to agree that from one hundred and eleven samples of my collection I can choose, compare, make unbiased conclusions. All the categories of ages and social circles are covered by me—in my collection you will see marvelous examples of presidents and generals, poets, philosophers, actors, bishops, bankers, monarchs, vagabonds, bandits, and, of course, rapists, although all of them essentially are rapists. In addition—regardless of race, religious conviction, citizenship, or their size. I approach their study from the position of strict scientific fact and with the intent to completely exclude any kind of arbitrariness or postmodernist lack of obligation in treatment. My conclusions, I must say, are far from consoling for the arrogant self-satisfied hero of this research: he degrades, and the earthly era of his hegemony is approaching the end! *[Applause, whistling.]*

Finally, what should one expect from a career, at the basis of which force is always exhibited everywhere? This cane, this cudgel, this whip was summoned by the darkest powers of evolution to affirm its superiority

Ada once again made a sheet from the ball sent to her and read on its crumpled upper portion: "I want to be with you. I so want to be with you. And I will be with you! For I will be with you. For you will be with me. For we will be together. Alone with ourselves. For you want to be with me. For not being with you—for me is not being. But it is better not to be than to not be with you. With you. For you. Above you. Beneath you. In you."

Ada joined the applause and then wrote the following back to Perfetsky:

"Be careful, little brother. For I might believe you."

only through attack, breaching, and invasion. The taking of someone else's city by the army of an aggressor immutably accompanied Mr. Ph with a wild orgy. For him there never existed any other methods besides force. Already in ancient Egypt we find preserved for us in papyrus form attestations to the conveyance of female blood to the most horrifying of the gods—Sobek, this Crocodile's seed. Mr. Ph in all this acts as the closest companion and even as an instrument, in as much as they sacrifice not just blood, but first blood. It will not be superfluous also to mention the special subdetachments of Phoenician warriors, who made use of their bronze members for breaching the gates of enemy fortresses; about the Sumerian reproducers of holy writings, who, through the use of their above-mentioned offshoots, wrote on clay tablets (that is why the letters have a cuneiform character); about the ancient Greek athletes, who used the ballistic possibilities of their implements to fling cannon balls to a far-off distance. The cult of Mr. Ph in fullest measure appeared in the form of the erecting of sacred edifices, convoked to depict the vertical idea

"Believe me."
"*Nevermore.*"

"Believe me. Believe the poems. Believe the breeze of poems. Believe the battalion of poems. Believe the vortex of verses—tear off a tear. Believe the realm of poetry at least."
"But you're a beast!"

"And you're my anguish. And my onus. My possi-impossibility. My constant erectility. My consternation. Illumination. Imagination. Destination. Give me some leg for consolation."

Having read the newest epistle, Ada cheerfully flashed her green eyes and sliding forward far off the chair, answered:
"Which one for you—the right one or the left?"

of being: temples, obelisks, chapels. The bell tower of a Christian church or a Muslim minaret—equally unsanctioned by me—with that very immutability remind one of the true subject of reverence in these confessions. Not to speak here about the columns of the temple of Zeus or the Roman Coliseum, and finally, here, in your damp little town, we will find far too many similar monuments, about which I have already spoken. One of the oldest cities of Russia carries the name of Kyiv, which we can approximately translate as "the city of Mr. Ph," its dominion, its sphere.[1] In fact, the inhabitants of Kyiv and its surrounding areas from ancient times have the characteristic habit on Easter Sunday to festively eat horseradish, which emerges as a symbol of Mr. Ph, and the fact that eggs are also served with the horseradish just expresses the meaning of the ritual. Perfetsky, who happens to be present here could, of course, attest to the veracity of this example, if he weren't occupied with who knows what, if he weren't crawling under the table with his hand, if he weren't straining himself, if he weren't shuffling papers or someone's

"Both," Stakh wrote her and stretched out his left hand beneath the table with his incredibly long fingers. For a certain amount of time his hand made its way forward in emptiness and expectation. He had to help by bending his entire torso forward. Only then did it meet that leg, that foot, that soft suede shoe.

"Here's the right one for you. Two would be too much," a note from Ada explained.

Perfetsky thanked her with a nod of his head. The shoe—warm and pliant, came off easily and without a sound. Further on was the smoothness of her stockings, also warm, the roundness of her heel and the fabulous indentation right before her joint—two bony hills, a quiet stop just before the march further. But again his arm was too short.

Ada understood this and she slid even further and further off the chair. This allowed Perfetsky's fingers to move forward along her calf, which was both tense and tender.

"Feel good?" Stakh asked.

"Sure, just like at a doctor's office!" Ada answered.

"I'd like to be an anatomist. Your personal anatomist." He didn't manage to write anything more, for the fingers of Perfetsky

stockings, if this monkey had not tempted him, you can believe me! [*Everyone looks simultaneously in the direction of Ada and Stakh.*]

In a parallel in the most ancient of cultures, processes develop that reflect the ambiguity of the stunning rise of our impudent hero. Certain peoples already since primordial times have striven to shame this assumer of airs and to point out his place for him. The Semites actualized a decisive step in the direction of common sense when they decided to circumcise him. Other races went further—from circumcision to dismemberment, for example the Acephalians, among whom the above-mentioned dismemberment served as the necessary prerequisite of marriage initiation. Only with a completely divested sexual member could the Acephalian male youth begin his married life. The members of the council of elders took upon themselves the problems of the procreation of the lineage; they, with the great efforts of their important rank, were forced to maintain celibacy. From the parchments found in the graves of the ancient Sogdians we have found out about another no less striking

nearly completely spread on the table reached right to her knee, to this full goblet of pleasures. . . .

For some unknown reason everyone was looking in their direction.

"Oho!" Ada signaled, whose eyes had just gotten a bit tipsy. "!!!!!!!!!!!!!"—Stakh answered to this. His exclamation marks resembled staffs, sceptres, vectors. His fingers impetuously stretched further, there, above her knee, where already the lower edge of her skirt could be felt, and the thinnest spider web of her stocking acquired uncommon sensitivity.

But further on there was a chill. The distance within reach of his hand dug into this. Stas's fingers for a certain amount of time still stretched forward in despair, so that even his joints were cracking.

marriage ritual. The bride and groom spent the first night with a bisexual priest, a horned Bull-Sow, who from one side deflowered the bride, and from the other allowed the groom to penetrate. [*A voice from the audience: "Not true!"*]

As we see from time immemorial, people, especially those belonging to cultures advanced relative to their time, marvelously understood that sex can occur even without the domination of the whimsical Mr. Ph, that sex is never the matter of just two subjects-objects, but in the least—is a matter for all of society. The control of high priests over the process of conception, which is characteristic for the entire prehistory of humankind, fortunately, has not been exhausted as that prehistory has been itself.

Or we can take another side of the phenomenon—the artistic. Let's mention here at least the castration of young male slaves in Greece, thanks to which they could perform female roles in theatrical performances. This was a brilliant idea! With the help of an insignificant surgical loss to carry into effect the fact that in no way are men higher than

"????????????" asked Perfetsky.

"..." was the answer.

And Stas dove into patiently waiting, remembering that there was very little time, that in general time was against them, that soon the lecture of the Witch Shalizer would climax, that in two days they already would be going their separate ways, that at some point he would have to leave Europe, that actually, he and Ada don't have the right to delay even for a minute, and instead of fruitless perching in this so-called seminar they must be together somewhere with just the two of them—in a grove, an Eden, an orchard, in the sky, in the sea, in a boat, in a single bed. For failure stalks them everywhere. This table. This husband of hers. And this audience. And this entire city.

women, that they are less perfect, that the biological difference between a man and a woman is profoundly artificial and quite nonexistent. If one can speak to some kind of difference, then just in a single sense—any man is a woman just far removed from perfection, and the entire illusory ingeniousness of men lies just in the presence of an absolutely unnecessary (like an appendix) thing. [*Whistling, impatience of the audience, a few applauding while standing.*] I repeat: a woman far from perfection! . . .

Right from here—from the sense of one's own imperfection, of a primitive physiological authority—comes man's striving to have control over a woman. Being on top during the sex act, it is as though the man once more is trying to prove he is better than the woman and openly oppresses her. Conjecturing that with the equality of relations and status, they have to recognize their incompleteness and fragility, nearly everywhere men enacted a radical historical disturbance to overthrow the natural matriarchal customs and with the aid of their temporary weapons, impelling the anomaly of patri-

But Ada's eyes not for nothing became fogged with tipsiness. She knew what to do, she grew bold. And waiting for the appropriate opportunity, she fluidly and silently slipped beneath the table—so fluidly and so silently, the way for example, that her scarf made of light silk would float off in the air. So like an animal, nimbly and lithely, so unnoticeably and with self-sacrifice, as though one more time convincing Stakh (whose heart had stopped) of her perfection. And there, in this dungeon, in the crampedness of another's legs—in the stamping of feet, in jeans, in socks, in legs, that sweated, protested and grew angry—she instantly found him, Perfetsky, his endless legs, stretched out toward her, and she wrapped them with herself, as though with stiff lianas, and found there, in the far reaches, this living and strong creature, this weapon from the dawn of time, this young prince, this proud warrior, this egotistical assumer of airs, a well-built rider, a firm stoic, a tender rapist, a sweet killer, a free Kozak, a gentle giant. And so, making her way uninterruptedly onto his peak, she remembered: this is the

archies. They restricted women in everything, but mainly—in the possibilities of choice and the freedom of movement. They jammed them in the prison of domestic life, choosing alcohol and seafaring as an alternative amusement for themselves. [*An outcry from the audience: "She's a witch!"*]

greatest thing she can do for him, and the least thing she can do for herself, but in this cave, in this darkness another is not given—just love as wickedness and wickedness as love and hell as heaven and heaven as hell and the stamping of feet and fluttering of wings and flight and flight and flight. . . .

Here we must leave out a part of Mrs. Shalizer's lecture, in as much as the lightning streaks in Stakh's skull illuminated his path to near nirvana. Just a half glass of whiskey could save him, which he was not refused in such cases of the heart by the secretary of the foundation. Just afterward the straying soul of Perfetsky allowed itself to return from the tall Shangri-la in the library walls of the San Giorgio Maggiore monastery on the island of the same name in the Adriatic sea, in the city of Venice, in the south of Europe, and again to occupy the usual for it, over the course of the last thirty plus years, refuge in his, Perfetsky's, body.

"Amid the eternal plots of human existence," in the meanwhile becoming tame from the first attacks, Scoundrel Shalizer elaborated her version of the world, "there is just one that always gives me no rest and forces me to constantly worry, and I consider it the most essential. This is the fable of Red Riding Hood, who, swallowed by the Wolf, wandered in his darkness for long centuries, although all the same she emerged to freedom. The

The dissatisfaction of those present was becoming all the more obvious. The situation inexorably rolled toward a scandal which, after all, was for the speaker usual as well as even desired. But the mood of the audience remained rather humorous to that time.

For example, Gaston Dejavu, Wit personified, in a comic manner depicted in turn a Wolf, then Little Red Riding Hood, then Perfection or Lust, then suddenly a Blue Beard

history of the human race—this is the history of the battle of women for their liberation from the domination of Mr. Ph, from that Wolf. The history of women till now—this is the history of Red Riding Hood in the innards of the Wolf.

Even in the society of the Middle Ages completely controlled by men, our female predecessors pretended to vanquish him, Mr. Ph., his boundless license. Sexual relations between a man and woman conducted against her will and enacted with the aid of force were punished just as harshly as murder—under the condition that it did not concern a married couple (and in this lies the entire inadequacy of laws of the Middle Ages). The awful story of the knight Sam Nemyrych circulated throughout the entire world of that time. He was an inhabitant of the Sarmatian fortress of Leopolis and an ancestor of Perfetsky,[2] who is present here, who—not Perfetsky, but Nemyrych—at the beginning of the seventeenth century raped the local executioner's daughter with the poetic name of Neborak, for which he was conveyed into the hands of an inquisition, and then who looks for his next victim.

John Paul all the same still was residing in the glow of the mist of the valley peak. His lip-filled smiling face could accommodate itself to someone else far away.

The great-granddaughters of the hoary baron madly blushed after each one of Sheila's utterances. Casallegra himself did not even plan to react to anything in any way, growing still in his president's chair, like a pillar of truth and virtue. Ultimately his closed eyes might have meant that he was sleeping.

Alborak Djabraili at that moment was for the most part beyond the island—in the building of the *quaestura* not far from Rio di San Lorenzo he was writing the next in line complaint replete with culturally historical reminiscences regarding Rocinante, who had disappeared and who had not yet been found.

All the other guests, in one way or another expressing their sharp dislike of the lecture of the famous American woman (hoots from their seats in a similar manner to "Ooo la-la," stamping of their feet, whistling), but at the same time they did not show their intoler-

justly chopped into sixty-nine pieces by the father of his victim. The member of the above-mentioned miscreant—Nemyrych's, and not Perfetsky's—today again resides in my collection, purchased during the worldwide sale of antiquities four years ago in Thessaloníki.

The beginning of the end of Mr. Ph is his insolvency, which becomes more and more evident. In ceaseless battles of the past millennia our hero—the aggressor and rapist—has already lost a good half of his previous might. Each time all the more often the unpleasant old charlatan complains about partial or complete impotence. And this is a fact already recognized by world medicine!

Today we can speak of completely real successes achieved by womanhood, especially of my country, regarding emancipation from this overage Lovelace.

First and foremost I have here in mind the juridical construction of the very concept of "rape," to which today quite deservedly we also consider any attempt of a man to enter into sexual contact with a woman, if that attempt occurs not at the initiative of the woman, but the man (or both the woman and

ance to such a degree to break off the action and not to allow Shalizer to have her say.

But, abruptly sharpening her tone and shifting to personal insults (namely this is the way the intimation against the gray-browed president Casallegra was taken, about whom the speaker said "an unpleasant old charlatan"), Liza Sheila sowed a storm. The fact added to the tension that from a certain moment a small, but nevertheless active number of male and female supporters of the American proclaimed to themselves—some kind of at first glance suspicious, unshaven guys, and totally shriveled painted honeys, obviously hired and brought by Shalizer herself for applause. Becoming from the very beginning somewhat restrained in such radiant company, for a certain amount of time they acted shamelessly right before our eyes. At first this appeared just in individual hoots in the manner of "*Brava!*" "*Molto bene!*" and "*Ben gli sta!*"[3] But after sensing

man). The excessively diligent servants of Mr. Ph, these last Mohicans, concordant with certain of our laws, today can be dragged to court and, as in ancient times, like the bandit Nemyrych, chopped into pieces, even in the case when their victim herself seemingly has convinced them of sexual union, in reality just trying to check on their restraint, which they failed to exhibit. Several test cases and quite successful trials have been facilitated the fact that our men much more infrequently are tempted by the inciting of Mr. Ph and seek the pinnacle of physical delights not inside of a woman's body, but rather inside a beer mug! . . .

Shalizer's voice became more nervous, because quite distinctly the prospect arose for her not being able to finish speaking.

"I will say it, all the same I'll say it!" She threatened with her witch's finger in the direction of the incited audience. "I will force you to hear out this bitter truth! Mr. Secretary, I demand order. . . . Shut up, *bastards*! Male members disengaged from men . . . have a life of their own. . . . We don't need to have them attached! Mr. Dappertutto! . . . *Kiss my*

that in this way they definitely won't earn their promised honoraria, this strange team divided up and occupied all the approaches to the podium. . . .

No one noticed when precisely, at which moment and after which words of the speaker, and also from which and from whose side the first book took flight—a serious chunky tome in quarto. This, however, served as a signal for the unfolding in time and space of the entire battle. Fortunately there were so many books close at hand that after several minutes they were strewn all around. Other books flew like bombs, in the air, exploding like mushrooms of five-hun-

ass! . . . We have the need to use them when we want, clear? . . . Clear for you, too? . . . *Fuck yourself!* . . . The millennial drama of Little Red Riding Hood awaits its final resolution in the new millennium! . . . Raped by the Wolf Little Red Riding Hood. . . . I spit in your snout! . . . Little Red Riding Hood chooses for herself! *Go to hell, you shitass!* . . . She is going on the right path! You will become witnesses of your own worthlessness. . . . The future is not in your favor! . . . You'll say this to your granny! . . . Pigs! If there's insemination already, it's artificial! . . . And no one of you can be compared. . . . They are being prepared—shut up, you *motherfucker*—they are being prepared from rubber substitutes! . . . Go away! Take away your *pricks!* Mr. Secretary, for the last time I ask. . . . Get away from me! . . . Make way for Little Red Riding Hood!

dred-year-old dust and scattering on a sheet of paper, pages, words, letters.

The enraged guests of the seminar moved to a decisive assault and, also taking advantage of ashtrays, spittoons, bronze statuettes, and candleholders, began to actively press the lumpenized hirelings of Liza Sheila to the facing, quickly emptying stands. . . .

How good that right at that time, this time of discord and hate, Stanislav ended up next to Ada and, taking her by the hand, tore away beyond it all. And just there, not seen by anyone, we leave them right now, and may they have good fortune!

There was entirely no opportunity to speak further. The performance ended up in a blaze of glory. Demonstratively stretching a red virgin wool beret on her head, Liza Sheila Shalizer stepped off the podium and long leggedly left the hall.

Dappertutto flew after her with apologies in a tobacco smoke aura.[4] But the passions among the listeners were still seething. Some astrolabes, ashtrays, and inkwells were still flying above the table. Fortunately, neither Ada nor Perfetsky were in this hurly-burly, the end to which was finally put by as old as the world Leonardo de Casallegra, rising up and leaning on the pillars of his great grand-daughters.

"Discussion, it seems, is already unnecessary," he moaned, and following these words, again grew silent for the next few hours.

■ □ ■ □ ■

1 4

csxt-dl

To Monsignore I sincerely report:

Today, the eighth of March, around noon, I managed to carry out an adroit and entirely successful operation. While the Respondent was at the seminar sessions, unnoticed by anyone (!) I penetrated his room. I entered through a window in the Respondent's bathroom. Taking advantage of the fact that the above-mentioned window that looks out onto a courtyard was open and (moreover)—some kind of gaping fool had left a rope ladder on it, I (an old alpinist) without any particular problems, but with risk to my health or life at least, crawled into the Respondent's apartment. As a result of an investigation of the Respondent's things, I managed to obtain his (the Respondent's) notebook—at first glance, an ordinary notebook of pocket size with a glossy jacket, covered in a dark brown ersatz leather, the paper inside pigmented like parchment, on the glossy cover the title DIARY (golden embossing). The notes of the Respondent encompass approximately half the notebook. They are copied by me in their entirety, without even the smallest cuts and in the same order in which they are entered by the Respondent. I pass them along for Monsignore's disposition. I continue not to be enamored of Cerina's mood. The Fourth Extraordinary Subcommittee could exhibit more activity. I wish Monsignore pleasant reading (this was a joke).

Forever to the ready—

The Doctor

***

What will I fill this first page with?

With my names. And I'll begin this way:

They called him Stakh Perfetsky and Carp Loverboysky and Sheatfish Saintlymansky and Pierre Fukinsky and High-as-a-Kite Birdsky.[1] But they also called him Gluck, Bloom, Vrubl, Strudl and Schnabl.[2] In addition he was Jonah of the Fish and George of the Fowl and Shura of the Fish and Siura of the Balls and Glory of the Days. But he was also Sargent Pepper, Juan Perez, Petey Peppa, Pepperonimon, and Ertz-Hertz-Pertz.[3] Some knew him as Persiansky, Parthiansky, Personsky, Profansky, and Perfavorsky. His closest friends loved him for the fact that he was Kamal Manchmal, Johann Cohan, Buddah Judas, Yukhan Bukhan, and Pu Fu. But all without exception called him Bimber Bibamus, Agnus Magnus, Avis Penis, Shtakhus Bacchus, and Cactus Erectus. Therefore no one could even guess that he really was Antinoah and Zorro Vavel and Hams/m/bur/g/er and Savior Orpheusky and P.S

All together he had forty names, and not one of them was real, for no one knew his real name, not even he himself.

Nachtigall von Ramensdorf: 618-22-21 (the Berlin area code?)˙

The institution, one of those where we often had to be. Tons of people in the corridors by the offices, some kind of little rooms, a lively line of people, an argument. It seems she can't go. She can't stand up. I hold her under her elbow. Then someone from the line turns around—a massive and nondescript guy—and asks: "Might you perhaps be gay?" Not enough fresh air. A dream in Prague, the middle of December, I don't remember more details.

GERMAN WOMEN. Mostly with big breasts, but, in fact, deprived of behinds. Nature wanted it that way.
(From the notes of a certain wanderer).

At 4 P.M. tomorrow: a meeting at a Chinese eatery (get off at the Zoo)

rhythmomelodics arithmetics poetics rhetorics

In general: the impression of complete exhaustion. Devaluation of the lofty word: to write as much as possible unpoetically. This is the schizophrenia of the older generation. The young are doing something else (if they are doing anything). The possibility of a "new Rilke"? Benn? I'm afraid not.

In the best case—Artmann. A petrified language.

Zoya: 7:30 P.M.

She did not believe that she was the first for me. That I didn't cheat on Her, I didn't cheat on Her with anyone, not at all. She didn't believe that I wrote letters to Her, but didn't send them. She didn't believe that I could live for weeks in the garret, where Slavtsunio brought me coffee and waffles with jam. The coffee shop was on the first floor, a jukebox. *Special for me* Slavtsunio made it louder. She didn't believe a single of my nocturnal stories. When I had been beaten in the park, She washed the bloody snot from my *morda* with cotton soaked in warm water. And she didn't believe me. She didn't believe me that they pummeled me purely by mistake—I simply answered the wrong way to the parole "What time is it?"[4] Etc. If this requires explanation, I implore: She loved me. Not to believe was easier for Her. MAKE A "PROLOGUE" FROM THIS.

Greek food: called gyros (they can be with hot red, but most often *tzatziki*). Souvlaki.

of arithmetics—nymphettes—pathetics (?)

VENETIAN MORNING[5]
To Richard Beer-Hofmann
Tall windows regally command the view
which we can only sometimes look upon:
the city tentatively made anew
each time the sky lets its reflections shine

upon a gleam of tide—ever redrawn
yet never quite achieved. Each morning she
requires the heavens to show her once again
the opals which she wore the previous day,

and every morning her canals present
the images which are her memories.
She gives herself, her chiming ornaments

(an amorous nymph surrendering to the God),   !drawing near,
lifts up San Giorgio above the flood   like a nymph to
and smiles and gazes, lazily content.   Zeus!

UROBOROS—an ancient symbol of eternity, a Serpent that
bites its own tail.

BAPHEMET—in the most ancient literatures an image of an
idol or the devil with a woman's body and a bearded man's head.

MAFEDET—an ancient Egyptian lion with a neck like a serpent.

LACERTINE—a two- or four-legged eellike chimera of Middle
Age illuminated book painting.

                            to find an image

poplars—poplar, poplarian
lindens—linden, lindenian

The beginning of August in Lviv. Heat. The buildings and side-
walks burn. Too little water. Rust, the scent. We drank a lot of wine.
We moved from garret to garret. We didn't wake up from the tram
cars, but from pigeon cooing. Every night I undressed Her for bed.
The wine was mostly red. Everyone said it was Algerian. It smelled
of the earth and I liked that in it: the clay, the cold. The stairs
creaked awfully when we returned to the garret. Once on the stairs:
a pensioner in a military-trophy hunting jacket over his
T-shirt. He fired at us several times but missed: he was over the hill.
In Max's studio there was a book, which must be read only from
right to left, flipping the pages with the tip of a sacred knife. After
the reading of each page one must utter nine prayers out loud.
Once I found Her over that book. She was holding a glass of red
wine in Her hand and was reading the book without following the
prescripts. She said that it's a not too bad novel, a bit old worldish
and boring, just as much as good literature must be boring. I nearly forcibly tore Her away from the book and never again brought

her back to Max's studio. Then for a time we lived in the Pohul-yanka neighborhood.[6] There I found a lake.

Regarding the matter of Munich: tel. 23-77-15

"The Firm"—4600 Am. dol.
Janeczek—310 Am. dol.
"Finance and Comfort"—2500 Am. dol.
LDP-Bank—7000 Am. dol.
Kulya—500 Am. dol.
Tsuikovsky—2100 Ger. marks.
Joint Venture "TENT-M"—780 Am. dol.
Yura—450 Ger. marks.
Pyrohiv—1500 Sw. francs.
Lawyers—1500 Am. dol.
Krokhoborov[7]—530 Fr. francs (I gave back 70 in April).
"Vampire-Import"—900 am. dol. (without loan shark fees).
Ahmed (Abdurakhman)—1200 p. sterling.
"NIGHTINGALE-trust"—335 Am. dol.
Small Business Concern "Blef"—1000 Am. dol. + 1000 Ger. marks
(to be returned in Japanese yen)
All together 27,730 Am. dol. !!!!!!!!!!!!!!!!!!!!!!!!!!!!

from this arithmetic.

Also, you need to say Bosch, and not Boskh. In Berlin: second time. In Vienna I saw "Carrying of the Cross." Now "John the Evangelist on Patmos." A red-haired boy with a quill pen and a book. Reading of apocalyptic signs. The Mother of God with the baby Jesus (the left upper corner, in the sky, a bright capsule—Bosch!). A tree with birds. A linden? Every tree's a linden. The violation of the perspective so brazen, that just from the tree alone you experience the full and eternal seventh heaven. The lower left corner—again a bird (like a falcon). An angel on a hill. Azure blue with white. An intercessor. A messenger. A lot of water and boats far off. I feel like being there. In the city by the water. And this monster in glasses! A troll? in a coat of armor? a tail like a salamander? A demon. Find out more about the brothers and sisters of the Free Spirit. Green, ochre. A cape: white, pink, red. Close to the text. Objects spread out on the ground. One object? Attentiveness. Sending us signs. We are not ready.

I'm growing hoarse—I'm restless—I'm sticking out—I'm going blind (!)—I'm creaking[8]

It turns out, they also have someone in Munich. AN INEX-ORABLE SCENARIO.

a number of passing Munich inhabitants with hair colored green or red grew with each hour of my stay Among such emerald purple water nymphs even seventy-year-old babes were not excessively rare The winter trees were spattered with lanterns Moors and clowns traveled in the evening train cars and throngs of FemAngels in punk style fluttered from one tavern to the next following Devils and Roman Legionnaires Besides this the general atmosphere was sufficiently peaceful not criminal at all and for this reason because in my view not entirely festive
BETTER WITH PUNCTUATION MARKS

Finish writing the story of Pavarotti in the Vienna opera—for *New Millennium News*.

Text of an announcement: "A tall extravagant foreigner looking for single Bavarian lady with traditional cookery for the joint celebration of Fasching.[9] Age: not older than forty. I speak Italian. Where are you, my love?"
This will be the sign.
And if someone really responds?

I suggested to Her that we leave Lviv. I know perfectly well that She wouldn't agree. For my own sake actually. "What are you going to do among your Romanians?" In Chortopil: She didn't like it. I played out the business to the end. I showed everything: the neglect, the dug-up streets, the mountains in smoke, a sulfur miner, rainfall nine months of the year. Old buildings crumble by themselves. Gathering berries beyond the train tracks, She saw a snake. Then three more. It's always that way: worthwhile just to see the first one. I warmed up some wine for Her. The same "Algerian." We barely made it through that week. We nearly argued. When we returned to Lviv, I borrowed the keys for Frantz's apartment. We lay down right on the floor. Then we filled up the bathtub with water. I was without my glasses, but I saw all of Her with my fingers.

lindenian—look at (look at what?)

A big argument with Dr. Stein. Whom did Rilke give birth to? Dr. Stein!

Life as a means of utilization. Someone said this.

SAN MARCO[10]
Venice
In this space (inside), that as though scooped
bends (in an arching vault) and turns in golden smalt,
with rounded edges, in a smooth, well oiled with refinement,
the entire murkiness (darkness) of this country is kept
and secretly amassed, like equilibrium
to light, which in all its objects
makes itself so much larger that they (as such) have nearly
disappeared.—
And you suddenly doubt: are they not vanished (entirely)
and you squeeze out the firm (stubborn?) gallery,
which, like a gallery in a mine, side by side with a flash
an arching vault suspended; and you recognize the blessed (*heile*)
shining (*Helle*) of perspective; but somehow
sadly measuring its weary moment
(temporariness?)
near the steadfast (immovable) four (quadriga?).
!! clarify the "four"!!

Idea: a complete translation of *The Book of Images* and *New Poems*. Rilke here is without shamanism ("without fools"). I love him for this.

a coat (jacket)
a pair of new shirts
shoes
handkerchiefs
ties
at the post office: send Zoya a funny package

Reception in the old city hall. Don't forget to have dinner.
Right away—the night club Casanova. Am Platzl. ???? But they pay
really well.

the drowner the drownedess drowning

One time, while licking streaks of strawberry juice from Her
body, I found something like a pea under Her skin with my lips,
below her right breast. Then She was lying on Her stomach, and I
slowly, ever so slowly, kissed all of Her, I kissed out of Her—
what?—until finally She

*a July of nymphettes
a drowning river a drowning time*

Edgar Allan Poe begot Baudelaire. Baudelaire begot Mallarmé.
Mallarmé begot Rilke and Valéry. Rilke begot Count von Lanz-
koronski and an entire armada of poets. Valéry for the second
time begot himself. Nearly all his predecessors (evidently) begot
Eliot, but mostly—his contemporaries (secretly). Another
branch grows from Rimbaud. Antonych said that he was born of
Whitman. In the Lemko village of Duklya? Bertran de Born and
Joachim du Bellay begot Apollinaire. Apollinaire—this is premature. Develop.

a piano!!

Pinzenauerstrasse, 15

Have to write back to Ewa!!!

Have to check if it's true that "carnavale" in Italian means "farewell, flesh."

***

Winter in Bavaria is like
any other winter,
when, wandering alone,
you look for a young lady like a rhyme
or—in other way—you look for a rhyme
like the wafting of some kind of news,   of sparkling
                                                        tidings

for the young women here know no restraint
and have all become antifascists.   harpists

Winter in Bavaria is slow
and lasting. The years pass.
Some kind of retarded melody
trashes my soul, until
I walk through the park. The dark sap
of trees without movement or labor.
In this silence, as though at the bottom of a bay,
I dream of red-haired Gertrude.

Winter in Bavaria is constant.
This isn't winter. Something's wrong with me:
my being that loves travesty
becomes a wintry pine.
I exist in memory. I exist
in the spring, thinking about Gertrude's
breasts, I sob like an echo,
like snow to the mountains and buildings.

Winter in Bavaria is moderate
and short, and not eternal.
My high-mountain soul
deals with dark events.
A hole in the soul—this is the semantic
chasm between "me" and the world,

when my beloved from the other side
calls with decay, with the mortal, with summer.

Winter in Bavaria is needed
just by me and by no one else,
but to the south—the silver streak
of the tallest Alps! I place a comma
in premonition. I've become the sand in
an hourglass. There is just a little more of me—
and I will acquire weightless
presence in the hole of the epoch.

MAYBE LEAVE IT WITHOUT A TITLE

The last S-Bahn: 00.28 (from Marienplatz).

after all poetics (crossed out)
after the rhythmomelodics of arithmetics (crossed out)

And the best days were those when Roman and Marta let us into
their museum. We came for the night when the museum was
already closed. One of them—they took turns separately—allowed
us inside. We had dinner off the museum dinnerware and slept in
the museum beds. Good that it was a museum of antiquities. At
seven in the morning (at the latest at 7:30) we had to fade away. A
portchaise. She shook her foot so furiously that her sandal flew off.
Roman came in on us. Later somebody found us. They chased out
Roman, and Marta didn't want to risk it anymore.

antifungal ointment!

Who is this N.? (crossed out)

coat (jacket)
socks
shoes
2-3 new shirts

TOO MUCH OF VENICE! "so that people would not feel a firm hand on the nape of their neck and the Venetian carnival was for all the capitols an unattainable example of experiencing life in all its beauty and fullness."

Rilke wrote his poems about Venice in Paris. This was news to me. From a distance. Which on the other hand is not there.

Casallegra Dappertutto

Foreigners in Venice. Always surprised. Mozart met with the local masons. Byron told them to lock him in prison beneath a tin roof (his right to a creative experiment). Handel, Gluck (one more?), Haydn. Peggy Guggenheim. Houyhnhnms." Hemingway. Wagner: fell down on the steps of the Vendramin-Calergi Palace. They carried the body to the train station by gondola. There are these kinds of funeral gondolas. Look at Bosch in the Palace of Doges. A collection of contemp. art (Dali, Mondrian, Legér, Picasso, Chagall, Pollock). Do I want to see it???????

After all poetics, arrythmias, arithmetics
I step out into the heat, I melt and go blind.
I'm in July. The time of nymphets.
I entered the river, drowning and lindenian. *definitely this way*!!!

FOR AN ACCURATE SHOT YOU NEED TO
1. Take a deep breath and hold it.
2. Lean the butt end into your right shoulder. The barrel has to continue the line from your shoulder.
3. Close your left eye.
4. Guide the sight in such a way that the target stops at the point of intersection of the vertical and horizontal axes in the scope.
5. Check if everything is okay.
6. Quickly, but sincerely, say a prayer.
7. Together with an exhale steadily press the trigger mechanism.
8. Ka-boom!

ORPHEUS IN VENICE

An opera buffa in the form of a pasticcio
in three acts and numerous scenes

Original idea and libretto—Mathew KULIKOFF

Cast:

Orpheus, poet and singer .... *tenor or baritone*
Rina, a Venetian beauty .... *soprano*
Asclepio, her guard and an evil spirit .... *bass*
Inquisitor .... *baritone*
Sparafucile, a hired killer .... *tenor or falsetto*

Smeraldina ⎫
Clarice ⎬ courtesans .... *soprano and*
Rosalinda ⎭   *mezzo-soprano*

Carambolio ⎫ young officers
Pantalone ⎬ singers .... *tenors and baritones*
Galileo ⎭ philanderers

Man-Dragon ⎫ agents of the inquisition ... *contrabass*
Woman-Viper ⎭   *alto*

Voice of Eurydice .... *soprano*

Masks, dancers, ghosts, castrates, *sbirros,* acrobats, monks, Moors—
in a word, the people of Venice.

The action occurs at all times and everywhere, but this time—
in the Teatro La Fenice

The music of Italian and other composers will resound in the per-
formance: Claudio MONTEVERDI (*Persephona*), Antonio VIVALDI
(*L'Olimpiade*), Domenico CIMAROSA (*Il matrimonio segreto*),
Gioacchino ROSSINI (*L'Italiana in Algeri*), Gaetano DONIZETTI
(*Enrico di Borgogna*), Vincenzo BELLINI (*Norma*), Giuseppi VERDI
(*Ernani, Rigoletto, La Traviata, Simon Boccanegra*), Gian Francesco
MALIPIERO (*L'Orfeide, Tre commedie goldoniane, Il mistero di
Venezia*), George Frideric HANDEL (*Acis and Galatea, Rinaldo*),
Christoph Willibald GLUCK (*Demetrius, Orfeo ed Euridice*), Wolf-
gang Amadeus MOZART (*Don Giovanni, Cosi fan tutte*), Igor Stra-
vinsky (*Orpheus*) and . . . several measures from Richard WAGNER![1]

Director-Producer—Mathew KULIKOFF
(Los Angeles—Paris—Melbourne)

Orchestra, choir and ballet of the Venice Teatro La Fenice.
Orchestra of mechanical and pneumatic instruments.
Crew synthesizer support of voices.
Crew for laser support.
Computer graphics and holography.
Dance-ballet "Sexappealer."
Striptease group "The Bacchanalians."
Dressed creatures and circus illusionists.
Fire extinguisher crew.
Crew for sabotage activities (pyrotechnics).
And a lot lot more—all together 2,000 performers

ACT I

For an endlessly long time the tragic singer and poet Orpheus wanders about the earth. His wife Eurydice at one point dies from a
snake bite. Perhaps this has occurred just because some among the
gods were terribly jealous of Orpheus's art—his superhuman gift.
Orpheus recalls that once he had captivated Hades himself with his
playing on a golden harp and thanks to this has pleaded for him to

release the Shadow of Eurydice from his underworld kingdom back to the earth. Vicious Persephone, interfering in the course of the action, hampers the miraculous resurrection of Orpheus's wife. Sad and inconsolable, Orpheus wanders from country to country, from city to city, from hotel to hotel. His renown and the renown of his music have transcended all the glory of the world. This, however, has failed to make him happy.

On this occasion Orpheus ends up in Venice—a fairy-tale city above the waters of the Adriatic. He had been told much about this haven for artists and loners, and also about the fact that Venice knows how to celebrate a holiday. Right now, just before the end of the several-month-long joyfully bitter carnival, on the main square of the city, next to a lagoon and an ornate cathedral, continuous revelry and diversions take place. Dressed in colorful costumes, with masks on their faces, the Venetians and visitors give in to unbridled pleasures. An ardent dance is replaced by fencers battling, and to the snapping of petards, singing, and the music of a hundred street *cappellas* that gushes from the square and canals, *volo del turco*[2] occurs—a young boy acrobat fearlessly leaps with a bouquet of mimosas in his hand along a cable, stretched between the spire of the Campanile bell tower and the loggia of the Palace of Doges.

And just Orpheus, covered in a black cape and hidden beneath the mask of sadness, is not exceedingly happy with everything that he has seen on this extraordinary holiday. Blacker than a storm cloud hanging over Giudecca Island, he walks among the reveling throng like a flotsam and jetsam sinful spirit.

But what is this? The competitions of singers and musicians grow silent. Anyone can take part in them, anyone who considers their voice and musical ear good enough not to embarrass themselves. For the Venetian public is terribly exacting. The venerators used to strict coloraturas have put many an ambitious seeker of vainglory in his place.

Three friends—Carambolio, Pantalone and Galileo—sure that today in the city there are not any who can be compared to them in the art of song. It is just the competition that will show who is the best among the three. With derisive smiles and mockery they listen to the performances of other participants: not a single of the performed numbers (arias, duets or trios) elicits a particular rapture among those present, and they cruelly whistle down the losers. And the prize in the competition is quite valuable—a kiss from Rina herself, the most beautiful of the Venetian women and (as the whispers of wicked tongues confirm) the mistress of the chief Inquisitor.

Here she is, in a pink velvet *portchaise,* held up by four athletic Moors, and listening to the course of the competition. To which of the luckiest of men will she bestow the paradise of her lips today for a single unforgettable moment? With impatience everyone awaits the decision.

But who is this who has turned into stone in the loggia of the palace—unmoving and gray, as though debris from a cliff? And even the doge, the chief leader of the city, gazes at him with fear, remaining unemboldened to be the first to speak. Yes, this is he—the terror and trepidation of the happy republic, Monsignore Inquisitor, the punishing sword of order and decency. Not far from him, now and then whispering something into his ear, overgrown with ruddy-colored hair, Asclepio stations himself—they call him the guard of Signora Rina, but in reality he is, rather, her warden. Commenting to the Inquisitor about several performances during the singing competition, Asclepio jokes quite saltily and laughs sarcastically.

And here the turn of the three officer friends approaches. They really have beautiful voices. And each one in his own way conquers the audience, it's also nearly impossible to designate which one of them will be victorious all the same. "Ca-ram-bo-lio!" Shout out some. "Pan-ta-lo-ne!" Others respond. "Ga-li-le-o!" The third group does not let up. On whose side will success be? Whom will Rina kiss?

At that moment an unknown man in a black mourning mask and a black cape announces his participation. The audience with disbelief and a chill greets his entrance onstage. The hottest heads, without having heard the stranger, strive to whistle him down: how does this self-assured intruder have the audacity to compete with their three favorites! But no one present knows that this is Orpheus himself—the living legend of music and poetry.

Yet, Orpheus begins his sweetly sorrowful aria, from which everything becomes quiet and turns to listen. All of Venice grows silent in unprecedented rapture: the canals, the towers, the palaces, the gardens, even the waves of the lagoon strive to help the singer. Tears of ecstasy and heightened sensitivity appear on their faces and pass through from beneath their masks. And here an unearthly woman's voice combines with Orpheus's song—yes, this is Eurydice reminding her beloved about her.

There are no doubts—it was the best performance! Their anger changing to kindness, the Venetian people go wild with applause and gratitude. The ashamed trio of officers, enraged, abandons the square.

The beautiful Venetian woman, graciously leaning over from the *portchaise,* sticks her lips to the victor's lips. For some reason this kiss lasts exceedingly long! Once again orchestras reverberate, and the audience manages to count to twenty-five in unison, until that passionate moment ends. Of course the Inquisitor is forced to harshly punish his young lover for her inability to control herself and to hide her passions of the flesh as deep as possible! . . .

ACT II

From the time that their lips fused together in a torrid kiss, neither Rina nor Orpheus had any peace. Having returned from the holiday square to the hotel, Orpheus can't find a place for himself. Two opposing forces rend his singing breast: the fidelity of the memory of his wife and his new incomparable enrapture with a young Venetian woman. His friends had told him that this was a dangerous city! Orpheus does not even see how the Dragon and the Viper were dancing and singing around him—the evil spies and investigators of the Inquisitor.

At that time Rina, aware of the fact of how much she is risking, intending to betray the Inquisitor, summons to her room her guard, the lanky Asclepio. She orders him to find out everything about the mysterious foreigner: who he is, where he is from, where he is staying. And, if he succeeds in finding him, then let Asclepio definitely pass along to the foreigner her, Rina's, invitation to dinner—for tomorrow evening. She dreams of getting to know him better. Asclepio goes to fulfill her orders.

And although at that moment Orpheus and Rina are living under different roofs and in different corners of the city, it is as though they hear and see one another. Their voices merge in a harmonious, sensitive duet.

In the meantime the three officer friends—Carambolio, Pantalone and Galileo—in the hopes of dispelling the bitterness of their defeat manage to join the company of three well-known courtesans—Smeraldina, Clarice, and Rosalinda. But neither the playful maidens' caresses, nor the noble wine, nor the silence and spontaneous conversations are able to cheer the mood of the guests. Then the courtesans begin to question carefully the reason for such insurmountable dispiritedness. The sly foxes, certainly, also were at the festival and understood everything perfectly well, but it's important that the losing singers express it all themselves. When finally after lengthy entreaties the visitors through their joint efforts relate the fantastic victory of some unknown parvenu, Smeraldina, Clarice, and Rosalinda laugh loudly and pacify the vanity of their friends. "We know who he is and know what can mortally wound him," the courtesans say. Having heard this, their guests noticeably cheer up. It seems, is the good gladness of spirit returning to them? Also, is it not time to move on to the battles of love? Well then, from the six of them there would always be a wonderful SEX-tet! So it turns out that way—a grand scale copulation begins and they even imagine that it's not just six, but a full six hundred and sixty-six female and male lovers simultaneously taking part in lovemaking on the theatrical stage! . . .

Asclepio, like a faithful dog, runs to his master—the Inquisitor. He has much news for him. The latter, however, already knows quite a bit—it's not in vain that the shadows of the Dragon and the Viper expressively lay on the grass of his secret garden, in which he has the habit of hearing the reports of his *sbirro*-spies. He just didn't know the most important thing—Rina, it turns out, has invited this clear-voiced newcomer to her abode for supper! Well, then, it will be that much simpler to resolve the problem. Clearly, the all-powerful Inquisitor could simply proclaim Orpheus the servant of the Devil and, subjecting him to the most varied tortures in the most horrifying *carceri*, to publicly lose. But this could elicit dissatisfaction among the people—the throngs all too well remember his, Orpheus's, singing. In such cases the Inquisitor has other, far more promising means. Then Sparafucile, the hired killer, appears in the garden, on whose hands there is so much innocent blood that he never removes his sticky red gloves. . . .

ACT III

It is unknown by whom and how Orpheus is warned about the threat of death hanging over him; however, he does not refuse Rina's invitations. This woman for him is now the most important thing in the world. But just in case he puts on armor on his chest, arms himself with a sword, and wraps himself in a lengthy black cape. Now he is ready to go to a rendezvous with a beauty.

In the meantime, in Rina's palace, a boisterous reception has already begun. Today, as often happens, it is filled with guests. Almost all of them are in masks and carnival clothing—from room to room strings of dancers stretch, songs and music everywhere, the luxury of inner elegance adds to the luxury of the tables covered with drinks and food. The three courtesan girlfriends—Smeraldina, Clarice, and Rosalinda—particularly distinguish themselves with their celebrating. Just their cavaliers are nowhere to be seen. For Carambolio, Pantalone and Galileo also had been invited to the nocturnal feast of the incomparable Rina! Also the hostess herself is nowhere to be found. Some of the guests suspect that the capricious woman has again intended some kind of stunning surprise. But others had already sensed something bad and quite bloody in the wind.

Right at midnight, as the beauty had requested, Orpheus signals from the gate to her palace. The ironclad doors open as if by themselves—and here the singer enters the lower vestibule. But what is this? Be careful, Orpheus!—a mad, enraged bull runs right at him down the steps. The blow from his horns lands in Orpheus's armor, otherwise it unavoidably would have crippled his singing chest, the way that an awl would pierce newspaper. The bull revs for another blow, but here Orpheus's sword that he had clutched mortally wounds him. The bull falls over onto the floor and, trickling black blood, tosses his animal accoutrements in every direction: his head with horns and ring in the nose, his hooves, his tail. This is the hired killer Sparafucile! Dying, he pleads that Orpheus forgive him, for it is through the Inquisitor and his sycophants that he has destroyed so many innocent people. Orpheus forgives him and, calmed, Sparafucile gives up his soul with a gladdened smile and froth on his lips.

But where is Rina? Orpheus ascends the stairs. There orgiastic diversion is going on. Each of the three courtesans—Smeraldina,

Clarice, and Rosalinda—pretends in turn to be Rina. Each time Orpheus believes this, but tearing off the mask from the lovely face and leaning to the honey lips, he is convinced that it is not her, that these are not her lips. . . .

Searching through the entire palace, he does not find Rina, then in one of the most distant rooms he comes upon her servant Asclepio. He is bitterly crying over an empty goblet. For his entire life he had secretly loved Rina and for that reason had been aiding the Inquisitor in relations with her in order to save her from the courting of others. But these three miscreants—Carambolio, Pantalone and Galileo—today had scoffed at him. At the order of the Inquisitor, they forcibly have taken Rina from the palace. The Inquisitor allows them to have their will with her. Asclepio will not endure this. He has already taken poison. He implores just one thing from Orpheus—to forgive him, Orpheus forgives him and, gladdened, Asclepio gives up his soul with joyous sparks in his eyes, which are becoming more and more glassy.

Orpheus hastily sets off after the kidnappers. Someone had seen their boat set off in the direction of the Grand Canal with Rina tied up in it. Sustained by a tail wind, Orpheus quickly overtakes the rogues. He jumps into their boat. An unequal battle takes place in which he turns out the victor: he drowns Carambolio in the water, he pulls off Pantalone's head, and Galileo kills himself. But why can't he see Rina? Pantalone's severed head explains that the beauty has managed to jump out of their boat and go to the bottom. She preferred death to derision. The bound body of a young woman, which floats up the surface of the water and lazily continues to move with the current, serves as the proof for this.

Orpheus shudders from grief. He can no longer stay here. He wants to go far away from here. He abandons the city: decisively and immediately. His boat holds a course into the open sea. The voice of Eurydice accompanies him. On the shore of the lagoon the petrified Inquisitor stands, like a Commendatore.

Note: Between the second and third act no intermission is expected.

Mathew KULIKOFF (born 1956) is one of the most well known opera directors and innovators of the contemporary world. The artistic credo of this master of stage sensations lies in the return to the theater of theatricality through the living and blistering deluge of eternal childlike amazement and even shock. A viewer of Kulikoff's performances must be stunned and shattered. "Only then, from those pieces, can he be assembled together again, but much better," the director says about his aim. Twelve years ago, having led a live elephant (instead of a donkey) onto the Paris stage in the first act of *The Clowns* of Leoncavallo, the artist apparently proclaimed: "This is just the debut. There will be more coming up." Then there truly was an entire series of stunning successes: Mozart's *Don Giovanni*, New York, 1983 (a two-meter-high statue of the Commendatore, manipulated with the assistance of electronics, self-destructed during the finale through an atomic miniblast), Mozart's *Zauberflöte*, Amsterdam, 1986 (the serpent, that at the beginning of the performance chases after Prince Tamino, was 148 yards long, made of plastic, plasteline, and fish husks, which used 1,219 giant carp; it spit fire and a special odiferous gas, the result of which, after the first scene, the performance was stopped, and they had to air out the theater over the course of two hours, first emptying it; and only after this did the action continue), or the unforgettable *Night Flight* of Dallapiccola, Moscow—Casablanca, 1987 (the performance occurred in a plane that took off in the evening from Moscow, after an eight-hour battle with the natural elements of wind, had landed near the shores of North Africa by morning, thanks to which one hundred and seventeen Russian dissidents invited to the performance finally ended up in the free world).

Without any hesitation Mathew Kulikoff accepted the proposal to perform the opera in our city on the water, for a certain time setting aside other urgent projects (Rome, Berlin, Tokyo). We are profoundly grateful to the Maestro first and foremost for his kind agreement to embody on the stage the musical idea of Venice, the city in which three hundred years ago sixteen (!) opera theaters already were operating.

La morte di Venezia Foundation

Mathew KULIKOFF:
I was terribly enthralled with the idea of doing an opera in such a legendary city. Because right here, in this island state saturated

with culture and its imitations, is quite appropriate for embodying one of my mad intentions—to create an opera beyond operas, an opera of operas, where the very elements of *operaness,* its inner actuality, its substance, is parodied, rethought and, if You accept this, is elevated even higher. To my assistance came the old Italian experience of the seventeenth to the eighteenth centuries (to the point, the centuries of the most luxurious flowering of Venice). I have in mind the so-called pasticcio, when new operas were created on the basis of the deconstructing and recombination of elements of operas that already existed. The historical-cultural space of Venice, its topoi, its genius loci, it seems, assisted me in my work. The spiritual landscape of the Italian opera tradition had no less meaning for me. Finally, the space of the stage and the hall—the magic of this fantastic space, the Teatro La Fenice, its aura. And countless other spaces in addition—the individual creative spaces of each, who believed me and worked with me on the same team. I thank all of You without exception and invite You to the premiere.

I hope my pasticcio will be to your taste!

רָבִי-דָ-אַכ

I request to bring to Monsignore's notice:

As Monsignore surely must be aware, that evening one of the grandest musical sensations of our time occurred, the news of which first flew throughout Venice, and then—the rest of the world; I will begin, however, with the fact that I accompanied the Respondent over the course of the entire day, we boated a bit by gondola to Dorsoduro, the Respondent ate sugar-coated nuts and looked somehow distinctly unsettled; the gondolier was enraptured with the Lemko[1] songs which the Respondent sang endlessly, and the Doctor remained in the hotel (busy with his stupid little fish, rather than with our joint enterprise) until evening, and we set off together just to the performance—all three of us, but in the throng of opera fanatics, which, just as we, had pushed to the direction of the Teatro La Fenice, along the Calle del Piovan, much too cramped for such pilgrimages, we were rubbed and driven back from one another. Right before entering the theater, I again managed to press close to the Respondent, I hid my face in his shoulder, and he managed to kiss me behind the ear, but right after this we took notice of Dappertutto waiting for us at the doorway: in his hand were complimentary tickets for all the participants of the seminar, he had no less than five hostesses beside him, "you look like the most beautiful of Venetian women, Ada," this master of viscid compliments puffed smoke, "be careful, Perforatsky, this is a fatal woman," he said in English, so I didn't have to translate, there was still a good half hour until the performance, the Respondent answered this "for me she's sooner a finale woman," Dappertutto pretended that he understood his joke, tickets to the performance cost from two hundred thousand lire and more, but the foundation paid for everything; finally, the Doctor, who had just been lost, was elbowed over to us, "I didn't think that," said the Doctor, but Dappertutto managed to inform us of several of the latest news items: first, Mavropule did not show up, although they say, he apparently showed up not far from the Rialto Bridge, at a fish bazaar, where he inquired about the price of an enormous skate fish, and second, Alborak's horse made of nickel had not been found for the time being, we pretended as though we were terribly struck by his announcements, I even slapped my palm once, we grabbed our three complimentary tickets from his hairy little hands and pushed through inside. The exterior is not particularly showy, but the Teatro La Fenice simply glitters inside—the gild, the stucco, the decorations!—I am not going to draw all of this in detail, in as much as Monsignore in his infinitely long lifetime must have been within these walls appointed with opulence; between the first and third bell we had walked around nearly all of its nooks in search of our seats, the Respondent continued to eat his sugar-coated nuts, he gazed about all over, as though he were straining to see someone, but the majority of the audience was in quite variegated masks and fantastic costumes, *venite pur avanti, vezzose mascherette,*[2] some Kynokephalos stepped on my foot with his hoof, and then I bent over the Respondent's shoulder and whispered something into his ear, of course, he apologized, our seats turned out to be in the balcony of the fourth tier, this is really high, nearly right below the vault, the Respondent twiddled his binoculars in his hands, if I managed to hear correctly, that Kynokephalos whispered something in his ear like: "He's here look out for the second tier they're here so be careful," again they rang the bell, "be careful, Orpheus," I jokingly said to the Respondent when we were walking up the stairs, because he didn't look down at all and nearly stumbled, on one of the floors we overtook the half-sleepy Casallegra, who, accompanied by two female body warmers, conquered step after step out of breath and did not answer the respectful greetings of acquaintances, just constantly nodded his head, as happens among such old farts, Madame Shalizer, as though she wasn't haranguing us with anything special today, waved from afar at the Respondent and, perhaps, invited him to her private loge, fortunately, the Respondent did not notice this licentious gesture, evidently preoccupied with something else, he was gazing all over, with the binoculars; Dejavu, this time dressed as Harlequin, dragged behind himself an entire Train of Antiquity and Tradition; someone under the guise of a hired killer glided past him, but the Respondent did not notice him; "in 1836 this theater burned down," I said, "but it was rebuilt to its inaugural form of 1792," the Respondent answered this, gulping with a look from behind his glasses along the balconies of the second tier, however our seats were located right above the middle of the hall, they were quite good seats. The Doctor as though by accident sat down between the Respondent and me (I so expected one more meeting with his virtuoso fingers, with this Monti czardas!),[3] below us Alborak Djabraili said something loud about "the rules of the game without the rules of the local police," the ladies flapped their fans, the left part of the parterre below us was completely occupied by the Friends of the Teatro La Fenice Society headed by their female president; quite decisively incited, they had begun to chant something as a sign of protest; through the entire hall a golden cable was stretched at a slope—from one side supported on our balcony, the second end had disappeared somewhere in the drapery in the depths of the stage, I read from the libretto in the program that along this cable, evidently, the "Turkish flight" would take place, several times the name Kulikoff flew through the hall, someone clapped weakly, someone impatiently whistled, the decorations represented everything in the world, San Marco Square, the waves of the lagoon, the Grand Canal, the Golden Palace and much more; John Paul Oshchyrko sat down on the floor in the passageway between the rows of the partere, "they're here!" the Respondent said, tracing his binoculars along the balconies of the second tier, the third bell rang, somewhere to the right of us Andrew Lloyd Webber coughed, from this point they began to turn out the light, the conductor's hands emotionally flew above the pit, thanks to which the overture began, comprising countless other overtures that lay one upon the other in layers, so I succeeded in differentiating at least ten composers, but I surmise that in reality there were considerably more.

With the first measures the Doctor fell asleep, hanging his balding head on his chest and gazing at his favorite fish in his dreams, all around us some kind of technicians were bustling about with shortwave portable radios and in bulletproof vests, some kind of guards maybe; I guessed one of the themes to be that of Donizetti, but an orangeade seller corrected me, whispering "bello Bellini,"⁴ in that case it could have come from his opera about Romeo and Juliet, although it wasn't announced in the program, and I know it just in fragments; the conductor had gotten so wound up from the very beginning that he nearly jumped out of the pit, but, reaching the end of the overture, the orchestra immediately had to hit the floor, since three multicolored explosions occurred onstage one right after the other (the director Kulikoff's find), fortunately, no one was killed or even wounded; this gave the opportunity finally to begin the action: the stage was stuffed with people, the mismatch of clothing screamed with bad taste, the personages of antiquity from Vivaldi, Monteverdi and Stravinsky—in bright tunics—were complemented by Middle Age capes from *Rigoletto* and crinoline from *La Traviata,* some of the actors remained in jeans, other brutes bustled about just in their underwear, and yet others—even without it; all this moved, percolated, and waved, from all directions it was penetrated by underlighting and rays of laser light, above the stage there were luminous outlines of the Campanile⁵ and the towers of the Orologio,⁶ the Syrian columns, a flying lion, an overturned galley, special wind machines raised up the waves of tin water, ships in a small bay cracked and bent, the stage turned together with dancers, the inconsolable Orpheus sang his own aria from Gluck's opera, but in an unbelievably quickened tempo, for it had to be timed to the beginning of the rain, a black cloud, hanging over the Island of Giudecca, poured out onto the audience rain and hail (each piece of hail was made of mountain crystal by Burano artisans, each contained a different painting on itself and there were all together four hundred and forty thousand of them); wild beasts howled in the area of Zattere, but they grew silent from Orpheus's song, the lead performer was quite fat and had short legs, not even the spacious black cape managed to hide the roundness of his gut; the vocal parts performed from the stage entirely did not correspond to the content of the opera, several male and female singers suddenly joined into play from their decoy seats in the partere and in the balconies; in order somehow to hold the action within the shores of the plot's riverbed, the director contrived long and dull recitatives, from which, actually, we found out (apart from the libretto in the program) what was occurring in this mixed-up reality. One must give their due, pieces of various operas were looped one after another quite successfully and imperceptibly, but even to an ear unarmed with knowledge of the art of opera it was quite clear with which open threads all this material was sewn; during the recitifs the audience became inattentive, guzzled Pepsi, and cracked salt pretzel sticks, there were those who were playing cards or dominoes—so as not to permit complete disorder in the hall, the director from time to time introduced a new surprise for them in the form of an explosion on one of the balconies or chandeliers, that from the sky painted in allegories began to fall rapidly onto the heads of those sitting in the parterre, however it was stopped at the last second, about a meter's distance above the heads of the terrified music lovers; "Malibran and Patti sang on this stage," I said to the Respondent in such moments, "and Tamagno," the Respondent added for me, pushing away the sleeping head of the Doctor from his shoulder, in general the Respondent was wonderfully collected and attentive, he almost never tore away from his binoculars, the arias of each of the three officer rogues in turn during the singing competition gave the Respondent the impression of something well known, and, in fact, the first of them corresponded to the aria of Polythemus from the second part of *Acis and Galatea,* the next one was the serenade of Don Giovanni beneath Elvira's window, and the last—the dying call of Simon Boccanegra with Count Enrico's falsetto spatterings; in any case, this was better than the victorious appearance of the fat man Orpheus; right after this a dazzling azure flash pierced the hall, reinforced by the howling of unendurable, but not mythological, sirens, which accompanied an exceedingly long kiss of Orpheus with a beauty Rina who was two heads taller than he; she in fact (one should note) was not really such a beauty after all and her voice could certainly have been better. Instead, the favorite of the audience turned out to be the Inquisitor—you could deny or refute the mastery of his performance, his voice, successfully made monstrous by a synthesizer, recalled horrific croaking and brought a part of the women in the crowd to ecstasy—one pregnant woman even started to give birth, shortly it was successfully completed in the foyer, although the majority of those present were left with the thought that this was the next in turn director's fiction, and the newly born baby—a four-kilogram little boy—indeed wasn't real; the first act ended with a striking choral *murmurando* and with the orchestra's crescendo, part of the audience was already ordering snacks in the buffet, when together with the last measures (Wagner) the curtain fell—a dark green velvet with giant wine and blood stains.

The Doctor remained asleep in his chair, in the meantime the Respondent and I went out into the corridor and, finding a more or less unoccupied corner, began to kiss furiously, we moaned and bit each other, our tongues probed throughout each other's mouths, the Respondent pressed me to the wall, he wasn't wearing his glasses and couldn't see how all kinds of women and men were surrounding us, glaring in our direction, one judgmentally, one with greedy envy, a certain character, dressed as a hired killer, openly looked us over from a distance of ten paces, this gaze so closely attached to me appeared in the least to be shameless, and I shut my eyes so as not to look at this homegrown Sparafucile, nor the hideous Liza Sheila with her camera, nor Dappertutto running back and forth surrounded by his flock of hostesses; we kissed as well as we could—with our entire being, word of honor, this was done significantly better than that Orpheus's licking onstage, our mouths smelled like mint, this was grandiose, like mouth-to-mouth resuscitation, from which you get ringing in your ears and your head becomes detached, and your legs give way, we stopped doing this just after the third bell, barely managing to run to our seats right before the raising of the curtain. The Doctor wasn't sleeping, "I'm not an aficionado of the opera at all," the Doctor announced, "but I really like this thing," soon he sniffled again steadily and deeply, but almost no one paid any attention to this, because the ballet Sexappealer was prancing onstage, and the Orpheus and Rina duet turned out in reality to be a duet of Ottavio and Anna, bulky glass aquarium bowls raised on lances above the stage created a strong impression on the audience, all kinds of living reptiles were in them—crocodiles, toads, snakes, salamanders, iguanas, and others; these great glass vessels threateningly swayed above the heads of the singers, symbolizing, certainly, that danger which the further plot of the opera was preparing for them, one of the female violoncellists fainted during this and they carried her off behind stage, together with her instrument, in a spasm pressed between her legs; she came to just after the next electronic discharge of thunder and lightning with the following shock for the largest part of the audience, the Respondent took off the Doctor's hand from his knee, "this is already too much," the Doctor growled out in sleep, the performance continued, the three friend scoundrels were already duping their courtesan acquaintances, in reality these were no Carambolio, Pantalone and Galileo, as well as no Smeraldina, Clarice and Rosalinda, but Alfonso, Guglielmo, and Ferrando together with Dorabella, Fiordiligi and Despina, and everyone who loves *Cosi fan tutte* could easily recognize this; the left side of the parterre, bought up by the Friends of the Teatro La Fenice Society, ceaselessly protested with whistling and chanting, and the vice president Sergio Cameroni even opened up an enormous umbrella above himself with a circular inscription "Down with Show Business in Opera!" the umbrella was especially noticeable in the cases of subsequent atmospheric shaking; then something awful happened—countless (more than six hundred) semiclad boys and girls were released onto the stage, who, accompanied by a choir of druids from Bellini's *Norma,* began to create a great voluptuous game, each with one other and everyone with everyone else, they interwove together and unwove, crossed each other's paths and squeezed together, crawled and clambered, and also licked, this was some kind of avaricious anthill, a many-membered body, drenched in fluid and tenderness, the choristers barely contained themselves, the Society of Friends first grew quiet, bodily thirst was transferred to the spectators, the auditorium became bloated with moans, shrieks, appealing female screeching, something dully wallowed in the parterre, pieces of ladies' clothing flew from some balconies, the druids further gathered a higher magic force, I barely contained myself, the Doctor's snoring roused me more and more, and everything worked toward the director's conception: lasers, computers, flashes of light from everywhere, three magical orchestras, two thousand living performers onstage and beyond that and three and a half thousand more in the spectator's auditorium—everything, everything, everything worked in a single transport to a communal and grand orgasm, but right at that minute, in the moment of the simultaneous and riotous climax[7] of the episode, the door creaked behind us, turning around I saw the silhouette of someone who stepped onto our balcony, it appeared to me to be the hired killer seen during the intermission, but I wasn't sure, because, I repeat, I just saw a silhouette on the backdrop of the opening of the door, but then something nudged me, forced me to scream "be careful!" and Stakh (crossed out) the Respondent seemingly understood everything immediately: a blade was flying at him, and a bullet released from a pistol, and a cyanide capsule, and a curare-tipped dart, and two big clumsy goons, dressed in the magnificent garments of the hired Venetian killers, snuck up from behind to strangle him with their bare hands or with a silk rope, or with a leather strap, or to slit his throat with a serrated knife, this was his death, I don't even know why, who would need this, they sought him out in this theater jammed with people, followed him right here, where nearly everyone was wearing masks and where countless times they were dying onstage—the Respondent flashed through the balcony with his long legs and, for a thousandth of a second hanging in space filled with sparkling and vapor, with both of his hands grabbed the cable stretched for the "Turkish flight" and then, arching his head back so as not to lose his glasses, and from time to time breaking above the enchanted public below, he lowered himself to set off in the direction of the stage, the projector immediately found him and did not release him, the heroes of massive adultery were already crawling in various directions when the Respondent jumped off onto the stageboards somewhere in the depths of the stage behind the curtains, something thudded heavily on the floor, the audience beat "Bravo!" and three hundred fanfares announced the continuation of the action.

I heard as here next to me, they were gnashing their teeth, cursing and arguing among themselves, they reeked of garlic, sweat, and a mixture of expensive deodorants, from bits of phrases I concluded that they will try to make their way backstage, to finish off the Respondent there, I, perhaps, didn't have the right to do so, but in such a situation I resolved to resort to desperate means . . .[8]

■ □ ■ □ ■

1 7

. . . THAT'S WHY I WORK IN THE THEATER. IF NOT THIS—THEN I'D be selling real estate or raising hens on a farm. But to me it is given to create action. In order to see *everything* or to hear *everything* in my performances, you have to have a hundred pairs of ears. And you might as well have a hundred of any other organ. Because I give a *thousand* parallel actions. At least through their physiology, perhaps, and for other reasons, people are powerless to embrace all this *simultaneously*. Just I on my director's rostrum, surrounded by monitors and mirrors, can embrace—no, also not *all* of it—but, I expect, at least a considerable part—about ten percent or so—of what I myself have intended and set into action. Interesting whether God is capable of controlling the Universe set by him into action to the same degree. [*Laughs.*]

That's why any of the testimonies—of the *eyewitnesses?*—regarding the actions in the Teatro La Fenice on the eighth of March this year at the premier of my show *Orpheus in Venice* can in no way be exhaustive, even my own, which at the same time as this is the *most complete* anyway. I must pause at this episode in more detail because of the fact that tens, if not hundreds, of speculations regarding it have been circulated. There was a particularly big ado about nothing over those two corpses at the finale of the story. For me this already had turned into certain significant unpleasantness, which I don't see an end to even now. You have before you a victim of police protocols and investigatory experiments brought to bay. [*Laughs again.*] It turns out the investigators also have a right to experiment, not just directors! [*Laughs more cheerfully.*]

A certain foundation, about which I had not heard earlier, turned to me with the idea to create an opera for them in Venice. It said, at the beginning of March there will be a certain seminar crucial for the fate of humanity, to which only stars are invited to participate. By the way I note: the stars turned out to be suspicious, because not a single of the names of the participants said anything to me. But this is a trifle. At the same time and *in the same city,* one other extraordinarily interesting activity is taking place—a semisecret conference of the transcontinental mafia organizations, but, as always happens, apparently under the guise of a conference on the battle with the mafia. Ultimately, I won't say anything superfluous—you understand me. [*Laughs.*] For the former and the latter—I have in mind both the seminar and the conference—they propose that I create an opera. I refused for a long time, tied up by several previous contracts in other cities, but the sum of the honorarium was *such.* . . . This in light of the fact that, as you know, you won't astonish me with *any sum.*

I really have grown accustomed to terribly high honoraria. I could have invested them in business, trade in cocaine, for example, or grow pearls in clams. I would be one of the richest entrepreneurs in my field or in many other fields. And finally, I would know quite well what to do with my honoraria for everyday stuff, I could buy diamonds for Alex or an entire park of cars for her. . . . But I am a creature gone astray. [*Laughs.*] And do you know what my honoraria are spent on? On *my very performances*! For every new effect, for every fantastic idea, for every occasion for the sake of your spectator's amazement I will pay with *my own* money. Alex wisely says that someday we'll end up as bag people. When we met for the first time I said it to her this way: "Woman, you're twenty-two years older than me, but always be by my side!" Since that moment we've never parted. [*Lights a cigarette.*]

The sum that they promised me in Venice gave me the possibility to do an opera that *never had been seen* before. And counter to this, I decided to compose it from operas that *have already existed.* In August of last year Alex and I first visited the Teatro La Fenice. All this inner opulence, this gold, these paintings, these carved arcades, the inlaid loges and balconies—all of this Alex recognized as old-fashioned and irritating. I didn't have the right not to respect her opinion. It isn't easy to work in these kind of theaters because of their exceedingly stalwart, stifling atmosphere. Alex and I call these kind of situations "naphthalene." There remained just one out—a complete inner *redoing* of the theater (the funds allotted by the foundation even permitted this). Too much dust had gathered in this velvet over the course of the centuries! [*Smiles wryly.*] I would have agreed to this despite even the protests of this stupid Friends of the Theater Society! In Venice there is such an hysterical collection of all manner of aristocrats that have totally given in to fate. But this isn't important.

We left the theater and began to circle around the city. Only *then* did I understand: everything must remain *as it is*. Yes, for otherwise Venice will not work out! This pretentious collection of objects and luxury. This antiquarian mold and absolute lack of taste. For I truly have not seen a more monstrous city, for you must know me: I particularly seek *monstrousness* everywhere and always. It particularly attracts me and adds at least a bit of sense to my inane ideas. [*Jokes.*] All together—the stench of the water, the scent of the women, the dying buildings, the grass in cracks between stones, cheap hideouts, sentimental legends, each one of which they believe more than the Bible, half-rotted books, watery wines, damp ceilings, satin pillows, bottles of a thousand sizes, pigeons, tourists, streetwalkers, ghosts— this entire mixture lay as an intolerable ballast at the bottom of my future opera, suffocating and humid. I managed to convince Alex. In general she nearly ever meddles in my work. The premier was set *for March.*

I squeezed out everything that I could. My opera was a spectacle so slaying that even Savary with his *Zauberflöte* at the Bregenz Festival can not be compared, and there was something to see there! I played for the whole pot. If I should have suffered a fiasco [*laughs*] in Venice, I would have abandoned the theater forever as well as myself, and the rest of *the days that aren't my own* I would do something completely different, like, for example, selling old skyscrapers or collecting stamps.

I've listened to about five hundred operas. Every day I've walked around, stuffed to the brim with arias and duets, at night I dreamt this all up, I combined and mixed up things, but I don't know what already—whether they were fragments of operas I had heard, or excerpts of dreams I had dreamt. Each morning Alex gave me a single egg in bed, boiled *soft*, and a big glass of orange juice. She checked that *there were no draughts* in the palace we had rented. So that each of my ideas wouldn't fly out the sash window! [*Waves his arms like wings.*] The selection of performers also did not occur just any which way. I looked over and, as they say, felt out several tens of thousands of sopranos, mezzo-sopranos, dancers, tenors, bases, castrates, conductors, pyrotechnicians, programmers, trainers, costumers, choristers. . . . Later there was that awful love affair with Smeraldina, from which Alex simply tore me away. I left those performers for the project who managed to understand *what* I was getting out of them. Although for a long time I didn't know myself what that was. [*Jokes.*] At times I simply went mad from despair. Two thousand people waited for me anticipating their instructions, and I just wanted one thing—to hide my face in Alex's checkered skirt and cry my eyes out. [*Sadly wags his head.*] Undoubtedly in such moments I must have had the look of a real idiot. Just like this! [*Contorts into a grimace.*] On the twenty-first of November I came on the *Festa della Madonna della Salute*[1] and it seemed to me as though I had seen *something*. This meant that I had to begin *everything* from the beginning. Not a single of my previous ideas suited the embodiment of the new concept. Our money was melting before our eyes. Some of the performers betrayed me and switched to other projects. In addition an announcement came from Australia that our house had burned from a lightning strike (I suspect the long arms of the Friends of La Fenice!). And Smeraldina told me that she was pregnant. And before I found my lawyer via Bangkok, and my psychoanalyst via Montreal, Christmas had come, and the entire cast expected me to let them off for vacation. I thought of ending this all in a quite traditional way, but Alex, sensitive in everything that concerns my moods and intentions, managed with scissors to snip the rope on which I had just been dangling, feeling with the tip of my shoe the alluring nothing of emptiness. This happened in the very same La Fenice on one of the balconies of the fourth tier. Later this very episode gave birth in me to the idea of the cable for the "Turkish flight," and from that very balcony I stretched it into the depths of the stage. "You wouldn't dare!" Alex said to me. How right she was!

In about the second week of December I flew to Australia, where with my last money I bought a new house. Alex was *incredibly* happy with it. In addition, it turned out that Smeraldina had lied about her pregnancy—if she had gotten pregnant by someone, then it wasn't by me, but by one of the castrates. Only Clarice could have gotten pregnant by me, but she was silent on this topic, although Alex knew about *everything,* and she had forgiven me.

The conditions were changing for the better, the carnival was gathering swing, I already understood *what* I had to do. Then when Fat Tuesday came on the twenty-fifth of February, my opera happened in *me.* Three days before the premiere I began to produce it in the theater. There already wasn't a lot of time. [*Laughs.*] Just the fantastic piles of money promised kept the performers there. Not everything clicked with the torch lights and displayed decorations. We were two to three canals short for the simultaneous transport of the necessary quantity of old ships. A sea monster, caught on my order in the Bay of Taranto two months ago, broke loose during transportation from Chioggia Island and began to wreak horror in the waters of the lagoon. The authentic Voice of Eurydice, taped by me digitally not far from Delphi in Greece, was accidentally erased by some abortion from the technical staff. Additionally, I became the victim of several adolescent cyberpunks—in the computers a "Paganini" virus created by them spread that devoured nearly everything. As a result of these and many other reasons I was able only to show *half* of what I intended. But this was enough so that at the end of the premiere, when the audience went wild from rapture and demanded my appearance onstage for the seventh time, and from their steady roar, it was not just the Teatro La Fenice that moved and swayed, but also the entire sestiere of San Marco, and Alex, wiping my perspired brow with her kerchief, announced: "I am proud of you, Matt!"

And there was something to be proud of! I was astounding as never before! So much fire, light and water, those favorite of my elements, had not yet been in a single of my performances till now. I overturned boats and burned palaces with a lightning bolt, shot living flowers and dead pigeons from arquebuses and cannons. The explosions occurred not just onstage, but among the spectators, where, lastly, there were several hundred performers seated by me. Every explosion spread in all directions in splotches of honey and wine, and in its spot in the air, there hung voluminous depictions of Venetian landscapes, the heavens, reflections. Half the stage was covered by a tortellini[2] made of actual dough and cut in half. Inside it, instead of filling, there was a thirty-seven-musician orchestra—a *nearly complete* group of strings! [*Laughs boisterously.*]

I must admit that among those three thousand spectators, from which the most honored seats belonged to the participants and guests of both suspicious gatherings, there were very few dissatisfied patrons. There is a certain class of devotees of the opera—all kinds of doubtful aristocrats—who always fly into a rage with everything I do. The voices of the performers were really barely audible, they didn't manage to sing out all the *half notes,* and the orchestra didn't always manage to follow the changes in stage decorations, and in addition, ferociously argued with the main conductor, whose scent of eau de cologne irritated Alex, in his place I was forced to appoint a suitably prepared robot. On the eve of the premiere they shipped him in to me from Japan. Although right before the beginning of the performance, poor *Herbert* had become shorted out, most certainly, the Venetian humidity had made its power fully known. Thus, the orchestra was left undirected. Just for looks I put a spare juggler on the dais before them, whom I asked to wave his hands as energetically as possible, so that those who could see him got the impression that he was flying. But all this angered the music lovers. Even the recitatives written by me, in which so much choice fantasy had been placed, failed to save the situation. In the intermission, I already sensed how clearly it smelled of disaster. Some of those decoys, running up to me after the first act, informed me: grumbling was spreading among the audience, reinforced by the fact that not everyone had perceived the explosions, downpours, the falling of the seats beneath the ground, and the penetrating March wind from the mountains in the same way. I gathered the chief Inquisitor, the chief plumber, the third assistant for flying constructions, and the responsible rosin-master for a short consultation. We managed to begin the second act in a little more lively way, and the blow-up crocodiles, pythons and dragons, skillfully guided by the aid of radio waves, became an absolute adornment of the first episode. It smelled of blood. [*Laughs.*] Mine, too.

The object of my highest ambitions, joys and torments was the grand erotic scene with the participation of nearly all the performers. Half my life I've dreamt of enacting it on one of the world's stages, and now I feared that it could tear the entire fabric of the performance, illuminating it with a premature climax. But Alex said to me: "Do it! Do it or die, Matt!" And she was right.

Right then I undid Rosalinda's corset; she unexpectedly jumped to me between two of her entrances, when I noticed something unforeseen on the eighth screen. A young man unknown to me lowered himself through the entire hall along a cable from a balcony, of the fourth tier, *exceedingly well known to me*. This was not a decoy performer. I saw him for the first time. Here I sent out a radio question to all the assistants and helpers, but no one knew anything. If we had not delayed so, the assistant lighting master would have managed to cut him with a laser. I guess the audience would have understood such an improvisation. But we lost several seconds on fruitless venting. The stranger gathered more and more speed. To tell the truth, I expected that he would slip out by himself—he was carried along above the hall with such whistling, approaching the stage. You never know what to expect from these Italians. I chased away the unhooked Rosalinda and, against my will, gave the order to Orpheus and Asclepio to intercept the stranger when he jumped off the cable in the depth of the stage, and to immediately pass him into the hands of the firemen or the inquisitors. But there was no way at that moment for the lazy Asclepio to manage to run from the makeup room, which you could see marvelously from the fifth screen, the vertically challenged Orpheus so clumsily rushed to meet the flying violator, that running across from the third screen to the fourth, he flew with his chest and stomach at the legs of the latter stretched in front of him. He, right then, just descended down the cable. The collision did not turn out to Orpheus's benefit. He just constrainedly whimpered and crumpled onto the floor. Losing memory and unconscious.

The catastrophe gathered head. Fanfares had already announced it. Besides all the other failures of this premiere, I also lost the performer of the main role. Fortunately, the depth of the stage was draped. The audience didn't see what had happened. I hesitated just for a brief moment, and then gave the command to drag away the big-bellied Orpheus's body behind stage and to try to set him back on his feet. In the meantime, to capture the unwanted performer with the projector and to show him to the entire hall. Let him be perceived as intention, as my intention. . . .

I came to my senses after a good five to eight minutes. The performance continued without any hitches. The orchestra finally caught the right tempo. Orpheus was performing the next of the arias belonging to him. Only this was a *different* Orpheus, a new one. The one who flew down onto the stage from the very top of the arched roof. He entered the reality of my opera just as to his own home. He was easily recognizing the musical phrases and was getting into them without straining. Beyond that, the orchestra began after him. His singing gave harmony to these distinct and egotistical virtuosos. They listened to him and followed after him, as though they were the gentlest beasts. *Where* did he come from?

Now I am already inclined to think that he came that evening to save me. His warm baritone, not exceedingly strong, but very expressive and unique, his plasticity and art of mime, his movements and gestures of the incontestable Orpheus, his ability to orient himself lightning quickly in the development of actions on the stage and to act in the way that my intention and libretto demand, all this became the reason for that almost hysterical success that shook the walls of La Fenice and the entire *sestiere* of San Marco immediately after the final chords of my opera. [*Crosses his arms on his chest.*]

He was the first who introduced *soul* into this mechanical performance. I am nearly sure that he is a real Orpheus. For I tormented myself for too long to summon him from nonexistence. But from my torments *he* appeared at the most difficult moment, my materialized dream, my Venetian madness. Right now it already seems to me sometimes that it had been *my* intention all the same, that from the very beginning I had planned to do this. Perhaps Alex suggested it to me.

She and I stepped out seven times for ovations. Flowers were strewn from every direction. Even they, those intolerable degradations from the Society of Friends, applauded me. Wiping my perspired brow, Alex said: "I'm proud of you, Matt!" "Otherwise I'd be busy doing something else," I said. "I'd be collecting old cars. I'd be selling decorative trees." We wanted to find him and bring him onstage. He was sitting in the wings on the step of a cardboard palace and was wiping the moist lenses of his glasses. "That was fantastic, sir!" I gave him my hand. He put on his glasses and, perhaps, recognizing me, answered nothing. "We want to invite you to our place for dinner," my quite practical Alex said. "Unfortunately, *another* supper awaits me," he answered. And we understood everything. They were really expecting him somewhere else. The Olympian gods at their banquet, for example.

Something entirely different than this, I understand, interests you. You still regard me an accomplice to those two corpses found after the premiere in the vestibule of the theater, one on the left, and the other on the right of the entrance. What, I'm really an accomplice. [*Laughs.*] Every good artist is an accomplice to situations invented by him. Imagine this throng, this audience of several thousand, in masks, covered with gypsum and ceruse, in clothing from various times and lands. They go crazy over my performance. This is something on the border of psychosis. This is my victory over Venice. And if someone's heart doesn't hold up with this, and he falls under someone else's legs, then reckon that he had bad luck for the last time in his life. And I don't see anything mysterious in this. Even if those unlucky guys turned out to be two. Even if both of them appeared in the clothes of *hired killers*. Am I right? . . ."

(Reprinted from the book *Mister Shock: Five Monologues of Mathew the Frantic.*)

1 8

NO, I DIDN'T SENSE, I DIDN'T SENSE ANYTHING—ONE SHOULD USE A considerably less sensible verb here, we don't even have such a one in our language. What lay before me? The abyss of the hall, filled with pyrotechnic flashes and the projector's aureoles. A gold cable that offered the opportunity for escape.

They could cut through it or finally untie it. Just then, when I jumped up on the handrail of the balcony and, grabbing it with my arms and legs, I moved forward and down. They could cut through it with their cutlasses, which they carried on their belt, as though they were real hired killers. I would clatter down from under the very ceiling, from under the stucco, the paintings, from under the chandelier, onto the heads of the monsters sitting in the parterre. I would surely make some big noise and rattling. I would have shattered ten or so bodies. And I would have splattered all of myself throughout the hall. But they didn't touch my rescue cable.

I ended up in the garden. I was lying in tall grass, resounding with cicadas. I recognized several of the grasses by odor, others I didn't know at all. I looked around in every direction—all around there was a stone fence overgrown with greens. I rose up and lay down again: the gate screeched, the two appeared in the garden. I recognized both of them: the first—tall, massive, gray, and the other—dressed as a servant, with high receding bald spots, cringing, like a dog.

I hid behind the white pillar of an ancient platan.

"Explain already," the first droned.

"I found out about everything, lord." The second bowed down his head.

"About what?"

"The foreigner, who has so interested my lord, is called Orpheus. He has come to us from quite far away, if I'm not mistaken, from the island of Lesbos or from some other Greek island. In his time he has played for the pagan gods at banquets, achieving wild success in deportment with the most varied musical instruments, as, for example . . ."

"Enough!" the gray one interrupted him. "I know all this."

"His concubine, according to other versions, his wife, was bitten by a snake while gathering berries in the July grass. Today she dwells in the underworld kingdom, as we say, in hell, without any hope even of purgatory . . ."

"Enough!" the gray one again interrupted. "I know all this."

"Then my lord, perhaps, in no way knows that the above-mentioned Orpheus is fully undergoing accusations of sorcery and witchcraft. About him we know that with the help of his diabolical harp[1] and pipe playing he is able to calm the wildest of animals, and the hyacinths and cyclamen bloom from his voice in the gardens of spring—just like these here that spread in the garden of my lord . . ."

"Enough!" For the third time the gray one snapped and distrustfully scanned the garden, but didn't notice me. "I even know this!"

"Lord, I am in difficulty and hard pressed." The cringing one was perplexed. "Is there anything in God's world about which my lord would not know?"

"Ha-ha-ha!" the gray one victoriously exploded. "That's it, good-for-nothing. I have eyes, ears and noses everywhere! I feed my spies with raw meat, and for that reason they rush to investigations. My agents are everywhere and vigilant: they sleep with you in your beds, they listen to you from your pots in the kitchen and observe you from your cesspools. They are capable of crawling inside you and reading everything that is written here in the most secret of holes and depths! . . .

No one anywhere will escape me.

I know what and where and whom to burn.

Though I'm silent, I'll wring your necks!

And I'll burn your asses with a poker.

And I'll screw off your whatevers!

the gray one finished with a song.

YURI ANDRUKHOVYCH

192
▾

His servant, having understood the insinuation, totally trembled and, with chattering teeth, hastened:

"But I venture to guess that not everything till now is known to our dear lord. Rina. . . ."

"Rina?!" the gray one roared.

"Rina, to whom I am assigned with the aim. . . ."

"Rina?! What Rina?!" The gray one raised his fists up.

"Rina, to whom, with the clearest agreement of my lord I am in the role of a most obedient slave, scorned and vile, ordered me to find the just mentioned reprobate Orpheus, for she would have fallen head over heels for him. . . ."

"Rina?!"

"Rina, who has red hair and a fiery soul, as well as alabaster skin and a birthmark on her left buttock. . . ."

"Rina?!"

"Yes, and she has invited the above-mentioned vagabond to her place for dinner, to the Palazzo Azzo, tomorrow, at midnight, my lord. . . ."

"Oh no!" The gray one wrenched his hands in despair. "You're lying, vile bastard! Anyway, you fear me too much to be bold enough to lie to me. . . . Oh, Rina, Rina! . . . Have you really thought to do this, my girl? Has not my love and my ardent intercession before all the powers of the earth and heaven changed your childlike and pristine, your female soul? Oh, woe to me that I so fell in love in my declining years with this harlot, this hooker, this whore!

Oh woe, woe—what abyss
Swallowed me on this day!
This slut Rina tore apart my soul!
What the hell, what the fuck, why?!

She tore apart my soul, stole my heart.
What will my answer be?
Like rain crying, I'll cry: "Rina!"
You are unfaithful, so you must die—

singing the rest of these tragic couplets, the gray one wasn't able to stop his tears that began to flow from him in two bitter streams. The servant cried with him.

"So, ne'er-do-well," the gray one finally began to speak after blowing his nose. "You will relate her invitation to this wandering clown. You will convince him that he must come to her. After all, he is thinking only about this right now! I saw how they were kissing! How long this shameless, this greedy, this precious kiss lasted there in the fourth tier! He wants her! She wants him! Ha-ha-ha! They'll have each other!" And the gray one rubbed his hands.

"But lord," the servant snorted, "why drive the matter to their union? Does my lord not have sufficient grounds—the serving of pagan gods and the devil, sorcery, debauchery, drunkenness, spying for the benefit of Genoa, perhaps sodomy—doesn't my lord have sufficient grounds to immediately take the good-for-nothing *pagliazzo* under arrest and, driving him away with brine-soaked branches along the Bridge of Sighs, to pack him away in one of the famous *piombi*[2] beneath the hot tin roof, where his vile skin will peel off his villainous bones from the death-dealing scorching heat?"

"Be silent, fool!" the gray one scolded virulently. "Your advice is good but one shouldn't listen to it! Regarding this swain I have somewhat other intentions. Ha-ha-ha-ha!"

He clapped his hand and, the cringing one, bowing every moment and smiling obsequiously, moved away backward. Just exiting beyond the gate and sitting on his boat, he began a song, of which I managed to hear only the first couplet:

What vile torment—the splitting in the soul!
One born in hell does not reach virtue.
I'd live in nature, I'd write poems,   ⎫ 2 times
If not for you, my love, if not for you, my Rina. ⎭

In the meantime from the opposite gate a certain character entered the garden, similar to a gorilla and completely spattered in blood, with an immense rusty cutlass, jammed behind his multi-colored Turkish belt.

"You've come?" The gray one looked at him.

"As you commanded." The spattered one flashed his single eye.

"Well. Come a bit closer. Stand here. Fie, how you stink of death!"

"I just finished off a certain fencing teacher at the behest of Signore Pezaro and his family," the long-armed one explained.

"Well, fine, fine, turn this way. Stand against the wind. Good. Now pay heed to what I say. . . ."

But after these words the gray one began to speak so quietly that I wasn't able to hear a single word. Even after I stepped from behind the platan, which was such a cozy shelter for me and stopped next to them. I saw only how the bloodied one from time to time nodded his long unwashed head, obviously agreeing with the whisperings of the gray one. Finally the latter finished and, reaching to the slit in his baggy robe, he pulled out a taut leather pouch that clanged pleasantly with dinars.

"This is a down payment," the gray one said and slapped the dirty one on the shoulder, and then he quickly went offstage.

I hid myself behind the tree again. My soul became cold and anxious. And the long-armed one, ominously stamping and dancing, in his angry falsetto started singing something like:

All the living have a right to goodness,
Everyone knows his paragraph and column.
Just I alone—a knife in the ribs!
The wretched and unlucky Sparafu . . .

All the living have a nice trade—
One disposed to plants, another to stones.
And I am just—a walking slimeball:
Rub out, snuff out—and amen!

All the living have the sun and a window,
I only have a screw loose cause I'm nuts;
Cause I'm such a dung and fated
To circulate among the dead and living.

The singer should be very careful now,
Putting the harp and strophe aside.
A single knife into the chest—and the corpse
Into the water! And a curse on Sparafu!

PERVERZION

The one-eyed guy danced to the end and then expressively and distinctly uttered, "So tomorrow. Tomorrow at midnight."

He laughed loudly and ran offstage. I sensed unseen motors beginning to work, plungers moving, a little garden with cicadas collapsed right before your eyes, the stage began to turn.

I ended up in the cramped subfloors backstage.

"Are you ready? Your entrance is coming up right away. The night visit of the palace," some mistress of ceremonies dressed as the Dogess told me.

A bunch of the performers in magnificent garments were trying to revive some big-bellied man in a tunic who had lost consciousness. A lyre trimmed in gold leaf lay next to him on the floor.

"Finita," Asclepio ascertained, checking the pulse of the guy.

All kinds of Sailors, Monks, and Spirits were scrambling all around, in makeup and not too much, several were running onstage, others were returning from it, someone was avidly drinking a black liquid right from a bottle, some swindler Castrate right away was feeling up two ballerinas in the corner.

"Are you ready yet?" the Dogess repeated. "It's the third act right now. Without an intermission. And you haven't even put on your armor! Here it is!"

She showed me the costume room where two costumers flew at me right away—one ancient babe, another—nearly a child—and they began to hook onto my chest impenetrable convex armor. Their hands were practiced and quick. In a minute I was already not only in armor, but also in an incredibly wide dark red cape, although, as much as I remember from the libretto, the cape was supposed to have been black.

"Here, here." The Dogess led me through the backstage labyrinth. "There, behind this curtain. Are you playing in a production for the first time?"

I nodded my head. "In this one—for the first time."

"Don't be afraid. It'll all be okay." She winked. An old dust-covered Italian woman. "Well, onward! *Buona fortuna!*"

But right there she grabbed me by the sleeve.

"Stop! What, you're without your sword?!"

I spread my arms apart.

"A sword for Orpheus, a sword!" She began shouting, and some fat little boy dressed as a dwarf, rolling toward me gave me a sword.

"Go now," the Dogess said.

All around me there was night, pitch-dark night, I stood above an unknown canal and tried to remember where the Palazzo Azzo[3] was, where I had been invited. From the mountains a cold, gusty wind blew. Hail sprinkled from the sky and knocked onto the tightly closed window blinds. I covered myself more tightly with the cape and moved toward a solitary light that shone to the left of the bridge I had noticed.

I had no doubts—I was standing in front of the palace that I needed. I rang the large ship's bell hanging in front of the gate. In the peephole someone's bloodshot eye appeared. Then someone opened the gate, and I stepped inside.

I hadn't even managed to shake off from the folds of my cape the big hailstones that were as large as crow's eggs, when I heard awful stamping and rattling. Right at me, running down the steps, some kind of big clumsy goon with a bull's head on his shoulders. From his inertia striking me with his horns in the chest, he, evidently, expected easy victory. But my armor, fortunately, held up.

"Oho, bully!" I shouted and again received a blow with the horns.

This time I failed to keep my feet and fell backward. But when the beastie came at me the third time to drill me through while I was lying down, I managed to turn and meet him with the flawless prick of my sword into his heart. The monster began to roar with its entire stout long-armed body. I rose up and placed the tip of my sword to the "bull's" throat. The malefactor snorted and thrashed back and forth; finally, he tore off the bull's head by the ring in his nose and flung it far to the side.

"I knew, I knew that you would be victorious, foreigner!" He snorted. "This vile life had to be torn asunder at some point!"

"Who are you and why did you attack me?" I asked imperiously.

"I am Sparafucile, a hired killer," the scoundrel said, oozing thick black blood. "All of Venice knows me. I've killed people not for the sake of evil, but just for money. It's not my fault! This is the Inquisitor, this is all the Inquisitor! I implore just one thing of you, foreigner—forgive me if you can! . . ."

And he intoned a sorrowful aria, from which I remembered just the penetrating and pathos-filled finale:

Oh, how am I to be forgiven
For everything I've done, for everything I've striven,
Will no one in this world be able to forgive me?
I'm dying! My black blood is pouring out! . . .

"I forgive you, in as much as this is in my powers," I said, listening to the truly touching melody till it ended.

"Then slit this throat with your weapon, foreigner, and put an end to my suffering," the killer Sparafucile joyfully laughed.

I was just preparing to do as he asked, but noticed that even without that, he already was no longer breathing. The stage crew dragged him backstage to the roaring applause of the hall. And I ran up the steps, from where quite appealing, fiery music was playing.

There a noisy party was going on with dancing, ardent Venetian melodies alternated one after another, but this did not gladden me until I saw her. Was she really there at all? At times it seemed to me as though I recognized her features among the masked dancers. They called me to them and asked me to dance with them.

"Who are you looking for, darling?" One of them breathed into my ear when I put my hand on her turning waist.

"The one like her, Rina!" I answered.

"You don't need to look for her. I'm Rina," she showed me the tip of her tongue.

And really, this could have been Rina. Because I never saw her without her mask. And anyway, how could I be sure if this was she? With my lips I found her lips. Her mouth reminded me of a flower. It was sweet and stupefying. With her tongue she was doing impossible things. My eyes grew dark, but not for a second did I believe that this was Rina. I recalled that kiss, it was different. Then I forcibly tore myself away from the temptress and chased her away.

"My love, how good that you are remaining faithful to me," a different mask began to sing into my ear, "I'm so happy that you haven't forgotten your Rina."

"Soon we'll feel," I decisively said in response instead of "soon we'll see," and once again lowered myself to meet the fragrances of the two maiden's lips opened just right. It was like a goblet. It was unforgettable. So much submissive tenderness and ardent self-sacrifice was quaffed by me from that goblet, so much select honey licked from the moist walls of this cave by my tongue! It was as if I had fallen under ground, but I was utterly sure of the fact that it was not Rina. That's why I finally chased away that liar from me.

"You've worthily endured my examination, my dove," a third mask rustled into my ear. "I was making certain that you love your Rina. . . ."

Her corset for some reason was badly tied, and she did everything she could to take me to oblivion, but she smelled too strongly of wine and some men's eau de cologne, and her mouth was open like a wound, and all the same I was soaked in her kisses, her sucking, her burning, subduing myself and my forced arousal, I separated myself from her, but all the same this was not her, Ada. Or maybe Rina?

All three maidens, somewhat angry at me, circled around and began to sing in their licentious soprano voices approximately like this:

You just look—here is a Lovelace!
And each one of us would give ourselves to him!
Further away from such a Lovelace,
Who kisses the soul out of us.

Girls, don't believe singers!
They just have flutes and music on their mind.
They play bows! Our poor virtues!
Don't believe them, O sisters, woe to you! . . .

But I didn't have the time and desire to listen to them to the end. I quickly walked from room to room, examining out of the corner of my eye the beautiful furniture, rugs and paintings, stopping sometimes, to drink a goblet of wine and always in new company and again began to search, past the portraits, *portchaises,* canopies, wardrobes, cages with singing parrots, chessboards, tapestries, oboes. In the furthest of the rooms I finally stumbled across a single tall skinny guy with bald patches, whom I had already seen today. He was holding an empty goblet in his hand and, examining me through his Venetian glass bitterly sang an aria, the beginning of which I didn't catch. But inside was the following:

Die, Asclepio, unworthy
of love, of happiness, of pity,
No one needs you anymore,
You didn't say "My Love"

To the lovely Rina, for whom you
Could give your life. But now
Ask repentance from the hemlock!
Why haven't you died yet?!

Fall asleep, Asclepio, fall asleep. ⎤ 2 times
You won't see spring again.   ⎦

"Where is she?" I interrupted his singing, for the matter wouldn't wait.

"Oh, how far away she is!" The bald guy sighed. I knew her when she was such a little girl. I used to buy sweets for her and peach-flavored water from an old Albanian, when I strolled with her to the Giardini Pubblici. . . ."

"Where is she now?" I insisted.

"In any case, she isn't in this arbor where I used to bring her sherbet, back then in the summer, when days at a time she sat there in her little straw hat with enormous brims to keep from getting sunburned. . . ."

"Is she at least here, in this house?" I glanced in his eyes, becoming more and more glassy.

"She's here. And not here. She's with me. And without me. I'm without her. I feel like sleeping. I want to have an eternal dream about how again and again she captures a butterfly on the steps of the San Gregorio Monastery, just like fifteen years ago. Or plays on a lute in the Ospedale della Pieta orchestra. Or eats grapes, tearing off each berry separately with her tiny fingers. With her tiny fingers. Tiny fingers. . . ."

"Tell me at last where to look for her?" I raised my voice. And this seemingly led him to consciousness.

"They abducted her! Just you, foreigner, just you can manage to catch up to her, if your pagan gods will help you in this. These thrice-damned villains, Carambolio, Pantalone, and Galileo, abducted her at the order of Monsignore Inquisitor and right at this moment are taking her along the Grand Canal to carry out a vile atrocity. You can catch them, you'll still catch them, foreigner! . . ."

I understood that his death was already quite at hand, and he, probably, will be not able to finish the aria interrupted by me.

In addition it was necessary to catch up to the boat of the abductors. Therefore I rushed away from the palace, and in my footsteps the final words of the dying Asclepio gushed forth:

O Orpheus, eagle, defender!
The one who has ruined himself
Now is pleading passionately
That you believe him and forgive.

Fall asleep, Asclepio, fall asleep. ⎱ 2 times
You won't see spring again. ⎰

I don't know whether my constrained shout reached him from below: "I forgive you, Asclepio!"

In the wings it smelled of perfumes, sweat and apparently garlic. The Dogess pecked me on my cheek and praised me for my good performance. The dwarf was running around and screaming for them to set up a sailboat quicker.

"How is that poor fellow?" I asked about the little potbellied guy in the tunic.

"He's already better," the Nun answered with a bowl of blood in her hands. "They just bled him."

"Two men were just looking for you here," an athletically built Moor announced.

"I thought they were ours," Smeraldina added. "But everyone's saying that they're not ours. They're somebody from the audience."

"Today you won't be able to figure out who is from the audience and who is ours!" The Dogess flicked her hand, wiping the sweat from my brow with her scarf. "The boat is ready. Your entrance, Orpheus! . . ."

The waves of the Grand Canal beat the sides of my light rowboat right and left. The weather really was not the best for a chase: a heavy wind from the mountains, perhaps, a mistral, smashing on the marble walls of the palaces, whirled in the canal as though in a canyon. Dirty salty splashes fell on me from every direction, and my glasses were even dripping water.

I caught up to them right between the Corner Palace and the never completed Venier dei Leoni. I managed to latch on to their bark with a grapnel, and with difficulty keeping my balance from the swaying, jumped across to their deck.

"Ha-ha-ha-ha!" The most impudent of them, Carambolio, began to laugh loudly in my face, pulling out a stiletto with a poisonous blade from his belt.

I, however, wasn't about to wait until he set it into action. Putting all of myself into the strike of my right foot, I just managed to see how his good-for-nothing body plopped overboard and in an instant went to the bottom, leaving behind himself just a three-cornered hat, which for yet a certain amount of time was carried by the waters of the canal from the walls of one palace to the other.

"Here is death for you!" Pantalone began to scream through the wind, but I was the first by my sword, and the lopped-off head of the wretch fell at my weary feet. I had the least problems with the third depraved one: having seen the fate that had befallen both of his cronies, Galileo pulled a flint pistol out of his trousers and without any lengthy hesitation discharged a bullet into his brow. His stupid brain flew in every direction like bird excrement.

But Rina! She was nowhere to be found. I was certain that I would find her on that boat. And what of it?

"It's futile, Orpheus," the lopped-off head suddenly began to speak. "It's futile. She's not here." The head frowned contritely.

"And what do you want to say by this?" I asked harshly.

"Just what I said," was the answer. "Rina, ah, beautiful Rina, how she loved life!" The head let out several hot tears.

"Finish saying what you have to say!" I shouted. "Finish saying it, vacuous egotistical blockhead, you dead head of cabbage, you bellfry with bats!"

But instead of an answer the head began singing:

Like a tiny fish, nimble and supple,
She freed herself from us squirming and darting.
And she took a dive into the canal,
Although we shouted: "Wise up, bitch!"

Why does a poor head have to be lost?
Why, foolish ram, must I die?
For two legs, for two tits, for two
Eyes of the blackthorn that pierced my soul?

My lost soul, fly off,
Uncaptured by earthly lanterns.
May the Venetian silence of silences ⎫
Meet you beyond other shores.   ⎬ 4 times
                                        ⎭

I saw a large blow-up doll. The murky waves of the canal carried her toward the lagoon. She was held up on the surface just on the parachutes of her countless skirts. I lowered my hands. I had grown weary. I recognized that gray shadow on the water. I was carried away into the open sea. I passed the Treves Bonfili Palace and Santa Maria della Salute with the customhouse.

And the voice, the voice, I recognized it, too, Her voice, through the wind and storm, barely audible, far off, from the other side, She was saying something, repeating something, it seems, my name, but which of my names, I have forty of them. I would have fainted if not for an explosion, the great explosion of the finale, from which the theater was to be spread to a hundred thousand little theaters, this explosion blended into the final chord of all thirty-three orchestras, I would have fainted if the curtain had not fallen. . . .

I didn't come out onstage anymore, although there was an ovation. I sat on a piece of waxwork stone and waited until they came to get me.

■ □ ■ □ ■

1 9

WHAT DID THE VENETIAN PRESS WRITE IN THOSE DAYS?[1]

About politics, sports, the economy, and the weather. Great changes were foreseen in all these fields. Everything concerned prominent disturbances, especially in the weather. The meteorologists recommended getting raincoats and stilts ready.

About the solitary and unknown horse that appeared in Cannaregio, then in Dorsoduro, then in San Polo, then in the area of the Arsenal. His horseshoes echoed in measured clopping on the oldest cobblestones, on the most distant meshes of streets and alleys. Sometimes he appeared on bridges. Tourists fed him sugar and marmalade, and the Venetians—young grass. Someone tried to capture him, but in those cases he began to move faster, shifted to a trot, and soon disappeared from the field of vision of his persecutor, knowledgeably maneuvering in the capillary wickerwork of old Venice. That is how the version was born about him being a ghost.

A lot has been written in general about ghosts lately.

About the tragic death of the thirty-four-year-old trumpeter, in the flower of his strength, Giuseppe Antonio Aldrovandini, who, returning from sensational reveling, ergo, being quite unsober, one night in 1707 fell into the canal and drowned.

About the brazen robbery from the Sansoviniana Library of a very rare and attractive volume—a collection of frightful stories and horrific retellings *Hypne-rotomachia Poliphili,* written in the *koine*[2] and published in Venice by a certain Dr. Franciscus Columna in 1499 (the printing house of Aldus Manucius).

About the conference covered in secrecy and devoted to the war against the mafia. It went on exclusively at night and was protected from unfamiliar visitors with a triple guard. The place of the conference was different each night, although one can be nearly certain that the previous meetings were in the Ca' da Mosto Palace, known also as the Hotel Leon Bianco.

About the attempt being readied on the life of one of the foreign conference participants, as per rumors flying around. He must be an extraordinarily significant personage in his country, since not a single attempt to determine anything concrete about him led to anything good for those of the reporters who tried. Last night one of the most intrusive reporters even had been beaten by cudgels on the twisted steps of the Contarini del Bovolo and was pushed down from the noted steps. All the attackers were cursing, as much as the guy being beaten up understood, in Russian.

About the colorful blade who arrived by ship from Egyptian Alexandria and for the third night had been amazing the public in the winter casino of Vendramin-Calergi, making incredibly high stakes time after time. The results of his unusual gambling talent already were one suicide (*luminal*) and one family poisoning (according to other versions—a family insanity). As concerns the young Baron Barbarelli, he has just been transported to the King Umberto Psychiatric Hospital, and only time will tell how deeply his high-born and noble soul has been traumatized by the sudden loss of all his lands and family's valuables.

About the unqualified success of yesterday's premiere in the Teatro La Fenice and the fantastically successful director's contrivance, the replacement of one of the performers in the lead role by his antipode in the course of the very performance; the appearance onstage of a little known novice in the role of Orpheus at first gave birth to a certain skeptical misunderstanding among the exacting audience. Then the distinct organicity of the performing method of the latter, the expressiveness and refinement in each gesture or bend of the head, the decorous vocal gifts and his top physical shape provide all the grounds to affirm the appearance of a new star on the Venice opera horizon. The director of the performance, unfortunately, refuses to give the name of the novice, obviously tying up with him some distant plans for productions.

About the two dead men found in the foyer of the Teatro La Fenice right after the end of the boisterous premiere. The identity of neither of them has been established. Both came to the theater in past centuries' costumes and black masks. Traces of violence were completely absent on both of them. Leading court medical examiners consider the death of both to have been a heart attack. It was interesting that no one of the several thousand in the audience who had left the theater through the foyer had noticed even one of the dead bodies at their feet. Perhaps the impression from the stage action was so intense that any kind of appearances of reality simply was not accepted by anyone seriously. It might also have been something else: the bodies were noticed by the majority of theatergoers, but evaluated as the gag next in turn of a director bountiful in imagination. The previous investigation of the decedents leaves the impression that neither one of them is an inhabitant of Venice or a citizen of Italy. Both of them belong to a highly conspicuous Turkish or Persian type, and a certain sign, linked to the appearance of their childmaking member, permits us to suppose that they belonged to the Islamic tradition.

But in those days the press wrote not just about this.

About the intention of the greatly respected professor of thanatology and carnavalistics, the eternal Venetian Leonardo di Casallegra, to abandon Venice forever in the nearest future. One can only guess just what the praiseworthy elderly man has in mind with this expression—"abandon." One wants to believe that it in no way refers to his own death. The newspapers submit that on the decline of his lengthy years filled with complex searchings, the professor was having a harder time enduring the capricious Venetian climate, that the all-pervasive dampness affects certain unexpected mutations in his organism, and Signore Casallegra needs to change his permanent residence immediately.

About an entire series of completely unexplained phenomena and occurrences, which, during the last days and nights, grew more frequent in various sections of the city, after all, sufficiently used to all manner of strange things. So, a certain inhabitant of the sestiere of Santa Croce, who wished to remain nameless, after the ebbing of the water in turn and a corresponding lowering of the water level on the wall of his building, covered all over in mollusks and algae, noticed a certain blood-red inscription in letters unknown to him (Sanskrit? Hebrew?). The inscription was swallowed by the water during high tide, and with the next low tide it no longer was there, an ill-defined ochre drawing had replaced it, which generally recalled the outlines of a fish skeleton. The same way Mrs. F, a housewife, an inhabitant of the sestiere San Polo, recounted the appearance of certain ghostly lights in the adjacent long-abandoned building; over the course of the entire night unknown but extremely suspect subjects carried off their boats and dragged to the above-mentioned half-demolished hovel countless suitcases, traveling bags, sea lockers, smaller boxes, and other caskets that looked like coffins. Yet another mistress, this time from the environs of the Vecchio ghetto, Signora Galuppi, was complaining about intolerable feline concerts. At that time of the year it was a quite natural matter. The entire unnaturalness lay in the fact that the word "concerts" in this case is used literally: the feline playing was not simply occupying the surrounding roofs and terraces for the love games of March—all the way till daybreak they really were ecstatically playing music, using the strangest instruments like a *torban,* and their solo singing in turn recalled the best vocal parts of Giuseppina Pircher; the strangeness, however, did not end with this, because at the same time as the feline music was playing from all directions, an unpleasant odor moved in furiously, to put it more accurately, a stench, which penetrated the houses through the walls and the cracks in the plaster; the scent, in some way close to the miasma of a sulfuric spring, disappeared just with the morning consummation of the feline roulades. Besides this, there are several testimonies by women about the appearance of a nocturnal satyr on Giudecca and near San Trovaso, who was depositing his excrement all over, ecstatically laughing and keeping people from sleeping. Some have been confusing him with a maniac who had escaped a few weeks ago.

The account of a seventy-year-old drunkard Pietro G. is especially noteworthy; while wandering home from the restaurant Da Ivano, obviously, between the hours of one and two in the morning, he observed on the Piazzetta, between the columns of Saint Mark and Saint Theodore, yet a third column, incontestably the very same one. By morning once again there were two columns.

They also wrote about the fact that the third and next to last day of the grandiose seminar "The Post-Carnival Stupidity of the World" was coming up, conducted with the participation of celebrated intellectuals on the island of San Giorgio Maggiore. In conjunction with the seminar's program today, two concluding lectures will resonate—that of Mr. Tsutsu Mavropule, having arrived several days ago in Venice by ship from Alexandria, and that of Ukrainian poet S. Parafinsky, the author of five collections not translated into a single other language and three or four doubtful concepts that will be declared in his lecture, the title of which is being refined.

What didn't any of the morning papers recount?

About the exceedingly obvious love affair of the above-mentioned S. Perforatsky with his translator Mrs. Z. (by other sources—Mrs. A). About the mysterious plans of Dr. of urology Mr. R., the husband of the above-mentioned Z. (A?). About the strange character who is masquerading as a Kynokephalos, that is, a Doghead. He always appears not very far from the twice-mentioned S. Preferansky. About the light that wasn't turned off till morning in the hotel room of the latter, and you could see this not just from the Accademia bridge, but even from the windows of the Genovese Palace, considerably farther away.

About the nocturnal rustling and muffled sounds, and the splashing of the water.

■ □ ■ □ ■

2 0

SO IT ALL HAPPENED, CAME TRUE, WAS FULFILLED—TSUTSU
Mavropule! At 9 A.M. in the corridors and halls of San Giorgio
monastery, above the island by the same name and the entire
lagoon, his deep, reverberating voice was already echoing, from
time to time reinforced by the laughter of a cannonlike clamor. He
still wasn't visible, but Ada already knew that he was here and let
Stakh know: "Mavropule."

He truly recalled a drunken Noah as he leaned against the
Palace of Doges. Gray with the mightiest lion's full black head
of hair, disheveled every which way, a beard, uncombed for a
hundred years; if you so desired, you could find countless tiny
objects, blackened teeth, used to chewing up lamb thigh bones, a
checkered linen shirt, a grand and nice stomach, gold rings, chains,
ringlets, earrings, bracelets, scales along his entire body, hirsute
ears, eyes black as a pit, the scent of sweat, wine and onion reaching everywhere, and more than anything else—the voice, the
voice of some prehistoric pagan god, the master of the bowels and
heights. Tsutsu Mavropule recalled Saturn, who ate his own
children.

He embraced and kissed everyone coming across his path, press-
ing them to his stomach so strongly that their ribs cracked. He
appeared first there, then here—with a goblet, a canapé, a pipe,
from everywhere his frenzied laughter rattled, the hostesses
squealed, whose bottoms, judging by everything, he was constantly
pinching, Liza Sheila literally tickled to death, poured out after him
in a murmur, even Dappertutto didn't look like such an incontro-
vertible, as always master of the situation.

Then having caught sight of Ada with Perfetsky, he spread his claws to half the room and moved toward them.

"Ho-ho-ho-ho!" He greeted Ada and raised her on his hands high above his head, and then, putting her down, he squeezed and licked her for so long, that a storm nearly was evoked inside the faintly smiling Perfetsky.

"I believed, I knew, and I expected: we'd see each other!" Mavropule roared in not too bad English. "What's new, daughter?"

"Get acquainted, Tsutsu," Ada answered. "Mr. Perfetsky from Ukraine."

"Ho-ho-ho-ho!" Mavropule pealed volcanically, shaking Stakh's right hand. "Is this him? This is your Perfetsky?! I'm very happy, very happy! *Ochen rad!*" For some reason he translated the last words into Russian, and then, leaned toward Stakh's ear and, sensitively touching him with his pockmarked tongue, roared so loudly that everyone within six paces heard him: "I expect that you haven't been wasting your time for nothing with this lovebird, hah?"

After this he started laughing again and smacked Stas on the back with his big paw.

"And what's this to you, you big elephant?" Perfetsky answered smiling, but in any case, in Ukrainian.

"I won't, I won't get in the way of two hearts in love!" The big thug answered, and, winking in turn to each of them, but with different eyes, he left, engaging someone else at once.

In about a minute his colossal howling reached them from yet another spot.

"Now I understand why everyone was talking about him," Stakh said.

"You still don't understand anything," Ada mysteriously responded and moved to her spot in the translators' booth, because Dappertutto, appearing on the podium, suddenly announced the next day of the seminar and summoned to his lecture, the topic of which does not submit to formulation, the fervently expected by all and at last safely arrived dear Tsutsu Mavropule, fire swallower and Bessarabian-Transylvanian prince.

This announcement forced the audience to sit down around the library table and gave the newly arrived lecturer a downpour of enthusiasm.

Stas was moderately struck by the fact that after yesterday's devastation by certain invisible waitstaff, they had managed to bring an ideal order and luster to the building: all the books were in place, broken inkwells and spittoons had been replaced by new ones, even more ancient, and the quantity of globes and astrolabes had even grown. But all these appropriate observations didn't exceedingly bind Stas's attention: a certain new problem had enveloped him with an impenetrable wall and kept him from concentrating. Perhaps it was worry just before his own lecture, from which so much depended?

And Tsutsu Mavropule, with microphones stuck at him from all directions, plaited all over with ropes like Laocoön, in his unnatural voice began reading the text, the title of which did not exist in any human language.

"The essence of my appearance today," the great heresiarch filtered each splash of his rumbling, "lies in the acknowledgment or lack of acknowledgment by you of certain criteria, for which the caravans of days and nights have already been stopping. To acknowledge these criteria one can either completely and totally, or partly, either not acknowledge them at all, in no way and to its entire extent. In the first case we have what has caused the infamous opposition of the superhard metals to other natural phenomena already known by you from previous lives, as, for example, the striped representatives of the feline family. This became possible only in combination with further occurrences of the civil code. In two other cases the transition from nothing to an egg will arouse your anxiety anyway in a longitudinal slit, through which the personal agents of new copulation are not guaranteed always or everywhere. I would at least like to rely on rookeries, in as much even the minimal approach to a fading telegraphic style does not bring anything more than bean pods. On the other hand, the continuance of any one of us in the state of postbirth psychosis itself drags the renewal of grape (gastric) juices and the impeccable exhaustion of all the suitable centipede members for this, true, with the adherence of several mysterious directions concerning the expansion of borders of the newest parastate mechanism to the west and to the moon at the same time. Among other decisive parameters I will also name the depth of the location of vegetables, the temperature of the roads and the height of soaring of the first spring comets, if such a height can be accepted by us as constant. Now, coming out of sketched preconditions, from which the greatest meaning does not have absence or all the same the omnipresence of dead points of dew in the general scheme of the use of hot dishes, but—I ask you to take note!—only in the case of hot baths can we cross to the recognition of ordinal numbers of their completely established vegetation. I say "vegetation" and see smiles on the faces of many of you. True, in this context one can yield that the stream of consciousness of the Alamanni long ago has left the boundaries namely of the rice biofield and become a negative aspect of woodworm processes, in connection with which it would be much more expedient to speak about the "effect of middle-ear ultraviolet." But I ask you not to forget with this that the coefficient of participation of tomatoes to the turning blue of extreme flesh can in no way be compared to the beginning of an important dialogue regarding the regulating of external blood pressure on the underwater irrigation system of coordinates of the surrounding environment. In this way, with all boldness we can make the first far-reaching generalization: the presence in the cape pockets of turtle eggs does not obligatorily cause a worsening as dreams in color themselves, as their material proofs! . . ."

The unseen secretariat worked faultlessly. Mavropule's lecture, printed on the whitest paper, lay before every listener. It was translated into the Italian, French, Arabic, Albanian, Japanese, Sorbian, and Bengali languages. However, you could not understand it in any language. Although each one in the auditorium gathered all of themselves to grasp its content, which was truly important, and who knows, perhaps, even sacred. From time to time Liza Sheila flashed the lecturer an okay sign. Alborak Djabraili, who spent last night in the prefecture, slept and had a dream in which he was rushing on horseback on a flying jumping steed from Mecca to Jerusalem and back, ultimately, it seemed to him at times that this was a ride through the city on a bicycle. John Paul was here this time, he didn't set out on distant journeys, but listened quite attentively, just from time to time quietly uttering "*bloodclot.*"[1] Gaston Dejavu, for the time being Restraint-in-Evaluations, all the same pretended that he had been understanding nearly everything and even had been differentiating certain humorous notes in the flow of the heresiarch's dense speech, deeply hidden from the understanding of others—that sly smile of his large red lips, that wouldn't leave the powdered white and the red paint of Gaston's face, served to witness this. Finally ancient Casallegra. He, perhaps, for the first time over the course of these days did not doze off during the recited lecture. Quite contrary—with extraordinary civility for his age—he listened, from time to time approvingly nodding his head. Both his female companions had stares that burned with open lust—they gazed at the monumental Mavropule, at his shaggy Minotaur head, at his hirsute chest that bulged out of his low unbuttoned shirt; their mouths were half gaping and yearning.

Stakh Perfetsky looked over the table. This was one of the wonders of the library, memorabilia of olden times and the present. In the thirteenth century artisans from the island of San Pietro first made it. This occurred after a well-known earthquake, as a result of which the monastery was forced to be rebuilt from scratch. At the same time a great amount of furniture was ordered for it. The table carried the imprints of all times and strata, through which it had flown its seven hundred years. First of all, it was made of various pieces of wood, fused together in various epochs and in different ways. Today one can say that this lengthy oval monster, at which you could easily sit from fifty to eighty people, made of beech, ash, African ebony, yew, boxwood, and sandalwood, encrusted with mother-of-pearl, but in spots with ivory and dragon's teeth, although at first the table had been considerably smaller in size and destined for tarot readings. Along the edges the table was held up by four legs, each one of which today looked different. The first was four-sided marble, on which there was carved out an endlessly long string of bowmen who were riding on elephants and singing some kind of battle song. This leg was brought from the ruins of Carthage sometime in the seventeenth century. Of course it was significantly older than the table itself. The second was round in shape and came from an unknown country to the East from the island of Caucasus. It was made of the polished horn of a giant aurochs, stoned and shot to death by cannonball during one of the expeditions of the seafarer Alviso da Mosto. The third one was a copy of the Tower of Babylon, made of the petrified remains of an eternal fish, caught a hundred years before Columbus in the Danube delta. And just the fourth leg, the furthest from Perfetsky, was the only one of them retained from the original table, that is, made by artisans from San Pietro out of beautiful fumed oak, which nothing ever would have been capable of harming.

In the middle the table was held up by two additional pedestals, quite probably of extraterrestrial origin, both one and the other were covered with allegorical carvings, and today used for a technical purpose—the sockets for connecting the headphones and Dictaphones were located right inside them. The table top with its layers generally was very dark and rough. But within the boundaries of his comprehension, Stakh Perfetsky managed to read something on it, something distant and past. Amid the traces of this past Stakh noticed several deep blue stains, unequivocally a blueberry ink, put there by the inexperienced transcriber of books Fra Michelino during work on the later canonized text of Jacopone da Todi's *Stabat Mater*—the young monk, perhaps, was really nervous, first dipping his quill pen like a good spear in the thick blue abyss of the inkwell; right here several dark brown stains, which with equal success could have been the blood from the nose of the eternally sickly librarian Fra Amadeo (fifteenth century) as well as the carelessly splashed leftovers of an incredibly sweet malmsey, which abbot Benedetto used to abuse while sitting over a good book or philosophizing in the company of three icon-daubers—Titian Vecellio, called Titian, Jacopo Robusti, called Tintoretto, and Doménikos Theotokópoulos, called El Greco. There also were someone's tears (eighteenth century) dried up on the pockmarked surface, and also a Latin poem scratched out with a shard of an empty green bottle of a cabernet, that by all signs of language and style had come from times in no way later than the rule of doge Gradenigo (1289–1311); in Stakh's approximate translation it sounded like this:

. . . for which tortures and bitter vexation
if I knew it wasn't in vain and there'd be no regret
to be madly in love to lay down my head
but to steal a touch of Rosalba's bosom . . .

You could read much from this deep surface and its annual philosophical rings!

And the unsolicitous Mavropule subsequently did his own thing, "I will move on to the accounts about something more well known and known to many," he continued. "In '38 I noticed that the inclination of an Abyssinian ambassador to blank verse poems had not ceased to amaze rat catchers caught red-handed. From everything it flowed out that the diapason of the glimmering of the doors at seven-eighths is not capable of being the subject of parliamentary listening and gradually turns into a classic chimera for the raking out of trash. Thanks to this, the possibility of acquiring an eternal pen prompted me to an examination of several buttons and minerals, from which, I underscore, there wasn't a single one like its own reflection in milk and especially coffee crockery. This circumstance could not help but lead to the fact that the abiding of the president of Sweden in the soul of the then autopilot stretched beyond all measure. Taking advantage of this, macaroni disappeared without a trace, and dirty wash appeared long deprived of any kind of author's rights. This could not suit either the Ossetians, or more so the ship builders, the result of which any kind of citrus hint at the beginning decisive reforms had been accepted openly as hostile in the lower corridors of the duodenum and met with furious resistance among the orthodox partisans 'on the sly.' Such a situation had to be marked on the quality of telephone conversations! In relation to this, that a nearly critical level of extraatmospheric precipitation on the damp heads of newly appeared fanciers of the Western Hemisphere of last year went beyond the level of sound of the composite orchestra of mathematicians, the next action failed to find anyone suddenly, although the conclusions of the philatelists were somewhat distinct from oranges. The action, about which we are now speaking, so that it would be more understandable to you— this is the complete accomplishment of the process of larks' survival in the conditions of essentially quantitative (it's still far from the qualitative) transition through the collaboration of third cock crows with Mexican cactuses. It's enough even to describe all the results of the above-mentioned cataclysm! First, for once and for all the music lovers were spurned and the Museum of the October Copulation was remodeled into the residence of the archbishop of all foreigners. Second, exaltation far from stability appeared in pyramids, to which not a single of the existing hellish substances succumbed. Third, every attempt of the Turkish security minister to place a limit on the perpetual growth of strawberries led just to the next outflow of prostitution and seafaring. And, finally, fourth—although I could count to the "tenth" and to the "hundredth"—the chain of consequences stretches without end and has had no borders, so here, fourth, the close to the truth pseudotheory of the Mongoloid (read: colloidal) origin of butterflies and electric light switches was destroyed forever. . . ."

"Something's not quite right," Stas Perfetsky thought, "something's wrong with my English today! I can't comprehend the direction of this big oaf's thoughts in any way. That's the kind of day it's been!"

And he managed to reach the headphones with synchronous translation and there he heard Ada's voice, and that voice, unequivocally, was directed just at him, at Stas Perfetsky, for who else among those present could understand her: ". . . so I don't know, I don't know what we should do further, but you already can't mend what's happened, I wanted to avoid this, but it's happened, it's happened. You'll forget me completely in two weeks, well, it'll hurt a little bit—and you'll forget, I know, every day you're in love with another woman, but me, what can I do, won't you tell me? I've cared least about myself, but I never think about myself, I was born this way, in love I have to take it to the end, to the final sob, you know? You won't even think about tomorrow, maybe it's our last day and we, I'm sure of this, never anywhere anymore—do you hear?—never anywhere, it's as if we'll die together this way, but for some reason it just hurts me, I feel just like scratching the walls from all this, and you just listen, just listen to the lecture, satisfied, smiling, you're always smiling like a Japanese. I would rip up this smile of yours from ear to ear so that you'd walk around like this forever, because this from your side, my jewel, is too cruel (how do you like the rhyme, poet?), it's too cruel—always to walk around with a smile, when I'm nearly agonizing here as the slave of your penis or of something else, the brow above your left eye, for example, how can I know? . . . I'm cheating on my husband, I'm sinning for you, and you just smile, you haven't even said a nice word to me, just quotations and word play at every step, word play and quotations, and some kind of stories that I don't want to know, some kind of allusions to what I don't know. You'll soon return there, to your home, to Ukraine, again you'll end up near your friends and lovers, so, and you'll have a lot of everything, and. . . . But I, eternally alone, am alien to each and everyone, what I recall of our six-day love, besides this smile of yours, with which you, maybe, even sleep—I don't know, because I haven't seen you sleeping, I haven't slept with you! . . . Did you at least once say something warm, tender, alive to me? I haven't asked for too much, I simply thought that you needed me—not less than I need you, but it doesn't happen that way, love isn't equal, love is inequality, one has to give more, and the other just takes, takes, takes. . . . Sorry."

"That's not true!" Stas shouted from his seat, and everyone looked at him, understanding that he disagreed with the lecturer's last assessment, which was about "the causing of agrarian abundance to the samurai of the first type caused by the catastrophic absence of the latter in the upper regions of the atmosphere."

"That's not true," Perfetsky repeated already more quietly, almost in a whisper, when everyone began to hiss at and shush him. He could have refuted very much of what Ada had said, he was quite different from what she imagined, because he knew how to love not less devotedly, because all of Venice had become a witness to his love, and no one ever had loved with such persistence and courageous hopelessness, as he, Perfetsky, no one had ever loved this way for over a thousand years. But Ada's voice in the headphones kept him from answering anything, to retort, it was as though she had gone to another circle, again repeating that he had a smile on his face, like a Japanese, like a Japanese, like a Japanese, then he had to take off the headphones, smiling.

And then an episode occurred, which all kinds of eyewitnesses often recalled contradicting each other.

Tsutsu Mavropule, the bare-chested potbelly with the head of a fairy-tale giant and the teeth of a cannibal, the fire swallower and unacknowledged academic, suddenly began to choke on his own language, the words crawled back into his wide-open gullet, some unknown power crushed his throat, he turned crimson and convulsed, and someone else, in a completely different voice, squeaky and grating, began to speak from him, from his maw: "Listen to me everyone! I am the spirit of Bakhafu, and I am twenty-two and a half thousand years old. I was born in Mesopotamia of the four-winged demon Patsutsu and the goatfish Sugur-mas. The last five hundred years I have been a fly and have been slumbering in a droplet of amber on the shore of the German Ocean. From there I was finally called at the will of my highest master! I turn to you, brothers and sisters: awaken from your sleep! Awaken and go forever to the flowering garden of ours and your sovereign!"

After these words it was as though he had become stuck, the way sometimes an old worn record gets stuck, and in the room for several minutes there reverberated an incomplete "ve-reign-so," "ve-reign-so," "ve-reign-so."

Finally Mavropule, on whose mug the sequence of the fierce duel was painfully reflected, stifled this rebellion and chased away the shameless voice somewhere to an unreachable depth. The audience, for a certain time dumbstruck, exploded in joyous applause. The drunken Saturn bowed in all directions, dangling his beard and curly locks.

"He's here," said Leonardo di Casallegra.

"He's everywhere," Dappertutto added, lighting up a cigarette.

"One more speaker," Ada hmmmed from the booth.

"One more—that's me," Perfetsky failed to understand her.

■ □ ■ □ ■

2 1

ΥΖЫΑ-ДҌ

To the attention of Monsignore—the text of the talk, given by the Respondent at the seminar "The Post-Carnival Absurdity of the World: What's on the Horizon?" on March 9 this year in Venice. The Respondent's presentation began at 11 A.M. and with a brief break lasted until 12:23.

Cerina

I

Dear ladies and gentlemen! My task is not one of the easiest, and not without grounds I am abundantly fearful that I will be unable to manage to deal with it as one should. And the fact of the matter isn't that I don't have anything to say. It's all just the opposite—I have so much to say about everything in the world, that the rest of the time allotted for our seminar wouldn't even be enough, but also not even, I venture to assure you, the remainder of the days and nights allotted by Providence for the human race. And all the same with importunity, worthy of better and more realistic application, I throw myself at these windmills in the hope at least of somehow making you aware of something.

I've come here from a country about which you know either very little (calling it either Ukrainia, or Urania, or Ukrenia), or nothing. Those of you who know "nothing" truly know much more than those who know "very little," for the latter know just distortions and mutilations. I will be quite happy if I am fortunate enough to correct a few of the distortions and mutilations, and for those who till now know "nothing," to give luster in the form of "something." I imagine this is important not just for me.

But how should one embrace the unembraceable? From where, for example, should one begin? From the egg? From the first day of creation, "when just the Holy Spirit flew above the water?"[1] From the Neolithic abodes of the primordial people? Perhaps from paradise lost?

I'll begin with a lost manuscript. This happened to me about seven years ago when, just having graduated from the university, I was hiding from military service in the Red Army in one of the Lviv garrets. Lviv—that's the city from which I came here. In Italian it might be called Leonia, and in Sanskrit Singapore. This city is nearly nine thousand years old, and it lies in the middle of the world. Of that Old World that was flat, that was perched on whales, turtles, whose most distant region was India, on whose shores the waves of either the Nile or the Ocean broke.[2] Surely that's why so many madmen and fantasizers live in it, each of whom is exceedingly convinced of the fact that he, indeed, is the center of all the world's processes. Besides this, Lviv has its own demons, its own ghosts, its own genies. You could write a separate book on each one of them, something I'll do someday. Finally, I must say that it constantly rains in Lviv, from which the garrets smell of elderly ladies and decayed flowers.

Seven years ago I had been hiding out in just such a garret of a certain well-known political activist who, at that time, had been working as a bartender in a coffeehouse. The coffeehouse was located on the first floor of the same building as my garret, and the building itself was from those dark times, about which we cannot say anything for sure other than they just happened to have been at one time. Concordant with one assertion, this building had already numbered a good five centuries and at that time had been part of a fortress wall. Concordant with another—it had been erected during the Austrian changes and a filial of local psychiatry for especially gifted patients had been located in it. Concordant with yet another—the building had really been ruined in the 1930s, that is, under Poland, and today only its semblance existed, not lastly for preserving the activity of the conspirational coffeehouse, where three times a week artist-avant-gardists, prisoners of conscience, and deserters like me used to appear for secret meetings.

Out of a great and constant love of old objects, and speaking sincerely, out of boredom, I began to sift through everything that I came across in that garret. Unable now to do an overly detailed enumeration, anyway I'll mention birds' nests, a music box, garters for stockings, glass jewelry, unglued artificial eyelashes, the neck of a mandolin, a collection of gramophone records, and a lock of someone's gray hair. I also can't be silent about an abundant collection of old Habsburgian Sezession pornography on fragile yellowed cards, on which the models of that time, as a rule, turned their large naked bottoms to the observer, acutely recalling young hippopotami.

I, however, have digressed, because I'm supposed to be talking about my country.

Thus among other things that I found in that secret haven was a thick, homemade book, copied by hand on over seven hundred sheets of various—from crayon to cigar and even toilet—paper, sewn together, tied with string and numbered, and also covered in the remains of covers of other books, in particular, an apocryphal Gospel of Adam, a black magic Andalusian treatise "The Indestructible Loins of Fecundity," and the memoirs of an Austrian cavalry general von Böhm-Ermolli.

The manuscript had been written by one and the same hand, but in different languages: the most numerous were fragments in Ukrainian, but sometimes when the author lacked a particular term or something else there, for example, certain idiomatic possibilities, then he shifted to Polish, German, Yiddish, several ample passages had been written in Armenian, there is also a fragment each in gymnasium Greek, Gypsy, Turkish-Tartar, Old Church Slavic, Karaite, and Genovan. There wasn't a single fragment in Latin.

All this together had a name from which not a single one of you will smile on hearing it. The author aimed a blow at everything and called his fundamental work neither more or less *The Eclipse of the World.* We will still return right away to the person of this brazen one, but for the time being I must say a few sentences to relate the fate of the manuscript itself.

To my great luck, it was mostly summarized by me in hours of the night and day of sitting in the above-mentioned garret. But, to great misfortune, one day in late autumn of that same year the underground secret abode was cut off, the coffeehouse closed, and I was forced to relocate to a reserve hiding place—the tower of the train station. After several months, returning to the old place with a single aim—to carry out the manuscript—I found it burned to a crisp. It fell apart from the touch of my hand, and I wasn't even able to gather up the remains. Someone had been there in my absence and had destroyed the only evidence of a great and unusual soul.

I have here in mind the author of the manuscript. His name— Yaropolk-Nepomuk Kunshtyk—was noted on the title page. With the aid of not all that burdensome research I managed to clear up nearly everything about him. A student of philosophy and law, from childhood he was gravely ill with consumption. The son of a well-known government official in Lviv, with whom, however, he breaks off at the age of seventeen. About the mother—a single fact was known—that her father's maid could have been she. In 1909, not having yet reached twenty-seven, Yaropolk-Nepomuk dies, having left for us the manuscript of *The Eclipse of the World*. A fate typical for young intellectuals who have appeared on the borderline of two centuries. Consumption, decadence, debts, Nietzsche, tragic love, misery, books, distress, an early death by one of two kinds— consumption or suicide. . . .

Today I intend to tell you something about my country, based exclusively on the notes of Yaropolk-Nepomuk Kunshtyk. There are several reasons for this. First, I do not consider my own views as particularly new or more interesting. Second, the legacy of Kunshtyk looks exceedingly appropriate namely for our time while we are approaching a certain horrific point of instrumentation reading— the chronological mark 2000. The author of *The Eclipse of the World* sensed this nearly as strongly as we do: his century also fell on a serious threshold of the system of chronology (the beginning of the twentieth century). And third, namely to him, to Kunshtyk, one of my favorite assertions belongs, which is formulated this way: "Truly no reality exists. There exists just the boundless quantity of our versions about it, each one of which is erroneous, but all of them, taken together, are mutually contradictory. For the sake of our salvation it remains for us to accept that each of the countless versions is the true one. We would do this if we were not sure of the fact that the truth must be and is a single one, and its name is— reality."

I would want these bitter and wondrous words to serve as an epigraph to my further exposition, which I ask you to accept exclusively and only as a collection of certain judgments, that in and of themselves are not true and do not even correspond to the truth, but quite self-sufficiently they are its, the truth's, versions.

2

Next I will begin with things which, although they externally appear the most objective, in reality always are perceived with the greatest doubts. I'm talking about history and geography. It would seem that nothing might be truer than the judgment "River N. flows to Lake P." or "The battle between the Arnauts and Atlantians occurred such and such a year?" But try to rely on these judgments as one should, and you will hear the loud catcalls of the audience, for each one present has their own view on these rivers with battles. And such a view is determined—as in any other, so called science— by the point of observation. For what is the Far East to a Japanese?

The country from which I peregrinated is determined from the east to west by four large rivers—the Don, the Dnipro, the Dniester, and the Danube. Each one of these names echoes with the Sanskrit root "dana," which signifies water. One wise guy, somehow having heard this from me, cunningly frowned and asked whether I really know Sanskrit. I answered him that, unfortunately, no, but when he uses the word "clitoris," not for a second do I suspect him of a knowledge of Latin. Having dealings with separate words, we almost never know a language as we should. But this is already a passing observation.

Determined by these Four Rivers, my country, then, from time immemorial has had its most fatal problems with its geographic location. The essence of them lies in the fact that this land is mountainous and hilly in the west and northwest, forested and swampy to the north, abutted to two relatively warm seas to the south, thus it would be a completely normal European exemplar, well, at least just a bit too large—if not for the east—the northerly, the southerly, and simply the east: the steppe, the plain, the field, Asia. The battle of these two, or more precisely, two hundred and twenty-two geographical tendencies, has defined the entire dramatism of our situation from the very beginning. Where Europe was just beginning to arise, to grow, to be constructed, at that same instant Asia revolted, demanding the establishment of its despotic and simultaneously anarchic status. At this moment I am not saying that this is bad. But I am just saying that this is its essence, and this essence vehemently contradicts the other essence—the European.

Therefore any kind of stability, constancy, and endurance in the conditions of this land appear quite hazy and indistinct. Some kind of mysterious autochthons in actuality had grown grain on it and had worked metal already three or four millennia ago. But what else do we know about them? The temptations of archeology remain temptations—all the same you won't find out about the main one. What do I have to do with a beaten skull and to bones painted red? I want some text, and not separate signs. We know much more about foreigners, nomads, intruders, as well as specters similar to them instead of about the autochthons. Let's look deeper into this carnival of tribes, each of which from time to time proclaims itself to us as a forefather, and each of which in truth is not, but all of them together actually poured their nomadic blood into the veins of the nation, to which, it seems, I also belong. It is best to seek depictions of them in the literary monuments of the distant ages, all those capital accounts of Herodotus, both Plinys, Strabo, Ptolemy, Ovid or the bit later—Ammianus, Jordanus, Procopius, Pseudo-Mauricius, or even the Arabs like al-Mas'ûdi or Abu 'Amr, in all these beautiful ingenious inventions that with their truthfulness are able to debate perhaps with the testimonies of Saint Augustine about his trip to central Africa: "Still being a bishop in the town of Hippo, with several slave-Christians I started off to Ethiopia to teach them the Gospel of the Lord. There we met many men and women, who had no heads at all, their eyes were located on their chests, all their other members were identical to ours." And we have no bases not to believe him! These "other members" that are "identical to ours" exceedingly allure us!

Ancient Ukraine is a no less fantastic space than the Ethiopia described by Augustine. Sufficient at least would be a passing enumeration of all these inhabitants of the field, forest, mountains and waters. The Cimmerians, cloaked by Homer in the fog of *The Odyssey;* did they exist, you will ask—did Homer exist, I will ask; about Cimmeria we only know the fact that Rimbaud considered it "the homeland of fog and whirlwinds"; the Scythians, who are the direct descendants of Hercules, or Zeus himself, and therefore live in felt sheds on carts; the Isedonians, who drove away the Scythians from above the Caspian Sea; the Arimaspians, who drove away the Isedonians, just have a single eye in the center of their forehead and eternally do battle with griffins for gold; the Taurians, who have bull and goat heads, and the Neurians, each one of whom once a year over the course of a day turns into a wolf; the Amazons, who do not have a right breast to shoot better from a bow, and the Sarmatians, whom these Amazons gave birth to after widespread sleeping with the Scythians; the Androphagi, who eat human flesh and do not recognize the truth of any laws; the Amadoci, who also eat human flesh but while it's still alive; the Melanchlaeni, who dress only in black; the Saudaratae, completely identical to the Melanchlaeni, however, according to other sources, are more inclined to the Iazyges, the Saii, the Thisamatae, and the Roxolani; with the latter you shouldn't confuse the Rheuxinali or the Rosomoni, nor even moreso the Coestoboci, who were renowned for their robberies in the Balkans, as a result of which they are compared to the Bessians; in the meantime the Carpi gave the name to the Carpathian Mountains, although at that time these mountains were named either the Peucinian or the Caucasian—to each their own; the Agathyrsi, who sang instead of spoke; the Dacians-Showers-of-Airs and the Getae-Immortals,[3] who truly understood the mystery of eternal life and therefore the majority of them are alive to this day; the Bastarnae, from whom the Goths developed, the Sciri, Heruli, Rugii, Vandals, Taifali, Gepidae, the Urugundians, also known as the Burgundians and other bastards; in their place the Huns spread out, who came from the nonexistent deserts where they had slept up to their necks in sand, afterward they went into the nonexistent forests, where the wild greenery hid them; along the road to the west they vanquished all the other nations that they came upon, including the Fanesiers,[4] who lived on an island covered by water today in the Sea of Azov, they were thirty feet tall, had marble white skin, and such large ears that they could totally shield their bodies with their ears in bad weather; however, there were too few of them—eight in all. After the Huns the Kutrigursand Onogurs swept through on steppe mares, although others say it was the Unugurs, Utigurs and Unugundurs; the Antae, also known as the Veneti, or to be more precise the Pelasgians, rolled through under the name of the

Etruscans here, to the north of Italy, although I don't have preten-
sions to the fact that Venice may have been an ancient Ukrainian
city; however all this turned to dust after the invasion of the
Avars, after which there stretched again and again in streams of bar-
barians all kinds of Bulgars, Khazars, Black Hats, Karakalpaks, Obri,
Ugrians, the Pechenegs, the Kynocephalians, the Cannibals, and
Polovtsians—and not any of the earthen defense ramparts could
save from onrushing Asia these languageless, mysterious and still
unnamed autochthons, with whom we finally emerge out of nonbe-
ing somewhere in the ninth century, when a flock of Scandinavian
easy riders decided to unify this voiceless society, all these Derev-
lians, Dulibians, Krivichians, Drehovichians, Ulychians, Tivertsians,
Polianians, Croats and "White-eyed Chuds" into a single state,
headed by them, that is two or three Norsemen, tenacious drunk-
ards and robbers, who didn't even know a word in the local language, and who called themselves the "Rus." The last condition,
perhaps, impelled the autochthons to recognize foreign rule over
them.

What did these people, generally called the "Slavs," look like?
Light-haired and physically not badly cut out, with light skin that
easily burned in the sun, they most struck civilized foreigners first
and foremost with their slovenliness. In Procopius we read that the
Slavs sleep and eat in dirt, like cattle, and not just any kind, and Ibn
Fadlan writes of merchants of Rus, who, over the course of a week
washed up ten at a time out of a single bucket, without changing the
water, blowing their noses and spitting. It's a small consolation—if
such disillusions require any kind of consolation—there are echoes
of the very same educated and well-washed Arabs about other peoples of the European Middle Ages (so al-Qazwini says about the
Germans of that time, that "there is nothing dirtier than they are,
they wash once a year, maybe twice—and at that—br-r-r-r—in cold
water!" and Ibn Rusta, after meeting with the Vikings, pronounces
that "rarely will you see such handsome people, but at the same time
they are stupid as asses, and stink from a mile away"; I suppose that
for a contemporary Swede or a Norwegian these observations could
be quite unpleasant).

What can you do? A hundred something tribes had arranged for
a perpetual carnival in our genes.

And why just in genes? Do we not believe in other things less palpable? In these energetic draughts between the centuries, in this uninterrupted sowing of auras through all of space?

I have become used to regarding difference and complexity. Right here, today, before you [*the Respondent looks at his watch*], I am forced to recognize in myself—in more or less measure—a Taurae and a Neurae, a Saudaratae and a Thisamatae, a Bastarnae and a Vandal, and Androphagae and Pecheneg, and perhaps someone else, a Gypsy, a Jew, a Pole, and it's entirely not out of the question, a *Dovhan.*[5]

And now, my ladies and gentlemen, I'd like to request a short break.

■ □ ■ □ ■

2 2

YOU CAN REALLY GO NUTS LIKE THIS—DOWN THE STEPS TO THE corridor on the right—not stuff too much in your pants cause everything'll slip out—and I gotta finish my lecture—all this is ridiculous—what situations crap carries me to—either die or take a shit—such a bitch—a bummer and that's it—I'm to blame myself—I'm sick of myself—a bit of a schizo—if only something'd stop me—slip fall break my leg—talk be quiet talk again—now it looks like it's to the right—yep—there's a certain corridor—let's a let's a keeler boy—we've been sitting in this monastery for a week and if only just one monk'd be praying by the window—or wacking off—nobody—which window there is the third huh—from which side is it the third—aha this—even better open like we arranged—all's kleear—veerdohs eeen akshun—pretend like I'm breathing the sea air—a little queasy—barf or what—instead of a shot—ah, what air—I'm freakin' from the landscapes—the killer was an aesthete—what's going on with our little carrying case ha—there, it's a really light little case—here this way we pull out our little pigeon—our little swan—and how do you say *glushitel* ["silencer" in Russian] in Ukrainian—*zahlushnyk* or what—and what's ass in Polish—that's also nice—I screwed it on—raally raally raally nice—right now ven vee shoooot—aha, here we'll brace the tripod—and hautoMATically—like the drill sergeant says in the joke, if your mother's a whore, then you're a sonofabitch hautoMATically, so shoot hautoMATically—how's Venice there through a scope—to draw a bead on eet—looks like it's steaming out—eleven thirty-nine with a millimeter accuracy—don't forget about the gloves later—the corpse into the water as a certain happy Venetian once said—and how is this thing in their language—*fucicare*—somehow that's not it—*fucilare* because a rifle is *fucile*—a rifle or a rod—a rod or a rifle—what's the diff—in Ukrainian *fuzeya* and that's it—or a cannon—so they've turned around the cape—first ship second ship—in a straight course here—to Canale di San Giorgio I guess—they're floating away floating away—Stenka Razin's boats—float little swans—float—that it was written there to breathe the air in or what—shoulda gone to the army—and not goof around coffee-houses—eef your a *mon*—and eef not then right between the eyes—this technology's a bitch—if it's the optics—I seez everything just know dat—optics for synoptics—we won't touch the first boat it's a nice one—float, float my little boat—along a pretty golden moat—boat number one, and the second boat—I'll nail your golden throat—complete schizophrenia—they're floating along not too badly—with champagne on the lower deck—or maybe the name of this thing isn't a deck—it was a deck it'll be your final wreck—the deck of the sky burns to the sunset—a genius and evildoing—my own biography by my own hands—we'll let the first little ship pass and we'll cheerfully greet the second one—well what—vere ees our deear guy—if he'd just be sitting there without lollygaging in front of the mirror—if only he knew—if only a man would know where he'll fall said a certain old Galician high schoooolteacher now deceased—is that so—he and no one else—he—of two opeenions to kill ees not—what an ugly kisser—an ordinary bandeet—interesting but the funeral will be at Baikovy—they'll take him in some refrigerated truck—a shot through side of beef—and who is this—this is "kevin costner"—his personal "kevin"—a bruiser the way it should be—well a bruiser where your intuition is—for what do they pay you moolah—well good—momma I love a sniper—say a prayer kiddo—ten—nine—eight—seven—six—five—three—why three—four—now it's three—two—one—amen—

   that's it—I'm done—and you—you thought that I'm—well well—then you thought that I'll—I'll shoot—well you're a real scumbag and already—how do you take this thing off—does it screw off or what—aha, right—so I should wave my hand to him—let's a let's a—float shit float—I won't kill—I don't kill people cause I've got a soul[i]—bye-bye.

YURI ANDRUKHOVYCH

3

I am happy once again to see your attentive faces. I am left to continue and finish my lecture.

Movement, incessant movement, black holes of entire centuries, abysses in memory, the absence of form and hierarchy, plasma, fermentation—this is what falls into your eye while diving into the depths of the earth, about which I had begun to tell you. From local and foreign chronicle writings, at least those, which have remained safe and sound in the conflagrations of a thousand and one wars of all times—before the Mongols, during the Mongols, and after them—from songs, legends, myths, and other beautiful nonsense, or better to say—versions (for that is what we agreed) there emerges an image of a land incredibly more chimerical than the India or China of that time. The swords of comets eternally cross above it. The processions of corpses emerge from underground burial places in the light of day. Calves are being born with eight legs and dogs with two heads. The churches are sinking beneath the earth, and in their place black lakes appear. Dry winds and whirlwinds are rising to the sky and carry off entire cities together with gardens and buildings somewhere to the abyss of Tataria. The figures of the Lord's crucifixion at the crossroads are themselves turning their faces to the west. And it's not strange: this land does not know the Lord's laws, for it has been abandoned by God.

But at the very same time how bountifully it has been favored! From the "Treatise on Two Sarmatias" such riches arise before us of a virgin nature, that the allusion to Biblical milk and honey begs involuntarily. "There are so many fowl that with spring the children fill boats with the eggs of wild ducks, geese, cranes, and swans. They feed dogs with the meat of wild animals. The rivers are stuffed with an unheard of countless number of sturgeon and other great fish, which come from the sea to the surface of fresh water; the river so fills with fish that a lance thrown into the water gets stuck and juts out, as though it had been hammered into the earth." The Wild Field, that beckoning terra incognito of the Ukrainian South and East, attracts newer and newer pioneers into its fatal expanses—something like the American Wild West over four or five centuries.

The grass there is taller than a horseback rider. The oaks are ten thousand years old—you can carve out an entire ship or a palace from just a single such tree. Half-imaginary aurochs, buffalo, and antelopes with golden horns and diamond hooves in a giant fearless cloud push from border to border of this borderless plain. In burial mounds heaped up to the sky sempiternal sorcerers, dreaming in expectation of the X-hour, guard countless treasures. But in the winter all this disappeared beneath the snow. So much of it falls that, just like the grass in summer, it is capable of covering a mounted warrior. With the spring these snows melt and for two or three weeks flood the entire surrounding plain. Then the local inhabitants float out into God's World in their boats and throw out their fishing nets, with the help of which they capture a great amount of all kinds of things: quail nests, Roman coins, mammoth tusks, the skulls of unknown monarchs, from which the mirthful nomads used to drink wine.

Of course such a land could not help but pull in numerous flocks of especially colorful people from various berry fields and lands. Noblemen deprived of their estates and clerics deprived of their rank, wandering beggars who have an understanding of chiromancy, chirotony, and chiropractics, singing blind men who took upon themselves the mission of both troubadours and chroniclers, runaway villagers, nonguild bunglers, seminary students expelled for their free thinking and sodomy, knights with suspicious genealogies and reliable genitalia, professional card players and charlatans, Jesuit preachers, black-skinned acrobats, unrecognized kings of nonexistent countries, scholarly vagrants, seekers of the philosopher's stone, sellers of air, followers of the blooming fern,[1] tasters of the salt of secret knowledge, tavern keepers well skilled in

Chaldean papyri, children of first communion, witnesses of the second coming, adepts of the third night, adventists of the fourth day, pissfaces, rational protestants, aryans, rastafarians, trinitarians, antitrinitarians, however first of all—free lovers and kozaks, madcap crazies and heroic warriors,[2] drinkers and slashers, angels of the steppe. . . .

Our carnivals have maintained the distinct personal characteristics of several of the enumerated series for us. For example, the suzerain of the Carpathians and Danube Prince Yaroslav the Octopus, named this for his omnisagacity and omnipresence. Or Jamaica the Kozak—a seeker of adventures of a rare kind, who, having stolen a Turkish galley on the island of Chios, made his way to the Antilles shores and there began the Oshchyrko line. Or the philosophizing executioner Pavlo Matsapura, one of the godfathers of the Middle Ages drug mafia, who was hanged for his love of the human body. Or the Scottish wizard McNeese, who served to the rank of a Kozak colonel and today is known to the entire Polish-Lithuanian Confederation as Maksym the Crooked Nose. . . .

Foreigners in Ukraine—this is an entirely different subject for a lengthy and separate talk. I'll pause just on several Italians—first and foremost out of a love for everything Italian, but also because Ukraine could have become the native mother for every Italian.

Passing over the widely well known names of all kinds of epigones of the high quattrocento who, not having found for themselves a market in other western lands, came to us stuffed to the brim with architectural, artistic, musical, erotic, and philosophical ideas, all these heroes of the cape and sword on the pattern of Pietro Barbon, Paul the Roman, Ambrose the Supporter, Callimachus Buonaccorsi, and still later Rossi, Rastrelli, Corasini and those with them, in passing, I'll recall those here, who are much less well known, but who are completely extraordinary and even exotic types. First and foremost this is the owner of a movable menagerie Michelagnolo Romano, who was the first to show the inhabitants of my land a living rhinoceros, about which they earlier had read only in popular "Physiologues," obviously of Byzantine origin. This, absolutely, was the consul of the Venetian Republic Bandinelli, who lived in a building with a winged lion on Lviv's Market Square and organized unforgettable ship regattas with music and song on the River Poltva with its canals. This also was a diplomat and poet, the ambassador of Venice to the Kozaks, Alberto Vimina da Ceneda (actually Michele Bianci), who partook of the local mead and fruit liquor, and who had no wish to return and therefore remained with the Lowland Army under the name of the scribe Mikey the Drunkie, dying from delirium tremens in the Budzhak steppe. There also is the son of the wandering gypsy and Capuan washerwoman Pietro Moghiliani, who came to the Greek faith, made his way to become a metropolitan, and then founded the Academy in Kyiv where by the Italian model they taught the seven free sciences; to the rest of his days this serious hierarch could not rid himself of a light Romance accent in his speech, through which he was called the "Wallachian" or the "Moldovan." Then, finally, there's Giovanni Mazeppa, a remnant of the extinguished Lombardian line who made a complicated political career first during the reign of Peter I, and afterward in the court of the King of Sweden Karl XII. I could continue this wondrous list.

However, so as to finish up with the theme of our historical ties, I must underscore that also *bella Italia* has attracted quite a few Ukrainians to her. They supposed they could learn something here, so they walked across the Alps and lay down to rest in sweet grass not far from Bologna or Padua, above the shores of eternal rivers, in the shadow of orange trees. With this I'll at least mention Yurko Kotermak, also called Yuri Drohobych, the author of the first book published in Rome, a doctor of philosophy, medicine and astronomy, the rector of the University of Bologna, whose lectures even Nicolaus Copernicus attended. The latter was considered, true, one of the pupils most lagging behind, often times he stood out at lectures, because he was bold enough to prattle all kinds of antinatural idiocies, that for example the Earth circles around the Sun. We atone for the inheritance of these mystifications of Copernicus till this day.

I already won't mention the fact here (though it would be worthwhile) that the famous Venetian painter Vittore Carpaccio clearly came from the Carpathian Mountains, just as I do, and his real last name was either Hutsuliak, or Budzuliak, or maybe even Buzhduhan.

Now, beloved ladies and gentlemen, first before turning to the concluding part of my pouring from pitcher to pitcher, I want to complain about a certain petrifaction of my tongue and a dryness in the throat. Would you not give your kind consent for me to quickly empty some recent vintage wine from that silver goblet over there. [*He receives their consent, drinks the wine.*]

But enough puppets and masks. From the presentation of exotic birds and plants it's worthwhile to move on to subjects of higher content. Because we have gathered in the epoch of the "post-Carnival absurdity of the world." And we are asking: what is on the horizon? But for a good hour I've been talking about what is beyond the horizon. Although, perhaps, the horizon—that is not only what flashes of unattainability somewhere ahead. Perhaps are we given to see the true horizon, just having looked back and just having covered our eyes, blinded from the setting sun with the roof of our hand? In fact, the ancestors of my people felt that namely there, beyond the horizon, the souls and bodies of the dead live. If this at some point turns out to be the truth, then I'd really want to go there—to the contrary, back, backward, not looking back. Only in this way are the chances preserved to reach this invisible, but also in no way provisional, line.

4

This land, about which so much has come from my lips, could not, as you already understand, help but give birth to countless poets. There is an entire legion of them, and they, for the most part, are not known to anyone other than to themselves, yet among them there are several thousand lucky people who have published them in newspapers and even in books. More than even poets, we have songs. One quack tallied them up to nearly thirty thousand. I can boast of the fact that I know a good ten of them.

But neither the poets nor the songs comprise the essence of our carnival. There are just adjunct seasoning, spices for the especially sensitive. There exists another factor, another stimulant. Thanks to it we've survived even after the most devastating wars and, according to the words of Paul of Aleppo,[3] we remained "more numerous than the heavenly stars and the sand on the shores." Finally, thanks to it we always become ourselves despite all the temptations to be someone else.

Here I have in mind the great mystery of men and women.

I can only compare Ukrainian women to the Italian or the Greek. Each one of you can see ones like them in Titian. A visiting philanderer from Armenia some five centuries ago wrote about them as follows: "In height more tall than short, hair more dark than light, eyes more brown than gray, although you come across green, too. Teeth large and white, but not exceedingly so. Lips rather thin than thick, but pleasant for kissing. Brows, as they themselves say it, in a line, and there are various kinds of noses, although not as beautiful as our women have. Fresh breath, a good voice for song, a lively tongue. Smooth necks, but not too long, just right. Broad shoulders, but in the right measure, nice. Breasts for the most part large rather than small, at times very large, in extremely rare cases very small. Wonderful tummies, large, moon white. I could go on endlessly about their thighs, about their bottoms—even longer, but I won't. Knees, like the elbows, firm, pleasant to the touch, sensitive. Calves, like the shoulders, full, smooth skinned, hairless. Feet generally larger than among other peoples, but it suits them. Regarding the area between the legs—again we won't say a word, though it's nice, too. I've forgotten about the ears—sooner small than large. And about the hands—capable of all kinds of work, clean."

Unfortunately we're rather ungrateful creations. Our menfolk to this day have not learned to value what has been bequeathed to them as they should. The Tartars, who rushed from the south over the course of centuries just for these "living goods," apparently have turned out to have been the best appraisers. In all of the Mohammedan world, and also here, in the Mediterranean area of Europe or even Africa, they sold women stolen and raped by them, women "with hair more dark than light." The fashion for Ukrainian concubines easily took the place of the previous enthusiasm of harem erotomaniacs for emaciated Cherkessian women, stout Amazons, or frigid Lesbians.

Our men generally have turned out to be unworthy of such riches. What did the best of them do to hold these women and keep them? They ran away into the fields, beyond the rapids, to kozakdom, to celibacy, to monasticism. For what reason? To get drunk as much as they want, to go fishing, to be in the company of other men. In the meantime they left the women, "about whose thighs one could talk endlessly," to be loved by all kinds of idlers, plowmen, traveling lovelaces, and wandering magicians. And when the catchers of women's bodies flew in from the southeast, then there was already no one left to defend them, for the idlers were waiting out their rough times in the taverns, the lovelaces set off for more distant, untrampled lands, and the magicians simply dissolved in the air, for that's why they're magicians.

Once a young Greek woman had told me that all other women in her country commonly have just as lofty and nice breasts as she does. This is accomplished thanks to a certain secret. Their girls are fed a special grape snail from an early age. I joked then—don't they give other snails to their boys? But still: how many efforts the Greeks make for their men to want their women! So that this frantic drama, this carnival of feelings would never end.

As for us we still have a great misunderstanding of the sexes. Our girls continue to remain unloved by us. Any kind of manifestations of the fullness of being, this eternal bittersweet holiday with its gifts and rifts has been replaced for us by a place at the table—this ersatz of carnival, where they drink, eat and guzzle much too much, where "coitus doesn't even occur," where "arses are constrained by nails," where "we go on the assault and sink into our rations and, like knights, we will lay down our bones at the feast."[4] And from this our women become overweight and caught in a trap.

The most feminine of them flee every day to harems overseas— in greater measure today than three hundred years ago, but tomorrow in the greater measure, as today—they have adorned themselves with the sweet-smelling societies of the West and East on all levels of their existence: from dirty port brothels to exclusive snobbish clubs.

Contrary to all this there are those among us who continue to love one other. Thanks to this we are living even now, when all the angels have turned away from us. Thanks to this till now we still are "more numerous than the stars in heaven and the sand on the shores." Finally, thanks to this we all become ourselves, although the temptations are so strong to appear as someone else.

Allow me a single truism just before the end of my talk. I expect that it won't excessively irritate you.

Only love can save us from death. There, where love ends, the "absurdity of the world" begins. And I don't think then that "anything" can still remain "on the horizon." Besides emptiness, of course. It attracts, it calls, it pulls—how can we render resistance in this time of "postlove"?

At the least I would want to be like a prophet and forecast something here today. I proposed to your inattentiveness all of just several versions, each of which separately is erroneous, and all together contradicting each other. But all the same I will attempt, even out of such a hopeless situation, to emerge with honor, that is, with a certain conclusion. This is extraordinarily necessary for the compositional completion of my text. But not more. That is why I ask you not to take this conclusion overly seriously. Consider it as you would a period at the end of a sentence. Or ellipses or a question mark.

I hold to the traditional system of notions. If we understand carnival as the extreme strain of the powers of life in all their fullness and inexhaustibility or also the loftier manifestation of the battle between love and death (death as emptiness, as antilife, as nothing), then carnival truly should never end or, at least, last as long as we have not spent our credit given by the Heavenly Observer. I assert this, no, I don't assert—I admit, although with this I can look just as old fashioned as the inopportunely contrived by me Yaropolk-Nepomuk Kunshtyk, who, in due course, died from an eclipse of the world.

■ □ ■ □ ■

2 4

MY GUEST SMOKES A LOT. HE HAS THE HABIT OF TAKING OFF HIS glasses from time to time, during which his eyes take on a completely different, slightly perplexed expression. We're communicating in a somewhat strange language, in which two-thirds of the words are German, and the rest English. Our mutual understanding in these two languages is sufficient to come to an agreement somehow. I can't help but turn my attention to the extraordinary shape of his fingers. I wouldn't be surprised at all, having found out that they belong to some virtuoso. With them—the fingers—I begin our conversation that is taking place in the apartments of the hotel where my guest is staying among tapestries, mirrors and old candelabras.

Mr. Perfetsky, Your fingers, it seems, betray You as a musician?
I actually can play several instruments. Believe me, though, far from professionally. But there are moments when I can play some things.

And if I should ask You to play something on that spinet?
The spinet, like the harpsichord, like the cembalo and clavichord, is one of my favorites. When I was a child living in a small town, surrounded by mountains all around, I took private music lessons from a solitary old Jewish woman. In the town they called her "ditsy Celia." From times unknown she had inherited a wonderful Dresden harpsichord, which in his time one of the greats had played, apparently, Mozart, but not that Mozart, whom everyone knows, but Franz Xavier Mozart, his son, who used to live in Lviv.

Celia was terribly forgetful and untidy; in addition, she kept thirteen cats on the veranda, and it really reeked from all this. But I loved those music lessons: the scent of old wood, collections of notes, the quivering of timbres, the stench of the veranda. . . . One day she stepped out of the house and never returned, just as if she had never existed. Considerably later I found out that there was a Saint Cecilia, the patroness of music and the inventor of the organ.

I see. Now from your fingers—to the jewelry on your fingers. Does this ring have any kind of interesting story behind it?
The master of the lodge Toward True Unity presented it to me during the initiation into the fifth level from the bottom. I'm joking, of course. It's a family ring, or better said, ancestral.

As much as I heard from Your lecture today, are the problems of descent, heredity and tradition in all their dimensions key for your worldview?
Maybe, You're not mistaken. Although I haven't thought about it. My descent is not something all that unique. For the longest of time it caused serious suffering for me. Suffering? Yes, apparently this time I can use this kind of resonant word. Suffering.

Do you have in mind some kind of persecution on the part of the regime?
Not in any way.

Then what?
It's too private. But, I can sketch the conditions in the most general outline. Once upon a time I was married to a person descended from the truly most noble upper crust. She was a countess, maybe even a princess. Her parents refused to bless us as a result of my commoner's descent. At first they demanded a genealogical certificate from me that showed that at least one-sixteenth of my blood had a bluish tinge. But I couldn't manage to acquire such a certificate, although I had written desperate letters to all the monarchs of the world. Just the king of Nepal had been kind enough to write me back and enclosed a color picture of his favorite elephant for me. . . .

And this became the reason for your breakup?
I guess that's true. Not directly. Generally there are never any direct reasons.

Thank you for the maximum openness you've expressed here. But our readers would be quite interested in learning a bit more about You and Your life. I don't doubt that in Your homeland You're a pretty well known figure. Don't judge us harshly, but here in Venice no one had known anything about You earlier. So please, a bit about yourself.
In general I love to talk about myself—that's why I willingly agree to all kinds of interviews. I also love to go to confession—priests can be attentive. I was born approximately in the center of Europe. In my childhood I took private music lessons, then went to the secret gymnasium where they taught us language, poetics, fencing, and reading music. . . .

How many languages do You know?
Not a single one. I know a lot of words in different languages. I've already spoken about this today. Then, in childhood, I learned to tell musical instruments apart. I understood that the clarinet is the exalted young master of the time of maturation, inclined to pathetics and the sudden rising of its voice. An alto—an externally superfluous dandy of thirty years, profound and passionate in reality. The violin—an aging maiden, whose totally nervous fervor is based on the terrifying premonition of an eternal life as an old maid. Instead of the violoncello—the serene and harmonic mistress of her fate, the erotic queen of fiddle sticks and bows. I became a man thanks to the harp—to an experienced aging courtesan with certain exceedingly romantic views on life and sex.

Have you tried to write music Yourself?
I've always tried to do that, for as long as I remember. By this music I understand poetry. And words in general, in combination, texts. Regarding music as such, music per se, I've never written it in the literal sense, although I could play anything you want. In Lviv, where I moved from my hometown at seventeen. . . .

Lviv—this is the city You mentioned today that's ten thousand years old?
I said that it's ten thousand years old? Crazy! So, right away in Lviv I came to be in the warm company of some juvenile delinquents. We used to sit in the cellars, smoking, drinking cheap wine and playing, what seemed to us to be rock. Or the blues. Quite often they caught us, and the police, which we call the "militia," took away everyone to the slammer without exception. They didn't hit me a single time there because I started to recite poetry aloud or read their palms. You meet all kinds of people among them, not just shitbags.

Really?
I'm sure. I wised up and enrolled at the university. Then there were a lot of other interesting activities—I got married, went into hiding, published books, flew above the city on a delta glider, transported banned books and grass, for half a year I played the kettledrum in a symphony orchestra, worked as a grave digger at a cemetery. . . . Now I can't even recall everything.

What are your poems about?
About the silence that arises at the moment after a nuclear explosion. Don't look at me with those eyes, it was a joke. Definitely, the best of them are the ones you can recount, but how much they lose from that! Ideal poems, which don't exist, had to be the kind you could simply recount with the least amount of loss. Recount in your own words.

Perhaps you'll try anyway?
It's hopeless, but listen. I've always gotten involved in hopeless affairs. So, imagine. . . . Imagine the July heat. A large stony city, gray, and yellow buildings. And the dried pipes of waterworks—they smell of moss. There's not a drop of water anywhere. You have just half a bottle of wine left. It's warm and musty. But you're carrying it for someone to save them from. . . . The heat? From thirst? From death? And then on the crossroads of two dead silent little streets in the dense forest of the Old City a patrol stops You. And finding the wine, right in front of Your eyes they slowly pour it out, it flows along the sidewalk to the drains, and You begin to understand that this is all the end, and

You crawl along the wall of the building against which they've pressed Your face during a body search. But this is a poem that's all too sad. There's another. It's like this. A boy and a girl are sitting at two pianos pushed together. One against the other. They're supposed to play a piece for four hands. Further on is the description of what they're playing. He—about rain and falling leaves. She—about cold empty rooms. He—about hope for the better. She—about a rat seen yesterday on a trash can. He—about how good it is for him with her. She—about parting. He shuts his eyes. She's gone. He opens his eyes. She's gone. But who then is sitting at the second piano?

Death?
No. He's alone. Reflected in a mirror. Like me now. Did you like it?

Not particularly. It rather reminds me not of poems, but of dreams.
These are still unwritten poems. And unwritten poems are dreams. You're right.

Thank You. In that case, will You allow me one more personal question?
I don't know, we'll see.

Won't You tell me something about the milieu You belong to in Your city?
Oh, it's a beautiful collection of real idlers and blockheads, among which no one has treated anything seriously in their life. Besides painting with crayons on asphalt and ballroom dances, of course. But above all they value themselves most and talk about this constantly in coffeehouses. I love them above all else; in addition, it's just they who give a certain sense to this city, I don't know. . . .

How do they make a living?
For the most part they make their living like the birds in the sky. Though once in a while one of them sells a painting or two here, to the West. Or graphic works. Or, for example, a family diamond. Or one of their internal organs—say, a lung. They pay pretty well now for those.

And how do You make a living?
In a few hours I have to be at a stately dinner where I'll be bestowed with an honorarium for today's lecture—a million lire. That's about six hundred dollars.

But how about there, at home? How do You make a living there?
First, I'm eternally in debt. It's not easy for me to speak about this, but that's the way it is. Second, I saved some from those times when I worked as a grave digger, and then a trumpeter at the city hall. Since the former and latter make decent money, but the former make more. Sometimes I'm able to sell a certain amount of my books or give a Zen philosophy lecture in a penal colony for juvenile criminals. But there were times when for weeks I didn't have anything to buy bread or cigarettes with. The last recourse was to take my favorite books to the bazaar or the graphic art given to me by my friends for my birthdays.

That is, You've sold Your friends?
No, I didn't sell my friends. I'd say it a different way: my friends saved me from starving to death. Oh!

Do You believe that a better life will come in Your land?
It's beautiful right now. Life isn't better or worse. It's life. I'm in it. I'm pleased that it is.

Even when You don't have enough money to buy bread and cigarettes?
Even more then. Then everything intensifies. Then you're light and clear.

Then, after Venice You're returning home?
I don't know. I'd want to travel a bit. Cross the ocean. Write a book about New York.

Will there be a book about Venice?
That would really be a crazy idea! To write about Venice? Can you write anything else about Venice? After thousands upon thousands and thousands of the pages already written? No, I'm nobody's fool, sorry.

YURI ANDRUKHOVYCH

Anyway. What are Your impressions of Venice?
I've had a lot of anxiety here. And trouble. Do you know how I spent
several of my afternoon hours today when my lecture finally took
place at the seminar? I've been trying to lie low to keep from seeing
a certain woman I know. She arrived from Poland and apparently
already has been looking for me all over Venice for three days. But I
just can't see her right now. Don't laugh, this isn't what You think.
And thus, so as not to meet with her anywhere, I've been choosing
certain far-off and unpopular quarters of the city for my strolls,
where there are nearly no museums, monuments, restorations, and
things like that. I must admit, it's not easy to find places like that.
Anyway in the afternoon today it seems I found something like that.
I wrapped myself in my coat and trembled in the fierce wind. . . .

The weather lately has really been startling. . . .
I walked under that wet snow, no one was beside me, and I saw a
certain impoverished and really ailing city. And my body clenched
with something cold when I suddenly became conscious of the fact
that even we, the current generations, can become witnesses of how
they're evacuating everything living from this city, because living in
it already will simply be impossible. In it I saw the awful metaphor
of human feebleness to save the world through culture. Just a
momentary mood for me. . . .

**Something very compatible with Your lecture, yes? To the point,
that passage about the young Greek girl with large breasts—isn't
that also a metaphor? Didn't You make her up—the same way as
You did with Your poor consumptive philosopher?**
I didn't make her up. She worked as a waitress in a Berlin tavern and
really had wondrous breasts. Her name was Zoya, that is, "life," if
I'm not mistaken. Right now, apparently, she's in Greece.

And what will You have to say about the local women?
I like the fact that they look at men. That makes them nice. This
century-old mixture—the blood of courtesans and nuns. . . .

Don't women in Your land look at men?
I think they still do. They've simply reached the point of disillusion.

Have You also been the reason for disillusion?
Certainly. I loved my woman all too little. I have in mind duration.
That is, again I haven't expressed it right. It's hard for me to be
understandable.

Excuse me. Perhaps I'm a bit capricious with impropriety. By the
way, You also will be able to receive an honorarium for this conversation. For the time being I want to thank You. I must be candid—I liked Your lecture best of all the ones I heard, You won't
believe it, but even more than the lecture of Mr. Mavropule! I
wish You and Your country only love. Now one more thing, the
last question, which You can refuse to answer. Observing You
since early morning, I noticed that different from previous days,
You had some kind of black leather case which You didn't part
from. What's in it?
Firearms. A sniper's rifle. Because I'm just pretending to be a participant of the seminar. Really my task was to finish off an important bird.

Did you manage to do that?
I expect no. I didn't shoot. And it was just a joke.

You don't say! A joke? How You've disappointed me! But then, I
thought so. Thank You one more time.

For the photo: Our guest S. Perfetsky looks at Venice from the
window in the monastery of San Giorgio Maggiore.

■ □ ■ □ ■

2 5

"I DON'T DOUBT THAT YOU BOFFED HER," ADA SAID AND PRESSED HER lips together tightly.

"Who?" Perfetsky didn't understand.

"Of course that slut from the newspaper. She's constantly sucking Tic Tacs. Do you think your stupid interviews interest her? The chick is just looking for thrills."

For a good half hour they wandered beneath the wet snow through some dark alleys in search of the mysterious Farfarello house, where they had been invited to a stately dinner. Judging by the marks on the map that Dappertutto had presented to them today, the place of the great evening concourse was somewhere right nearby. But just where?

"The devil himself would break his own leg in these quarters for the lumpen-Venetians." Perfetsky stated the obvious, and right there nearly fell, stumbling on some invisible step, at which he cursed not too angrily. "Why do you think so?"

"You sat with her for too long in your room," Ada explained. "In general. But anyway, what business is it of mine?"

She again feigned that she was looking over the map, standing closer to a solitary and for the time being unbroken lantern. The wind from the north stirred up in the alleys, spattering more and more handfuls of snowflakes. It struck the lanterns and shook the shutters.

"But that's nothing. Just one more night, one more day" Ada continued. "We'll go our separate ways, and my ass is grass! Look for the number on the building."

"Three thousand two hundred and sixteen," Stas informed her without blinking with what first came to mind. "You're being unfair to me. I just need you. I just want you. I just don't see anyone else because you are in this world."

He ventured to kiss her somewhere on her face, but his lips caught just a snowflake.

"In that case we're almost there," Ada deduced and decisively turned to the right. "I've wanted just one thing—for things to be good for you."

As always she walked a bit in front.

"Well here it is," she said after a minute and looked at the map one more time. "We're here."

The map fluttered in the wind and tried to break away from her hands. It suddenly appeared that this was a piece of living skin that really wanted to fly. Overcoming the birdlike resistance of the map, Ada folded it up and forcibly put it away in her handbag, procuring one of many countless guides in its place.

The building, opposite of which they were standing, was located on the other end of a narrow canal and an unnoticeable bridge led to it from the outside. Despite the surrounding darkness, the building was lit by some inner illumination that penetrated through slits in the boarded-up or broken shutters. Besides this, the building made sounds. You could hear it from far off. The entire facade was adorned with tin-sheet metal suns, stars, half-moons, play windmills, and little devils—and all this frenetically turned, clapped, and buzzed amid the strong nocturnal cyclone. It seemed that some juggler in a second childhood had decided to dress up his place in all kinds of magic trinkets in order to chase away or, just the opposite, lure spirits passing by.

"Casa Farfarello," Ada read from the guide. "Today no one lives there. Earlier the house had belonged to a family of foreign trade negotiators that had arrived in Venice from somewhere in Calcutta. Or from Madras. At the beginning of the century they all abruptly disappeared. Here it's written that they turned into strange-looking birds. Now our foundation rents the building. For all kinds of undertakings. Go in?"

Stepping onto the bridge, Perfetsky heard as it began to moan beneath him. His spirit was becoming sad. The wind knocked his slightly wet head of hair. With both hands Ada was hanging on to her beret.

"In either case, I love you!" Stakh tried to outshout the wind, but it's possible Ada did not hear him, because she answered completely missing the mark:

"Try not to leave me with other people."

Inside it smelled of desolation and fungus, bits of velvet tapestry hung from the walls, from some kind of holes in the walls water gurgled. But this entire ruin was mightily illuminated by multicolored candlesticks and countless fragrant candles—thick and thin ones, arranged on the steps, galleries, and in the upstairs rooms.

"Your coats." A Chinese servant bowed, rising up before them in the vestibule and, as it appeared to Stakh, smiling malevolently. Somewhere upstairs Mavropule began to laugh boisterously—you wouldn't confuse that with anything.

"Here it's sufficiently cozy," Perfetsky said as though he were being ironic, shaking off bits of wet snow from his hair.

"Since long ago the foundation has been carrying out plans for a total remodeling and rebuilding," Ada explained. "For the time being there's not enough money."

The Chinese man took their capes and went to some cupboard to the side, from which he no longer returned. Instead, a hostess emerged to them in a moon-white dress, incomprehensibly somehow similar to the wardrobe keeper who had just disappeared, although without even the tiniest bit of a Chinese feature. She accompanied them up the steps, avoiding the candleholders, the holes in the floor, the basins, troughs, and pitchers set up here and there, as well as chimerical chamber pots—all this earthenware was already filled to the brim with water that dripped from everywhere.

Ada was in dark green—for all these days it was the first time that Stas had seen her in such an unseemly color. On her chest she also was wearing a brooch which he had not seen till now in the form of a tiny, delicate, silver frog. Surprised, Perfetsky discovered that it suited her. The hostess walked a bit ahead. Reaching the top floor, she turned around and suddenly turned out not to be any hostess, but secretary Dappertutto in an artfully sewn exclusive suit. He cut loose a tiny cloud of tobacco smoke into their faces and unhappily said:

"Everyone has been already here for a long time. We can't begin without you. Where have you been roaming?"

"I lost my way several times," Ada responded, guiltily shutting her eyes from the light.

"You've always been careless." Dappertutto wagged his head and stopped before the doors spattered with chalk, from behind which not very expressive voices echoed, Mavropule laughed boisterously from time to time, and certain distinct musical chords could be heard above everything—it happens this way when a smallish orchestra is just getting ready to play, tuning their instruments.

"Are you ready?" Dappertutto asked harshly, looking them over cloyingly from head to toe.

"As always." Stas smiled dourly.

"You aren't ready," the secretary pronounced resolutely, and with his index finger first touched Ada's and then Stas's brow. "Now you're ready."

His finger was smeared with a sticky oil that must have left a trace on the brow. Perfetsky tried to wipe away the unpleasant sensation of a stain, but Ada grabbed him by the hand and whispered "leave it be" through her teeth. Once again Dappertutto enveloped them with a harsh gaze and, suddenly melting into the smile of the wardrobe keeper Chinese, said, "I wish you good entertainment and unforgettable impressions!"

He bowed, turned his face to the door, and pressed against it with both hands.

The room where they had ended up truly was not an overly spacious hall; it was also generously filled with lights. The windows were covered with old hole-infested shutters, into which handfuls of wind and snow were tossed from outside. The entire company really was already here. The guests looked totally special and festive: the Brylcreemed and grease-painted Dejavu, the embodiment of Elegance, Alborak in a new hunting jacket and leggings and in horseman's boots with spurs, Liza Sheila in a man's hat so wide that her sharp-nosed face nearly completely fell in its shadow, John Paul in countless shirts and sweaters of countless colors. Mavropule was wearing such a caustic-red jacket and such an emerald-violet-orange-gold tie that it was impossible not to be blinded; in addition, he con-

YURI ANDRUKHOVYCH

250
▼

stantly seized and grabbed by the waist the enticingly whirling hostesses, who in fact were finishing up setting the table; with arms
spread like a scarecrow he followed them through the entire hall
with just the aim of squeezing them alternately and, getting an
enthusiastic erotic squeal from each of them, guffawing victoriously.

Casallegra himself was sitting closer to the lighted stove in a
grand and nearly Vedic armchair, more similar to a throne—in a
black tailcoat up to his waist, with a bow tie and a vest, also sprinkled with a starry-lunar, still-warm dust. What was below the waist
is harder to say, for this half of the old man was carefully wrapped
in a plaid kilt, above which in an honor guard there leaned over him
Concita, then Lucia, in turn stroking him and whispering something sweet into the great-grandfather's ear.

And further there were still other guests—numerous world luminaries or, perhaps, just their doubles. Some were even dancing,
although it seemed that there couldn't be any dancing or any
schmancing to that disharmonious cacophony that gushed from the
amplifiers from every direction.

And right at that moment there flew, as though a murmur, light
and indistinct, from mouth to mouth one and the same thing:
"Let's begin, let's begin. . . ."

The music (if you can call it that) ended, and everyone grew still in
the corners of the hall. Dappertutto stood in the middle, holding a
microphone in his hand, which looked more like the head of a
snake. He tapped on it with that same greasy finger, and complete
silence fell. Even the wind halted beyond the windows.

"My beloved friends." The executive secretary turned to those
present. "According to the everlasting traditions of our society, we
begin these long-awaited festivities at the moment of general unity
and deepest concentration. I ask you to start the sound recording."

After these words he nimbly came to attention and spit a just
extinguished butt out of the corner of his mouth. This served as a
signal for the invisible choir and orchestra. The melody was just as
incomprehensible as the entire previous musical accompaniment.
Actually, there were at once several various musical themes, played
simultaneously and without the least amount of taste. With his perfect ear Stas managed to delineate just some elements of the holy

cacophony in full bloom with the mirrors and candles. The "Minor Masonic Cantata" lay as its basis, on top of which separate syncopations flew in from the "March of the Rosicrusians" as well as buffoonish rhythms from the "Waltz of the Sorcerers."[1] But not even Perfetsky could catch what else was there, although from all this, ten or so kinds of classical and neoclassical layers were drawn. The majority of those present stirred their lips—in a way as though they were singing softly in some quite difficult language, maybe Latin. Slanting his eyes toward Ada, Perfetsky noticed that she, although she wasn't singing, was struggling with the temptation to do this the entire time: the twitching of her lips clearly attested to her condition. After a certain amount of time he even caught himself with the itch to join in the song, which was becoming more and more intolerable; it did not matter that the words were unfamiliar, more than anything he felt like singing along with at least the last syllables. Fortunately this ended soon, and everyone applauded.

The table was covered with such hysterical generosity that for some time Stakh was about to stop complaining about his appearance at this suspicious dinner. So, it's as though everything was occurring not for the great fast, but for the very height of the carnival. In fact, he had to sit at a table rocking so terribly, which, additionally, was entirely blotted over with chalk and splashed with relatively fresh paint, but Ada managed to whisper furtively that these are the remnants of the recently commenced remodeling. Besides this, right opposite them Mavropule perched himself. He called Ada "my darling daughter" and greasily winked herewith. When a thick black liquid, for some reason called *sangue del drago* by everyone, had been poured to the brim of tall glass goblets, Dappertutto stood up and, from time to time, leaning his ear up to Casallegra dozing next to him, as though seeking confirmation about his speech, announced the following:

"My glorious folks! My celebrated folks! My none too rarely extolled folks, but first of all my illustrious and renowned, my radiant folks! Here the hour of our supper has arrived. You've earned it completely honestly—over the course of these four unforgettable days you've courageously competed with your intellects, inasmuch as they've permitted you to do this, in order from all of this absurdity of today to strike at least some spark of pleasure and joy. Not all of you have come intact to this evening. Some have had their horse stolen, others their heart. In the name of my patron and from myself, I sincerely thank you all for this. We have invited you for no particular reason, and not because you are some kind of special people. Because in truth you are completely ordinary people, there are bucketloads of you, and your name is legion. No one of you—neither my patron, nor I would cast an eye in the direction of any of you if there weren't some feature which makes you—I won't say interesting, but I'll put it this way—entertaining. Each one of you marvelously knows this feature; I also am not even going to name it. I have to underscore: you've earned not just this abundant supper. Much more important rewards will be strewn tonight over your heads, filled only with your selves and other emptiness! And the matter isn't even about honoraria, which, by the way, I count to three—*uno, due, tre!*—you'll find in your pockets! . . ."

Reaching in the bowels of his jacket, Perfetsky indeed felt a long, sturdy envelope, which ended up there from who knows where. But he wasn't able to be surprised enough at this as he should have been, because Dappertutto continued: "Did you find it? That's it! But all these payments are zero in the face of the abysses that we are going to open up for you today. For this, just one thing is demanded of you—drink and pour, gobble up and stuff yourself, and so as not to fall asleep prematurely—drink to excess, slurp away, munch away, in a word—frolic and play, be happy, so that in full luster and till morning we could unfold an action before you, whose name is "Comical Battles with Drowsiness in the Widest Circle of Friends!"[2]

Then it thundered from outside so hard that the walls began to shake, and the flashes of lightning could be seen through the boarded-up shutters.

"We were heard!" The secretary was pleased and drank his considerably large goblet to the bottom.

"Don't drink it," Ada whispered. Stas was already about not to listen to her, fixing his attention on how greedily, in large gulps, those present were guzzling their black wine—until it flowed in jets beyond their mouths and splashed in every direction. But raising the goblet right close to his nose, he shuddered from the foul odor that struck his nostrils.

"You're right," he answered to Ada in the same way nearly in a whisper and completely unnoticeably to others, as it seemed to him, he poured out his dose under the table. Herewith he noted for himself how the floor beneath him began to hiss and became charred. Fortunately, he had a little bottle just for such cases in a pocket with his favorite Carpathian balsam, the last one of his reserve from home—in color the balsam didn't look any different from the "dragon's blood" at all; it also went down into Stas fine and dandily, strongly warming and cheering his soul.

"Well, you're drinking!" Mavropule conspiratorially winked to him and once again began to guffaw.

"But not human blood,"[3] Perfetsky quoted in answer, perhaps not entirely appropriately.

And there was great guzzling. And kaleidoscopically the plates and the victuals changed. And time after time the goblets with the black liqueur filled up and again were emptied. And cheeks and eyes got puffy, and noses got irritated. And the hostesses squealed, whom Mavropule constantly and tirelessly grabbed, tried to catch, and groped. And tails grew, and hot hooves beat the floor. And Dapper-tutto wandered about the hall, devoting to each a little bit of atten-tion and favor, a tiny bit of especially mysterious sympathy, shoving out some kind of papers for a signature, puffing smoke, rolling his eyes and scratching his chest with his fingernails. And the music didn't stop; although one couldn't dance to it, or even breathe. Some kind of fantastic couples swirled all around nevertheless. And even the ancient Casallegra, propped up by his tender female companions, shuffled out to the middle of the hall and ended up in the very cen-ter of the furious round dance—it didn't matter that he had nothing below his belt besides his lilac drawers. And flashing from beneath her hat with her sullen bird's eye, the incomparable Liza Sheila said with playful intonation, "Hey, *buddy*, the next dance is mine!"

"I don't dance," Perfetsky replied harshly, but from the balsam that he had drunk up, it suddenly seemed to him that it wasn't spaghetti winding on her fork, but live worms, that still continued to writhe in her mouth.

And here he observed many other metamorphoses with the food, which, it seems, no one could see anymore. And it wasn't mushrooms baked in the pizza, but tadpoles, and Dejavu poured out not tortellini in red ketchup, but dog's ears, and Djabraili let blood not from a steak, but from someone's hairy cheek cut while shaving and now lying on his plate, and the ramous Mavropule wasn't stuffing sausages in his mouth, but a certain misfit's severed fingers with dirt under the fingernails. And what should one say about everything else—about the fruits, salads, or *frutti di mare*—if not leeches, then caterpillars, if not centipedes, then wood lice swarming in a swarm on the plates, salad dishes, and platters. And looking at all this vileness, Stakh wasn't able to keep from locking his lips on the bottle concealed on his chest, otherwise he'd be barfing. . . .

"I have to invite the old man. Today's his evening," Ada said. "Try not to lose me. From your field of vision," she specified, as though she were laying a claim on this.

And she left, rounding the table, and there, at the very edge of it, she kissed the ancient Casallegra on the hand, all dark green, but possibly she simply kissed his ring, and after a minute she was leading him in a strange slow dance to the sounds of the tuned instruments, the snakelike hissing of the public and the thunderous peals beyond the windows.

"The lights!" Dappertutto commanded into the microphone, and it became semidark in the room, that is, intimate.

"Bravo, patron!" Dappertutto shrieked again.

"Bravo, patron!" Nearly the entire hall followed the cue, joyfully observing how in a childlike way the old head bowed benignly somewhere there, very close to Ada's full breasts.

"But where is her husband, that German?" Mavropule asked, with his unbreakable teeth crushing a tailbone.

"Disappeared since yesterday." Stakh shrugged his shoulders.

"Disappeared?!" Mavropule covered everything all around with a new wave of Homeric swaying, so that even the gold on him clinked. "Disappeared! Then one shouldn't waste time!" Afterward he, just as always, winked to Stas, but this time simultaneously with both eyes.

"What do you have in mind?" Perfetsky decisively fixed his glasses and swigged the balsam right from the bottle.

"To definitely have a dance with her!" Mavropule explained and licked his fingers. In fact Stakh hadn't noticed whether they were

Mavropule's own or the other guy's chopped off ones. "And do you have a problem?"

Stakh wanted to throw the pig ear at him, but at that very instant he saw that it already was not Mavropule sitting there opposite him, but a donkey with a black coat in a bishop's tiara and sultan's clothing.

"My glorious, my notorious folks!" The flying Dappertutto pressed close to the microphone. "I ask that you all turn your attention to Mrs. Ada Zitrone, a collaboratress of our foundation and queen of today's reception!"

Everyone began to applaud simultaneously with successive blows of thunder, from which the old Casallegra staggered and turned terribly pale.

"Well, that's it. It's starting," the donkey said, drying up a full goblet of "dragon grog."

"He's feeling weak, he's feeling weak" buzzed through the hall.

The party continued.

"He's feeling weak, he's feeling weak." This refrain pulsed in Stakh's roused head, and he didn't know whom it referred to, but he could suppose that it even referred to him.

"He's feeling weak, he's feeling weak." With these words they led out the old man by the arms from a room into some far-off corridors, and the tailcoat and drawers hung from him in mute, sad folds.

Stas also was feeling weak. Ada was dancing. She was having success. Someone was asking her to dance the entire time. In answer to this Stas smoked relentlessly and excessively often took off his glasses and put them back on. Thunder and lightning. Cruel unmusic. A dark green dress. It was too much of everything.

At first it seemed to him that Ada had been openly rubbing her cheek on Alborak's chest much too much. That John Paul's hands had wrapped around her waist below and wove into a lock in the most frivolous place. That Gaston Dejavu had licked her neck. That some handsome dude, quite similar to Eros Ramazotti, wound himself around her moving thighs. That even Liza Sheila was dancing with her for some reason.

How many of those dances were there? An intolerably endless amount! And for how long was Perfetsky being tormented, trampling his misfortune in a bottle of balsam? A thousand years!

But the end to his gnawing did not come even then, for suddenly the penetrating voice of Dappertutto began to buzz into the microphone: "And now my glorious notorious, a tango! The Mavropule tango!"

Red in his jacket, the hairy giant flew above the hall like fire and grabbed Ada like a stalk of straw in the thorns of his clutches. And the tango began—though it was not entirely a tango, but just a knife into Perfetsky's heart. And there was bending and petting, and constantly slobbering something into her ear, and she just tossed her head back and laughed, and Dappertutto shrieked "the best pair, the best pair!" and this fusion of venomously red and dark green was so wild and indecent, like Mavropule's tie, and to the applause of the entire menagerie, which was just freaking out, both danced from the hall and disappeared somewhere in the corridors blocked by sand and crushed brick, where streams of rainwater ran from the ceiling.

"That's it," the black donkey said to Perfetsky, although no longer a donkey, but rather the wardrobe keeper Chinese, who kneaded spaghetti with chopsticks, but in just a minute he was no longer a Chinese, but a large spotted cockerel in exactly the same kind of eyeglasses as Perfetsky.

"You just shut up!" Stas struck his fist on the table, and the cockerel flew up somewhere to the ceiling, fluttering its wings in fright and remained there, transmuted into an ancient seven-sticked candelabra with buck horns.

And splashing as one should from his bottomless bottle, Stas finally rose up and firmly decided that it was time. . . .

In the corridors there really was a lot of lime, sulfur, and crushed brick, and the streams of rain flew from above, and Perfetsky stepped right into puddles and painfully whacked himself on some strange boxes, placed everywhere and locked, on some unwieldy suitcases from antediluvian times, and coffinlike crates. He looked into each door, but no one was anywhere, and just now and then one of the hostesses nervously passed him shouting: "A cold compress for Baron Casallegra!" "Hot camphor for Signore Leonardo!" or "An oxygen tent for Mr. President!" They knocked Perfetsky aside to get him out of their way, and each time he was forced to clutch the moist walls, the cobwebs, the emptiness.

"And if she's right there next to him?" Stas thought and decided to run after the next hostess in order to end up there where, perhaps, they were saving the life of the inappropriately for his age danced into the ground doctor of thanatology. But just when he thought this, as all the girls in the corridor had disappeared, no one was running anywhere already, and out of anger Perfetsky sat down on one of the wooden boxes. That very same instant a knocking could be heard from inside and some nasty voice pronounced in a nasal voice:[4] "Get out of here!"

Stakh just spat and moved farther. . . .

A good hour of his uninterrupted wandering through the endless corridors and floors passed, until he finally heard an exceedingly familiar loud laughter. He jerked at the sound and soon saw an entire flock of hostesses who, chattering and laughing, formed a line in front of the door, from behind which the characteristic call of Mavropule flew, which recently had been heard by Stakh.

"What's he doing there?" Perfetsky asked the girls, barely catching his breath.

"He's impregnating," the girls proudly answered.

"Whom?!" Stanislav startled at the shout, for in his particular mood there apparently was just one object for impregnation in the world.

"Anybody," the hostesses said. "All of us."

Right here the door opened and with the words "Who's next?" a cheerful beauty emerged, pulling up her stocking while walking and fastening the zipper on her narrow skirt. While she was walking out, passing the next one entering at the door, Perfetsky managed to look over the large bed and the head of a bull that was snorting in satisfaction on it and, it seemed to Perfetsky, even winking at him. The rest of his body was beneath the cover; it was also difficult to say whether it was a bull's.

"So, is that what's guffawing?" Perfetsky asked, licking his dried lips.

"Not it, but he," the girls corrected him. "Our good-looker!"

"And where's Mavropule?" Stakh betrayed himself.

"Somewhere," the most derisive of the hostesses said, and they all laughed for a long time at his heels. . . .

Jealousy, fierce, insane jealousy drove Perfetsky further and further. Where is she? The night was passing, thunderous discharges were shaking the earth and sea, the building was continually whirling and, it seemed, could collapse any second. Suddenly Stas saw a figure at the end of yet another corridor, who, with no less decisiveness threw himself at him. He had already prepared to strike the attacker with his foot, or, better, with a karate chop, but then, fortunately, he understood that it was himself reflected in the mirror.

"And what are you doing here?" Perfetsky asked and smiled crookedly.

"The same as you," the reflection answered him and took off its glasses, squinting blindly.

Stakh felt the bridge of his nose. His glasses were in place.

"So, maybe, have you seen her somewhere?" He stuck his finger in the reflection's chest.

"She doesn't want to have anything to do with us, old man." He heard an answer from the mirror. "They're all whores! Remember: it was this way, is, and will be. They betray always and everywhere. Our foolish hearts—they're just an object of play for them. You just have to screw them screw them and forget them, and go on! . . ."

"What time is it?" Stas asked for some reason.

The reflection looked at his watch and said, "Twelve-fifteen. The tenth of March has arrived, old man."

"Happy birthday," Stas said and offered his unfinished bottle.

But he couldn't make his way there, beyond the mirror, behind the smooth and cold surface.

Then there were all new trials: a rotted-out beam that had fallen from somewhere on Stakh's head; a puddle of blood, from which five rats were ladled out; a frothing mad black Rottweiler that was trying to rip free from its chain, tied to a giant ship's chest; a frightened flock of bats. But nothing could stop Perfetsky.

Don't leave me with others. Don't lose me. That's what Ada said. And he circulated each time through new nooks of this strange building, in which something exceedingly abominable was happening.

And his despair was so fierce that he grabbed a small piece of brick and scratched out on the wall in huge letters: ADA I ALREADY HAVE THIS UP TO MY EARS THEY'VE GOTTEN ME I'VE HAD ENOUGH!

But all the same he continued to search for her.

"And if she's already returned to the hall and is dancing with someone again?"—all at once came to mind for him. Then he rushed back, but in a few minutes he understood that he wouldn't find a hall today— all the corridors were dead ends and, throwing himself in one direction, then in another, each time Stakh returned to the spot where he had left his desperate appeal. Out of such hopelessness he had to liplock himself to his beloved bottle, and right there heard a harp. Its sounds, arranged in a completely harmonic sequence, in no way fit with the general cacophony everywhere. Perfetsky moved toward them, just as to light, the sounds were already near him, and he quickened his pace when he suddenly sensed how he was falling who knows where; in an instant he was bustling about inside a glassy space filled with water, some kind of aquarium, where all kinds of multicolored little fish were swimming past him with black spots on yellow fins or vice versa. A large head with a beard and bald spots bent over above him and malevolently grinned. Perfetsky wanted to hide from it in one of the shells on the sandy bottom, but right there alongside the head arms grew, two incredibly large five-fingered ones, and they began to rock the aquarium to every side, from which an awful agitation began, Perfetsky and the other fish were thrown from wall to wall, the head was happy and laughed loudly, and then the aquarium slipped out from the head's hands, Stakh's eyes grew dim, once again he sensed he was falling, the glass was breaking, and together with the water, plants, and shells he was abandoning his very self.

He came to his senses on the cold cement of the floor.

The harp echoed above him and when he, moaning from the pain, opened his eyes, first caught sight of a black she-monkey who was skillfully strumming strings and winking at him the entire time.

"One more winking babe," Perfetsky thought, rising up on his legs and slowly shaking himself free of the water plants and the wet sand.

"Hi," the monkey said in a human voice, which wildly surprised Stakh.

"Ciao," he finally answered, and at that very instant recognized her—by the expression on her face, by her manner of playing, by several other intimate details—it was that woman who had been sixteen years older than he and who once, a really long time ago, almost in his childhood, had invited him to her place right after the end of rehearsal and had led him to her mysterious garden where he came to know the hurricane of becoming a man.

"You haven't broken your glasses?" The harpist asked.

"Apparently not." Perfetsky touched the bridge of his nose. "They're in place. And how did you . . . how did you end up here?"

"Good evening!" The monkey answered without halting her play even for an instant. "Do you always ask such stupid things?"

"No, not always," Stakh guiltily denied.

"Then ask something smarter."

"You . . . do You⁵ know this building?"

"Happy New Year!" The woman answered, and Stakh recognized her even better. "This is what you consider smarter?"

"Well, then, um, tell me, whether then, tell me, um—I forgot how to you, well um, I have addressed You. . . ."

"You didn't address me in any way. You just clattered with your teeth, such a thin boy," the monkey reminded him.

"Maybe," Stakh tossed in, "but tell me how to find the large hall where everyone is singing and drinking. . . ."

"*Buenos dias!*" the harpist interrupted him. "Be so kind to tell me, why do you need that hall if she's not there?"

"Which she?" Perfetsky didn't understand.

"Well this one, yours. . . ."

"Do you know where she is?"

"Posolutely," the monkey said and mysteriously grew silent, completely surrendering to the music.

"Then might you tell me?" Stas began to seethe, rummaging through all his pockets in vain, apparently for his lost bottle.

"And what's in it for me?" The woman coquetted.

"A million lire." Perfetsky crawled after the long envelope.

"No way, man!" The harpist said to this. "Why the fuck do I need your lire?"

"Well, then I don't know what else I can do for you," Stas babbled, thinking with horror that right now, for sure, he'd have to screw her.

"Just kiss me." The monkey finally expressed her desire. "But not here. And not here. Do you know where? On my butt!"

"Ma'am, forgive me, I, perhaps, how can I say this to you . . . ," Perfetsky purred, imagining the red monkey's behind and feeling so faint as though he were sixteen again and the madame twice as old as he were inviting him for tea after rehearsal.

"What, you don't want to?" The monkey pretended to be dejected. "You liked it once and called it your sweetest melon. . . . You shameless cad! . . ."

"I don't remember." Perfetsky wiped his brow. "Maybe it was somebody else who called it that?"

"Well, that's your problem." The monkey was insulted and with her entire look decisively showed that the conversation was at an end.

Beyond the walls it was still thundering, the storm had not calmed down for a while, in the echoing corridors a strong wind whistled and rose.

"Okay," Stas sighed, and the harp stopped playing.

He shut his eyes and struck his lips on something cold and metallic. It was the knob of some door that he had not seen before. From the touch of his lips the door opened up slightly. Perfetsky rose up from his knees, but he didn't enter the room that had opened up beyond the door. He could see everything anyway, even though only a few candles were burning in the room and a thick gloom ruled.

In the middle of the room a really old cast iron bathtub was standing on four legs, blackened with smoke and cracked. Obviously it was supposed to fill the function of a bed, for the pale yellow Casallegra had lain down right inside it. Next to the bathtub the perspiring Mavropule had fallen to one knee. The President's arm had grown still on his wild gypsy head, bent over as if it were a flag. Both girls—Lucia and Concita—stood at the head and feet of the bathtub in the poses of mourners. Besides them, there was one more person—someone turned with their face to the wall, some woman in a dark green dress, in front of her there was a thick open folio volume, from which she read something softly and monotonically, in a viscid, completely unknown language, perhaps *koine* Greek.

"And then the hour will come," the old guy said, barely stirring his thin gray lips.

"And then the hour will come," Mavropule repeated after him.

"And another will come at the will of my Master. . . ."

"And I will come at the will of my Master. . . ."

"And you will not believe and will say to your Master. . . ."

". . . to my Master. . . ."

"My Master, I have not been in the world enough, I have not enjoyed myself enough. . . ."

"My Master. I have not hurled enough, I have not destroyed enough."

"You, my Master, I have not praised enough, have not drawn near enough, have not savored enough. . . ."

". . . not hazed enough, not drunk beer enough, not disfavored you enough. . . ."

"and for five thousand springs served You fairly, and have served you well."

". . . and for five thousand springs have served you vilely, and go to hell."

"And I ask You, my Master: "Why today?""

"And I ask You, my Master: "Why not today?""

"And I sense You in my gut, as you say: "It will be today!""

"And I sense You in my ass, as you say: "It will be today!""

"For the hour has come and the night has come and he has come. . . ."

"For the hour has come and the night has come and I have come. . . ."

"To whom you give My strength My beauty and My charms. . . ."

"To whom you give His strength His beauty and His charms. . . ."

"And I take You unto Myself for eternal delectation in the garden dell!"

"And I take You unto myself for eternal devastation in hell!"

"Thus it must be so. . . ."

"Thus it must be so. . . ."

"Thus it must become. . . ."

"Thus it must become. . . ."

"And if not to be or to become, then nothing can be or become!"

"And if not to be or to become, then I'll let you have it, scum!"

And following the end of these words, from which Perfetsky's breath had been taken away, the old man uttered yet one more charm, and Mavropule mumbled them after him, the perspiration rolled from Mavropule like Babylonian rivers, so that the caustic jacket became dark cherry colored, and thunder split the sky somewhere beyond the walls, and dark blue sparks flashed through the hand of the dying man and crackled in the wild hair of his successor, and all this gurgled in an unknown language and perhaps in various unknown languages, for Perfetsky did not know any language, but just knew words. . . .

And then the bathtub with the old man's body rose up nearly to the ceiling and began to circle the room, and everyone, even the woman in green, led their gazes to it, as though to the image of their higher master, and for an instant it was not the grayish old man who had just uttered the charm in a drumming sound, but a lion with wings, and you could take him for that very same sacred lion if not for the tiny horns that stuck out from beneath his bright mane; but everything lasted just for an instant, for the bathtub exploded together with the lion in a blinding flash, and there was much yellow smoke, and stench, and again just for a moment, for after the explosion just an egg remained that had fallen from beneath the wall onto the floor, but it did not break because it was so hard, and it was not given to break, for it was its destiny.

The egg rolled, and Mavropule was already rising up from his knee. Catching the egg, he swallowed it. At that very moment a large fiery pillar stood in his place, along with an insane, loud laughter and heat, and Lucia and Concita actively began to dance around him. Just the lady in the dark green continued to stand with her face in the book, from which she was reading something mysterious out loud. . . .

Along the rotten boards, along the pools, along the pieces of the aquariums, along the slippery and crooked stairs, along the bowls and buckets with rainwater, along the candlesticks and lanterns, along everything that came under his feet, Perfetsky ran wherever his eyes could see, although his eyes saw nothing. Some kind of raven's nests were strewn on him from the ceiling, some kind of mouse paws and snails fell behind his collar, and there was sand everywhere, gypsum, cement, and bits of bits of wallpaper, and suitcases, and boxes, and coffins. . . .

YURI ANDRUKHOVYCH

"So it all happened, came true, was fulfilled!" Dappertutto shrieked into the microphone.

Everyone greeted this announcement with applause. Only Ada, the queen of the reception, in a dark green dress with brooch frog (frog Brooch), stood in stasis before the open book, the extraordinarily thick half folio.

"My celebrated guests!" The secretary continued the night's activities. "My supervenerables! Our frolic continues, though it's already not too far from dawn. But what are those earthly dawns to us—the main thing is still just ahead of us! How's your mood, my luminaries?"

Everyone began to roar and stamp with such roaring resolve that Dappertutto bloomed like a monstrous dwarf tree.

"The moment of the final reward is upon us," he began to speak after a minute when the throng had grown silent. "You recall that the foundation has promised us considerably larger blessings than the supper, to the point happily gobbled up by you, and honoraria, which have been placed in your pockets. But what, what can it be? What do you want the most?"

In response innumerable answers began to echo, among which one could manage to hear something about cars, oil stocks, airplanes, and real estate, for each had a different desire.

"No!" Dappertutto contested, shaking his head. "No! You'll not receive that today, but something considerably loftier, more valuable, and more incomparable. But what is this? What is it you desire the most?"

This time fewer answers came, but some ventured anyway to conjecture about the most intimate thing out loud:

"A sex gland transplant!"

"Interplanetary sex!"

"Extending the life span!"

"Life on the islands!"

"Eternal bliss!"

"You've nearly guessed it, my sweet people, you've nearly guessed it! Just a bit more—and you'll forever remove from yourselves the burden of the impossible! Think more unfettered, easier, freer—remember: nothing is impossible! Today everything is given! Just a bit more—and we will hear that word, we will reach the unreachable, we will attain the unattainable, that mysterious idée fixe, of which you still, perhaps, are embarrassed, but you really really want this, in dreams, in your subcortex, in your insights you see this. . . ."

"Immortality," Perfetsky joked, and everyone looked back at him.

"Yes, yes, the devil take you!" Dappertutto jumped up. "Yes! Who said this word? Who was the first to utter it? Where is he? Show me this jokester!" At least fifty percent of the people began to shout, competing with each other: "I! I said it!"

After which such mad joys had already begun, such cat screams, such wildness of temperaments, that the secretary for an intolerably long time had to tame and calm down the company, in reality provoking it even more.

"Yes! Yes! Immortality! Eternity! The Universe!" He screamed incessantly, sweeping his tail and running back and forth through the hall.

Anyway, this squall had to come to an end, and silence finally fell. Everyone grew silent because they wanted to know to an excessive degree what was to come, which game will be played with them today.

"But for immortality, my eminences," Dappertutto intrigued them, "for immortality each one of you needs to adjust something in themselves. You are just worthy of it, immortality, if you have become yourself, otherwise—drat it! But you—for the time being, you are not you, my dear friends! Because at this moment you still are not yourselves! Right now you are nothing, fie, emptiness, intellectuals! I wish you to become yourselves! The real you! Different! Incomparable!"

"But how?" In a single unified voice the guests of the house of Farfarello began to drone.

"A magic book!" Again the secretary outshouted them. "The magic book in the hands of our queen Ada! A magic book that is four hundred years old! Four hundred times by four hundred years! It will judge everyone and will transform them for immortality!"

After the umpteenth storm of calls and exaltations had abated, Dappertutto once again took the microphone snake in his hands.

He spoke now without exclamation points, peacefully and con-
cretely—as an instructor of alpinists before the ascent on an especially prominent crag:

"The procedure will be simple. Each one of you who agrees to
immortality, and I expect there aren't any who don't here, goes up
to the book in turn and utters just two numbers: the first of them
designates the page from the end of the book, and the second—
the line from the bottom of the page. There are one thousand one
hundred and eleven pages in this book, and forty lines, that is, a
multitude, on each page. You name the two numbers, just the two
numbers, without any superfluous chitchat, and Ada will read the
spot you've mentioned out loud. And then, if you're worthy of it,
you will be re-created for a new life, for an immortality in accord
with what is written and read!

And you really should have seen how all the guests dashed
toward Ada, to her queen's podium, how they began to quarrel
tenaciously over a place in line, how they scraped elbows, shoulders
and stomachs! . . . (Although the impetuous Shalizer outsped everyone with her hat cocked.)

It was just Perfetsky, somber in his glasses, who didn't dash anywhere. Didn't he thirst for immortality, or what?

Between five and six in the morning the shutters flew open, and
together with the whirlwind that circled through the hall, a fiery
pillar grew on the windowsill, in the middle of which stood the
red caustic Mavropule, accompanied by two small comets and a
trail of heated gases. And the first comet was called Lucia, and the
second Concita. And Mavropule began to scream from his very
bowels:

"I am the great spirit of Bakhafu! I have come to summon you.
Go with me to the flowering gardens of our and your master and
sovereign!"

"Arise!" Dappertutto roared from his serpentine microphone.

"Arise!" The daintily weak voices, the name to which there is a
legion, sang out after him.

"Let us arise," the guests demanded.

And they were carried off from the windows into the stormy

predawn sky, one after another, one before the other, one ahead of the other, accompanied by the fiery sorcerer with two comets at his sides. But it already was not Liza Sheila among them, but a snake-bodied winged lamia, a succubus by the name of Lilith, and it was so good for her. And it was not the impersonator Alborak Djabraili who flew up into the endless space after her, but a spirit without a name, who had stolen a winged stallion from the prophet and was about to acquire his name for himself, but by the will of Allah was deprived of it, and the aforementioned horse returned to the golden stables in the seventh heaven; but this was good for the nameless spirit, for he became his true self. And it was not John Paul Oshchyrko who took flight into the cold heights to the bottomlessly blue other grass, but the spirit of the African forest Dada, present in every plant, in every flower and reed, in every speck of dust, and then forgotten, but today from oblivion made into a blade of grass again, that is, resurrected—an earth, grass, leaf spirit, and it was good for him. And, of course, it wasn't Gaston Dejavu, the expert on Choreography, who burst into the Ocean of Air after the saved ones, but another winged creature—for all of them were winged—Marquise of Frogs, a thin-legged croaker, a great aficionado of black masses and sabbath games in the otherworldly marshes; and it was so good.

And after them—yet a whole slew of other guests; but not actors or ministers, and not models, and not bankers, but mostly lemurs and vipers and sirens and eight-eyed dragons and manticores with lacertines. . . .

And the entire lengthy cavalcade flickered spectrally and fluttered in all directions in smoke, and shot off gases and hummed, and roared and howled. And finally, at six-fifteen in the earthly Venetian morning, in an instant at the first flash of day, it disappeared in the darkness among unknown constellations.

And Stakh Perfetsky ended up in the book, no, in the Book, in its garden, among the bushes and flowers of old woodcuts, among the birds and bees of Greek writing, among the *koine,* among enchanting stories, among scents—of old paper, wine, type fonts, watercolors, golden embossings. The garden was stifling and dark, and the grass in it reached up to Stakh's waist and higher, and snakes hissed everywhere. He already had nearly caught up to Her—for he was sure that it was She, although he saw Her just from behind—he had been running after Her for a long time, but nevertheless was unable to catch up, further on, the grass was higher, the hissing became louder, it smelled of the fruits of all the trees depicted on the page, thus, he caught up to her anyway, just to ask Her and not find out, just to look and not see, just to stretch out his hand and not touch Her, and he already was stretching out his hand with his endlessly long fingers, when suddenly he heard that he was being called, that the voice of another, the voice of Ada was incessantly calling him, that his name had been uttered already tens of times and, maybe even hundreds of times. And when this finally reached him, he stopped, then everything stopped, and the just revealed garden gathered together into an infinitely small meaningless dot, the last dot at the end of the last sentence of the already nonexistent Book, no, book, for again and again from somewhere, just a single word made its way to him: "Stanislav!"

■ □ ■ □ ■

2 6

༡༊-པ༡༠༠:
In this last of my dispatches I want to inform Monsignore about the following:

a. On the morning of March 10, I entered the hotel room of the Respondent and saw him sleeping in bed, but in his clothes, including his coat. This looked like one of the consequences of last evening's supper that occurred at Casa Farfarello. I was forced for an intolerably long time to call Stanislav (crossed out) the Respondent from his dreams. I had the impression that it was as though he heard my voice, but he didn't want to submit to it, but preferred to abide *there* (possible variants: an old building, night skies, a dark garden). But anyway my persistence achieved the goal: the Respondent returned to reality (?) and looked at me with his eyes wide open. It's hard to say how he saw me without his glasses.

b. I was the first in this world who wished the Respondent a happy birthday. In answer to this, the Respondent announced that he was counting on a gift from me. I promised that we'll just be together the entire day. The Respondent retorted that it won't be possible, for today's the concluding day of the seminar, a quite important memorandum has to be approved and—most important—in the program some kind of raging supper-maestoso with grappa was anticipated.

c. While Stakh (crossed out) was soaking in the bathtub and bringing himself into shape, I thought about the fact that tomorrow at this time neither he nor I will be here any longer. I didn't want this "tomorrow" to come, but it was coming, it was drawing closer. In the meantime he (crossed out) the Respondent was splashing in the bathtub and at the top of his voice singing a Ukrainian song, the content of which lies first and foremost in the fact that out of a hundred thousand pairs of lovers just one succeeds in not parting.

d. During breakfast an unpleasantness occurred: feeling in his jacket an envelope, presented yesterday by the foundation, the Respondent decided to boast how rich he was. But upon looking inside, he turned pale and rigid with his entire, even without that, longish face, strewing all kinds of trifles from the envelope. Instead of twenty new banknotes for fifty thousand lire each that, according to the words of the Respondent, still were in the envelope last night, today he found in it: a scrap of the city map of Venice with the location of Casa Farfarello marked; a used ticket for a city traffic boat (one trip); another used ticket—this one to the Correr Museum; a yellowed page from some Italian cookbook that contained a recipe for making *broeto de pesse;*[1] an invitation to a benefit concert of the works by Giovanni Legrenzi that took place in the Ca' Rezzonico yet on February 13 a year ago; an ad for a Macintosh computer system; a newspaper announcement for services in fortune-telling, massage, and the formulation of horoscopes; a used telephone card with a reproduction of *Porticoes* by Canaletto; a newspaper clipping photograph of the Italian prime minister; a page from a school copybook, on which was drawn in a red flowmaster a heart with an arrow through it; a Xerox, folded in four, of the last page of a lecture on the topic "Sex without Cudgels, or Little Red Riding Hood on the Right Road" (in English); a leaflet of a secret Maoist organization with a call for a one-hour sit-down strike; instructions for the use of the bidet basin in the restroom at the train station in the city of Venice; a postcard with a view of a lagoon from the bell tower of San Marco in evening, on the other side a handwritten inscription "Dear Lesia!"; a heavily marked-up draft of four terzinas from canto 21 of Dante's *Inferno;* a page of a telephone notepad with the single notation, "My little partridge: 505-99-12"; a receipt with a bill for dinner in the Luna Restaurant; the label from a wine bottle, "Merlot di Pramaggiora"; a piece of thick cover paper with the text of the main Krishna prayer jotted down in Urdu, and also in Latin transliteration; a dried laurel leaf that crumbled at a touch.

e. The noted find, as I've already announced, did not leave a positive impression on the Respondent; he just kept repeating that he was left almost without any money, that he wanted, no, he had dreamt the entire day of spending it on me, that now he (crossed out) Stanislav will be unable to buy even a goblet of good wine for me, not to speak of champagne. I calmed him down, telling him that money isn't the main thing. I have quite enough of it for us to celebrate this day without any particular restrictions and wouldn't deny ourselves anything.

f. Then the Respondent wiped his brow and said that all this, absolutely, is one of those hocus-pocus tricks, many of which occurred last night, and to which he was a witness. I became interested what exactly he (the Respondent) had in mind. In answer, I heard Stakh's confused and contradictory impressions about flying fiery pillars, a monkey that played "The Minor Masonic Cantata" on the accordion, a black donkey under a bedcover, and other fairy tales. I surmise namely in this chimerical manner, his (Stanislav's) head was reflecting the nocturnal ceremony of the Baron's transition into a flying substance and the raising by him (the Baron) of the newly appeared Prince to a rank of power and grandeur, as well as the general naturalization of the other respondents, successfully accomplished with the assistance of the Book.

g. I managed to rid the Respondent of his doubts that what he saw last night had any kind of real underpinnings. A cup of coffee quivered slightly in his (Orpheus's) hand and, in order to cheer up his sullen soul on such a day for it, I turned the Respondent's attention to the sun-drenched world beyond the window.

h. After the night mistral, Venice truly looked freshly created and was a fine gift for the Respondent. The skies were clear and grand, bright buildings were reflected in the waters of the canal next to the motorboats, agile produce barks and, obviously, floating gondolas. The night wind, in fact, had done some damage to the city, flooding the lower floors of buildings, breaking piles here and there, overturning garbage cans, and shattering lamps. However the main thing is that it raised the water and substantially renewed it, driving away all the previous dirt.

i. First and foremost this struck me just as Stas and I had started off after breakfast to the shores of San Giorgio Maggiore, although

I was sure that it was in vain. When we stepped out onto the wide strand of the San Marco Canal, Stas squeezed my shoulders. I placed my cheek on his large hand. His hair blew in the wind and touched my face. He whispered in my ear: "I can't without you." I had to keep silent for three minutes in order to handle myself and not give myself away with my voice.

j. In the building of the monastery, of course, no one was there and nothing happened. Attached to the doors of the Cenacolo a piece of paper brought to the attention of all the seminar participants and guests that last night the president of the Foundation *La morte di Venezia,* Dr. Baron Casallegra, had unexpectedly died. Linked to the sudden death of its inspiration and ideologue (how does Monsignore like this?) the seminar must put a halt to any kind of work, in as much as the collaborators of the foundation should concentrate all their attention on a worthy disposition of the burial ceremony. The participants and guests over the course of the day were asked to leave the city.

k. Having *kissed the monastery's doorknob*[2] (my émigré Ukrainian expression "to kiss the doorknob" at this point made a great impression on Stakh), we returned to the boat. The steps before the Church of San Giorgio were flooded (*acqua alta*).[3] Stakh was quite unhappy with the fact that now he would be unable to complete the closing memorandum, to which he, as he says, had some ten extremely essential propositions. But it seems to me that his unhappiness more likely was linked to the promised and lost concluding supper. That's the way he is, this Respondent!

l. I reminded him that all this was just for the better, because we would have each other all day, unconstrained and free. To say farewell to Venice and to say farewell to each other. It was not simple for me to express this. Something got in the way in my throat, it was too much when Orpheus touched my neck with his soft lips, somewhere there, right beneath the nape of the neck, sweeping aside my scarf and sweater (Monsignore must remember which of the sweaters I'm talking about!), he (crossed out) the Respondent touched me from behind with his kiss as though it were a golden seal.

m. Again, while we were already in the boat, the theme of the Doctor arose. I answered Stas that the Doctor has been interesting me less and less. I have several suppositions about him. First, the Doctor could simply have wandered off somewhere in old Venice and rented for himself a place for the few days that remained. The Doctor's passion for aquariums and fish, which never had been embraced by me with great enthusiasm, most recently had grown into a completely transparent mania. It is sufficiently possible that the Doctor is carrying out his usual aquarium machinations elsewhere.

n. Third, I would not cast aside the possibility of the Doctor's flirting with some nice Venetian guy. I would least like to appear before Monsignore in the role of a slanderer, but let Monsignore judge us. In my opinion, the Doctor, from beginning to end, with a consistency peculiar to him has tried to undermine this matter for which we've come here, and, truly, has used his entire time in Venice for the settling of his own interests, reaping the fruits of his distance from Monsignore.

o. I would not resort to such accusations and I would have hidden his, the Doctor's, improper conduct before Monsignore, if the news had not come to me about the fact that this ungrateful and treacherous creature had already managed to scribble to Monsignore a dispatch completely contrary to the truth, in which he vilely besmirched and even recommended my person for investigation by the Third Extraordinary Subcommittee. No matter.

p. The water rose so much that even the gondolas could float completely freely across St. Mark's Square. As regards the pedestrians, they were forced to move on specially laid out boards or on stilts. The water completely flooded the atrium of the basilica, which we reached by boat without any difficulties and we floated there for a good hour (until the water had noticeably fallen—so that the bottom of our boat began to scrape on the stone slabs of the floor).

q. The sun gleamed on the water beneath us and on the mosaics above. The splashing of the waves echoed inside the cathedral. Stanislav showed me each tiny stone of this Bible strewn on the ceiling—from the creation of the world to the exodus from Egypt. We stayed for a time in each of the seven small naves, where, next to us, above us and a bit right inside ourselves, the most varied wonders, which under other not so bitter circumstances you would never turn your attention: the Jerusalem black and white columns with eagles and lions, the marble shell of the arcade, fifteen paintings of the world's great flood, all very appropriate today.

r. Old apostles, Saint Mark in rapture, the remainder of the evangelists, the prophets, the floor also was set out in mosaics, they shone from beneath the water, the death of Noah floated above them and above us, the Tower of Babylon, the court of Solomon, the life of Joseph moved in a semicircle, the culmination of which was the Gate of Flowers, and then

s. all of this flowed in reverse order, that is the Gate of Flowers, a semicircle with the life of Joseph, Solomon's court, the Tower of Babylon, the death of Noah floated everywhere, the light of the underwater mosaics, the prophets, the evangelists, the rapture of Mark, the most ancient of the apostles, the great flood of the world in fifteen scenes, but in reverse—begun with an olive branch and completed with the building of the ark, the arcade of a marble shell, eagles and lions of black and white Jerusalem columns and still countless other things, which we did not manage or were unable to see.

t. When we ended up on dry land again, Stas took me by the hand. I told him that all this is not so simple. Pigeons flew around without having anywhere suitable to land. I said that we will try at least not to regret. Stas answered that there is a certain sense in everything. I said that he's right. Stas noted that it had to be this way. I agreed that it couldn't be helped. He let go of my hand.

u. Suddenly he (crossed out) my poet sat next to me and hid behind me, telling me not to move. As it turned out, he had just noticed a certain familiar young woman with whom he had arranged a meeting in Venice. She had come for his sake, but over the course of four days had been unable to find him. Right at that moment she herself got onto the vaporetto. The tourist, of which there are countless numbers—in dark glasses and a sweater below her knees, not interesting in any way. Only a dope like Perfetsky could find anything special in her. She apparently already had to leave Venice, poor girl. On this topic my vagabond announced that he felt bad for her and that she was a true friend.

v. This late sympathy of Don Juan sufficiently angered me, and until the pallid seducer had stooped down quieter than a mouse behind my back, I stuck my tongue out in the direction of the vaporetto, which, fortunately, was moving off somewhere far away, to the Lido, and, perhaps, to Chioggia, Pellestrina, Sicily, or even Poland.

w. Waiting until its complete disappearance from his field of vision, the hero-lover stood up to his full height and immediately attempted to obtain my indulgence, licking my hand in the depression between the bones of my thumb and index finger. I gave the appearance that I wasn't angry at all, though inside I was unnerved and angry, ultimately, not having any right at all to this: his relations with women of different countries—that's his problem, tomorrow we won't be here, we're nothing to each other, just accidental passersby, who wanted to spend a little time together. I even feigned coughing so he wouldn't think anything.

x. I ultimately managed to chill out after just about an hour when we sat down to lunch in a cramped *ostaria* at Campiello Corner not far from the post office. I noticed an unpleasant character, who, with his entire appearance, really reminded me of a hairy monster, some kind of Kynokephalos or something similar was eating overfried fish in a quite slovenly manner, spitting out bones in every direction and nearly without taking his eyes off Stanislav, who was sitting with his back to him and therefore couldn't see this. From the fact that he (the monster) was greedily downing the fish with the cheapest red wine (!) I concluded that he absolutely must come from the same country as Stanislav.

y. Monsignore certainly understands completely that as the favorite pupil of Monsignore, I have learned some things in Monsignore's school in my time. For example, I could have made the repulsive devourer of the fish accidentally choke on a bone and in just a few seconds, as Monsignore likes to joke, he'd stretch out his fins. But I have an overly soft heart, even concerning such people whom I decidedly dislike. That's why I just put a little spell on the abomination, and over the course of the next half hour, until Stas and I were drinking our coffee with liqueur, the Kynokephalos spent in a complete stupor, with glassy eyes, a gaping mouth, and a goblet raised from the table. It was like this until we left the *ostaria*.

z. And here again such despair came over me, such an intolerable faint feeling wound around from my head to toes, that I thought to myself: no room for you to breathe, toots. Though we had nearly sixteen more hours to be together. And if you translate this into minutes, then it's even longer. And I thought that we really, really have to spend them the best way we can, the closest we can, to give each other as much warmth as we can, and that's incredibly a lot. And I am crossing out this word forever—the Respondent (crossed out), I have not completed my mission, I've intentionally not completed it, because I've had enough—of missions, of secrets, of sacrifices, of reports, for from tomorrow on even more so it's all the same for me, and I am leaving the Pyramid from under Monsignore's guardianship, and—beyond this—with all my heart I renounce Monsignore.

With respect—Non-Cerina

BARON LEONARDO DI CASALLEGRA, A DOCTOR OF THANATOLOGY, A learned carnivalist, an eternal Venetian, a tireless seeker of truth and virtue, has finally left this life. This occurred the night of March 10, when the elements were swirling above the city, and the invisible wings of the powerful demons of foul weather fluttered outside the windows of our homes. His death was sudden and categorical—it comes exactly this way to the greatest of the great.

Word of honor, we can't believe it. We can't believe that Leonardo di Casallegra is no longer with us. It is difficult to imagine this city without him. It seemed that he has always lived in it. It seemed that he has been its master, its phantom and its husband. This was the most faithful of marriages that one has seen anywhere ever—his marriage with Venice.

It is deeply symbolic that Leonardo di Casallegra has left us at the climax of the activities of the seminar about our city that was set into motion and made a reality by him. Embodying one of the most grandiose of his ideas, he certainly was completely happy and with a light soul stepped into the streams of other music, as happens with people who fulfill their earthly predestination till the end.

The scholar did not will that he be buried in the ground. For one such as he, flowing, changing and different—the idea of a normal and even trivial repose in the ground was profoundly abhorrent. Today we are doing as he ordered, and his ashes will be scattered from a plane above the lagoon.

The memory of him remains with us. Eternal memory of the eternal Venetian.

Foundation *La morte di Venezia*

CARNIVAL MUST CONTINUE ON, OTHERWISE IT MIGHT END!

The concluding memorandum of the First Venetian seminar
"The Post-Carnival Absurdity of the World:
What Is on the Horizon?"

*Resolved on the tenth of March on board a Bucintoro airplane,
from which the remains of Leonardo di Casallegra were scattered.*

From the sixth to the tenth of March 1993 in the city of Venice the international seminar "The Post-Carnival Absurdity of the World: What Is on the Horizon?" took place. About 330 participants took part in it, with seven main speakers from more than eight countries of the world.

The seminar participants and guests gathered in the capital of carnivals in the first days of Lent with a single joint aim: to express their suppositions on the further possibilities of humankind to remain, to be, and to become itself. Any kind of possible reflections on this topic particularly happen to be tangible for us today, in the time of the approach to a certain chronological boundary, beyond which there is an ominous unknown.

During the course of the seminar there were:

—7 main speakers with a total speaking time of 16.5 or even more hours;

—1,213 addresses in discussions and other remarks—as immediately relevant to the theme of the seminar, as well as completely far from it, and even inappropriate;

—nearly 14,537 hermetic metaphors, rhetorical figures, pointed paradoxes, transparent allusions, mysterious quotations, other means of black humor, and national dishes;

—over 817 original ideas released into culturological circulation; and

—a striking quantity of white and colored liquids imbibed, first and foremost of grape, grain, and blood origin.

The seminar participants and guests came to the following main joint conclusions:

I. The city of Venice (together with the suburbs of Mestre and Marghera) today numbers approximately 370,000 inhabitants.

II. On the threshold of the new millennium the chances of humankind's survival and subsequently remaining itself (and what is this?), are not excessively great, but they do exist.

III. In conjunction with the not quite realized participation of soapmakers and wiseacres in the recent (read "future") attempt at the recreating-the-world syndrome of the spring-autumn hunting of witches should be considered "unlimited" and should be immediately withdrawn from all periodical tables.

IV. Carnival must continue on; otherwise, it might end!

Our memorandum is resolved in the sky above Venice during the ceremony of the scattering of the immortal dust of our Friend and Teacher, Professor Leonardo di Casallegra. From a bird's eye view Venice has the shape of a *fish*, bisected by an upside-down letter "S" (Canal Grande).

We call all the nonapathetic to support us in our strivings. People, be vigilant!

Dr. Leonardo di Casallegra, Baron. Amerigo Dappertutto, Executive Secretary. Dr. Gaston Dejavu, France. Psuedo-Alborak Djabraili, Sheik. Guru John Paul Oshchyrko, da-da. Liza Sheila Shalizer (Lilith Zuckerkandel), Writer. Tsutsu Mavropule (*BKF*), Prince of Fire, Fire Eater. Slavistan Prefektsky (*CIS*), Author. All together 329 signatures.

■ □ ■ □ ■

2 8

[*Videocassette, a retelling.*]
Introductory Remarks
The action occurs in one of Venice's small restaurants. In these dinner
hours it is nearly filled up. This, however, is just a general (background noise) impression, because in the frame we don't really see
very much. The left side of the frame contains a fragment of a mirror,
in which the opposite side of the room is reflected with the bar and
old exotic bottles, big bellied, longish, flat, and ball-like, often woven
over with straw. Sometimes in the mirror passing visitors appear and
disappear. In the right side of the frame you can see just the edge of
someone's table, but it's not known who is sitting at it, and, perhaps
it's immaterial. In the center of the frame, closer to the mirror is a
table at which two people are sitting—we recognize Stas Perfetsky
immediately, next to him a young woman in a dark cherry-colored
jacket, as we surmise, Ada Zitrone. A lit candle is standing between
them. They apparently have just finished dinner. Perfetsky from time
to time locks lips with a narrow shot glass, from which he draws
something that burns going down. His companion has a bit of red
wine in a goblet. What else? An ashtray with a pile of butts testifies to
the fact that it's not a very high-class restaurant. The conversation
doesn't always sound clear, but after three or four listenings it yields to
a nearly complete deciphering. An unknown camera, obviously hidden, works in a static position, there is not a single edit over the course
of all the taped material. Constantly a general view.

STAKH PERFETSKY [*sipping from his flask in turn*]: It burned. Total seventh heaven. Why have you hidden that thing from me for so long?

ADA ZITRONE: You can't know everything, kiddo. I can't know everything. . . .

STAKH PERFETSKY: I have in mind this vile stuff. [*Nods at the liquid in the shot glass.*]

ADA ZITRONE: Ah, that! Well, if you don't like it. . . .

STAKH PERFETSKY: I like it. It loosens your tongue and then weaves shut again. It's warm from it. It fills me with an inner humming, like Houdini. Harry. I echo with life around me.

ADA ZITRONE: And the cortex of your brain?

STAKH PERFETSKY: I sense it dying. Beginning from the subcortex. Soon it will be completely gone. Can you imagine how good it is without your subcortex? It's the same as without. . . .

ADA ZITRONE: This, for sure, is a tragedy for a poet?

STAKH PERFETSKY: Not for certain. Maybe I'll stop having these damned dreams at least. You didn't answer my question.

ADA ZITRONE: Is this important for you?

STAKH PERFETSKY: Very important. Both for me and for you.

ADA ZITRONE: I don't know what to say to you, Stanislav. I was fearful of our relations, this getting close. That it'll go too far. Do you remember that day when I didn't come? [STAKH *nods his head.*] I had to be alone. I thought it would help. But by evening I was already moaning without you. I pounded my fists on the wall. On my pillow. And writhed on the bed, as though. . . . Actually, you don't have to know such things. . . .

STAKH PERFETSKY: Talk, talk. That's nice for me. [*Takes her by the hand.*] I'm a little sauced, but I'm allowed today, ain't I?

ADA ZITRONE: I'm fearfully awaiting the hour when we part. . . .

STAKH PERFETSKY [*looking at his watch*]: It's ten right now. We still have nine hours. At least. If not more. Everything depends just on you.

ADA ZITRONE: On me? You've proposed something extraordinarily unexpected. I'm not ready to answer you.

STAKH PERFETSKY: And in nine hours?

ADA ZITRONE: You should have understood me. You're proposing something from which my head is swirling. Maybe it's just the wine? Just think—how can I say yes when I know almost nothing about you till now. Do you remember then in San Marco, I told you about myself? Everything you'd want to know. To personal trifles. But your life? I don't know anything about you. Besides the fact that you've crawled inside me and are sitting there, and don't leave me. Who are you, Stanislav? I don't know anything about you personally. About the women in your life, your lovers. No, not that way, sorry. I don't want to have anything to do with your lovers. But how, well, how can I answer "good" to you when someone is certainly waiting for you at home? Tell me honestly, is she waiting? . . .

STAKH PERFETSKY: It's been seven years already since no one's been there waiting for me.

ADA ZITRONE: You're divorced?

STAKH PERFETSKY: She died.

[ADA *drinks the wine.* STANISLAV, *catching the reflection of the* WAITER *in the mirror, makes a sign to come over.* STAKH *drinks up from the shot glass.*]

We lived together for not quite five years. I tore her away from her father's home. I took her by the hand and led her away, although I didn't have anywhere to go. They hated me and considered me a redneck from Chortopil.[1]

ADA ZITRONE: Who?

STAKH PERFETSKY: Well, not someone whom they'd want to have for a son-in-law. They were from really old nobility. They lived in a mansion on the slopes of High Castle. There were lots of wild grapes there and ruined birds' nests. At night, when I was accompanying her home, their servants suddenly jumped from behind a fence and beat me with sticks. I made my way to her bedroom through the chimney, sometimes through the window, up sheets tied together. Her younger sister spied on us, but didn't say a word to her parents, otherwise the old man would have shot me on the spot like a vile criminal. . . ."

[*A young dandyishly dressed* WAITER *appears. He tries to catch* ADA's *eye. But she doesn't answer him.*]

WAITER: *Qualcos'altro?*[2]

STAKH PERFETSKY: Order me one more of these.

[STAKH *points to the shot glass.* ADA *orders and the* WAITER *moves away, casting a look at her one more time.*]

ADA ZITRONE: What happened later?

STAKH PERFETSKY [*lighting up a smoke*]: We got married in the Church of Sts. Peter and Paul. Her parents, of course, chased her out of the house. We were students and had nowhere to live. We stayed up overnight at anybody's place who'd take us in. Sometimes for months we lived at some summer houses outside the city or in old dilapidated buildings, designated for being moved. It was a dog's life: eternal garbage cans, basements, someone's dens where they let us make love for three rubles. . . .

ADA ZITRONE: Love? You loved her?

STAKH PERFETSKY: With every minute more and more. I quivered when I would get too close to her. We very rarely had the chance to be alone, just the two of us. Sometimes I took her to the woods, sometimes to the park at night. It was hardest in the winter, as you surely must understand. We had several friends, and they looked for all kinds of temporary havens for us—in garrets, in studios of various artists, in basements. After a year of this kind of life she began to take ill: colds, fevers, lack of food, nervous problems, all kinds of female problems. I went to her parents, but the old man didn't even want to hear about any kind of reconciliation, in our conversation he just called her a whore, a bitch, etc. When I was walking from their porch outside, they set two enormous dogs on me, and I was in the hospital for a couple weeks. . . .

[*The* WAITER *approaches with a small platter, which contains just a single greenish shot glass.*]

WAITER: *Per Lei, Signore.*

ADA ZITRONE: *Per favore, ancora del vino. Grazie.*[3]

STAKH PERFETSKY [*swigging from the shot glass*]: Good stuff. I begin to flow from it. It carries me off somewhere. Do you see this scar? [*Rolls up his shirt above the wrist of his left arm.*] These are the teeth of one of those monstrosities.

ADA ZITRONE: And what happened then?

STAKH PERFETSKY: Afterward we finally graduated from the university, and I suggested that we move to my hometown, to Chortopil. You, maybe, have never heard of it. It's a little town in the mountains not far from Romania, nearly next to the center of Europe. I was born there. A lot of drunks and all kinds of misfits live there, who've experienced defeat in life and who've eaten shit. I knew that to return there—would be to acknowledge myself as the same. But in any case there was a roof over our heads. The house of my parents, a garden with old apple trees. Cherry trees. Have you ever picked cherries? [ADA *drinks the wine.*] And the linden tree, the linden tree, the linden tree. In July[4] this was a true kingdom. I crawled along its branches, my head went topsy-turvy, it was a sweet, fragrant labyrinth. An ancient linden tree. [ADA *drinks the wine.*] Today you're so . . . special. -

ADA ZITRONE: I want you to remember me. This way—special. But you'll be that way for me, too, kiddo! . . . [*Touches* STAKH *'s face with her hand.*] What happened then?

STAKH PERFETSKY: We arrived there in the summer, every day it rained. You couldn't even see the mountains. In two weeks she couldn't handle it. She began to beg to go back. She couldn't live without her Lviv. Once a week they brought a new film to Chortopil. From early morning I used to buy tickets for the last evening show. This was the only diversion. Besides strolls through the rainy forest, of course. During the film the local boys whistled from the back rows and rolled empty bottles of *shmurdiak* along the floor.

ADA ZITRONE: From under the what?

STAKH PERFETSKY: Well, it's a kind of wine. If you drink it right from the bottle, then the next fifteen minutes your life seems fantastically beautiful.

ADA ZITRONE: And afterward?

STAKH PERFETSKY: Afterward, as a rule, you vomit.

ADA ZITRONE: I know that. I'm asking what happened with you afterward?

STAKH PERFETSKY: Afterward, clearly, we returned to Lviv. She was an absolutely worldly lady. She couldn't live without parties. Without theaters, without new clothes, without fine underwear, without morning cocoa, without poetry evenings and bohemian nights. . . . A noble woman, what can you do? . . . Barbara Langisz! . . .

ADA ZITRONE: Could you guarantee all that for her?

STAKH PERFETSKY: I managed to do some things. It happened that for a whole week I'd unload wagons at night, or buy something for her from the black marketeers—underwear that she liked, for example. . . .

ADA ZITRONE [*semiironically*]: You were the rarest of husbands! . . .

STAKH PERFETSKY [*not noticing the irony*]: What are you saying? I was really at fault. I was overly occupied with myself. Poems, drinking bouts. At times I disappeared for long weeks. Afterward she didn't believe me. She was sure that I was hiring some babes and sleeping with them. At times I even screamed at her that it's not true. But all the same she didn't believe me.

[*The* WAITER *appears with a not very big pitcher on a tray. He pours wine into* ADA's *goblet and herewith inseparably gazes into her eyes.*]

WAITER [*having filled up the goblet*]: "*Prego, Signora.*"

ADA ZITRONE: *Grazie, lei è molto gentile.*[5]

[ADA *also looks right into his eyes. This lasts about a minute; in the meantime,* PERFETSKY, *submerged in his own thoughts, continues.*]

STAKH PERFETSKY: The police often stopped us. Or their volunteer helpers. They didn't like that we were kissing in the park. Or that we're lying next to each other on the grass, just lying there. That's why we always carried our passports with us and a marriage certificate. To prove we're husband and wife. Because they wouldn't trust a church certificate.

[*The* WAITER *moves away, tossing a quick glance at* STAS.]

ADA ZITRONE: Did you have children with her?

STAKH PERFETSKY: We were supposed to. Six, apparently. We thought up all kinds of extraordinary names for them. The oldest was supposed to be called Avallon. Then a girl whom we called Marmolianda. Then another little boy—with such a long name Live-in-Harmony-and-Abundance. After him there was a little girl again, Marika. And so forth.

ADA ZITRONE: They weren't born?

STAKH PERFETSKY: It was impossible.

ADA ZITRONE: I understand. Sorry.

STAKH PERFETSKY: You don't understand. [*Drinks from the shot glass, frowns, begins to smoke.*] You don't understand, Ada. They couldn't even be conceived. Her illness.

ADA ZITRONE: What was it?

STAKH PERFETSKY: One of those that is considered incurable in my land. She was snuffed out over the course of a year. At first I kept her going on uppers. . . .

ADA ZITRONE: On what?

STAKH PERFETSKY: Well, on pills. Then we had to give her shots. As always there weren't enough needles. She believed that I would save her. She had dreams in which I saved her. In reality I destroyed her. All this happened with her because of me.

ADA ZITRONE: Why do you say this?

STAKH PERFETSKY: Because I took her from her home. If she had stayed in her family's nest, it wouldn't have turned out this way. I didn't have the right to take her to my mountains, she withered away in the basements. The underground isn't for everybody. There are people who pay for it with their life.

ADA ZITRONE: Did you turn to doctors?

STAKH PERFETSKY: We did just that. You know, at that time I had become a bit of a celebrity. Twice they showed me on television. We found such influential nice people who arranged for consultations with the best doctors. Strange as it was, their prognoses were unanimous: it was the end. Though I think there had to be a snake.

ADA ZITRONE: Without a snake?

STAKH PERFETSKY [*flicking his hand*]: Don't pay any attention. These are my hallucinations.

ADA ZITRONE: You don't happen to know that character there in front of the bar? [*Points at the reflection in the mirror.*]

STAKH PERFETSKY: It's the first time I've seen him. What about him?

ADA ZITRONE: It's nothing. I thought you might know him.

STAKH PERFETSKY: No, I don't know him. For the last half year we lived a bit differently. My benefactors found a place in Sykhiv for us. This is a completely disgusting area, far from the center of the city, total Soviet style, built in awful boxes. Someone gave me the keys from one of them. It was completely empty there. There weren't even faucets for water, just a floor, walls and ceilings. We lived in sleeping bags, as though we were some kind of mountain sojourners. We invited entire companies of our friends there, got drunk sitting on the floor, then we danced to the harmonica and jaws harp. She was crazy about dancing, to the very last. When her legs no longer held her up, I took her in my arms—she was becoming lighter as time went on—and carried her to the kitchen where I put her to sleep. Later she couldn't even walk, and I constantly looked for something for her to drink, because she was tormented by thirst, it was as though the summer were made of fire, and there was never any water in the apartment. . . .

ADA ZITRONE [*looking at the candle*]: It's almost burned out.

STAKH PERFETSKY: Two months before her death I went to her parents for the last time. They didn't even let me in the door. The old man talked to me through it. He said I should get out, because he was going to call the *polizei* right away and they'll put me away for five to seven for attempted assault and robbery. I didn't have the strength to convince him. In his own way he really loved his daughter. And that's why he hated me. Lord, how this burning stuff hums in my brain! . . .

[*The* WAITER *approaches and fixes his eyes on* ADA.]

WAITER: *Desidera qualcosa, Signora?*

ADA ZITRONE [*surprised, with laughter*]: *Come ha fatto a indovinare? Vorrei un'altra candela.*

WAITER: *Candela?* [*Smiles.*] *Questa non va bene?* [*He squints for a bit at the candle end, then for a bit at* STAS.] *Un attimo, Signora.*[6]

[ADA *laughs at his joke; the* WAITER *moves away.*]

STAKH PERFETSKY: They took her away right after she died. . . .

ADA ZITRONE: Who?

STAKH PERFETSKY: Obviously, her parents. They came in a black hearse and took her body from me. There were six huge servants, with brass knuckles and whips in their hands. I threw myself to defend her. It seemed she was still breathing, although it had been two hours since her pulse had stopped. They knocked me onto the floor, and two of them kicked me while others carried out the body. . . .

ADA ZITRONE: But how did you endure this? How was it that you didn't die then? How did you dare to remain and live?

STAKH PERFETSKY: Didn't I die then? In two days there was the funeral. . . .

[*The* WAITER *appears, takes the candle end from the table (during this time not taking his slightly moist eyes from* ADA), *and puts in a new lit candle.*]

WAITER: *Questa è veramente speciale, Signora.*

ADA ZITRONE: *Grazie. Non sembra male.*[7]

[*Both of them laugh, and the* WAITER *moves away.*]

STAKH PERFETSKY [*swigging from the shot glass*]: What are you talking about with him all the time?

ADA ZITRONE: You don't know Italians? . . . They always have the same thing on their minds! [*She takes him by the hand. He already is looking quite bleary eyed. At her.*]

STAKH PERFETSKY: They buried her at Lychakiv Cemetery, in the family tomb, beneath a black Virgin. All kinds of her great-great-grandmothers were already lying there. They didn't let me go to her. Some kind of lug was always standing there. . . .

ADA ZITRONE: Who?

STAKH PERFETSKY: Some kind of dipshit. He stepped in my way. I had bruises beneath my eyes and a swollen nose. The inconsolable Mr. Widower. This was still from the time they had taken her away. I just saw from far off as they carried the coffin into the depths of the tomb. It smelled of old stone and moss. And cemetery excrement. From very far off. . . .

ADA ZITRONE: You couldn't even go up to her?

STAKH PERFETSKY: They intentionally took care of that. Her mother had a nervous fit, she was in a wide black hat with a black feather and veil. They called the ambulance right to the cemetery for her. The old man barely shuffled his feet. I saw all this hiding behind an angel. Then I lay face down right on the ground, and I couldn't even breathe. . . .

ADA ZITRONE: I know, that happens.

STAKH PERFETSKY: For the rest of August every day I came to her. Dressed as a grave digger. Do you know how old tombs are opened? I learned how to do that. I broke the lid of her coffin. I kissed her and spoke with her out loud. Then I would bring an oboe to her, for some reason she loved that the most. This was after that incident in the museum. . . . It seemed to me that she was beginning to move her head. It seems I had gone mad, but this brought me faith. Then some jerk squealed on me—evidently one time hearing the sound of an oboe from the tomb, they decided to tell the old man about it. . . . In several days he had set up an armed guard around the tomb, and then bricked it up forever. That's it.

ADA ZITRONE: Do you love her till now?

STAKH PERFETSKY: I don't know. I thought—yes. Until . . . Well, you understand. Until we . . .

ADA ZITRONE [looking into his eyes]: But I can believe you.

STAKH PERFETSKY: Believe.

ADA ZITRONE: Are you waiting for my answer?

STAKH PERFETSKY: We have to disappear. They're hunting me. That's already another story, but they're hunting me. I shouldn't say this. I'm already drunk. Excuse me. But am I permitted the truth today?

ADA ZITRONE: Happy birthday. [Raises a goblet.]

STAKH PERFETSKY: Do you have enough for two tickets to Rome? Or at least to Florence? Or, maybe, to Ravenna? . . .

ADA ZITRONE: And what then?

STAKH PERFETSKY: And we disappear. And then—what I've already proposed . . .

ADA ZITRONE: Oh, Orpheus, Orpheus! . . . [*She puts her hand in his hair and tousles it.*] Who is that character looking at you?

STAKH PERFETSKY: You know, no one is really waiting for me. I have the complete right to disappear.

ADA ZITRONE: And your parents?

STAKH PERFETSKY: My parents? They're nearly sure that I set off into the world with a traveling circus. . . .

[ADA *shudders.*]

ADA ZITRONE: Anyway, who is that character looking at you?

[*Finally* PERFETSKY *glances into the mirror. In it he sees a gaze directed at him from the bar.* ADA *takes her hand away.* PERFETSKY *raises his shot glass and drinks to the face reflected in the mirror. It smiles.* PERFETSKY, *too.*]

STAKH PERFETSKY: Maybe he knows that it's my birthday today. Let's get out of here.

[*He begins to smoke again.*]

ADA ZITRONE: I'll give you an answer. By morning. We'll be together till morning. . . .

STAKH PERFETSKY: Till morning there's less and less time.

ADA ZITRONE: But there's still enough for you to hear my answer. So that you . . .

[*The* WAITER *approaches.*]

WAITER: *"Eccomi, Signora. Qualcos' altro?*

ADA ZITRONE: *Grazie, il conto.*[8]

[*The* WAITER *nods and moves away.*]

ADA ZITRONE: . . . so that you understand what kind of awful adventure you're venturing.

[STAS *bends over and kisses her. Right at that moment as he bends his head something whistles past him. The mirror cracks. Capillaries of cracks run along the entire surface.* ADA *and* STAS (*not immediately*) *look into the mirror, but there's already no one at the bar.*]

ADA ZITRONE: What was it?

STAKH PERFETSKY: Don't pay any attention. We have to get out of here.

[*Again the* WAITER. *Gives the check and winks to his distorted reflection.* ADA *counts out the money.*]

ADA ZITRONE: *Tenga pure il resto. Che cosa è successo allo specchio?*
WAITER: *Grazie, signora. Succede che anche gli specchi non resistono.* [*Both laugh.*] *Il suo amico non capisce l'Italiano?*
ADA ZITRONE: *No, come ha visto. Perchè me lo chiede?*
WAITER: *Perche vorrei rivederia. Ho una candela ancora più bella!*[9] [*Nods his head either in the direction of* STAS *or the candle. Again they laugh.*]
STAKH PERFETSKY: Well, buddy, bug off till I run into your macaroni mill . . .
WAITER [*to* ADA]: *Scusi? Cosa sta dicendo il suo amico?*
ADA ZITRONE: *Ha trovato il servizio eccellente.*
WAITER: *Si sarebbe trovata ancora meglio se fosse venuta da sola, Signora! Buona sera!*[10]
[*The* WAITER *moves away;* ADA *continues to laugh.*]
ADA ZITRONE [*looking back at him*]: Cocky guy!
STAKH PERFETSKY: Spread ketchup all over him? . . .
[*They get up from the table, evidently as* PERFETSKY *had swayed somewhere off to the side, beyond the borders of the frame. But he manages to blow on the candle. Subsequently both of them disappear from the frame, but* ADA*'s answer can still be heard.*]
ADA ZITRONE: What's with you, Orpheus. . . . Everything's in order, let's go. . . .
[*Maybe she took him by the hand and led him from the restaurant, outside. Most likely, that's how it was. In the frame for a time there still remain the empty table, a goblet, an ashtray, a pitcher of wine, a shot glass, the shattered mirror, the candle which had gone out. Then the image disappears.*]

2 9

THE LAST WILL AND TESTAMENT

of Stanislav Perfetsky, composed
March 10, 1993, in the city of Venice

I, Stanislav Perfetsky, the owner of forty names and several other doubtful valuables both of a spiritual and material type, in the face of impending death, being of full and sound mind, and also in a generally sober state, with this Testament designate the transferal of the objects belonging to me to the property of the below-named persons and institutions. Those very same agents, who are fated to find and elaborate the Testament laid out below, I humbly call to the measure of their possibilities about its enactment to care for and without exception to divide the described goods in concordance with my last will.

In this way, from the valuables present today at my disposal I bequeath:

I. *Objects of clothing and others*
silk shirts Angelo Ligrico, five items—give them all without exception to my friends in Lviv and in the area: the sky blue, dark blue, and lilac ones—to Yaroslav D. D. (Slavtsunio) and to both his brothers, the older and younger; one other lilac and yellowish green—to Anton Sulykovsky (Tsuikovsky, Tsiunkovsky) as an insignificant part of compensation for an unpaid debt. I'll leave a black shirt on myself;

—a white pinstriped shirt Emilio Perucci, with a bow tie—to Suleiman Davydovych Pyshner, the president of the Finance and Comfort Bank;

—a Giorgio Armani suit with the exception of the pants—to the creative society Hop-Stop-Shop, Lviv—Zhovkva;

—jeans shirts, jackets, overalls, handkerchiefs, and Bonanza brand pants—to the rock groups Doctor Tahabat, Station of Psychos, and the Dog Shit;

—a winter-spring Luigi Lazzari—to Maximilian Pohulyaisky (Max), the artist;

—various colored ties "Mauricio Lupo," four to seven items: to the young and youngest poets, artists, and actors who meet in the coffeehouse Under the Frog, with the exception of one, which I ask be given to the Museum of the Sovcommie Underground, if such a museum should be established;

—shoes, slippers, as well as socks I do not bequeath to anyone, because they're too worn;

—a lighter, an ashtray, a pen, a wooden spatula, a Christmas carol collection, and other trifles—to Jerry F. Janeczek (U.S.A.), a philologist with a capital letter, that is, Philologist;

—a suitcase made of fake alligator, given to me in Prague, apparently, by the president of the Czech Republic—to my close friend Josef Frantz (to Frantz Josef), a church choir conductor, ballet master of the variety theater the Black Kitty;

—a Nitech Dictaphone along with earphones and everlasting rechargeable Philips batteries—to the Service for State Security of Ukraine;

—a gas balloon "SG-gas" with an unused charge—to the bartender Zenyk (Ostap), the coffeehouse Under the Fly;

—As concerns the *Death in Venice* sniper's rifle, it's not my property, and I am not disposing of it.

II. *Books and other things*

—*The Lexicon of Prominent Vampires, Ghosts, Werewolves and All Manner of Corpses and Dead Bodies with Cadavers* (1992 reprint of a textbook written in 1332 in Marburg, in Low German, with illustrations and photographs)—to Father Remigiusz M., exorcist;

—*The Anarchist's Cookbook* (1990, underground publication in American—recipes for preparing explosives, narcotics, poisons, etc.)—to Lyubko Kak-ych, director of Small Business Concern "Blef";

—collection of works of R. M. Rilke in six volumes, a deluxe edition (with the preface by Beda Alemann, in German)—to Yuri Andrukhovych, Ivano-Frankivsk;

—*Porno Bible* (1992, illustrated, color positives are appended)—to Dr. Kost Pecherytsia (Champignon), exegete;

—*The Art of Defenestration* (the newest bestseller by an unknown author, reinterpretation nonsense-akshun and fantasy fikshun, in rheto-Roman)—to the Leviathanclub library, Lviv;

—map of the city of Venice (fifteenth century, Jacopo de Barbari printer, with the designations of places where we could meet)—to Ewa, a student of astrophysics, Warsaw;

—a map of the transportation connections of the city of Munich (S-Bahn, U-Bahn, buses, trams, taxis)—to the Munich City Administration with my gift signature;

—a map of the location of bordellos, striptease bars, and casinos in the environs of Charlottenburg, West Berlin (Xerox copy)—to the tourist firm Let's Get to Know Europe, Chortopil;

—a selection of postcards with views of Prague—to the married couple Marta and Roman Kh-sky, museum workers;

—a selection of postcards with views from Bratislava to Vienna—to the married couple Anna and Lesya B. rascals;

—an all-black postcard with the caption "Berlin by Night"—to the already-mentioned Maximilian Pohulyansky, artist;

—a postcard with a camel in the background of a pyramid and a caption "Greetings from Munich"—to the as yet unmentioned Olena Beebaby, artist-mannequin;

—a notebook with the golden embossing DIARY on the cover and with some of my newest texts, drafts, translations, and other things inside—to the compiler of my future collection of works.

III. *Cassettes (audio and other things)*
—Tom Waits's *The Black Rider* (1993, Island Records, Inc.)—to Ivan "John" Bombas, guitar, vocals;

—pirate recordings of Jim Morrison with the duet "Baccara" (apartment variant)—to Alex "Oleksa," rap and blues;

—complete collections of Jimi Hendrix and B. B. King (with the exception of Lou Reed)—to Ron "Seagull" Sigal;

—poeticomusical *Chrysler Imperial* (third edition), authentic digital recording, Vienna Opera, 1993, with Montserrat Cabalier in the role of Melisanda Harazdetsky—to Pavlo Matsapura, Kyiv;

—"El condor pasa," music of the Peruvian Indians from Marienplatz and other city squares of Europe—to the Lviv municipal police;

—a recording of my appearance in the opera *Orpheus in Venice,* the Teatro La Fenice, March 8, 1993 (pirate copy)—to the already mentioned Josyp Fr., director.

IV. *Magical and other objects*

—a silver signet ring with the anagram M.P.—"Melchior Perfetsky," which also means "Master of Poignancy," has the capacity to cast back an unexpected threat, to inspire lightness on deliberations and to fend off complete inebriation—to the Chortopil Museum of Carpathian Masonry, if they don't close the aforementioned museum; if they do close it, then smelt it into a bullet and shoot it from a rifle into the southern side of Mt. Hoverla, but just on the night of Saint John's Eve and not later, but not earlier than 1999;

—a needle for gouging out the eyes of vampires and for turning the pages in poisoned books (seal bone, walrus mustache hair, fine thread), a gift of the highly praised knight Nachtigall von Ramensdorf from Berlin, useful also for placing the countless horde of witches on the very tip—to Father Remigiusz, superior of the monastery;

—bone dice for Tarot playing, prepared in the sixteenth century from the bones of a prominent sorcerer and prophet Agrippa of Nettesheim—they relieve tooth pain and restore erections, and also bring victory in games of chance, as well as occult and political games—to Matsko Kulya (I don't know his real name), a beggar from near the Skvozniak Food Market, Akademichny Prospect in Lviv;

—a silver coin with the image (from one side) of a winged hyena and (on the other side) a Latin inscription, *Ergo bibamus,* stamped in the court of the Gothic king Winitar specially for the bribing of Byzantine eunuchs, acquired by me from the Dagestan gypsy Yashkin for eight American dollars (its nominal value), it possesses the ability to decrease and increase in diameter, to become black and red, besides that, it foresees the near future, but mistakenly—to T. T. Tvardivsky, editor of the weekly *New Millennium News,* Lviv;

—the root of the *mandragora officinarum* (*perestupen* in Ukrainian),[1] of the male sex, conceived by spermatorrhea of a mountain brigand executed on the gallows in the seventeenth century, it aids in the search for treasures, and herewith glows; unfortunately, it works just on the territory of the Kolomia area of the Ivano-Frankivsk region—to the Chortopil Museum of Carpathian Free Brigandry;

—a piece of skin and fragments of hair covering from the body of the famous Lviv swindler and card sharp Yuzio Dutsio (eighteenth century), maintained in a biosuspension, it does not possess any magical capabilities, a gift from the Museum of Pathologic Anatomy of the city of Lviv—to be returned to the aforementioned museum;

—a bundle of twelve keys from the habitations of my best lovers, from which (the keys) each now can be returned to its owner with expressions of gratitude from me: the first to Zoryana, the second to Marianna, the third to Roksolana, the fourth to Mstyslava, the fifth to Yaromyra, the sixth to Bohodara, the seventh to Olesya, the eight to Ulyasia, the ninth to Olyusia (Tsiusia), the tenth to Lada, the eleventh to Marena, the twelfth to Mrs. Stefa, but not the one who's now married to the poet Ruslan Smerechynsky, but the one who recently divorced the legislative deputy Rostyslav Smerekovsky (I ask that you not mix them up).

V. *Recordings of mine and about me, and the testimonies, papers, tapes, in short, a complete assemblage of documents,* concerning my person, if their authors or owners wish to give them up—to Yuri Andrukhovych, Ivano-Frankivsk, for further use.

VI. *My debts* in the general sum of $27,730—to everyone who can relieve or cancel them for the sake of my memory, which is what I really, really, really hopelessly expect.

VII. *My names* in the general quantity of forty I give to everyone who follows after me and continues my cause, with the exception of a single one (Stanislav Perfetsky), which I leave for myself for eschatological reasons.

This Testament has been composed without the presence of an appropriate notary clerk and not witnessed other than by my personal signature. The Testament enters into effect from the moment of my death, that is the early morning of March 11, 1993 (the hour will be specified).

Venice, March 10, 1993 A.D.
Personal signature (S. PERFETSKY)

3 0

IT WAS JUST AT THE RECEPTION I NOTICED THAT HE HAD GOTTEN so drunk, just at the reception, when we were entering the hotel. He suddenly got the urge to say something to the black porter, dressed in the fashion of a *cinquecento*[1] and, thanks to this, resembling Othello. The black man just smiled, and he badly fiddled something to him in sufficiently incomprehensible English, his cigarette constantly went out, and the black man courteously lifted up a lighter for him, this happened about five times, until I got pissed and nearly forcibly dragged him to the stairs, and the black man, flashing all his teeth, waved his hand at us. *I don't know why, but I really felt like chattering with a representative of a different race, to let him understand that not all whites are such shitbags, I began to explain this to him with the example of Shevchenko's friendship with Ira Aldridge, but she, that intolerant torpedo, didn't let me finish and dragged me somewhere after her. I didn't persist, I just itched to sing something of ours, something booming with my full lungs.*

When we finally reached the room, I took off his coat. So is this how you live, he asked, and, as though hypnotized, moved toward a wall hanging on the opposite wall. Right after a minute I figured out that he had seen a lute there. It was too late to stop him, *because I'm the kind, that music is paramount for me.* I thought: this is even good, let him strum for ten minutes until I wash up under the shower and get everything ready. I took off my jacket and entered the bathroom, but a troublesome surprise awaited me there. The bathtub was filled nearly to the brim, the entire floor was spattered with foam. Riesenbock was in the bathtub, he was quietly snoring, tossing his head back, and judging by the especially spicy odor wafting from him, he was totally drunk. I said "shit,"[2] slipped past him under the shower and, closed off the space with a curtain from every direction, I began to wash up for spite. At that moment a furious rattling flew out from the room—it was as though someone were pushing five-hundred-year-old furniture or had knocked an iron maiden against the wall. *I simply thought that they could come for me in the middle of the night, so I set the lute aside, as though I were a certain Vogelweide[3] and began to barricade the door, pushing up to it all kinds of antique crap in the form of walnut credenzas and ebony cupboards with stylized cupids and winged wenches.* This went on the entire time until I washed up, rubbing into me, into each one of my glands, a fragrant gel, and shuddering every moment from the rattling in the room; Riesenbock, fortunately, did not wake up, covered up to his neck in the warm bathtub. **I dreamed of dark glades, sleepy grass.**

Why did you do this, I asked, pointing to the barricaded door. *So that THEY shit in their pants, I answered and immediately apologized for the bad word. So that we fuckin' make it till the fuckin' morning somehow, I added, and began to untie my shoes, though it wasn't going.*

He didn't manage to take off his left shoe, I stood next to him on my knee. I hadn't seen this ring earlier, I said. *It often saves me from bad luck, I explained. Once it belonged to my grandfather, a post office clerk.* The shoe finally flew under the table, and he kissed me on the brow the way you kiss your sister. Here's one more for you, I said. Happy Birthday. This is from me. He opened a little gift box, *and in it I saw the most beautiful silver thing, a ring in the form of a fish that closes itself in a circle.* You'll wear it in the best of your days, I said. *Maybe. I didn't find myself with an answer to this. The ring was really much too nice for such a scumbag. I finally said this.*

We have too little time, I reminded him, can't you get undressed any quicker? *I expect you'll help me, the caprice struck me. The jacket flew somewhere by the window, in the morning you won't pick it up, she observed. You're right, I agreed, remembering that in the morning I had to act neatly and well coordinated.* When I had unbuttoned his shirt I noticed a medallion on his chest. That's her, I asked. Who else would it be, he sputtered, and I sensed how everything stopped in him. I kissed him—softly and warmly, just with my lips—not far from his heart and then, very slowly and nearly inaudibly, carefully, like a field minesweeper, I began to take the medallion off from over his head. You'd guess, it'd get in the way, but, for sure, so—*I didn't protest, but I didn't help her. She's no longer here, and we're still alive, she said, it seems to me, it doesn't matter for her. If she really loved you. Do you want to see her, I asked.* No, I firmly refused. Well, then I, I myself will take a look, he paid me back for my impertinence and opened the medallion in front of me. *As many times as I look, she's always different, thousands of women wear her reflections, each has stolen something from her, all women in the world walk in the radiance of her temporary presence.* I, certainly, also have stolen something, what exactly, I wanted to ask, but then from the bathroom we could hear the fanfarelike outburst of Riesenbock's snoring, fortunately, just one time. What's this, he asked without evident anxiety. *Music in the pipes, she answered, these Italians always have problems with their plumbing.*

Now these pants of yours, I reminded him. Yes-yes, the pants, he responded, the pants—my pride. I touched his hair with my hand because I really love that hair to the touch, our lips still really met, he, as always, knew how to drive me crazy, but those pants. They got in the way, have to do something with them. *Turn out the light and lay down, I said, I'll be there right away.* You've never slept underneath a canopy, I whispered, *and I answered, that I hadn't even lain down under one, but no, not really, in a museum, in a museum of antiquities where we made love several nights, friends let us inside, we spent the nights in the museum, each time in a different century, back then there weren't even any condoms, once upon a time it happened right under a canopy.* You're cruel, I reminded him about me, you could have refrained from telling me that, for five days I've just been thinking about the fact that we're going to be together under a canopy, I was sure that you'd never yet slept on these kinds of beds with those kinds of women, but, it turns out, she circumvented me, that dead lady. What, what are you saying, he tried to calm me down, I made up everything, there wasn't any museum, more accurately, there was one museum where I stayed over, but it was without her, without Her, and it wasn't on a canopy bed, but in a sarcophagus, alongside the skeleton of some princess, *I lied as best I could, savagely choking, somewhere there, into the space of the room, where she had moved away, then there was the rustle of sheets, from* behind the windows a quiet music floated up to us, someone had begun singing right from a gondola, several more voices supported him, in all there were three, fi-da-lin, fi-da-lin. . . .

For another good fifteen minutes he rolled about in his pants, folded them up on the edge of the bed, coins scattered out of his pockets, sugar-coated nuts, a ring of some kind of keys, dice, *no way could I pick up all the idiot's collection from the floor, finally I forgot about the nuts, because they had rolled all the way beneath the door, and in order to get them, I would have had to push aside that massive furniture, with which I tightly blocked off everything in the world. I'll turn out the lights, I said.* Why, I asked from the gloom, are just three candles lit here. *For snipers, I asked.* Paranoia, I sighed in answer. He flicked his hand and finally moved away to the bed, sitting down in the shade of the canopy. The bed was really wide, but his arms managed to touch me. I began to tremble. Why do you need your glasses, I asked. To see you better, was the answer.

I caught his hand, that virtuoso lily that forced me to breathe quicker, his long fingers. I paid respect to each one of them—all together and each in turn, there was a ring on the ring finger, I sensed the taste of silver on my lips, it's a fish, he said, I jerked his hand, the bedding began to rustle beneath him, he dove out of the room's darkness right above me. *And I began to unravel her like a doll from the countless bed coverings,* I took off his glasses and shoved them somewhere behind the headboard, behind the bright yellow curtain, that in soft folds flowed canopylike, there were now some four voices beyond the windows, *it was I who arranged for the musicians, she whispered, fi-da-lin.*

I nearly couldn't see her, just something white—rustling thick linen sheets, and something black, hair, strewn on white, and the warmth that twisted in my hands, answering each touch first with a flash, then with a moan, then with itself—with a half turn, a half bend, a half call. I passed through the bedding, through this fragrant rag, through the covers of all the fabrics in the world, in which she was wrapped, I finally wiggled out of all these magnificent garments, he stuck out like a giant above me, frozen in the flow of water, the song outside the windows continued without end, I swooned from his grandeur, I spread my legs and clasped my arms around his back. Then I understood that all this was in vain, and the song, fi-da-lin, ended.

PERVERZION

It's the alcohol, I said, excuse me, if you can. It's not the alcohol but your guilt, I said, you feel guilty before the one from the medallion. Mebbe, mebbe, he grimaced, laying down beside me. I want you to remember me a little bit and nothing more—I guided my hand along his hair. I wanted to bring you as much happiness as possible, sorry. *I should be sorry.* From the bathroom we heard a splash. Surely it must have been Riesenbock. He had stirred in his sleep. **I didn't give a rat's ass about that and right then started to prance after a young hamadryad with a face just like that pubescent flirt who had driven me crazy for two whole days; we were running near an ancient linden tree, and I laughed loudly, stretching myself out completely.**

I clenched my lips: damn these drunks—they're both the same. And you, girl, have to deal with it. *I lay beside her and breathed in her bitterness. Sorry, I said again. Not at all, she answered. You've gotten overtired in this Venice.* Overly tired, he corrected me. *The program really was packed, I agreed.* That's it, I sighed, and turned on my side. Why did they have such wide beds, he asked, did they screw ten at once? I don't know, I sighed, I don't want to know. Everything's against us.

The night was thick and viscous. We ended up on the very bottom. Darkness swallowed darkness, flesh swallowed flesh, objects became both darkness and flesh. I heard as the musicians floated away from beneath the windows. Anyway, I said, the bill will come tomorrow. Good night. What time should I wake you up so you're not late? Well, good, he said, although this didn't mean anything.

Well good, I said, hitting my fist on the pillow. If you think so, then it will be so. I sprang to my feet, tearing the tough bedding every which way. I saw him move toward the table almost by groping, with his arms outstretched in front catching just handfuls of the night air. Finally reaching the table, he nearly lay down on it with his entire chest and grabbed the table top with his hands. What are you looking for, I asked sleepily. Soon, soon everything will be okay, he answered, continuing to drum louder with his hands on the resonant wood, at times feeling for a goblet or an hour glass and pitilessly sweeping them onto the floor. Yes, here it is, he finally bubbled with constraint. It seemed that he was holding the medallion in his hand.

YURI ANDRUKHOVYCH

I managed to grope it. An abyss opened wide beneath me. If you think so, then it will be so, it sat in me like an echo. But I succeeded in grabbing him by the arm when he was already battling with the window, which, fortunately, was closed in such an old-fashioned way that you really needed to know how to open it. I grabbed him by the shoulders and dragged him back. The medallion fell on the floor. I finally wanted to get rid of it, he said, how much can you wear it, why did you stop me. You dope, I answered, later you'll regret it till your death. I don't want to be an instigator. I don't want to be the demon of your sin. I don't want to be your damnation, Orpheus. I jabbered some extraordinary stupidities, as though they were right out of a novel for hysterical teenage girls, we sat close to each other on the floor, *she held me by the hands so that I wouldn't cause any harm, but then I freed my arms, I was free to put those hands on her, I took her breasts that were awakened again, and then her neck, her shoulders.* I asked all the Powers of the World to take pity on us and to give him strength. *I went through her like a sojourner, slowly and precisely, recognizing everything from the beginning, I lay down into her as though into a stream.* I fell backward, feeling the rug's bristles with my shoulder blades and spine, but I did not release his bird, which was just so stingy and puny, and now he raised up his head and tried his wings, so he could fly from me elsewhere, to other lands, I helped him whatever way I could, I experienced the expression "hand tame." *I wound myself around her thighs, which you could talk about endlessly.* I thanked him with honey and milk that began to flow from me all at once. *And she exploded in zitrone juice.*[4] And with a golden rod he pricked me everywhere, and in the spots where he pricked me, a flower grew from me, or a wound, or. *And blood dwelled in me, like spring, I grew larger and continued in boundlessness.* And my lips sang for him without words and without. *And my tongue discovered the most mysterious hasps, in her.* And, although the other candles had already gone out, the best one still shined for us. For what was it fated to illuminate with a great, white flash?

The best of dungeons. The deepest of depths.

And in that darkness, sticky from every side and impenetrable, I suddenly saw something else—it crawled along on all fours: a large flat snout, a faun's face with a beard and bald spots, with a smile that perched on him like a slit for tossing in letters—Riesenbock, he rose no different than out of a tapestry (despite everything, I still sensed that the door from the bathroom was creaking and I groaned in anticipation), *for from here, from here could he still descend, if not from the tapestry's forests, where he had lain in the dark grass above the streams, until we tempted him to run over to us, to our glade?* **I really had awakened from the bustling in the room, the transition from sleep to wakefulness was momentary, I shook the suds off me, the water in the bathtub had already grown cold, I shook off the suds and began to smile, it was as though my eyes had glowed** (his eyes glowed, and the smile did not come off his lips, *like a criminal's special mark),* **I wanted to sneak up as quietly as possible,** but hooves tapped all too sonorously along the floor, **so I stood on my knees and moved on all fours . . .**

Here it's me, my two sweets, Riesenbock exploded into my ear (*I also heard this*), **here it's me,** *and here it's me,* and the two of them locked together above me, I never had any similar adventures, oh, two giants at once, it became terrifying and joyous, they were above me and below me so that I didn't know which of them was where, each could emerge from nowhere—Stakh's brow tossed upward, the slit of Riesenbock's smile, the heavy breathing, everything blended together, I divided myself, I split myself in two between them and united them in me, they are my wonderful guys, I loved them so right now, their bodies, although in such moments it's the very same thing—your self and your body, and they loved every part of me and all of me, and each one of the two of us. . . .

Then when I finally exploded and came onto the rug in a clear stream, my horror was in it. Never, never, I repeated, for never. Yet she rose up like the wave of a river, Riesenbock was snorting heavily and happily laughing in the grass, leaving the traces of his smile on all the living things like a dark milky stripe, and I already was falling into weakness and silence, I was still holding someone's fingers in mine, but, perhaps, it wasn't hers, but a faun's—bony, clinging, strong, someone else kissed me in my wound, but, perhaps, it was not her lips, but a faun's—dark blue, sticky, smelling of wine. Right at that moment complete darkness came.

■ □ ■ □ ■

3 1

VENICE, MARCH II, AROUND SIX IN THE MORNING. MY NAME IS
Stanislav Perfetsky.

An hour before I woke up in a completely different room. On a
really wide canopy bed. Together with a certain married couple.
Her name is Ada Zitrone, and his Janus Maria Riesenbock. It seems
I've already said something about this somewhere. The three of us
slept together. It's hard to recall how it came to this. I don't want to,
word of honor. In the end this already means absolutely nothing.

Ada was lying on her back between the two of us. I couldn't wake
her up. Why? Yes, I understood: drowsiness.

She had a different face. Some kind of shadow on it. A shadow
on everything, in every concavity, a yellow tint. Shadow and sleep,
sleep and shadow, the pit of the dawn, an abyss.

Riesenbock. His arm flowed beneath her head and his hand
reached me. My hair. Riesenbock slept on his side. His face, even in
sleep impudent, turned to Ada. A narrow smile. A crevice for flies.

I also was lying on my side. But turned away from them. From
the night the word "never" lasted. Where did I hear it? There's no
time to dig deeper. But that's the way it seemed.

I have to disappear before seven. The quicker the better. I have
my reasons for this.

I couldn't wake her up. I carefully untangled myself—crumpled,
some even torn, sheets, there were a lot of them, enough for a hundred brothels.

I was, obviously, naked. For a good fifteen minutes I looked for
my glasses in the darkness. Further it was easier. Although I found
my clothes in the most impossible of places.

What was this shadow that lay on her? Shadow and a dull yellow tint. The canopy.

Besides this, a bunch of all kinds of trifles that I have the habit of carrying in my pockets. I had the habit of carrying in my pockets, that would be more correct.

Time is left just for the completion of this [*pause*] epistle. Just to smoke a cigarette. Good that there's just one. I'd be a talented director, I always used to conjecture.

Ada: did she sigh? I wanted to kiss her silently, her, utterly burned out.

I've meddled in somebody else's affair.

I didn't have a right to do this.

What have I gotten into?

I don't know anything about her besides the fact that to the very. . . . I wanted to be beside her. To the very end. Not too loud? Maybe. Such is the time. It's floating in.

The instant before daybreak. All kinds of splendidly-worded dissolutions. Sorry.

That room was a trap. Some kind of monster had blocked the door with old, cumbersome furniture. I didn't begin to drag anything—I would have awakened the entire hotel. But just Ada. She would have slept through it. What was I to do?

I struggled with the window for a good ten more minutes. Some kind of medieval wiles. Then it became clear: the window was already open. But I finally understood how to do this. I won't have as many problems with mine.

The canal breathed cold on me. I stepped onto the ledge. I barely held myself back from the temptation.

Riesenbock. He started to rustle the sheets.

There were no chances of getting to my room. Meaning from the side of the canal.

Then I remembered: the bathroom. Theirs is right beneath mine, one floor lower. The bathtub for some reason was full of water. With the remains of fragrant foam. Right here another scent lingered—Ada's. She has many nice scents. This one belonged to last night. Bye-bye.

I opened the window. And what? And I thought about inexorability.

Pardon me. There was a ladder, left in its time by V. Like an invitation. The fear of heights, which I've been unable to get rid of.

From somewhere: fragments from operas. I recognized some.

What was left? To look into the room one more time? Was Ada sleeping alone? Did it just seem to me? Where did Riesenbock disappear? Has he become a faun again? I didn't approach her. *Bye-bye.*

Then I crawled up the ladder. Below me was a garden. Almost invisible. The last darkness of night. There was also a scent from it—myrtle and grass.

"Who will ever tell me where that barbarian is,"[1] Elvira sang decisively. I dove into the window of the bathroom. So I ended up again in my room.

It seems to me that I didn't forget anything. I have to hurry. The canal is coming alive. They'll come at seven. [*Pause.*] I don't want these tricks. With blowtorches etc. They'll make do without me. Who is this listening to bits of opera at six in the morning?

Maybe it's inside me?

The temptation of music?

I'll continue. I had to stop the Dictaphone. I struggled with the window. Now at last. All the paths are open. To give the sill a good push with my legs. Otherwise you'll be impaled up to your gut. Your typical Kozak story. What's the average depth of the canal? Who will tell me, hey?

Silence.

Why do I need glasses there?

So. Several final remarks. For those who'll listen to this later. My suicide: I ask you to judge it as an aesthetic act. There is no one to lay the blame on in this. The direction of the flight: where my shoes are pointing.

I'm completely tangled up. And that's it. These are essentially my problems. The angels are already singing for me. In Italian.

Who listens to angels at six-thirty in the morning?

I step out onto the ledge. I staggered. These gothic windows, they're high. It could be the first line of a poem: these gothic windows, they're high. Maybe I look comical. In this window opening.

Well, how is it here? Everything as it should be. Venice is rising out of the darkness. Santa Maria della Salute. This is instead of a prayer.

I'll wait for the barge now—and onward. Home. To the water. A fish wants to swim. The ocean awaits me. I'll make the flooded floors of those buildings habitable.

Give me the angels louder! Full sound! The splash of the water will be recorded last. The water that will close up. And it will save me. Sorry.

Thus. I thank everyone. I'm thankful for everything. It was wonderful. I have to leave you. Forgive me that it's taken so long. It's not every day! . . .

Thank you for your attention. Good-bye. Listen further. Listen to this life. Listen to the angels, listen to the splash of the water.

■ □ ■ □ ■

PUBLISHER'S AFTERWORD

WE DID NOT HEAR THE SPLASH OF WATER PROMISED BY STANISLAV
Perfetsky. Perhaps the entire reason for this lies in the excessively
great distance between the Dictaphone and the vortex of the last
dive of our hero? Perhaps. To the end of the tape we have just twelve
and a half minutes of silence. And that's it.

Categorically, having gone through the labyrinths of this book,
the Respected Reader will agree with me: in our entire history considerably more of the unexplained and unclear remains than one
would expect. And the main question, to which for the time being
we do not have an answer—was there really a jump from the window, and was there really a suicide?

Being occupied for a short (too short for Perfetsky!) time with
this matter, the police certified several moments. First, in Stakh's
hotel room all his things were left behind including his glasses,
which were left on a desk, next to the handwritten text of his last
will and testament, composed by Perfetsky the day before.
Handwriting experts corroborated that the testament was written
by the hand of Perfetsky. Second, the extraordinarily high window
(the last in the arcade) that looks out onto the Grand Canal, really
was open, and more, was thrown open, the wind pranced through
the room, all fragrant with southern groves, and Perfetsky's shoes
really stood on the ledge, which completely concurs with the
description of the situation, fixed in the last (?) monologue of
Stanislav, spoken into the Dictaphone. Third, the investigators had
the impression that between the moment of the disappearance of
Perfetsky and the appearance in his hotel of the room cleaner (who,
in fact, informed the police, and as a result the entire world knows

about the mysterious disappearance), between these two actions someone else had been in the room. The police could not (or did not want) to determine anything concrete about this visit.

In the meantime far more of all kinds of open questions and alluring lacunae remain. First of all, as I already have written in the preface, the body has not been found. This became the weakest link in the investigator's version regarding suicide. So the quite awkward buttressing emerged in the form of the supposition that Perfetsky's body could have been carried off into the open sea during high tide. For some reason the circumstance that the body had not been found also in the open sea failed to alert anyone. Perhaps sharks or other sea monsters had eaten him?

Second, the search for the people, the testimonies of whom undoubtedly would have shed more light onto this entire story, did not bear the expected results. Those mentioned by Perfetsky were not found, neither Ada Zitrone nor her husband, the doctor of urology. In fact, certain eyewitnesses tell of a car of unprecedented construction that had wildly flown along the Venice to Rome autostrade on that very same day. Behind its wheel (and this apparently struck the eye of encountering drivers) a balding bearded man was apparently sitting, who evidently was smiling the entire time. Next to him was some young woman, more attractive than unattractive, dressed in black and cherry red colors, stationary and apparently covered in shadow. It was impossible to notice anything more. The search for Dr. Riesenbock at the Meluzine villa in the Bavarian town of Possenhoffen mentioned by Perfetsky also came to naught, although the Italian police turned to their Bavarian partners; according to the facts there really is a villa with a similar name in Possenhoffen, but it does not belong to any Riesenbock, a doctor of urology, but to Wiesenbock, a doctor of ichthyology. They also were unable to find anyone of all the participants of the seminar: how paradoxical, but only a single fate is known for certain—that Casallegra had been scattered in dust. Today the very existence of other figures appears to be very doubtful and, if it were not fixed in its time in the Venetian mass media, then we would have had all the reasons to consider the entire company a wonderful fiction of the Creator. The investigators managed to find and lend an ear just to Mr. Amerigo Dappertutto, the Executive Secretary of the foundation that had organized the seminar. According to his words, Stanislav Perfetsky had made a dual impression on him during the seminar. The respected functionary did not even think to say more precisely what exactly he understood by that duality.

Among the objects mentioned by Perfetsky in his testament, there was listed a sniper rifle, which he, true, does not will to anyone, in as much as it, he said, did not belong to him. That rifle turned out to be the only one of the objects enumerated in the testament that already was not in the room when the police had come. Perhaps it never existed at all? Just like there was never a ladder lowered from the bathroom window to the garden?

Now some of my personal thoughts. I'm starting first of all with a packet of documents (or better to say—texts), which were passed along to me by an unknown Venetian and which I, previously having researched and adapted, have decided to publish as this book.

With all the tangled nature and discrepancies of the situation, all the same a motif stands out that can serve as a certain key for us. This is the motif (or mood) of the hunt. Perfetsky is being watched. A sense of quite serious danger hanging over him permeates everywhere through the diverse cloth of these texts (besides all their vagueness and stuttering). More than that, the peculiarity hits you in the face that there are at least several sources for such danger (one or another). Stanislav Perfetsky ended up in the intersections of some completely different and distant interests, encamped in entirely different surfaces. His position truly leaves the impression that it was a very complicated one. To add something more concrete or plausible to this, however, even if possible, then, beyond any kind of doubts, is not worthwhile.

In my preface I touched on the problem of the authorship of each of the texts that were passed along to me. I wrote about the fact that, besides the fragments, with the authorship of which everything is understood, there exists an insignificant but persistent number of pieces of another nature, as for example (corresponding to my numeration) the seventh, thirteenth, or twenty-fifth, the authorship of which belongs to a narrator who speaks with extensive knowledge of even the smallest details and at the same time in no way enters as a participant in the situations described. Who is he, that observer? Or who are they, those observers? Who is able to crawl into the spiritual depths of Perfetsky or his female traveling companion with such absolute knowledge of the matter and at the same time remain completely invisible?

The answer, in my view, can be just one. But we won't be hasty with it.

Not for a second did I believe (nor do I believe now) that Stanislav Perfetsky could die by his own hand. The only proof in favor of this absurdity is the documents Perfetsky himself left (in order not to say "dropped off"). And what a shaky proof this is! I'm not at all surprised by the Venetian police who acquiesced to such a trick—none of them personally knew Stas, nor took part in his adventures. But I have been surprised a thousand times by the gullible people here, in Ukraine, who, in their time being his close acquaintances and friends, so unconditionally have accepted this mystification!

And if it were only a mystification! If only you could say about Perfetsky just the fact that he's a mystificator, then that would be sufficient once and for all to abandon the version of suicide. But each of us, besides this, knew him as a fabricator, eternally delighted by life, an eternal player, an omnipresent performer, a grand master of fish slipping through the hands out of everything, even out of his own skin. Max Pohulyaisky said it best in his time: "When I hear from five different people that each had seen Perfetsky yesterday, but the first swears at the symphony concert, the second—at varnishing day, a third—that just the two of them had spent the entire evening getting drunk, the fourth—that he shared a girl with him, and the final—that just last evening the police had tied him up, when I hear all this, then I'm sure that all five told the truth, for at a minimum five Perfetskys exist on this earth."

And one more thing, very essential. We all knew a Stanislav Perfetsky altogether devoted to Mystery. One can say he was its knight (grant the distinctive old-fashionedness of such a characteristic). He lived by mysteries and for the sake of mysteries. Who can boast today that they knew a lot about him?

But from what we knew and know, it's entirely enough to affirm that Stanislav Perfetsky did not disappear in the waters of the Grand Canal on the morning of March 11, 1993!

YURI ANDRUKHOVYCH

He decisively and easily lopped off the Gordian knot that had been stifling him in those days—by his own dissolution. Once he said it to me this way: "I constantly dream of beginning everything from the beginning. You can't understand this, old man. This is a mad delectation: to get off a train at a station you don't know and each moment imagine the possibility of a new beginning."

Apparently I've now been given to understand this. I hope.

Corroborations of my conjectures have found me themselves. First, Bomchyk, the percussionist of the group Station of Psychos, talked about the smiling face of Perfetsky flashing past in the television supplement to *Playboy,* shown on RTL; our hero was scarfing down some exotic food in a tavern with prominently endowed topless waitresses—it's impossible to confuse his raised left eyebrow with any other. Not even this eyebrow established my certainty that Bomchyk was not mistaken, but rather the fact that I know perfectly well Perfetsky's propensity for protuberant women's breasts. Unfortunately, without a command of German, Bomchyk could not determine anything on the occasion about the country in which the above-noted original tavern is located.

Further, there was yet one more bit of news tied to television. Father Superior Petro M. had noticed the edge of Stakh's face during a telecast of the Christmas Divine Liturgy from the Roman basilica of Saint Peter's. Perfetsky, among other honored guests, had been sitting not very far away from the then prime minister of Italy.

Then there were several other bits of news that allowed us to follow the subsequent moves of Perfetsky through cities and countries. In recent times our people have been traveling more. Seeing the furthest corners of the Earthly sphere is no longer anything unattainable. Returning home, our travelers often share their recollections about wonders they've seen and experienced: six-fingered people, eight-eyed dragons, flying cars, and portable supermarkets. From such narratives I found out about a certain quite nearsighted acrobat from Florence, who rode along a cable stretched between the top of the bell tower of Santa Maria del Fiore and the loggia of one of the neighboring buildings; about an interesting shoe shiner from the Athenian Omonia Square, who over the course of every shoeshine managed to read a different poem each time for each client in an unfamiliar language—women loved his hair silky to the touch;

about some inventive musician, who for a time appeared between Hagia Sophia and the Blue Mosque in Istanbul. He set up in front of himself a totally countless number of larger and smaller jars filled with water and with delicate sticks made of bone, banging out on them the melodies of "The Turkish March," "A Little Night Music," the prelude to the Fortieth Symphony, and other things by Mozart; for some reason everyone without exception turned their attention to the fact that he had a silver ring in the form of a fish. . . .

Occasionally I ask you, who have already come across or happen to come across similar things, particularly street musicians, remember everything to the smallest details, to let me know.

For Stakh Perfetsky, who nearly everyone in the world considers a suicide-drowning and who is the real author of all (not just some!) of this book's excerpts, Stakh Perfetsky continues to be among us. He is alive and, I'll say more, he will return. First, just as a book, cunningly lain at my door by him.

I even see how, at six-thirty in the morning, on the eleventh of March 1993, he completes his last preparations, opens the window, places his shoes on the ledge with the toes pointing out (because these are not his only pair of shoes, my Lord God!), how he leaves his eyeglasses on the desk, looks at himself in the mirror, then puts on other glasses, new ones, once again looks at himself, to himself, to the mirror and to the entire world sticks out his tongue, one more time looks over the room, the Dictaphone is still on, he quietly (without a rustle!) exits to the corridor, his footsteps muffled by the thick carpets, he sneaks along the steps, slips past the reception area and at the same time, past the black man who looks like the Magus Kaspar and Othello at the same time, the black man opens his eyes wide, but too late, it's already too late, the entryway doors right then closed after someone, after whom, after him, after this eternal fugitive, so well, how's everything, Venice is marvelous and dawning, the canals smell of water, the sky has turned into broad daylight, the wind from the lagoon has filled with blooming groves, spring is just beginning, and half his life is still ahead. . . .

July 1995
Yu. A.

■ □ ■ □ ■

NOTES

Unless otherwise indicated, all notes are the translator's.

The epigraph is from Ukrainian philosophical writer and essayist Yurko Izdryk, coeditor with Andrukhovych of the literary almanac *Chetver*.

Publisher's Introduction

1. None of these newspapers actually exists. Literal translations would be *Bazaar Train Station, Kyiv Affairs,* and *Idea Twenty-First Century.* I've tried to retain Andrukhovych's mocking playfulness in the English translation. The headline is in Russian in the original text.

2. The traditional Ukrainian appellation for the secret service, army and border guards.

3. The name of a rather slimy stool pigeon Soviet type from Andrukhovych's novel *Recreations* (1992). In his earlier novel Andrukhovych describes him as a "blond-haired swine." The irony in *Perverzion* is that after Ukrainian independence, Bilynkevych has become a Ukrainian nationalist, a fact that is actually a rather typical occurrence in the new Ukrainian reality.

4. Meaning something like "Devilopolis" or "Demonopolis." The central action of Andrukhovych's novel *Recreations* occurs in the same city.

5. Lubansky (Loverboysky in the translation) was the Babe Ruth of Polish soccer in the 1960s and 1970s. The name also suggests the Hutsul word *liubasyk*, the condoned extramarital lover common among the Carpathian Hutsuls. Bimber Bibamus roughly means "moonshine let's drink." The name Pierre Dolinsky (Pierre Fukinsky in the translation) suggests the Polish verb *pierdolic*, meaning "to screw." "Gluck" ("Hlyuck") could also be translated here as "bad trip": it is the colloquial Ukrainian word for a drug-induced hallucination. Bloom obviously suggests James Joyce's Bloom. Vrubl is also the name of the famous turn-of-the-century Russian artist. I've translated *Syl'nyi perets* (literally "strong pepper") as "Hunkman." Kamal Manchmal, the first name in

Arabic and the last in German, means: "perfection sometimes." My gratitude to Sasha Hrytsenko and Antonina Berezovenko for assisting with the meanings of several of the various names, and to Kamal Aboul-Hosn, a Lebanese American student who illuminated the meaning of his first name for me.

6. I use the spelling "Kozak" instead of "Cossack" to differentiate the Ukrainian freedom fighters from the Imperial Russian Cossack regiments.

7. Andrukhovych dedicated a somewhat parodic sonnet to Barbara Langisz. She was a patrician woman from the seventeenth century in Lviv, whose portrait hangs in the city's Historical Museum.

8. Meaning "high castle." A high hill overlooking the center of Lviv.

9. The quotation from the lyrics of Queen, "a certain kind of magic," is in English in the original. It comes from the song "A Kind of Magic" from the 1986 album by the same name. *Chastka*, which I translate as "a certain little part," also means "host" from the sacrament of communion.

10. One of the oldest European-style parks near the center of Lviv. According to Andrukhovych, Steven Spielberg's *Jurassic Park* was extremely popular in Ukraine at the time he wrote his novel; thus the play on the film's title.

11. Actually Vidryzhka (The Belch) is the journal of a group of punk-oriented Ukrainians in Poland. Thanks to Mark Andryczyk for pointing this out to me.

12. Ukrainian bard Taras Shevchenko's famous long poem (1841) about the Ukrainian Haidamak uprisings against the Poles in 1733 to 1734 and 1768. Mickiewicz is the national poet of Poland.

13. One of the main brands of beer from the Polish city of Okocim, whose trademark on the bottle is a goat.

14. The gothic-style tower of the Polish Cathedral of St. Mary located near the center of the city in Cracow.

15. Protests against the Soviet government prior to Ukrainian independence in 1991.

16. Meaning "pigeon" in Czech [author's note]. The name actually means something like "roof shitter."

17. Nice neighborhood. [author's note]

18. Dishes of the Bavarian kitchen. [author's note]

19. Not particularly filled with content, but a rhythmical and rhymed selection of German words and expressions, borrowed by the publisher from a postcard written by Perfetsky on the road from Berlin to Munich [author's note]. *Nachtbumsik* means "night screw," from the German verb *bumsen* (to screw). My gratitude to Adrian Wanner for illuminating me on this.

20. My gratitude to Dr. Roman Kuc for fixing up my science on this point.

21. The last name means "shaggy haired."

Chapter 1

1. Her name is "Tsytryna," which means "lemon" in Ukrainian. I've opted for the German name for lemon, "Zitrone," to convey an echo of the name's meaning in the translation.

2. The artists' quarter in Munich.

3. I've opted for the literal meaning here. It is also an idiom meaning "regret having done something bad." Thanks to Olesya Shchur for pointing this out to me.

4. "Special effect" is in English in the original.

5. The appellation *kutsyi* is commonly used to denote the devil in Ukrainian.

6. The official language of Ethiopia.

7. The name of one of the points of passage between Germany and Austria. Perfetsky's mental state gives him to confuse *Kiefer* (jawbone, pine tree) with *Käfer* (beetle). *Kiefersfelden* means "field of pine trees."

8. Attention, attention my dear Riesenbock, please stop for a minute! . . . I have some problems . . . [author's note]. The correct German of this passage should read: *"Hei, Achtung, Achtung, mein lieber Riesenbock, bitte, auf einen Moment stoppen! . . . Ich habe manche Probleme. . . ."* My gratitude to Adrian Wanner for pointing this out.

9. It seems to be the aria of the Princess Eboli from Giuseppi Verdi's opera *Don Carlos* [author's note]. She wears a patch over one eye because of a riding accident and is the mistress of King Philip, but she really is in love with his son Don Carlos. This aria occurs in act 3. The English translation of the relevant lines would be: "Oh, fatal gift, oh, cruel gift, / Which Heaven bestowed on me in its rage!"

10. *Kushma kushem rozkus'* in the original. The magical charm is meaningless in Ukrainian, although the word *kushma* suggests the name of the current Ukrainian president Kuchma. I've chosen to create my own charm here based on the voodoo goddess of love's name, which is Oshun.

11. The original text comprises the corrupt German of the multicultural ethnic mix at the scene as heard and as translated into Ukrainian by Perfetsky for his diary. I have chosen to translate this and the additional passage below into Jamaican English to give a bit of the effect that a Ukrainian reader gets from the text. My gratitude to Dr. Michael Haughton, a native of Jamaica, for assisting me with the translation.

12. Literally "High German."

13. German poet-bards from the twelfth to the fifteenth centuries.

14. *Sovok* is a pejorative appellation for lackeys and drones of the old Soviet establishment. The "booklet" is his Soviet passport.

15. "Where the lemons bloom"—a line from Goethe's widely anthologized poem *Mignon* [author's note]. For an English translation see Michael Hamburger, trans. *Goethe: Poems and Epigrams.* Anvil Press Poetry, 1983, 29.

16. The name Riesenbock can be translated as a "large male goat." [author's note]

17. Personages from ancient German mythology: Egir is a sea giant; Grungnir a robber-giant; Fafnir a dragon and guardian of the sacred gold [author's note]. These are the Norse spellings. In German it would be "Fafner."

18. *Krasafitsa* in the original, which is a slight corruption of the Russian word for a beautiful woman *krasavitsa*. It is typical for the young urban Ukrainian intelligentsia to toss in a Russian word in conversation for special or ironic effect.

19. Known as Saint Roch or Saint Rock (San Rocco in Italy), a fourteenth-century French saint known as a healer, who was fed by a dog in the woods after he had contracted the plague. He recovered with the power to heal others. He was imprisoned as an imposter by his family who failed to recognize him when he returned home and died in prison. "Rokh" in Ukrainian is the onomatopoetic word used to describe the "oink" or grunt of a pig. So "Saint Oinkus" is another possibility for translation.

20. *Sviatyi dukh* literally means "Holy Spirit," but the use of the "saint" appellation in the sequence preceding the appearance of the adjective here sets up the anticipation for the reader to perceive it as "Saint" Spirit.

Chapter 2

1. We retain the spelling of the original in Ukrainian.

2. None of these is a Ukrainian writer.

3. A corruption of the Russian phrase *dobro pozhalovat'*, which means "welcome." Dr. Casallegra says *pozhaluista* (please, or you're welcome) instead of *pozhalovat'*.

4. Meaning: "everywhere." The name Dr. Dappertutto was Russian theatrical director Vsevolod Meyerhold's pseudonym for his highly experimental private theatrical activities. Russian poet Mikhail Kuzmin suggested the name to Meyerhold based on the character by the same name from E. T. A. Hoffmann's "A New Year's Eve Adventure." For a discussion of this see Edward Braun, trans. and ed., *Meyerhold on Theatre* (New York: Hill and Wang, 1969), 115. For an English translation of the story see E. F. Bleiler, ed. *The Best Tales of Hoffman* (New York: Dover Publications, 1967), 104–29. Dr. Dappertutto is a demonic figure who appears to the hero Erasmus in the Hoffmann story. Andrukhovych claims his Italian dictionary as his only source for the name.

5. The following two fragments are translated from Italian.

6. The title of Ukrainian writer Volodymyr Vynnychenko's 1919 novel. Alborak (also spelled Alboraq, Boraq, or Burak) is the name of the mythical creature that carried Muhammed to the seventh heaven.

7. The word *bib* (genitive plural *bobiv*) also suggests "sheep dung" (the diminutive *bobky*) or "mouse turds" in Ukrainian.

8. Polish "bison" vodka, Zubrovka, which is flavored with a stalk of buffalo grass (absinthe).

9. As usual, Andrukhovych embeds multilingual paranomasia in his characters' names. *Pule* is the f-word in Romanian.

10. The name of the carnivalizing literary group founded by Andrukhovych, comic writer Oleksander Irvanets, and poet Viktor Neborak, the author of the collection *Flying Head* and poem by the same name.

11. *Kapusta* means cabbage or sauerkraut and is the Ukrainian hypertranslation of Helmut Kohl's last name.

12. Schumacher is the famous racecar driver. The Mavrodi brothers were at the center of the Russian MMM bank failure and pyramid scheme. Ewa Cumlin is the wife of a Swiss ambassador who has organized a number of international fora for writers.

Chapter 3

1. The word "monsignor" is the way the devil is addressed in some Middle Age texts as well as an appellation for leaders in Masonic lodges. I have chosen the Italian spelling to avoid confusion in English with the appellation for clerics in the church.

2. The manticore from ancient fables is a monster with the head of a man with horns, the body of a lion, and the tail of scorpion or dragon, which can run faster than a bird can fly.

3. Western Ukraine was part of the Austro-Hungarian Empire during much of the nineteenth and early twentieth centuries.

4. The House of Gold. *Ca* is a Venetian dialectal word for "casa" (house).

5. Venetian for Saint Eustace.

6. Meaning something like "holy heck" in English—a mild curse in Ukrainian.

7. "Boy" in Italian. [author's note]

8. Flowery Gothic, the flowering of the Gothic style in Venetian art in the XII–XIV centuries. [author's note]

9. Literally "in Magus Kaspar clothing."

10. Neither Immanuel Kant nor Edgar Allan Poe, nor, for that matter, Pierre Menart, has ever been to Venice. [author's note]

11. The pun in the original *D'durnu* (meaning "stupid") is untranslatable.

Chapter 4

1. Meaning "suite."

2. Literally *do did'ka*—to the devil.

3. My dear sir, all this is for you. [author's note]

Chapter 5

1. Meaning "supper room" or "The Lord's Supper."

2. Zanípolo means "little gift of God" in Venetian dialect.

2. A traditional Venetian holiday that occurs on the island of Giudecca every third week in August. [author's note]

3. An extremely long horn used by Ukrainian villagers in the Carpathian Mountains.

4. Fruit of the sea (Italian). [author's note]

Chapter 6

1. Motor launch (Italian). [author's note]

2. "Brightest" (Italian), the most commonly used epithet for the Venetian republic. [author's note]

Chapter 7

1. Meaning "notions" store or "haberdashery."

2. The highest organ of Venetian power in the times of the republic. [author's note]

3. A neologistic tribe created by Andrukhovych from the Greek. The name means "shit eaters."

4. The word for lemon in Ukrainian—*tsytryna*.

5. The name given to the beliefs of the heretic Arius (250?–330?A.D.), which ascribed no divinity to Christ, and which were condemned by the Council of Nicea.

6. *Predyvna* means "really strange" or "wonderful."

7. Flight of the arrow (French). [author's note]

8. In English in the original.

Chapter 8

1. Fat Tuesday.

2. "Do you" is a cross-lingual pun. It also means "I'm blowing" in Ukrainian. It is in Cyrillic letters in the original, but separated into two syllables.

3. *Ad* means hell or Hades in Ukrainian.

4. A stylized fragment of a quotation from Martin Luther.

5. Anthropomorphic beasts from Greek mythology with the head of a dog [author's note]. Noted in Herodotus 4, 191, and Strabo 43. My gratitude to William Schmalstieg for assisting me with the Greek on this.

6. 1 Corinthians 12.

Chapter 9

1. Baked melon, a traditional Venetian dish. [author's note]

Chapter 10

1. *Haivky* are actually dances associated with the Easter holiday and have their origin in fertility rights. *Hai* means "grove."

2. Perfetsky intentionally gives Delcampo a false etymology here. A "chrismo" is actually a swaddling cloth and has nothing to do with the ice block.

3. "For the raising of the cup" (Italian) [author's note]

4. This is actually true according to Ukrainian catechisms.

5. The diminutive form of the name Hryhory (Gregory) in Ukrainian.

6. "How Hard for the Heart," "Farewell," "I Love" (Italian dialectal) [author's note]. In standard Italian this should be "Che pena è quest'al cor" and "Addio, addio."

7. "Where," "Ah, Children" (Italian) [author's note]. In standard Italian this is: "Ah! Figli."

8. "Oh, how it troubles" and "Oh, living flame!" (Italian) [author's note]. The former literally would be "Oh, how vague."

9. "Everyone in love is a warrior" (Italian). [author's note]

10. "The sweetness of life," "Here is spring" (Italian, archaic). [author's note]

11. According to two prayer books that I consulted, this is actually the tenth part of the "Symbol of Faith" in the Ukrainian version of the prayer.

Chapter 11

1. We leave this and further untranslatable Americanisms without explanations [author's note]. The words and phrases given in the original text in English are given here as italicized.

2. The world-renowned opera theater in Venice, the name of which means "phoenix"—named for the fact that its predecessor, the Teatro San Benedetto, had burned down in 1773. La Fenice itself has burned down a number of times itself—in 1790 during the process of construction, then in December 1836, and once again on January 29, 1996, in a devastating fire that totally destroyed the interior.

Chapter 12

1. To a Ukrainian reader, the normal word *bliakha* (tin) also suggests the augmentative version of the word for "whore" (*bliad'*).

Chapter 13

1. Kyiv, of course, is in Ukraine and not in Russia. The humorous false etymology here comes from the word *kii*, which means "stick, shaft, cudgel." Thus in the genitive plural, "Kyiv," in Andrukhovych's etymology, would mean "city of cudgels." Actually, the name of the city is thought to derive from a

prince named Kii; thus "prince Kii's city" would be the most likely historical-ly accurate translation.

2. Madame Shalizer is confusing things—shamefully and mercilessly. She is confusing Perfetsky with another well-known poet—Yurko Nemyrych. [author's note]

3. "Great," "very good," and "Deservedly so!" [author's note]

4. See Yaroslav Dovhan's poem "When the robber looks from the side." [author's note]

Chapter 14

1. *Kaif* is one of those nearly impossible words to translate in a single word. It means something like "state of euphoria" or a drug- or alcohol-induced "fly-ing high" in a colloquial sense.

2. *Schnabel* means "beak" or "bill" in German.

3. *Erz* means "archduke," or "ore," "brass" or "bronze" in German. *Herz* means "heart." *Perts* in Ukrainian is from the root meaning "pepper."

4. In Russian in the original.

5. Rilke's poem from part 2 of *New Poems* in the translation of S. Perfetsky [author's note]. "Venezianischer Morgen" in the original. I have opted to use Stephen Cohn's translation here from Rainer Maria Rilke, *Neue Gedichte/New Poems,* trans. Stephen Cohn (Evanston, Illinois: Northwestern University Press, 1998), 224–25. The line in bold is Perfetsky's variation of the line.

6. Pohulyanka, which means something like "strolling place," is the name of a recreational forest park on the outskirts of Lviv, as well as the name of a neighborhood and street adjacent to it.

7. Meaning something like "Bankruptcybattler."

8. A rhymed *khrypnu—nevsypnu—vypnu—slipnu* (!)—*skrypnu* in the original.

9. The south German (Bavarian) name of the great carnival that begins from Christmas and ends just before the Lenten fast.

10. A line by line (literal) translation of Rilke's sonnet from *New Poems,* part II [author's note]. "San Marco" in the original. For a bilingual translation see Rainer Maria Rilke, *Neue Gedichte/New Poems,* trans. Stephen Cohn (Evanston, Illinois: Northwestern University Press, 1998), 227–28.

11. The horses from *Gulliver's Travels.*

Chapter 15

1. The four Verdi operas were actually created at the Teatro La Fenice and had their debut there: *Ernani* on March 9, 1844; *Rigoletto* on March 11, 1851; *La Traviata* on March 6, 1853; and *Simon Boccanegra* on March 12, 1857. The other operas listed in the program must all have been performed there, too. Stravinsky's *Orpheus* (1948) is actually a ballet. I have been able to identify a

number of the cast names from existing operas: Orpheus obviously from numerous opera versions, Sparafucile from *Rigoletto,* Clarice from Rossini's *La Pietra del Paragone,* Rosalinda from Strauss's *Die Fledermaus,* Pantalone from *Le Donne curiose,* an opera buffa by Ermanno Wolf-Ferreri, and Fiordiligi and Guiliemo from *Cosi fan tutte.*

2. Flight of the Turk. [author's note]

Chapter 16

1. The Lemko region is an area of Ukrainian settlement that is currently is Poland. The area is known for its unique dialectal features and a rich tradition of folk song and the folk arts.

2. Here, apparently, is quoted the aria of Don Giovanni from Mozart's opera of the same name: "Come forward, mannered masks" (Italian). [author's note]

3. An extremely popular quick-tempoed Hungarian dance.

4. "The wonderful Bellini" (Italian). [author's note]

5. Steeple, belfry.

6. Clock.

7. The word *zavershennia* in Ukrainian also means sexual climax.

8. The fragment breaks off at this point. [author's note]

Chapter 17

1. The traditional Venetian carnival in memory of the miraculous deliverance of the city from the epidemic of the plague in 1630 (The Mother of God Healing). [author's note]

2. An Italian dish, something like potato dumplings or, sooner, blintzes. [author's note]

Chapter 18

1. Literally, the Ukrainian *tsymbaly,* a folk instrument played much like a hammer dulcimer.

2. Special lock-up rooms, situated right in the attics of the prison. Prisoners held in them grew weak from the heat. [author's note]

3. There is no palace with this name in Venice. [author's note]

Chapter 19

1. Il Gazzettino, Gente Veneta, La Provincia di Venezia, Mitteleuropa, Marco Polo, La Nuova Venezia, Corriere delle Alpi, and others. [author's note]

2. A simplified Attic and the common dialect of the Greek language and lingua franca of the conquered territories. Pidgin English might be a more contemporary equivalent.

Chapter 20

1. A dirty Jamaican curse. [author's note]

Chapter 21

1. Bohdan-Ihor Antonych, "Ballad of the Prophet Jonah" [author's note]. From Antonych's collection *Book of the Lion*.

2. Perfetsky, it seems, is confusing Lviv with Jerusalem. [author's note]

3. See Herodotus, *The Histories* 4.93–96.

4. A citation regarding this tribe can be found in the glossary of *Fabeltiere und Daemonen: Die phantastische Welt der Mischwesen*. Many thanks to the author for pointing this out to me.

5. The *dovhany* are one of the peoples who settled in Ukraine. This fact is established by scholarship [author's note]. *Dovhan*, which means "tall," or "lanky," is also, as a point of curiosity, the last name of the poet Yaroslav Dovhan, who is listed as proofreader for the published version of the novel.

Chapter 22

1. An echo of lines from a song about Ustym Karmeliuk's adventures. Karmeliuk was the legendary leader of a peasant uprising against serfdom and lived from 1787 to 1835. The relevant lines are: *Zovut' mene rozbiinykom. / Kazhut', shcho vbyvaiu. / Ia zh nikoly ne vbyvaiu, / bo sam dushu maiu.* (They call me a robber. / They say that I kill. / I never kill / 'cause I've got a soul.)

Chapter 23

1. According to Ukrainian lore, whoever finds a blooming fern during Saint John's Eve, the night of the summer solstice, will have great riches.

2. Literally *bohunstvo*—from the name of Colonel Ivan Bohun, one of the most heroic figures in the time of the Kozak Hetman Bohdan Khmelnytsky (1648–54).

3. A seventeenth-century Syrian traveling Orthodox monk who wrote travel diaries while visiting Ukraine. The diaries are extant.

4. We haven't succeeded in determining the source of this latter quote [author's note]. Actually, the quote comes from a poem by Viktor Neborak entitled "Den' narodzhennia" (Birthday Party).

Chapter 25

1. The "Minor Masonic Cantata" is the last of the complete works of Mozart, KV 623 (15.XI.1791). Regarding the "March of the Rosenkreutzers" and the "Waltz of the Sorcerers," we know nothing. [author's note]

2. A free translation of the Greek title "Hypnerotomachia Poliphili." [author's note]

3. From Shevchenko's poem "The Dream." The original Ukrainian is: *Ia svoiu piu, a ne krov liudskuiu* (I drink my own, but not the blood of the people). [author's note]

4. In the Ukrainian folk tradition the devil often speaks in a nasal voice.

5. The first "you" is in the familiar *ty* form in Ukrainian (this would be *tu* in French), while the second "you" is in the unfamiliar *vy* form (*vous* in French).

Chapter 26

1. Fish soup (Italian). [author's note]
2. Meaning to knock and find no one home.
3. High water (Italian). [author's note]

Chapter 28

1. Stas's hometown that means "Devilopolis."

2. Anything else? (Italian). [author's note]

3. For you, sir. [author's note]

Be so kind, a bit more wine. Thank you (Italian). [author's note]

4. *Lypa* means linden tree, while *lypen'* means July. The sound similarity is lost in translation.

5. Please, ma'am. [author's note]

Thank you, you're very kind (Italian). [author's note]

6. Have you called me, ma'am? [author's note]

How do you know? Please change the candle. [author's note]

The candle? This candle's already not suitable? Right away, ma'am. [author's note]

7. This one is especially from me, ma'am. [author's note]

Thank you. It doesn't look too bad (Italian). [author's note]

8. I'm here, ma'am. Would you like to order something else? [author's note]

Please, just a check (Italian). [author's note]

9. You can keep the rest. What's with your mirror? [author's note]

Thank you, ma'am. It happens that mirrors don't hold out. Your friend doesn't understand Italian? [author's note]

As you can see. What of it? [author's note]

I wanted to say that you should come by again. I have a much better candle than this one! (Italian). [author's note]

10. Excuse me? What's your friend saying?

That he really likes the service. [author's note]

You'd like it even more if you were without him, ma'am! Good night! (Italian). [author's note]

Chapter 29

1. *Perestupen* in Ukrainian from the word meaning "transgression" or "criminal." The folk belief had it that the root of the mandragora would grow beneath the gallows of a hanged criminal, whose release of sperm following death would pollute the ground. The mandragora with its magical properties would then grow on that spot. My gratitude to Yuri Andrukhovych for enlightening me regarding this folk belief.

Chapter 30

1. Sixteenth century (Italian), the epoch of the end of the Renaissance. [author's note]

2. In English.

3. Walter von der Vogelweide—the knight poet and Meistersinger from the Middle Ages.

4. As mentioned previously in notes, Ada's last name, Zitrone/Tsytryna, means "lemon." The pun is untranslatable here.

Chapter 31

1. Elvira's aria from act 1, scene 2 of Mozart's *Don Giovanni*. I am using Leonora McClernan's translation here, which is available on the Internet at: http://www.aria-database.com/translations/dongio03_ahchi.txt.

ABOUT THE AUTHOR

Yuri Andrukhovych, born in 1960 in Ivano-Frankivsk, Ukraine, is an accomplished novelist, poet, essayist, and translator. In 2001, he received both the prestigious Herder Prize and the Antonovych Prize in literature. His works have been translated into numerous languages, including Belarusian, Bulgarian, English, Finnish, French, German, Hungarian, Italian, Polish, Russian, and Serbian.

■ □ ■ □ ■

WRITINGS FROM AN UNBOUND EUROPE

For a complete list of titles, see the Writings from an Unbound Europe Web site at
www.nupress.northwestern.edu/ue.